ICON RAPTURE

By

Osman Khareef

NOTICE

This book contains provocative and adult subject matter. There are passages of a sexual nature, drug abuse and violence. The book is not suitable reading for children or young persons below the age of 18 or whose religious views or beliefs may be easily offended. Gaining access to the content constitutes legal acceptance of this warning and risk.

The right of Osman Kahreef to be identified as the author of this work has been asserted in accordance with sections 77 and 78 of the Copyright, Designs and Patents Act 1988.

Previously privately published as The Legacy of Carpocrates.

ISBN 978-1-9997416-6-2

About Osman Khareef

Osman Khareef died on St.Sulpice's Day, AD2001. His body was found in an apartment he was renting in Carcassonne in Southern France. The manuscript of this book was found on his desk. It appears here translated from the French and has been extensively edited to bring it up to date and more readable. Apart from this, little is known about him.

PROLOGUE

"All right, Gentlemen. Please be seated."

With much scraping of chairs, five of the senior officers of the Second Division of the New Army of the Russian Federation sat down at the long table in the otherwise deserted Officers' Mess of their headquarters on the outskirts of Minsk near the Ukraine border.

General Victor Morelin opened the folder in front of him, lit a thin cigar and quickly read again the Cyrillic printing on the sheet of paper. He looked up and surveyed a room filled with smoke, condensation and the stench of the damp uniforms worn by men who had not washed properly since the summer. The overhead strip lighting flickered in sympathy with the diesel generators whose muffled drone could be heard all the way up from the basement, two floors below. Outside, there was a full Siberian snowstorm raging.

The General didn't notice any of it. Five of his fellow officers, his comrades-in-arms (those who had survived with him in Afghanistan, Chechnya and other, less well-known, fields of battle) and his young nephew Sergei Yemeljan, a Sergeant in the Moscow Police who had flown in from Moscow for the meeting, stared back at him expectantly. All were smoking the cigars brought by the Sergeant who had liberated them from a criminal evidence room in the Dhzerzinsky Square FSB Police Complex where he worked.

"I'll get straight to the point, comrades," began the General. "We have three bids and today's meeting is to decide which of these we shall accept. Are we still in total agreement?"

He paused to look at those whom he now thought of as his co-conspirators. They all knew that if Moscow caught even a whisper of what they were about to do, they would be shot and their families imprisoned.

"Do you all understand the consequences?"

1

One by one each man banged his fist on the table to confirm his agreement.

The General nodded. Sighing inwardly, he read out the detailed offers for one or more of the stock of nuclear warheads that they were proposing to sell. They had good reasons for the sale. Firstly, to buy sufficient food and fuel to keep the soldiers under their command from mutiny or desertion and second for themselves. It was not being done through choice but through the necessity of surviving this and subsequent harsh Russian winters. These were professional soldiers, and although they retained a semblance of honour and dignity, the murderous Afghanistan and Chechnya campaigns had obliterated from their consciousness any regard for the sanctity of human life. They had experienced first hand how cheap life was and how randomly and regularly it was snuffed out. The thought that someone who bought a nuclear weapon from them might kill thousands of people was of little concern to them. What mattered was their own survival and the respect of their fellow soldiers – bonds forged in the mud and flame of brutal modern warfare. What also mattered was whether they could actually spend the money made from the sale. Whether they could get away with it.

General Morelin continued. "These are all acceptable bids, comrades. What we have to decide is to whom we shall sell. As you know there are many factors we should take into account. I think we are all agreed not to sell to the bastard Chechens whatever the price!"

There was a murmur of agreement. He paused to stub out his cigar in the overflowing ashtray.

"Even though the highest amount has been offered by Al Qaeda, I think there may be unacceptable repercussions for us if we sold nuclears to them. Also, they want to pay us in raw opium, which is difficult for us to deal with. If we suddenly entered the drugs racket, beyond our present level, questions would be asked that would cause us problems in the future."

"So how much are the Iraqis offering then?" asked one of the officers, a veteran from the Soviet Era.

"Yes, they have made a very attractive bid. They can pay in petrodollars or gold. But Comrades, think carefully about the consequences. The Yankees are still all over Iraq like a skin disease. It would be very difficult for us to deliver the weapon undetected. Also, I am a little dubious about their ability to raise the money. The Americans have a very tight grip on the movement of money these days. Also, the crazy bastards might trigger a final global holocaust starting with Israel, in which case we couldn't spend our money." There were further nods of agreement around the room.

"So, we come to the final bid, Gentlemen." General Morelin glanced around at his fellow conspirators as he told them the figure.

"That's less than half the other bids," came an immediate objection from one of the men.

"Yes, and we know nothing about them or of their possible motivations. Therefore, I asked my nephew here to look into it for us." General Morel waved a languid hand at an officer, the youngest and most junior, sitting to his right. "Sergei, please tell us what you have discovered."

"Comrades, I regret to say I have found very little out about the Priory Arcadia. My sources in the Police and FSB tell us next to nothing and I am reluctant to push it, in case they ask me why I want to know. After all, it is hardly a routine enquiry!" The other men nodded. He paused to cough and then continued.

"What little I have discovered I got from the Internet." He paused and looked at his uncle.

"Continue if you please, Sergei," said the General.

"It is some kind of European political society or cult based in France. However, what is significant to us, is they appear to be very wealthy, owning whole multi-national corporations and vast amounts of property throughout Europe. There is also a lot of rubbish about its history and involvement with secret societies and the Church - probably wild speculation. There are many crazy conspiracy theories on the Internet."

"How do you think they heard about our offer?" asked the General. "We haven't advertised this!"

"I've no idea, Comrade General. Anyone else have a suggestion?" All shook their heads.

"Somebody must have contacted them, for us to receive their bid;

for us to get this email on our secret account," persisted the General.

There was an uncomfortable silence.

Eventually, Sergeant Yemeljan coughed and spoke up. "Comrade General, I am not totally sure but it may have been through me that they found out how to approach us. As you know we have had some difficulty in getting the message across to the right people without compromising our security. You yourself contacted the Iraqis and others by careful phone calls and personal meetings. On your instruction, I sent carefully worded emails to various other groups; to individuals known to the FSB in the Tamil Tigers, ISIS, the Colombians, North Koreans and others. This is the only reply, in the correct format, which we have had. So far."

"All right, Sergei," said the General. "The message must have been passed on to these people in a manner, I suspect, we will never find out about. Keep digging into their background and keep us informed. Time is short and we must act swiftly."

"Yes, Comrade General," replied Sergei.

"Well, let's look at this in another way," suggested the General. "This Priory Arcadia has agreed to pay 40 million in used US dollars or the currency of our choice. They have agreed to pick up the weapon from us here in Russia. They have also stated that the weapon is unlikely to be used, because it's needed as insurance. They say..." he peered down at his notes, "they are not fanatics hell-bent on Islamic Jihad or World Annihilation." The General paused. "More like World Domination, I suspect!" he said.

"Well, that's a relief!" muttered one of the officers. There was a nervous note to their laughter.

"We have to make a decision tonight, gentlemen." General Morelin glared around at the others. "Does anybody want to contribute anything else? No? In that case, I will summarise. My friends, we know what Al Qaeda will do with it. We know what the Iraqis will do with it." He made a boom-boom gesture with his hands. "We do not know what this European lot will do with it, but they don't sound as bad." He shrugged his shoulders. "So, I propose we sell to the Priory Arcadia, even though their bid is much less."

He looked at the men. "Do you agree to my leadership in this, comrades?"

Slowly, each man raised his fist. General Victor Morelin raised his own fist and thumped it down violently on the table. The others followed suit.

"So be it," he said. "My nephew Sergei will complete the arrangements. I suggest the transfer is made on the Mushinsky Highway, a few miles West of us here in Minsk. I will, of course, check that they can come up with the money."

The others picked up their caps, buttoned their greatcoats and filed out to resume their normal duties.

Alone at the table, General Victor Morelin put his head in his hands. "God forgive us!" he wept. "God forgive me!"

He hadn't wanted to involve so many people, but there had been no choice. They had already located and extracted a suitable warhead from his inventory of intercontinental missiles lying rusting, mostly unattended, possibly unstable and some even forgotten, in their concrete silos. They still needed to rewire and reconfigure the controlling arming circuitry and to crate the warhead in something easily transportable by road.

Some of those missiles were more than forty years old dating from the Cuban Missile Crisis in the old Soviet days. In the last decade or so, most of these warheads, even those pointed at China, had been neglected so there was serious potential danger in disturbing them. Nuking the city of Minsk and its surrounding region was not the intended plan.

All this required the active collusion and involvement of others: his most trusted senior officers and one of the very few nuclear-missile technicians and key-holders left under his command. They all had their price. A high price.

The usual pay off of a crate of official unadulterated Army vodka and a couple of days leave to visit a Moscow brothel was hardly sufficient these days. Niet.

More like a forged US passport, a kilo of cocaine and a red Ferrari.

PART I

CHAPTER 1

His Supreme Holiness Pope John XXIV, recent successor to the German Pope, stared out of the window of his comfortable modern air-conditioned private office in the Castel Sant'Angelo. In the hazy distance, secular sinful Rome lay beyond the Byzantine edifices of the Vatican City, the administrative hub of the most powerful religion in human history.

A plain grey cassock with no decorative trimming covered the Pontif's small thin but wiry seventy- year-old body. Clean-shaven and hair tonsured in the Dominican manner, he stood still as a heron; hands clasped behind him.

Below, the oily brown Tiber bulged and roiled sluggishly past the footings of the ancient Roman fortress which used to guard the entrance to St.Peter's Square and the vast Basilica beyond.

Fiume Tevere, Old Snake Tiber, has dined well over the centuries, fed from the parapets, docks and platforms of the old Holy City. Cloaca maxima of Rome since the dawn of history, the great river has carried more dead Christians en route to the Eternal City than were ever consumed by the dog-eared, flea-bitten lions in the Grand Arena of the Coliseum less than two miles by Fiat to the South West. Pope, Cardinal, monk or pilgrim, it made no difference; all went to fertilise what used to be the rich vineyard- laden sloping plains to the seaward West, now an American-style desolation of suburban sprawl, airport and motorway concrete that stretched all the way down to the sea at the ancient port of Ostia.

In the small private office, accessed from the Papal Apartments only by a secret passageway built under the Via della Conciliazone by the Spanish Borgia, Pope Alexander VI, in 1493, stood a large leather topped desk. It was a Vatican treasure in English yew with ornately scrolled edges and holy scenes carved along its sides. Stacks of bulky

9

document files lay scattered across its surface. Of the two closest to the Pope's hand, one had the words 'Albigensian Heresy' stamped on it, and the other was simply labelled 'Q4'. Both had 'Top Secret' printed in red-inked Italian on the front cover. These documents were the modern equivalent of those hand-scripted by teams of castrated monks in the not-so olden days. The sharp laser print-outs on fine stationary showed that the Congregation for the Doctrine of the Faith or Holy Inquisition, as it used to be known, possessed tools equal, if not superior, to those widely available in the secular world. As the oldest and most powerful secret service organisation in existence, the Inquisition possessed technical assets equal to the CIA, MI6, the Mossad or even the US Department of Homeland Security.

Prayer alone has never been sufficient to maintain Roman Catholicism as one of the most potent forces in global politics since the Donation of Constantine in AD 312. To quote a phrase once attributed to God's Banker, Archbishop Marcinkus. 'You can't run the Church on Hail Marys.' Satan, heresies and the ungodly must be combated with every sinew, thought and tool available. But it all cost money. In spite of the hiccup of John Paul I, John XXIV considered that his predecessors had done well in that regard. It was a pity about Calvi, Sindona and the losses from their Enron and World Com holdings but, well, the Church had to continue in the face of error and casualty.

The Holy Father turned back to his desk and pushed a hidden button recessed into its side. A flat-screen VDU rose from a recess within the desk, and lit up with a beep. The Sun workstation was networked into a massive Cray Millennium Blue mainframe housed in a nuclear-bombproof bunker deep below Ground-Zero Vatican City. 'Armageddon Games' are a deadly serious application for the techno-bagarozzi assigned to serve as High Priests to this most modern neo-facet of the Almighty.

The Papal PC was whimsically nicknamed 'Abulafia' after a Jewish rabbi who'd made important contributions to the Judaic Torah and Kabalah. He was rumoured to have invented a primitive machine for enumerating and computing all the names of God, in the zealous hope and belief that this would precipitate the End of Time, the Apocalypse and the Coming of the TRUE Messiah. The Holy Father had commissioned a young computa-cleric to re-design the GUI of the operating system with Holy Icono-graphics. It provided His Reverence with mild amusement to access a private database of known personal enemies by mouse-clicking on the Veronica.

Increasingly often these days, he would withdraw to "consult the rabbi" clicking on the Acheropita, to bring up Sonic the Hedgehog, an old Nineties arcade game whose simple themes he often used in allegorical sermons delivered from the august High Pulpit of St.Peter's. The different levels represented, to his mind, progression in the attainment of Enlightenment; the bosses and obstacles representing Satan and the struggle against Worldliness. Pope John XXIV was an avid player of arcade games.

The world of computer games soothed his mind; in the same way TV snooker or English Test Match cricket might for lesser mortals. There are encyclicals and pastoral letters governing Catholic Doctrine on every imaginable pattern of human misbehaviour—console games are a patent invention of the Devil, railed at with holy invective from pulpits across the globe—but the Pope himself has yet to pronounce on this. After all, God works in mysterious ways, and D'Ascriba could hardly admit that he had been using a Gameboy for recreation during the interminable days of the Conclave of Cardinals that had chosen him to succeed and to be God's instrument to guide the Vessel of the Church through the stormy seas of the New Millennium.

It is a mistake to imagine that a reigning Pontiff spends any time thinking holy thoughts of doctrine. This is formulated for him by teams of earnest and worthy ecclesiastics who maintain the Sacred Continuity. The Pope's proper function is to be the Star of the Soap, Voice of the Faith, the Implementer of Policy, God's Politician and Prime Minister. His thoughts, therefore, were, at this time, to do with what he'd been studying on his desk—Q4, the Albigensian Heresy, and what the hell was Cardinal Joseph Mirphy, Legate of New York, doing?

"Rodriguez?" he called out. "Get me Secretary Von Helsinger on the phone. I need to speak with him. Also, make an appointment for three this afternoon for him and Assessor Paliato to see me here."

"I'll get on to it right away, Holy Father."

Canon Rodriguez Tolosa, personal assistant to the Pontiff from his Rio days, picked up one of the three phones on his desk in the outer office and dialled the code for the Department of the Curia in Holy Office Square which houses the offices of the Congregation for the Doctrine of the Faith.

Promptly at three that afternoon, Cardinal Otto Von Helsinger, a Swiss and the Italian Cardinal Guido Paliato, Secretary and Assessor respectively, presented themselves at the Pontiff's rooms in Castel Sant Angelo.

"What's going on, Otto?" asked the Assessor as they waited for the security system to check their coded cardkeys at the door.

"Some panic about security at the Ecole Biblique in Jerusalem and the Israelis, I believe," grunted the Grand Inquisitor. He was puffing from the exertion of the half-mile walk through the narrow tunnels from his office. The light flashed green and the door clicked open. Von Helsinger pushed the heavy padded armoured door open and went in, followed by his second-in-command.

The Pontiff was waiting for them in the inner office. As Canon Rodriguez closed the door behind them, he got straight down to brass crucifixion nails.

"We have another serious problem, gentlemen," he said. "I've received a report this morning from Father Vascone on the hi-speed modem link from Jerusalem. The Ecole Biblique has been broken into." He went on, "As you know, it is vital to continue our predecessors' policy of dis-information and prevarication over Q4 material. De Vaux and Benoit were brilliant at this, it seems, but now there is a new and unwelcome interest."

"Does Vascone know what is missing?" asked Von Helsinger.

"Nothing that we know about yet, but we know that they penetrated the Scrollery for over an hour. They must have taken photographs or videos."

"Surely, we don't keep much Q4 stuff of any importance there now," asked Cardinal Paliato "Do we?"

"No, of course not. Most of it has been here in the Secure Vault for more than twenty years, ever since De Vaux's time."

"So, what's the problem?" asked Von Helsinger.

"The problem, my dear Otto," snapped the Pope angrily, showing briefly the mettle which had led the Conclave to choose him as Pontiff, "is that there is a group of meddlers looking systematically for Q4 material and willing to take extreme measures. All the security devices were inactivated professionally in some way, and the two armed guards were found in the morning. Their throats had been cut. May their souls rest in peace." The other two muttered, "Amen" and crossed themselves perfunctorily.

"So what is it you want us to do, Holy Father?" asked Von Helsinger.

"For Christ's sake," blasphemed the Pope, "that's your job. I don't know. Just be on top of the problem. My every instinct tells me that ancient enemies are once more coming out of the woodwork. Satan is stirring things up. You know that we face a dangerous revival of the old heresy."

He picked up one of the files and waved it at the two Cardinals. "You see this? It's almost unbelievable but we are facing a revival of the Albigensian Heresy. In the twenty-first century, this is absurd!" He went on. "Templars, bloody shrouds, Rennes le Chateau, Gnosticism, Cathars, mysterious weeping icons!" He snorted with derision. "I thought we had all this suppressed and locked away safely. You know how dangerous our enemies in Priory Arcadia are with this sort of material. I want you to get a grip on this, right now!" he snapped. Lowering his voice menacingly, he continued:" I do not want to be the Pope that presides over the final humiliation and disintegration of our Church. Ancient bloody history will destroy us all, if we're not careful. There are people out there making a pitch for the Millennial high ground while we are scratching around, barely surviving the scandals of our support of the Banco Ambrosiano, Italia Forza and pederast priests in Boston and Ireland!" Turning away from his two shocked Inquisitors and waving his hands in the air, he continued: "I want our own relics dusted off and some new ones made. The time has come to raise the ante," he said decisively. "But no more Shroud cock-ups. I don't want any more dirty linen washed in public. Capiche?"

The two Cardinals nodded.

"I want you to come up with a bit of magic. How about splinters off the Cross? I know we have stored somewhere, a few real crucifixes dating from Roman Times. Surely, we can do something with those? Make them glow with phosphorescence on Easter Sunday. Project an holographic image, give out an electrostatic aura—you know, the usual stuff. We have a Special Team for this, don't we?"

CHAPTER 2

January winter, a transport cafe at the Polish-Russian border on the outskirts of Brest, 'gateway to the East'. A large articulated lorry pulls off the highway into the crowded car park. It was snowing, the neon lights of the café flickered dimly through the blizzard. No warmly welcoming windows in this café—just the neon over the darkened door.

Igor Golemov parked the artic carefully in line and climbed stiffly down from the cab. Slowly and methodically, huddled into his red checkered coat, he walked around the big vehicle, examined the tyres and the big new locks on the diesel-tank filler nozzles, and rattled the back doors to make sure they were secure. He armed the central-locking and alarm systems with the infra-red key fob and trudged through the slush to the sad café.

He threaded his way through the room crowded with tables looking for somewhere to sit. They're all like this now, he thought wearily. Capitalist fascist pigs. He missed the old days, his crisp clean uniform, the power to piss on this riffraff. The good Marxist certainties. Who would have believed the changes brought about by Perestroika and the collapse of Communism? Who could've predicted it? Not him, not Igor Golemov, a simple peasant, born of a Russian infantryman and a Polish nurse. I don't need all this shit! He thought bitterly.

He found a table by the wall. It was dirty with the food remnants and scattered cutlery of the previous customers. He sat down facing the crowded room and pulled the cap off his dark bearded face. He dipped a stubby finger into the gravy on the plate in front of him and licked it meditatively, letting his cold grey eyes drift carefully around the room.

He was early. Nothing yet. There would be time for a meal and a schnapps or three. Let the German bastards come.

He kept his coat on to conceal the Uzi machine pistol in its holster under his arm. Stretching his legs under the table, he massaged the calves of his legs and loosened the strap that held the spring-loaded throwing knife he kept there, day and night, when on the road.

This was his last job, he reminded himself. It was getting too dangerous. The long hours had taken a heavy toll on his health. It was not the driving; the big turbo inter-cooled DAF 280 they gave him to drive was modern, well equipped and as fast and as comfortable as a limousine. No, it was the fear that told on the nerves. Each flaring of the brake lights on the vehicle in front caused a jolt of anxiety and a stab of fear. No, it was definitely not like the old days. It was an age of chaos and lawlessness in which you resorted to desperate measures to stay alive and make a rouble, a kopeck, or a dollar. That was why he was here, waiting for the bastard German; waiting for his orders. No questions. Then Moscow and beyond.

They came while he was on his fourth schnapps. The food was good and plentiful here. Polish sausage, cabbage, boiled potatoes and coarse dark bread to mop up the thick gravy.

"Want some?" he asked as they sat down at the table. The German gave a grimace of distaste. Igor shrugged and looked at the other man.

"No, thanks," he said politely, "we must move quickly if we are to make good time to Moscow."

*

The Biophar Drugs Corporation management meeting had come to an end.

"Stay awhile, will you, Joel?" The CEO, John Visorkis, stood up and waved Joel Maniato over to the huge tall windows overlooking the night time wintery glitter of New York stretching towards the sea and the planes coming in to land at LaGuardia—a view now uninterrupted by the twin towers. On 9/11, John Visorkis had watched in fascinated horror from behind his desk, the mail unopened in front of him, as the World Trade Centre disintegration movie unfurled before his eyes.

The other senior managers and vice-presidents filed out silently to disperse to their homes and apartments, already mentally composing the complicated lies they would tell their respective wives, girlfriends, mistresses, partners, and dogs in response to the simple question… "Had a good day at the office?"

"They're on their way into Russia tonight, Joel." Visorkis barked. "I want you to supervise everything. We've diverted the orbit of the satellite to cover that area so you can be in constant communication with our people at all times." He continued harshly. "There will be no mistakes. The consequences of failure are unthinkable. I don't need to tell you how important this is to the Corporation, to us. We need a miracle and, by Christ, that is what we are going to get!"

Visorkis looked seriously ill. His normally smooth business-bland features were bruised and puffy with tiredness and fear. "You heard those stupid complacent bastards tonight, Joel. Christ! Every fucking R & D programme has gone down the fucking tubes and somehow those motherfucks at the FDA have gotten wind of the problems with FlavAdd. Jesus H! When I think of the money we've backhanded those greedy sons of bitches over the years and now they want to stab us in the back!" he ranted.

Joel had never seen the CEO so agitated, so coarse in his language. Knowing things were bad, he had secretly dumped his own BDC shareholding some time ago. He wasn't sure why he was still with the Corporation—maybe he couldn't really believe what instinctively knew. After all, it was incredibly difficult to face a catastrophic reality and a near-certain end to his career when life was outwardly so good, so prosperous.

John B Visorkis, CEO of Biophar Drugs Corporation, turned his full attention towards Joel Maniato, Head of Security, eyed him squarely, a strange unwelcoming glitter in his eyes. "I'll give it to you straight, kiddo. Get me that icon or you're doomed. I'll also see to it that everybody goes down with me from the fucking President, the Cardinal and every other poor son of a bitch I can think of who has ever had dealings with us." He handed Maniato a plastic key card. "Here's the ComSat code. Now get outta here and leave me in peace! I don't want to hear from you again until we have that picture in our Carolina research facility."

*

Igor's new companion for the ride into Russia was asleep, bundled up in a dark grey labourer's coat, although it was warm in the cab. Igor studied him carefully in the mirror, which he'd adjusted for this purpose. Definitely not German, he thought. A Westerner, maybe French or Nordic. Well, he won't know nothing, that was for sure. Not where he kept his stash of US dollars or his weapons. He figured no-

17

one would dream of looking in the place where he'd hidden his money—his future ticket to freedom. He was not thinking about the one thousand US dollars in the money-belt around his waist. The same amount was given him every trip by the transport company, for diesel and to smooth his way past the inevitable militiamen, assorted roadblocks and robber gangs that now plundered the Mushinski highway between Minsk and Moscow. If he had any left after running this gauntlet of plunderers, he kept it as a bonus.

His own money was hidden in the exhaust manifold, in a sealed ceramic pipe he'd had specially made. Sure it got hot but never enough to destroy the money, whatever the vehicle they gave him to drive. Officials didn't like getting their fingers burned, so they never checked. Anyway, he figured that they would think that the most likely contraband, drugs, would be destroyed by the heat. That's what Customs and other officials were usually looking for. Mainly for themselves, of course.

The journey passed without incident until three in the morning, about 150 miles from the border, when Igor heard an insistent buzzing noise above the drone of the big engine. His companion woke up instantly and fished a mobile phone from one the pockets of his coat.

"Yes, what is it? I was asleep." He used English. "Of course it's me. Who the fuck else do you know travelling about bloody Russia in the middle of the night?" he said irritably. "Sure, I'm OK. Yeah, yeah. I'll let you know what's happening. Any activity on the other front?" He listened to the voice and rubbed the condensation off the side window so he could peer out. "I can't see shit. It's three in the morning and snowing here. Goddammit! All right, we'll do a comms check. Give me five minutes."

He clicked the mobile phone shut and put it back in his coat pocket. Reaching under the seat, he pulled out an anonymous-looking briefcase and opened it. He took out an aerial device that looked like a Martian raygun and rubber-suckered it to the side window. The screen built into the lid of the briefcase flickered into life and he started tapping commands into the keyboard. High overhead, in its new geo-stationary orbit, the Biophar Drugs Corporation communications satellite paused for a millisecond in its ceaseless traffic of financial and business transactions to react to the private codes being transmitted to it from far below on the Earth's winter surface.

Peering short-sightedly at the screen, JeanLuc Kuovic studied the email messages that downloaded. He switched off the PC and closed the lid of the briefcase. "Mind if I take a charge?" he asked Igor in fluent Russian. Igor made a non –committal grunt. JeanLuc opened the briefcase again, took a lead from inside and plugged it into the dashboard lighter socket. Christ! A real Neanderthal, he thought. I could murder for a good cup of coffee.

It was a risk bringing the laptop which was still a high value commodity in Russia. However, it should be okay. In addition to diamonds, he had enough dollars and marks on him to buy off virtually anybody, except the nutters who were intent on killing rather than robbery. God knows there were a few of those about. There were also the Chechen rebels to think about, but he been told they were infrequent this far North and West. Anyway he needed it for the job, as well as the hi-res hand-scanner and the digital camera he'd had built into an old Praktica 35mm camera casing. There was also another piece of equipment in the case that he needed to validate the transaction he was due to make, which was the main purpose of the trip. A little red LED glowed in the handle of the case as the unit charged.

They hit the first roadblock at four in the morning just past Minsk. There were only a few trucks on the highway and they were third in a convoy of five, travelling more or less together. The highway was blocked by Militia in armoured vehicles, blue and white lights flashing through the driving snow. Igor changed down through the gears and brought the vehicle to a stop, headlights sharply illuminating the high rear doors of the old Volvo truck about ten metres ahead. He kept the engine idling to keep the heaters functioning.

Turning to JeanLuc, Igor said, "Don't worry. This is looks like a routine check. I will pay them. You will see." He stretched up and took a large bundle of paper money from behind the sun visor. "We try first with roubles," he said and pushed the notes into the pocket of his red-and-white check lumberjack coat. These coats were all the rage in Poland at the moment. Very mode, very Burt Reynolds! He put the coat on and they waited.

It wasn't long till a uniformed officer and a guard with a Simonov SKS appeared in the glare of the headlights. They beckoned to Igor and he opened the cab door to get out.

"Stay here. I'll deal with this," he said as he jumped down. JeanLuc fiddled nervously with the strap of his case. I am expecting this, he thought. Stay cool. He saw Igor walk over, head down against the snow, to the two militiamen and start a conversation in the bright halo of the headlights. Igor pulled out his sheaf of roubles, but the officer stepped back from him suddenly and the guard quickly brought the Simonov to bear on him. The senior officer shouted at Igor who stood still briefly but then started back to the truck gesturing at JeanLuc to get out.

"The bastard wants to know who you are," he shouted in his ear as JeanLuc climbed down. "Don't offer him money unless he asks. Watch yourself," he added.

JeanLuc walked carefully over towards the two men who stood waiting, the barrel of the Simonov aimed steadily at his midriff. The officer was a tall man in a thick uniform overcoat with the collar buttoned tight, the flat peaked cap with the red braid pulled down over his eyes. He was as tall as JeanLuc. With a sense of déja vu JeanLuc looked into a pair of intense blue eyes, rock steady and unblinking in their gaze. He looked away hurriedly.

"Name?" the officer asked flatly, looking down to study the papers that JeanLuc handed over.

"Alexei Fedorov." "Occupation and destination?"

"Historian. Zagorsk." Always try to tell some of the truth. Blank your mind, JeanLuc reminded himself.

"Why are you travelling now, by this route and with that ruffian?" he gestured towards Igor in the DAF, hunched gorilla-like over the steering wheel.

"The Institute gave me money to buy a ticket on the train from Warsaw but this way I can save money."

"Don't you have to pay him?"

"He is a relative. It is a favour for the family."

"Which Institute did you say?" The officer stared at JeanLuc seemingly intent on the reply.

"The Priory Arcadia in Sigor." JeanLuc lifted his gaze to the face of the man in front of him and waited to see if his coded message had registered. It had.

"Welcome to Russia, my friend. I am called Maraschino. I have your package ready," came the reply.

A blast of icy wind out of Siberia blew a flurry of glittering snow crystals past them caught in the headlights. "Return to your truck, comrade. We will move on these other vehicles and then load yours with its special consignment. Please pull off the road when one of my men flags you down ahead."

"Is the load heavy?" asked JeanLuc.

"Yes, very. That is why I asked your people to send a large lorry. Please return to your vehicle now. I will see to the loading at once. It is too cold and too dangerous to delay."

JeanLuc turned on his heel and returned to the warm cabin of the truck. General Victor Morelin, aka "Maraschino", disappeared into the darkness. Shortly thereafter the truck in front started to roll forward. Igor put the DAF in the first of its twelve forward gears and pulled away slowly. They passed a long black official car, and the two armoured vehicles pulled over on the side of the road, their blue and white strobes revolving slowly. Only the blurred outlines of the men inside could be seen through the condensation on the windows.

A few hundred yards further on and a soldier waved them into a lay-by and they stopped. The rest of the vehicles disappeared into the night. Igor and JeanLuc had only to wait a short time before a huge winter camouflaged Army lorry rumbled on caterpillar tracks out of the darkness and shrieked metallically to a halt beside them. Several soldiers emerged from the vehicle and stood waiting, sheltering from the wind on the leeward side. The long black official Zil they had glimpsed earlier drew up in front of them and General Victor Morelin stepped out.

JeanLuc turned to Igor who was staring ahead twitching nervously. "Don't worry. This is all arranged. We are picking up a special load to take back to France on your return from Moscow."

Igor glared at JeanLuc. "They didn't tell me about any of this. What's going on? Why all the Military? This is very dangerous! Who will pay them?"

"You don't need to know, Igor," replied JeanLuc more calmly than he felt. "Please now unlock the side panel doors for them, so that we can load up."

Muttering a string of curses, Igor grabbed the keys, opened the door and dropped out of the cabin onto the icy road. He unlocked the side panels and slid them back. Six of the soldiers quickly laid a metal ramp in position between the two trucks and, obviously struggling, rolled across a small wooden crate that carried no markings. The hydraulic dampers of the DAF wheezed and hissed noisily as the full weight of the crate was taken on board. The General directed the soldiers to rearrange the cargo of tractor tyres to cover and hide the crate as much as possible. The job was soon done. Igor closed the side doors and returned to the warmth of the cabin.

JeanLuc stepped down from the cab and approached the Zil, carrying his briefcase. He opened the rear door and entered. In the car it was hot, muggy and dimly lit. Condensation rivered down the windows.

Morelin had sat on the black leather, a thin cigar in his mouth and a half-empty bottle of vodka on the seat beside him. The uniformed driver stared straight ahead, unmoving; hands on the steering wheel.

"You have my payment, Comrade." It was not a question, just a plain statement.

JeanLuc nodded towards his briefcase as he slid into the seat facing the General. "It's in here. Diamonds you asked for and that's what we brought you, Maraschino."

"All right, let's take a look". Morelin screwed a diamond merchant's magnifying glass into his eye. JeanLuc opened his case and took out a small black velvet drawstring bag, which he handed to the other man. Multi-carat points of brilliance sparkled in his fingers as Morelin, taking his time, carefully examined each small glittering stone. Apart from the muttering of the Zil's engine which hiccupped from time to time on the poor quality Russian fuel, and the muted whoosh of the wind outside, it was quiet in the car.

"May God forgive us both," said Morelin, eventually. He took from around his neck a chain on which there were two small keys. He handed it over to JeanLuc who immediately put it over his own head and tucked the keys under his shirt, where they hung out of sight over his heart.

Business completed, the two men embraced clumsily in the confined space. There were tears flowing freely down the cheeks of the General. "You must go now. Destiny awaits you, my friend!" He cried.

"God be with us both!" said JenLuc huskily. He opened the car door, got out and, head down, returned to his vehicle. The other man poured a big slug of vodka into the glass beside him and raised it as if in toast to an invisible audience. He had what he wanted, what his men wanted – they hadn't been paid by Putin's government for more than two years and were on the verge of starvation and mutiny. Why then did he feel so bad? So guilty? He threw the contents down his throat and poured himself another. "Driver, take me back to headquarters. It's pay day!" he shouted.

"Is everything all right?" asked Igor.

"Yeah, yeah. Everything's cool. We can go now."

JeanLuc opened his briefcase, booted up the laptop and started tapping on the keyboard with stiff cold fingers. Igor turned the keys in the ignition and the DAF started with a diesel roar which drowned out the new noise, a rapid rushing tick- ticking noise that now emanated from somewhere within JeanLuc's bag of tricks on which he was tapping away. The big truck picked up speed, heading back out into the obsidian night, gusts of wind buffeting the high sides, digital lines of snow curving down, like heavy flak, out of the heavens into the powerful halogens.

Four hundred miles to go. Smolensk and then Moscow… for the next part of the operation.

*

John Visorkis, two thousand miles and a continent away, was staring unseeingly out of a window. But it was noon and the view, if he'd been interested, was across to the strange pigeon-encrusted Art Deco neo-Egyptian excrescences of the Chrysler building with Brooklyn in the hazy distance beyond.

"Your noon appointment is here, Mr.Visorkis," Shelley Lang, his secretary, announced softly through the intercom. JV walked back to his desk, an original 1951 black Cadillac sliced up and remodelled with desk surfaces for working on, a networked PC, and three VDUs built

23

in, permanently online and linked to share dealing desks in Wall St. He loved to sit at this desk in driving control of the vast empire of diversified business that was the Biophar Drugs Corporation. A naturally flamboyant character, his love of 1950s music, automobilia and films was indulged extravagantly and without discrimination.

Nevertheless, JV was a deeply religious Catholic and had been from his schooldays in Chicago's Cicero district. Nothing in a turbulent and vicious business life of corporate ladder-climbing had affected this man's unswerving faith and undoubted devotion to the Catholic Church of God and of his appointed authorised senior sales executive, Earth territory, the Pope. JV had never felt any incompatibility with the two aspects of his life. Archbishop Cody had always been most sympathetic and forgiving in the past when he'd made his confession in the privacy of the private steam baths they had both patronised in the Windy City. But now he really did have the 'Fear of God' in him and with good reason, he reflected bitterly.

He pushed the intercom button on the base of a solid gold Elvis statuette. "Show him in, will you, Shelley?" he said.

"Not your only icon, I see," remarked His Holiness Cardinal Joseph Mirphy ironically as he walked in. Imposing was a good adjective to describe Joe Mirphy, Cardinal of New York, Papal Legate. Street clothes for his Eminence consisted of a plain grey business suit of immaculate conception. Only the clerical collar distinguished his outward appearance from that of a high-powered executive. That and a lack of personal ornamentation apart from a large heavy gold ring embossed with a faint insignia barely discernible in the palely glowing, much kissed, 24-carat surface.

The Cardinal walked over to the tall wide windows and surveyed the scene below. "This view has given me a theme for Sunday's sermon, John," he said.

"Oh yeah and what's that, Eminence?" JV said cautiously. He was worried. The Cardinal's visits were infrequent and always a harbinger of dramatic change.

"The Temptation of Our Lord at the start of His ministry when Satan takes him to a high place and says "Behold! Follow me and you shall be master of all ye survey"," he misquoted smilingly at John

24

Visorkis.

JV fiddled nervously with the aerial of his Cadillac desk and looked down as the Cardinal turned away from the windows and came back towards him.

"We're releasing you from your duties as CEO, John," he said matter of factly. Cardinal Mirphy levelled his gimlet gaze steadily at JV. He seemed strangely uncurious, even bored, by the effect this statement might have had. JV felt as if he were about to be eaten alive by a lizard.

"Wha- What?" he spluttered, the first tears in more than forty years springing into his eyes, making him blink rapidly.

The Cardinal continued, a slight Irish lilt in his voice. "We think it is time for you to take a sabbatical, a contemplative retreat. You need time to study the Scriptures and learn God's Will. The Corporation has become a liability to us and Gelli's people have arranged for it to be sold. The new owners are godless Japanese who will move in next month. All is agreed," he said with an air of finality, brooking no argument.

"But ... But, what about Project Maraschino?" he cried.

Cardinal Mirphy steepled manicured fingers against a clean-shaven chin, as if in prayer. "Project Maraschino is to be transferred directly to my control," he said. "That is all. You may leave now. May the Peace of God go with you always." He paused and then said, "Oh and on your way out, please ask Shelley to send for Mr. Maniato."

The Cardinal sat down on the still-warm executive seating vacated by John Visorkis, who emerged on the cruel New York concrete sidewalk beside the Biophar Drugs building a beaten man. The word had gotten out so quickly— within minutes! He'd even had to open doors himself; to push the elevator buttons himself. Shelley had totally ignored him as he walked out of his office. His limousine had already been reassigned. His mobile wouldn't work so he couldn't contact his lawyer. He needed to call a cab but he carried no money. As far as anyone in the Company was concerned he was dead.

Shelley, the secretary, knocked her way in.

"Email for you, Your Eminence. Flagged Project Maraschino, so I thought you'd want to know," she continued sulkily. "Please look at

25

your personal directory on the network. Do you know how?" she asked prettily. "Shall I show you?"

"No, no! I understand!" he replied impatiently. "I will do it. Now please leave." Shelley flounced out. She had already found a new job with a PR agency so why should she care?"

Mirphy logged onto his email, hit the decrypt button and stared at the brief message. His lips moved in involuntary prayer. He read ... First transaction successful. Am proceeding as planned to Moscow for next objective. Wish me God speed! JeanLuc.

Mirphy deleted the message.

The die was cast. He felt a cold shiver of fear running down his spine. His stomach felt sick with tension. He should pray. He needed to pray. This was the beginning of the Fulfilment. This was what he, as a Seneschal of the Priory Arcadia, had been planning for so many years. This was what King Solomon's diamonds, which the Priory had looted from the Temple in Jerusalem over a millennium ago, was paying for. This was Fulfilment of Prophesy made at the 'Splitting of the Elm' in 1188 when the Knights Templar and the Priory went their ordained different Paths – one to build an Empire, the other to disappear into the shadows to work secretly to bring about what was to be known as the Fulfilment. This was the enactment of the Prophecy of Malachi. This was the enactment of the True Interpretation of the Book of Revelations by St.John the Divine. The cleansing and rebirth of Christianity. The flushing out of Satan.

Yes, it was time to reformat the hard drive of history and install a new operating system, to use the terminology popular with his Vatican master, Pope John XXIV.

Cardinal Mirphy turned back to the computer at his desk and keyed in some commands.

Do you really want to DELETE everything? This process cannot be reversed.

Y/N

The screen contents disappeared leaving only the cursor on the black screen that blinked steadily, hypnotically. Blink, blink. Blink, blink – a coded light modulation from a pulsar star at the far end of a distant galaxy. He stared at it and hit Y.

CHAPTER 3

In Moscow. In Izmayolovo Park. In the winter snow. Everything is for sale.

Often, there is a strolling band of tubas threading a jaunty way through the crowded pathways between the makeshift market stalls and the battered cardboard suitcases lids laid open revealing their pitiful tawdry contents; a pack of dog-eared playing cards, a left footed shoe, a tarnished toothbrush, three used Trabant sparkplugs.

Here, to the accompaniment of the cheerful oompah oompah, Muscovites sell their few remaining possessions, their family heirlooms, their aged grandparents, their hungry wide-eyed children, their own bodies and threadbare souls for a fistful of worthless kopecks or hyper-inflated roubles.

Here, King Dollar rules.

Here, if you are Dollar-rich you could buy; a grand-piano played by Stalin, Gorbachev's bedroom slippers, a full-dress uniform of the Red Guard, a priceless picture robbed from the Kolomshoi Museum, FSB special issue condoms, or a set of colourful Afghanistan or Chechen Campaign medals plucked from the chest of a 'zinky boy'.

In Izmayolovo Park, what is sacred becomes profane, becomes profitable.

The Park steams in the dim Russian semi-arctic sunlight, from the morose crowds in their heavy damp winter clothing, vodka cigarette halitosis and the greasy smoke of countless small kerosene cooking fires with their vendors selling potato soup and assorted indeterminate smoke-flavoured morsels of charred flesh of canine, feline, equine or rodent origin.

Coming to and leaving from Izmayolovo Park, there is a constant traffic of Moscow City trams, buses and rickety vans and lorries put putting along with their inefficient Russian-built engines and unrefined gasoline belching black exhaust fumes into the cold air. As each Trabant, Skoda, Lada, Mosgreitch van or lorry approaches the entrance to the Park, a crowd surges towards it, people clinging to the doors, shouting urgent questions at the driver. "What is it? What have you

27

got? How much?"

By every stark leafless tree, by every stone bench, by those statues of the Heroes of the Soviet Union that still remain intact, groups of men argue and deal.

In the ruins of the Soviet Dream, times are bad. The dialectic of Dollar is on everybody's lips.

"Why have we come here, JeanLuc?" asked Igor as they spilled out of the crowded trolley-bus onto the pavement at the entrance to Izmayolovo Park.

"We are to meet someone here." JeanLuc waved his hand towards the Park. "Then we can go and get a drink—and some girls?"

"Sure. But first I have to arrange transport and make contact with our guide. They said he would be here—amongst the wooden roubles."

"I could've arranged all that for you. Why didn't you say?" Igor asked somewhat petulantly. He had agreed to act as JeanLuc's minder during the last leg of the trip to Moscow. They had pulled off the road on the outskirts of the City and after half an hour's tinkering under the massive hood, a thousand more US dollars had gone into Igor's private stash in the exhaust manifold. Delivery of the tractor tyres was made on schedule, the truck locked up in Karasamov's warehouse in the Lyublino District, away from prying eyes and thieving hands. The return load was being brought in and loaded in the course of the next week. Igor had no idea what it would be.

Igor hated to leave the truck, even for a second, but in Moscow there was no choice. He had to risk that the stash might be found; that the truck would not be stolen; that Karasamov had been properly fixed by the Germans. He couldn't carry much money on him – that would be suicidal. There were some precautions he had taken, of course; the truck's engine was immobilised—he carried the vital components of the electronic ignition in his pocket. The vehicle was also fitted with a powerful movement-tripped transmitter in case it was towed or transported away. He carried a signal direction-finder similar to that used by the Chicago police to find stolen cars. If any fat Russian traitorous swine got into the cab, infrared and air-movement detectors would send signals to the miniature bleeper sown into the collar of his coat and the truck itself would squeal with electronic mega-decibelled hysteria. Oh, yes! It would be a bitch of job to steal his truck. But that's the way it was. All owners of vehicles from the West take elaborate and expensive precautions against theft. Most drivers carry handguns, mace canisters and other assorted special weaponry depending on which macho Rambo movie was in vogue with drivers at the time. Pissing against the Firestone of one of these big babes made you liable to get your dick fried. Igor held onto that comforting thought as they entered the Park.

From out of the crush of people, a couple of burly Muscovites, faces hidden in their greatcoats, pressed hard against JeanLuc, grabbing his arms, pinioning his elbows from behind. Quick as a cat, Igor spun around; a knife glittered into his hand as if by magic. "Bugger off, you two!" he growled. "Let go of my friend or you get this." The men released JeanLuc and backed away hastily, gloved hands raised in protest. "No offence comrade, no offence!" They melted back into the crowd.

An old crone in black beside them looked sadly up at Igor and JeanLuc from under her shawl with rheumy red marble-veined eyes.

"This is a dangerous place, Madame Comrade!" muttered Igor.

The crone nodded in agreement. "But only if you have a young hard prick and money!" she cackled suddenly.

The two men pushed away from her in disgust. Christ! The people here are ugly, thought JeanLuc. Fellini would have had no problem casting Satyricon here.

After about half an hour of searching, they found the section of the Park where paintings and icons were being sold. Propped up or nailed to timber backing boards, rows and rows of cheap, crudely executed devotional pictures had been painted on plundered wood panels from the altars and confessionals of churches, abbeys, monasteries and cathedrals throughout Russia.

In spite of the crowds, there was not much business going on. The foreign tourist parties had been and gone in the morning and were now back in the relative safety of the Hyatts, Hiltons and Holiday Inns that now surrounded Red Square like the oyster shell around a pearl.

"How will you recognise the contact?" asked Igor in dismay, as he surveyed the numerous vendors and crowded aisles ahead of them.

29

"He will have a reproduction picture on show like this. Look."
JeanLuc fished a colour postcard out of his coat pocket and Igor peered at it gloomily. The postcard depicted Leonardo da Vinci's fresco of the Last Supper.

"God. There must be thousands of these!" cried Igor.

"Not necessarily," JeanLuc said, "let's take a look. Here, you take the card." Together they wandered up the aisles, scanning the displays.

A band of tubas came marching down the aisle towards them, pushing them to one side. As they steamed past, all big swarthy men, cheeks puffing and blowing with exertion, eyes bulging rhythmically in tune with the funereal marching tune in bass E flat, JeanLuc's roving eye was suddenly caught and held ... by a face.

He waited until the last of the band had oompahed past. Yes! There she was again. JeanLuc felt a jolt of electric excitement run up and down his spine. Those were features that he knew! As if some long-buried memory circuit had suddenly switched in, he knew with magnetic certainty that this woman was to be his lover. He had never felt the pure blue flame of desire like this; totally unexpected and of mystical intensity.

Igor was plucking at his arm. "What the hell are you staring at, JeanLuc? Come on, I want to get out of this dump."

JeanLuc ignored him and walked across to the stand. The young woman who was the focus of JeanLuc's ardent attention got up from a folding chair and stood beside the rows of icons. She awaited JeanLuc's approach. A possible sale here, she thought. Those of her features that could be seen were Slavonic; high wide cheekbones and huge dark eyes set wide apart in a clear-skinned alabaster face above a flattish nose. A thin hand-rolled cigarette sat jauntily between full red lips like the stick in a lollipop.

Oh, shit. He's got a fucking Madonna complex! Just what I fucking needed, Igor thought. He couldn't personally see anything worth chasing after. There were a thousand tarts like her in bars and restaurants all over the city. He knew what his tastes were and they certainly didn't include her sort. Too skinny and dark. He preferred big comfortable flaxen-haired women with plenty of stamina and juice, with whom he could wrestle drunkenly all night. Give me a Wagnerian

30

Brunhilde trumpet-lady every time. Boom, Boom! Now that was his kind of woman—not these intense dark bitches with eyes like drowning pools and breasts like hard little apples.

JeanLuc and the woman had started an animated conversation. Igor turned away disgustedly and commenced scanning the many pictures in front of him. A framed print jumped into his consciousness like a jigsaw piece snapping into place. Yes! This looked like it! He compared it with the postcard he held in his hand. This was definitely a match. Well, well! It must belong to the girl. She must be the contact! Igor chuckled inwardly.

"Hey, lover boy!" he shouted New York style. "I've found it!" Igor beckoned JeanLuc who came reluctantly, followed by the woman. "Look! This is the one." Igor cried holding up the postcard against the print.

"I know, I know," JeanLuc said impatiently. "For Christ's sake put that thing away—you're attracting attention."

"How do you know? I just found it."

"Fate, probably," JeanLuc said cryptically and scowled. He turned back to the woman.

"Who is this?" she asked nodding towards Igor.

"Sophia. Meet Igor Golemov, my friend and protector." Igor nodded his head in acknowledgement and stared at her with the calculating eyes of a cattle-market auctioneer. She stared back unperturbed. "Igor, this is our contact, Sophia Yemeljan. Come, we must leave at once; there is a great deal to be done."

"Hey! Wait a minute" cried Sophia, "I cannot just drop everything you know. I have money to earn to feed my family. In any case, these pictures must be packed away carefully." Sophia looked anxiously about.

"Don't worry, I have money. I will buy all your pictures now," JeanLuc said impatiently. "Just leave them here and we'll go."

"How much?" she asked, standing her ground. "I want to know how much you will pay for all these?" she gestured towards the rows of pictures.

"One thousand dollars," JeanLuc said carefully. "For that price, you must also accompany me and become part of the team," he added.

For a long moment when time seemed to stand still, Sophia looked at him as if considering. A flash of understanding suddenly seemed to pass between them. She collected her bag and said brightly: "Okay, boys. Let's go!"

And they went without a backward glance.

CHAPTER 4

His Holiness, Cardinal Mirphy paced up and down the office recently vacated by the now-forgotten John Visorkis, ex- CEO of Biophar Drugs Corporation. Mirphy was angry with himself. Things had been allowed to slide. He had not exercised the rigid control he normally had over his own staff and the bishops of the diocese.

An ascetic man with scrupulous good taste, he felt distinctly uncomfortable in John Visorkis' overblown pretentious office with its Fifties paraphernalia. Sweet Jesus, he thought, how could a man have a Cadillac for a desk? Sure, it may be crucial good taste in the purple velvet twilight of some Black Baron's Harlem drug dealing den. But here? In the HQ of one of the premier pharmaceutical companies of the US? One of the best secret revenue-producers and money-launderers of the Catholic Church? No.

His thoughts turned to the upcoming sale of the company. The Church badly needed money now, squeaky clean or not. There was never enough, despite the huge revenues generated from the various business operations and share dealing scams put together over the past two decades—a fine legacy of Cody-Marcinkus.

The sale of BC would net a tidy three billion dollars. Not bad, considering the serious problems the new Japanese owners were about to inherit—the defunct R & D programmes and the carefully hidden problems with the best-selling FlavAdd product which appeared to have serious teratogenic properties similar to Thalidomide. This was a fuse burning towards a future time-bomb that even the Cardinal couldn't bear to think about.

Oh, yes! The Japanese would find BC a very slippery foothold in the US market, despite the well-located prime lakeside Chicago property and manufacturing facilities. They would find out soon enough that, in the thirty years of operation on the site, BC had been dumping leaky drums of radio-isotopes and complex organic solvents under the vast employee car-parks and piping, into the Great Lakes, waste of such toxicity that no fish, no aquatic life, no bacteria had ever been found within a four-mile radius of the outfall; not even the shit-loving algae could bloom.

Still, these were not his concerns. The Church wanted its money. The Holy Father in Rome had complained that revenue was down and this must be rectified. BC must also be sold before the employees found out that their pension fund had been Maxwelled. BC must be sold before the Federal Investigators finally unravelled the fact that the Church was the main aggregate stockholder through an intricate network of shell companies and private individuals who had been blackmailed into making over their earthly shares in return for protection from a premature early collection of equity in Heaven. And also before it became known that their accounts had been Andersonised. Ah, the sins of Sindona.

His Eminence was snapped out of his reverie by a knock on the door. "Come in. Come in! he called impatiently. "Ah. Maniato, is it?"

"Yes Sir. Joel Maniato. Head of Security."

"Good. Good. Come, sit down. I need a progress report on various projects and there's work to be done. Let me inform you, first of all, that Mr. Visorkis has resigned as of today. I am appointing you as Chief Executive Officer until the hand-over of the company to its new owners is completed."

"New owners?" gaped Joel. "New owners? Who are they? I've not been informed."

"Of course not. It's none of your business. Your job is to assist in the smooth transfer of the company to the buyers. I will assist you. Don't worry, it will all be okay. Now tell me what is happening on Project Maraschino. Where is JeanLuc now?"

There was a buzz on the intercom. "I have those files you requested Your Eminence. Shall I bring them in?"

"Yes, do that will you, Shelley. Thank you." The Cardinal released his finger from the button.

Shelley Lang, sexecutive assistant to John Visorkis, came in. Both men regarded her hungrily as she catwalked slinkily towards them. Shelley could provoke sexual interest from a blind castrated armadillo or pump up a truck flattened hedgehog. It would be inhuman not to lust after a body which had all the attributes of Roger Rabbit's Toon Lover: lustrous blond hair and a mouth like the swirl of raspberry syrup

34

in an ice-cream sundae, set in the face of an angel only recently kicked out of Heaven.

Dumping a couple of fat files on the Cadillac desk, Shelley turned on a high heel and slutted out, well aware of the Viagra impression she had made. She closed the door behind her.

"Does she come with the job?" asked Joel somewhat breathlessly.

"I suppose so," the Cardinal agreed reluctantly. He walked forward, picked up one of the files and opened it. "Ah, yes. This is your dossier I have here, Maniato.J. Let's see now." He quickly flicked through the pages of the personnel file.

"You have been a naughty boy, Mr.Maniato!" he said as he put down the file and looked over at the flinching Joel.

"How so?" Joel exclaimed. "You've got nothing on me. I'm Head of Security here. I'm the one that knows where all the skeletons are buried. I'm Mr Clean."

Cardinal Mirphy smiled. "You don't really think we would have promoted you to where you are now without having a hold of some sort on you, do you? Now be sensible, Joel. You're an intelligent man. It is in your dossier over there, the whole thing—enough to put you away for years."

"You're bluffing!" Joel said heatedly.

"Why should I? It's standard industry practice even in the Holy Church. Insurance for all of us—life insurance," he repeated with a meaningful look.

"I haven't done anything wrong."

"Well, maybe not by your set of values, Mr Maniato. But these are not shared by the US Legal system or the majority of US citizens. If I recall correctly, Exodus 22 has something to say about it too." He pursed his lips and looked judiciously at Joel. "I would say that the Polaroid pictures and the information about your cocaine use held in that file would get you five, maybe seven years. Given the right prosecutor."

Joel wracked his brain. Where had he slipped up? He couldn't begin to think how they had got hold of anything. He had been so careful. It must be more than fifteen years ago, long before he joined BC, when he was still at college...

35

"Oh, yes. I can see you thinking, Joel. How is it possible? Well we do have our little ways, don't we? Tell me, out of curiosity. What is oral sexual congress with a chimpanzee like? Was she cute? Lovely rubbery lips, eh!?"

Joel blushed crimson. He felt humiliated and shamed. Cardinal Mirphy heaved with laughter. "It was a college prank. Just a college dare," he mumbled.

"I dare say it was. But it's too late for that now. In any case, it hasn't done your career any harm. In fact, it may help to interest Shelley in you!" He roared with laughter again. He wiped his eyes with a tissue from the container on the desk. "We really must get down to business. Where were we? Oh, yes. Project Maraschino. Where is JeanLuc now?"

CHAPTER 5

JeanLuc and Igor followed the slight figure of Sophia, as she ducked and weaved through the crowd towards the East Gate of Izmaylovo Park. She led them to a large battered van parked in a side street leading off the main road that circled the Park. Fortunately, it had not snowed that day so they didn't have to dig the vehicle out. The two men got straight in, sliding across the hard bench seat. Sophia pulled the bonnet latch and lifted the hood. She fished a distributor rotor arm out from of her coat pocket and expertly snapped it back into place under the distributor cap. She pulled a small 6 cm length of rubber tubing out of the same pocket and, reaching down into the engine compartment, slipped one end over a small tap which had been welded to the cut end of the petrol feed pipe. The other end she joined to the other half of the pipe leading to the carburettor. She then connected the battery earth lead to a bolt on the chassis with a big butterfly nut. Finally, she replaced the windscreen wipers retrieved from under the driver's seat. Jobs done, she dropped the heavy bonnet down with a clang and clambered into the driver's seat beside the two men. "You can't be too careful these days," she explained. The two men nodded in agreement.

Although empty, the van smelled strongly of paint, varnish and turpentine. Sophia pushed the key into the ignition and turned the engine, which fired after the third attempt and settled down into a rough tappety rhythm. They backed out into the street.

"If you have dollars, we'll go to get some gasoline first" Sophia shouted above the noise of the engine.

"OK," agreed JeanLuc. "Where will you get it?"

"I know a place near here on the ring road where we can get good Army gasoline on the black market. There will be no questions—even members of the government get it there," she yelled flashing a smile at them, displaying a perfect set of white teeth. The two men sat back on the hard seat and let Sophia concentrate on driving the van, trying to avoid the potholes in the crumbling roads still mostly unrepaired from the days of the Union decades of hard winters ago.

They drove down a long dark unlighted underpass in the east of the city. "It is here, I think," Sophia said peering ahead into the gloom. Beside the road, in the other lane, there were two canvas sided Army trucks parked together beside the kerb. Deep in shadow, they could only be seen when a vehicle silhouetted them in its headlights. Sophia drove through the underpass and out into the greying dusk beyond. She pulled off at the next junction and drove slowly back down the other side into the tunnel entrance of the underpass. They pulled in behind a Lada saloon that had stopped behind the two trucks.

The curtains at the rear of the truck nearest to them were parted to reveal four men. All wore black balaclavas. Two were armed with Kalashnikov AK47 submachine guns while the other two worked humping the drums of gasoline that were stacked high inside.

"We should get one drum for about $100, here," said Sophia excitedly, the headlights of passing vehicles reflected like fireflies in her large dark eyes.

"I hope you know what you're doing," Igor said, eyes flitting back and forth trying to gauge the level of danger to which they were exposed. He knew this sort of black-market refuelling went on all the time, but when in Moscow he usually left all that to Karasamov. His own truck carried about half the necessary diesel to make the trip from Brest to Moscow, the balance he obtained with coupons from official diesel stations along the way, usually at Smolensk. He paid for it at the going rate, about a couple of dollars per litre.

The man in the Lada ahead of them was stacking jerrycans and containers of every description below a tapped drum in the rear of the truck. Quickly and efficiently, the two men dropped plastic hoses into the containers and started to fill them. Each time they moved the hose from one container to another a small amount of gasoline spilled onto the road. There was a strong odour of gasoline and exhaust fume in the underpass.

"I would put that cigarette out if I were you, Sophia," Igor said calmly. She hurriedly stubbed it out.

"I'll go and talk to them," she said and opened the cab door to get out. She walked around the front of the van onto the kerb and went up to the truck. She beckoned to the armed men standing in the back of the truck, one of whom jumped down and went to her. JeanLuc and Igor watched anxiously from the van. Igor fiddled with his knife. He'd left his machine pistol in the lorry and swore to himself that he would pick it up at the earliest opportunity. This was just the sort of time when they would need it.

Sophia finished talking with the armed man and walked back towards them holding up her forefinger and thumb in a circle of success. "Five drums for $520," she said smiling up at JeanLuc when he wound down the side window. "They wanted $600, but I said that was all we had and they agreed."

JeanLuc shrugged off his coat and pulled it round his knees to cover his movements. Under the coat he unzipped one of the compartments of his money belt and extracted, by feel, used ten-dollar bills. Most US dollar transactions in Russia are done with used small- denomination notes. Large denomination or clean money implies there is more where that came from, leaving one open to robbery or worse.

"Go with her, Igor," ordered JeanLuc as he handed down the George Washingtons to Sophia. "I'll stay here behind the wheel in case of trouble."

"Okay, Boss." Igor dropped down beside Sophia and they walked together back to the gasoline truck. Beauty and the Beast! JeanLuc smiled to himself and slid over to get behind the steering wheel. He turned the ignition on but did not start the engine.

The man in front, with the Lada, finished filling and capping his cans and loading them into the back of the car. There was a pool of spilled gasoline by the tail of the lorry. The fumes were overpowering. He handed up a thick sheaf of roubles the size of a house brick to one of the gunmen in the truck who pulled a torch out and carefully examined each note until he was satisfied. The Lada started, pulled out into the traffic and drove off into the dark.

Igor and Sophia watched as a block and tackle was set up hanging from a steel bar in the canopy of the truck. They rolled out drums and lowered them with a sling onto the road one by one. After a brief

39

conversation with Sophia, one of the men handed down two planks of wood to use as a ramp for the van. Sophia and Igor carried the planks to the van, opened the rear doors and laid the ramp. The drums were rolled along the pavement, up the ramp and into the back of the van with a lot of grunting and heaving effort from the two workmen. Eventually, they finished and Sophia slammed the rear doors closed.

One of the gunmen walked over to the van. He unhitched his weapon and held it loosely pointing at the road but with unmistakable threat. He stared in at JeanLuc through the slits of the knitted balaclava. "That was a lot of extra work, comrade. I would like some recompense for my hardworking colleagues," he said in a thick muffled voice.

JeanLuc stared back at him. "We have no more dollars. She told you that," he said and waved his hands helplessly.

"I don't believe you. I think it is only fair that we are paid properly for our trouble." JeanLuc heard the click as the safety was flicked off.

"Please comrade. We don't want any trouble. We are poor people. It has taken many months for us to save this money for gasoline. It is needed for our business."

"I don't give a shit. What else have you got?" he grated.

"I have some roubles, " said Igor who had come up silently behind him. The man backed away from the van holding the gun threateningly aimed at JeanLuc through the windscreen.

"I don't want fucking roubles. They are worthless," he shouted. Igor carefully put away the sheaf of roubles. "Okay, okay. Give me the dollars!" Sophia handed over the slim bundle. The man snatched the money and carefully backed away from them. He handed it up to the other gunman who proceeded to examine each note in the light of his torch.

Behind Sophia's van, a Lada saloon taxi had pulled up. The driver beeped his horn impatiently.

Igor and Sophia jumped into the cab and JeanLuc started the engine. The man finished examining the money and shouting a command at the other gunman, picked up his own weapon. They beckoned, machine guns pointed with unmistakable menace at JeanLuc. Oh, shit! thought JeanLuc.

"Sophia!" he said urgently. "Give me a cigarette, quick!". Hands shaking, Sophia spilled a couple out of the pack onto JeanLuc's lap. Pushing in the dashboard lighter, he stuck the untipped cigarette in his mouth; flakes of foul tasting tobacco sticking to his tongue in a mouth dry with tension. "You know what to do, Igor?" JeanLuc said. "When I drop the cigarette, hit the gas and go. I'll jump on as you go past. Okay? It's the only way—these boys are looking for trouble."

"Okay, Boss," Igor said calmly. Sophia, eyes saucer wide, was shaking and clutching her coat to herself with white-knuckled fingers.

The dashboard lighter popped out and JeanLuc pushed the cigarette into its glowing face. He pulled a deep inhalation of tart pungent smoke and opened the cab door. He left the cigarette hanging laconically from the side of his mouth. The van engine ticked over sluggishly.

"Put your hands in the air and don't give us any trouble, comrade." JeanLuc stood by the tailgate of the truck, hands raised. As one of the gunmen lowered his weapon to drop off the back of the truck, JeanLuc let the dully-glowing cigarette drop from his mouth into the pool of gasoline by his feet.

To hell with them! he thought. With a fearsome whoosh, the gasoline exploded. JeanLuc threw himself backwards into the road. The two gunmen, engulfed in a sheet of flame, tightened scorched fingers on hair-triggered Kalashnikovs spraying bullets wildly in all directions.

Igor jammed the van in gear and booted the foot-throttle to the floor. The van lurched forward into and through the sudden wall of yellow flame ahead of them. Twisting the wheel violently, Igor swerved the van out into the road and shot off into the underpass, dragging a corona of blue fire.

Behind, there was a tremendous whump, as one of the bullet-punctured drums exploded. A near silent river of flame zipped eerily down the sloping roadway away from the burning trucks. Men ran for their lives from the inferno. The Lada taxi-man watched in stark horror as the truck in front of him disappeared in a balloon of orange flame. He dived for cover to the floor of his vehicle.

Like a cork popping from a bottle, Sophia's van emerged from the underpass. Igor clubfooted the brakes bringing the van screeching to a juddering halt. He flung the cab door open.

"Looking for me, Igor?" JeanLuc let go of the wing mirror

stanchion and dropped to the road with a gasp. Sophia opened her door and he climbed in beside her.

"Come on , Igor! Move it!" he yelled.

JeanLuc turned towards Sophia. Leaning over he pressed his smoke blackened blistered eyebrowless features into her startled face and kissed her hard on those dark full lips. He felt what can only be described as a fierce biblical stirring in the loins. Sophia's hands flapped whitely like dying fish but her fingers soon dug into JeanLuc's coat clawing at his shoulders with an equal passion.

Igor sighed heavily and steered the van Westwards back into the city. "Hey! Where the hell are we going" he yelled in exasperation. Sophia pushed at JeanLuc who reluctantly heaved himself off her body and moved across the seat to stare out the window, breathing hard.

"Pull over, Igor. I'll drive us home," she said shakily. Igor did as was told and pulled into the kerb. In the opposite carriageway, a fire engine deedah deedahed at high speed towards where they had just come from.

*

"Papa, this is Alexei Federov and Igor Golemov. They are the people we were told to look out for. Sorry we are late but we had some trouble." Sophia gave a strained laugh.

The grizzled old man with long white beard and hair waved the weary travellers into the house with a welcoming smile that soon turned to concern when he saw the damage to JeanLuc's clothes and face. JeanLuc stank of gasoline and damp charred cloth.

A large operatic-looking woman emerged from the living room and emotionally folded her daughter into a capacious bosom. Igor's eyes flickered in his impassive face.

"Are you all right, my child?" she fussed. "Are you hurt? Who are these ruffians? My God! Your face is black and your lips are bleeding. What has happened?" she asked frantically.

"We went to get some gasoline from the black marketeers," explained Sophia. "But they wanted to rip us off. We were lucky to escape alive! Please, Mama, let me go. I expect Alexei and Igor want to clean up, get changed and have something to eat. I certainly do."

"Yes, of course. How stupid of me. Come in, come in. You can use

Sergei's room. I will make us some dinner."

"Thank you, Madame Yemeljan. You are very gracious and your hospitality is most welcome. We will, of course, pay you for any inconvenience." JeanLuc said formally bowing low over her hand.

"No. No! Don't speak of it. You are a guest in our house, it would be an insult."

"Shut up, Mother! Alexei has plenty of money. Let him give you some of it, " Sophia said harshly, a slight glitter in her eyes.

"Now let's stop this and let these gentlemen get cleaned up, shall we?" said Dmitri Yemeljan diplomatically.

JeanLuc and Igor went upstairs with Saskia Yemeljan and were each shown into a large high-ceilinged bedroom. In JeanLuc's room, the walls were papered with posters of Elvis the King—clearly a young man's room, the missing Sergei no doubt. At least the room was toasty warm. Both men pulled off their grimy clothes and JeanLuc went down the corridor to run a bath and do what repairs he could to his face and body. In his room, Igor fell asleep instantly, naked on the large double bed—a nasty shock for Goldilocks.

There was a knock on the bathroom door and JeanLuc opened it a crack after wrapping a towel around his waist.

"You can wear this until we fix you up with some clothes, Alexei. A slim bare arm stretched in holding out a white cotton robe. JeanLuc took it and the arm disappeared, closing the door softly behind it.

After bathing and washing off the accumulated grime of the trip, he felt good and relaxed. He examined himself critically in the full-length bathroom mirror. Not bad for forty years old, he thought. No fat yet. Firm belly and buttocks, strong muscled legs, a body much admired and fondled by women. In between bouts of passion several had traced curiously the distinctive rose-shaped birthmark between his shoulder blades. His Semitic nose and cheeks were now reddened and blistered as if sunburned and his eyebrows had been burned off short, giving him a strange startled look. His long dark golden hair was unaffected since he usually tied it back in a ponytail.

He pulled the robe over his head and tied the thin cord around his waste. Very nice, very Bedouin! he thought. He shaved carefully with the tackle he found in the medicine cupboard above the sink. JeanLuc finished his ablutions and padded back along the corridor to Sergei's bedroom. Igor was lying naked on his back, legs spread-eagled, cock stuck up in the air like a fat stubby cigar.

"Hey, beautiful! Wake up and go get cleaned up."

Igor grunted, shook himself and grabbed a towel off the bed.

"Took your bloody time didn't you? All pretty and perfumed are we now, ducky?" he muttered caustically and marched to the bathroom.

A wonderful odour of cooking wafted from the kitchen. JeanLuc was ravenous with hunger as he went down the stairs.

Dmitri Yemeljan, Sophia's father, was waiting for him in the living room. There was roaring fire lit in the large ornate fireplace. The bottle of Stolichnaya vodka was open on the mantelpiece with several shot glasses beside it. Dmitri poured. JeanLuc drank. "Nastrovia!"

Several Nastrovias later, JeanLuc felt a warm glow of alcoholic contentment seep through his bones. He started to feel exuberantly Russian.

"So. What of my stock, Alexei? What have you done with that?" asked Dmitri.

"I bought it all from your daughter. One thousand dollars." "All?" asked Dmitri incredulously.

"Yeah, all of it. Why? Sophia said it was all tourist stuff—trinkets. Do you want it back?"

"No, No!" Dmitri said hastily," I just wondered, that is all."

"We also bought drums of gasoline, most of which we will probably need for our searches. Did they explain to you why I am here?"

"Yes, of course. His Eminence Cardinal Mirphy, said to extend to you all the help we could. Naturally, I am only too delighted to further God's work in this unholy country."

"Yeah well, I don't know about that," JeanLuc said carefully. He needed food to combat the vodka. "Thank you for your hospitality. It is wonderful to feel accepted in your home," he said formally.

"You are very welcome," said Saskia, coming into the room from the kitchen. The smell of food was driving JeanLuc crazy. "We will eat as soon as Sophia and your tough-looking friend come down," Saskia said smiling warmly at him. "Please sit down by the fire and have another drink!"

CHAPTER 6

"He wants to see the Veronica? Tell him he will have to wait until the end of the next century, like everyone else. No! No! I don't care who he is, how many books he's written or who his friends are, he'll just have to wait. He says he'll be dead by then? Fine, that'll be one less meddling amateur. God spare us from these people, Guido!"

Cardinal Von Helsinger banged the phone down and pushed himself away from his desk. A big obese man with small eyes dotted like black shiny currants in a pasty moon face the colour of dishwater, suspended over a plump cushion of double chins, wisps of black hair combed back in greasy furrows—the very image of a dissipated mediaeval red hat so often reproduced in sinister portrait after portrait in the Vatican, Uffizi or Siennese galleries.

Here was a man who secretly hankered after the old days, not the Fifties or Sixties, no—the real old days, maybe sometime around 1300 AD when there were plenty of hapless heretics on whom to practice his Inquisitorial arts and inclinations.

Thoughtfully, he stroked his many-layered chins. The phone conversation had given him an idea. An idea of how to implement the wishes of the Holy Father and to distract the pesky unwanted attentions of holy relic investigators. He smiled to himself. Yes, indeed! Kill two birds with one stone. Drop a pebble into the lake of history and see where the ripples go! Put a cat amongst the flying peckers! It would need some planning of course and a Curial Special Projects Team for implementation.

Cardinal Von Helsinger stubbed the intercom button on his desk and spoke in his grating voice. "Sister Emmanuel. Please come in—there is the Lord's work to be done."

Sister Emmanuel came in with a secretary's shorthand notebook clutched in her bony hand. Face as yellow as tallow wax and as narrow as two hands folded in prayer, Sister Emmanuel's hard brown eyes—like those on a cheap toy teddy bear—stared out at His Reverence, from under the crow-black cowl of her nun's habit, with the fanaticism of terminal bigotry. "I am ready, Holy Father," she said.

45

"I need to go to Argentina tonight after evening Mass. Have the Vatican Lear Jet readied at Fiumicino. Call Claudio and Cardinal Paliado and have them meet me at the 'plane." He added, "arrange a private audience for Dr. Ian Milson for next Thursday at 2.00, for Mr Michael Bagent at 3.00 and Mr. David Pallop at 4.30. You will find their details in the file marked 'Pests'." Von Helsinger paused and tapped his teeth with a pen.

"I will be going to New York after Sao Paulo and will be back on Wednesday night. Please call Cardinal Mirphy in New York to alert him of my arrival. I may want to go on to Chicago. Ring Father Moloc in Paris and tell him to activate the Plan codenamed Atbash without delay. I want progress reports twice daily. Use the secure link to the Lear Jet only." He paused while Sister Emmanuel wrote it down.

"Oh, yes and make sure to order some decent food for the flight!"

"At once, Holy Father" said Sister Emmanuel obediently and left the room.

The Cardinal felt excitement rising in him. He hadn't felt like this since the heady days before and during the Conclave. Gross Gott but those were desperate hectic times, he recalled. But his man had squeaked in by the narrowest of margins after several burnings of the black smoke, many secret intercontinental phone calls, ultimatums and brazen threats.

Cardinal Von Helsinger, Grand Inquisitor of the Holy Roman Church, had started to feel hungry again—enough to spin out a complex web of cunning intrigue, at the centre of which he would sit with arachnoid patience, waiting for those delicious ambrosial tingling twitches which signalled the struggling of his political prey. Cocooned in sticky Vatican machinations, he could suck out their finances, their Mafioso muscle, their immortal souls, at will. The desiccated husks of Von Helsinger's victims littered the corridors of power within the volatile Italian government, the Curia, the EEC, the CIA and Civil Services of most Western governments. Men for whom there was no hope, no future, no forgiveness, interest on past misdeeds compounded hourly by relentless computers that never forget. Men and women with hollowed-out cheeks and the dull hooded eyes of advanced inoperable Kafka.

There was only one source of mortal dread in this world for Von Helsinger. Only one sphere of political influence in which he had not a fat podgy finger. This was the Priory Arcadia—perpetrators of Nestoriansism, Carpocratianism, Catharism, Albigensian Heresy, Modernism and sworn enemies of Roman Catholicism since the Council of Nicaea in AD325.

Not for the first time, Von Helsinger wondered what the Priory was up to. Were they behind this Jerusalem break-in? He was sure Licio Belli would have known. Belli's successor in Sao Paulo, whom he was travelling to see tonight, still controlled vast slices of the Vatican billions and share blocks that were used to finance what his CIA chums like to call 'black operations'—secret Inquisition Projects like Plan Atbash. But he didn't have the P2 sources that his dear friend Licio had had at his peak. Many of these had been murdered, 'suicided' or disappeared in the recent chaos of Italian government.

"Sister Emmanuel? I will take my afternoon tea now. Did you get that excellent torte from Fabriccio's bakery? Yes? Good. Please find and bring in the Project File marked Atbash as well. Thank you."

*

Across the courtyard, in the Papal Apartments, His Holiness Pope John XXIV lay on his daybed and stared at the small framed motto on the far wall. It was hand-scripted text on velum in black and gold letters. Taken from the twelfth century prophesies of the Irish monk Malachi, it read "John XXIV— Reaper of the Whirlwind." He didn't like the sound of that at all. He never had. His predecessor of the same name had been 'Shepherd and Navigator'. Now that was rich in hidden meaning and good connotation. But Reaper of the Whirlwind? That smacked of Divine retribution of some sort. He'd had a team of Curial semanticists working many weeks on finding alternative meanings for the original Latin, but all were essentially similar. There was no way around it; Malachi had predicted he would be a harvester of death.

The Holy Father had subsequently taken great pains to suppress this particular prophesy, even going so far as to author a Pastoral Letter castigating prophets of any sort—now adding Malachi, who was previously well regarded by his predecessors, to a list of proscribed visionaries which included such luminaries as St.Bernard, St.Dagobert

47

and Nostradamus.

At the age of sixty-eight, His Holiness was still in good health apart from some arthritis. His mind was still agile, but the tremendous workload and relentless responsibilities of the Papacy were eroding the cunning and poker playing skills that had led to his election. Born Emilio D'Ascriba in Madrid, the 'Spanish Pope' was chosen largely by the South American and Third World votes. Just before World War II, his parents emigrated with their only child to Brazil where they established a small shoe shop business. Showing an early vocation for the Church after seeing so many well-fed priests, young Emilio was educated in a seminary in Rio de Janeiro before starting pastoral work in the same sprawling city. Rising swiftly through the clerical ranks due to dedicated and unerring administrative skills in one of the largest hothouse dioceses in the world, he became the youngest Archbishop in the S.American Church. Paul VI posted him to Spain where he rapidly assumed important places on Vatican committees dealing with South American issues. In due course, with the backing and insistence of Opus Dei, this work earned him a red hat. He had made it known that he had voted for Benelli, Wojtyla and Ratzinger in the previous three Conclaves, thus establishing a reputation for 'political correctness' which stood him in good stead at his own election to the Ultimate Office.

Papa Emilio rarely delegated anything. His modus operandi was complete precision control of a few selected issues. Throughout his Papacy a multitude of urgent complex issues had gone unaddressed or put off because they weren't on the Pope's agenda. His attitude was if it couldn't be done properly, let it not be done at all. This approach had enabled him to stay clear of the various scandals that had rocked the Church hierarchy over the decades and had enabled him to carve out the niche of expertise for which he was known; giving the Papacy a clear direction. His refusal to delegate, make senior appointments or even spend money, had allowed power to concentrate in his own hands to an unprecedented extent with a concomitant weakening of the Vatican bureaucracy. Pope John XXIV was not a team player. He expected the Vatican to behave like a well-oiled machine to carve out and perpetuate his personal God-given vision for a recalcitrant unbelieving world. Tutored in the ways of Escriva de Balagua, he pursued his narrowly defined goals with ruthless efficiency, showing that he understood clearly the role and sources of money in power politics—lessons learned the hard way in South America which was still his political power base.

Like few of his contemporaries, he knew what real poverty was. He had understood early in life how Catholicism provided a bulwark and social framework against nihilism and militaristic capitalism. He had realised that he would stay alive longer as a dictator of the Church, than of a military junta. The same unwritten rules and skills applied to both jobs and as far as he could see, the only difference being one of sex. As a South American dictator you got plenty of every imaginable kind of sex, while as a Catholic churchman you got zip. Since he was not a highly sexed person in the first place and in the second there were well-established ways of privately indulging sexual appetite out of the limelight, Emilio D'Ascriba saw no contest in the choice of occupation. Power over others is the ultimate aphrodisiac.

As far as his personal beliefs were concerned, in his secret heart he was a Pauline Christian. The real Jesus had not been a factor in Catholic thinking for 1,500 years. He had no patience with simplistic visionaries and Jesus-based Fundamentalism. Since the time of Constantine, the Church had been, in his view rightly, suppressing or manipulating any information passed down about the 'real' Jesus who is regarded in the higher echelons of the Church as largely an irrelevance or, in the words of Pope Alexander VI, 'it has served us well, this myth of Christ.'

A rich married Jew of royal blood spouting regurgitated Essene dogma, military head of the zealots intent on wresting the throne of Israel from the Romans, a 'seeker after smooth things' and thereby suffering the inevitable crucifying consequence. He couldn't imagine why anyone, apart from historians, would be interested in such a person, let alone worship him. What Emilio did admire was what the Church had subsequently made of the basic story. He had to admit also to a sneaking regard for the way in which Jesus had organised his life to fulfil Old Testament prophesies so as to attain 'Messiah' status amongst the Jews. This showed sophisticated understanding of Jewish people and their mentality but no more than what would be expected of a trained Pharisee steeped in Biblical learning with years of intensive postdoctoral study at the Qumran desert university. Pope John XXIV thought he would probably have done exactly the same, given the same historical circumstances.

It was only after the Council of Nicaea that modern Christianity managed to acquire and consolidate the tools that would transform it into a world religion. With these tools, adopted and borrowed from other more successful religions such as Mithraism, Christianity finally acquired the right psychological formulae to strike a rich reverberating chord in the human psyche. Mysticism, revelation, crowd psychotics, archetypal symbolism, hierarchical structuring, repository of trust, leaps of faith and as an opposite counter-force evil in the form of Satan backed up by threats of real or social damnation. All the essential ingredients missing from Jesus' narrow political and militaristic aims of re-acquiring Israel.

The Church had re-written history marvellously, in his view. God knows they had more than enough material in the archives of antiquities in the vaults here in Vatican City—from the Dead Sea and Nag Hamadi Scrolls, the Mar Saba library and other records, to completely substantiate a mundane historically accurate view of Jesus the Zealot. But why? What purpose would it serve? It is debatable whether most people would even care. These stories were already about and passively sanctioned by the Church in that no active suppression was done—not these days anyway.

People do not want or need Truth. This was a lesson he had learned long ago in the slums of Rio. People want comfort in a harsh world, a belief in a hierarchical value system, an unattainable goal, a bit of magic and a champion of nebulous causes like the 'common good' or righteousness. These are summarised in the concept of God. This was not cynicism; this was action out of belief and knowledge of human nature.

The threat was not from historical revelations alone, no. It was from ambitious people who wanted to take over at the top. Replace him and the Vatican with another hierarchy essentially similar under the same banner of Christianity. The business and product of the religion would stay the same; just the people at the top would change—just like a corporate take-over. There would be changes in corporate policy, of course, to reflect the new men.

Emilio had always known who these people were—the Grand Master and members of the Priory Arcadia. Historical revelation, monarchic symbology and other psychological power tools would be the weapons of attack to undermine the trust in the present Church. This is why the Q4 material and the Podgorny File of '67 must never get into their hands.

The Priory would not want to destroy Christianity as a religion. Not now. It was a true psychic Cadillac with plenty of juice and deep comfortable upholstery. No! They just want to get behind that steering wheel and stick their own flat feet on the gas pedal. And they were coming in the guise of the Repo man! What bloody cheek!

The Pope felt a rare flush of anger that got him off his bed. He must get back to work!

CHAPTER 7

JeanLuc couldn't and didn't want to imagine how many hours of queuing in the snow or cooking effort had gone into the elaborate meal that Saskia had prepared for them. A fine Russian meal, in fine company; a few warm homely hours in a cold dangerous foreign land. Even the impassive Igor melted sufficiently to raise a strong baritone voice in Polish song followed by a rousing rendition of the Beatles song *'Back in the USSR'* sung with real emotion—as the vodka level dropped in the bottle and rose correspondingly in the bloodstream.

Back in, back in the USSR, You don't know how lucky you are ... Boy!

JeanLuc found it impossible to keep his eyes off Sophia who had changed out of the ubiquitous blue jeans and T-shirt of Russian youth, into a soft crimson dress in a heavy velvet material topped by a white peasant style blouse cut low revealingly. She wore her hair loose and it swung in shiny black tresses about her shoulders. Spots of ruby red glowed in her cheeks from the warmth and conviviality contrasting with the fine-skinned white of her face. Her full lips were bruised a dark cherry and she kept running her lizard tongue over them. Every time she did this, JeanLuc felt a match of desire flare in his groin. This was one hell of a beautiful woman—the living image of Rossetti's Ghirlandata but with black hair, he realised with a shock of recognition.

*

Suddenly, JeanLuc felt he was losing control. The warmth, the vodka, the day's events, Sophia. All conspired to -- --

He slumped and fell sideways off his chair landing with a thud on the carpet. The last thing he saw before passing out completely was Sophia's face looming over him, eyes dark and large with concern. And then he was spinning away down a dark vortex of unconsciousness ...

and now ...

... the soft touch of the desert wind carrying the well-remembered odour of sun-baked saddle leather and dromedary halitosis. Suddenly, he was in harsh hot sunlight at the foot of a huge ferric-red-brown basaltic cliff towering above him. Climbing up a perilous winding narrow path which looked out over spectacular views in a Martian landscape, he could see to the east the mirage-inducing haze that covered the silvery salt sea; to the West and South the desert ridges and mountains of Idumaea and the harsh sandy domains of the Nabateans. He himself must have travelled down from the north along the dusty road from Sekhakha.

The road had been thick with Roman patrols. Well, if he wasn't on Mars where was he? Yes, folks. You guessed it. JeanLuc is at Masada in Israel, Planet Earth—score ten points, give the lady a toaster-oven and a round of applause. The clue was the word, Romans. Lots of Romans, mean Romans, fed-up-to-the-back-teeth Romans, Romans who had not much else to do than play crucifixion lotto with the odd Jew, like him; laying bets on how many carrion birds it would take to tear out his liver. So, it cannot have been an easy journey and his stock of coin felt severely depleted by life-saving bribes to the abovementioned Latin types in a bad mood. Not to mention the trouble he'd had with the clapped-out camel he'd bought from the used dromedary dealership in Jerusalem's city limits. He should have tapped its teeth. His brother-in-law was always telling him to tap the teeth with a stick. That way you can tell if the animal is sound—and smell its breath. Jumping Jehosophat! Have you ever smelled a camel's breath? How anyone can discern subtle gradations in the foul foetidness that emerges from the camel's front orifice, he couldn't imagine. He could never do it and wasn't going to try. Let his stupid brother-in-law stick his nose into the camel's mouth and risk being bitten as well as the methane toxicity. Still, he really should not have listened to that crooked Egyptian with his smooth line about low mileage and the old rabbi who kept it only as a pet.

In a later life, JeanLuc would buy an Edsel. The Egyptian however was not reborn and is still consigned to that special inner circle of the Inferno which Dante has assured us contains car, camel, double-glazing salesmen, leech dealers and estate agents.

*

"Welcome to Masada, brother. How may we assist you? Will you stay and eat with us?" JeanLuc turned around to see that several Zealots with short curved daggers had approached silently behind him, having

53

used the rocks as cover.

"Forgive me," he said " I am a stranger unused to these troubled times and unfamiliar territories. I have come on a mission from Qumran to speak with Eleazar ben Ja'ir."

Thankful to have reached some sort of destination, JeanLuc followed the small band into the fortified walls of Masada beyond which lay the Palace of Herod still impressively intact despite its recent sacking. He saw that it was a busy place, many people and animals crammed into the narrow twisting streets winding down and around the central area which housed the deep life-sustaining Well of Masada. When JeanLuc arrived, the troop of Sicarii and a small procession of noisy curious children that danced and weaved about their feet, they found Eleazar supervising a team of diggers building a new tunnel to carry water from the Well of Masada to the garden terracing where the crops were grown.

Well, let's see now. I wouldn't want Charlton Heston for this one. JeanLuc thought. No. Perhaps Russell Crowe? Arnie? No? Maybe, Kirk Douglas then or the fellow that played ...

"Eleazar! We have a visitor from Qumran. He brings letters and news of the King," trumpeted one of the grizzled veterans leading the troop.

Eleazar ben Ja'ir , Commander of the Hasmonean Zealots of Masada, a Zadokite Pharisee of the old school, jumped down from the parapet from which he was directing operations. "Welcome to Masada, Cousin! I have been expecting you."

The news that Jesus Justus, son of the Messiah had arrived caused a sensation amongst the people of Masada. To JeanLuc's astonishment, the people began to flock towards him, falling down on their knees , crying and proclaiming "It is the Son of the King! Son of the Lord! Son of the Highest" and such like grandiosements.

It was ridiculous, of course, wasn't it? He thought. Surely the King's son would have had a better camel, wouldn't he? I mean the King's son should have a whole herd of soft-backed, perfume-breathing Cadillac stretch- camels to choose from, not just the ornery smelly beast of burden that he was lumbered with and had left tethered at the foot of the cliff, half hoping it would get stolen so he could claim on the insurance.

JeanLuc was still extremely confused. One minute he was drinking 120 proof vodka in twenty-first century Russia and the next he was being adulated as an heir of the King of the Jews in an ancient fortress town occupied by a fanatically religious sect who he vaguely recalled were due to commit mass suicide any time now. And why was he here? He hadn't remembered auditioning for the Quantum Leap TV series ...

Eleazar caught him by the hand and led him away. "Come, cousin. You are most welcome in my house. We have much to talk about. I was warned of your visit and have made the necessary arrangements. Everything is prepared for our holy task."

*

Some hours after these words, after a much-needed bath in cool flower-scented waters, precious water that, as Eleazar explained, was carefully recycled back into the terraced gardens, JeanLuc's memories of Russia, of his previous life, had faded completely.

He stood by one of the arched windows of Herod's great Palace in which Eleazar had taken rooms, and looked down into the cool shaded interior courtyard below. The blue mosaic floor was packed with Zealots listening to Eleazar preaching. There were no women and children present and they were listening in intense silence. JeanLuc caught the words as they hung like dust particles in the still air.

"Brothers, they are men of true courage who, regarding this life as a kind of service we must render to nature, undergo it with reluctance and hasten to release their souls from their bodies; and though no misfortune presses or drives them away, desire for immortal life impels them to inform their friends that they are going to depart ..."

JeanLuc turned away from the window, disturbed by these words. They didn't sound too cheerful to him and filled him with foreboding. His cousin was clearly taking a pretty dim view of the future and indoctrinating these Sicarii into a fatalistic acceptance of what was to come. And what was all this nonsense about immortal life and souls? He had obviously been listening too much to Uncle James. What had happened to 'zealous for the Law' and a healthy patriotism? They should be seeking a Kingdom of Israel here on earth, not in heaven.

The Jewish people had now been expecting an imminent Messianic

55

Kingdom of some sort for nearly seventy years. In those days, his Father, the King, and his Essene mentors in the Twelve Apostles had worked hard to make sure that every prophecy of Isaiah was fulfilled to the letter. His father had created the right conditions, was it His fault that His subjects seemed incapable of doing the rest or that the pagan Romans were such tough opposition? Mentally teetering on the brink of the Last Times, two generations of Jews had supported exhausting insurrection and guerrilla warfare against the foul Romans who, in reaction, had stomped up and down the length and breadth of Judea leaving a crucifixion trail of burnt-out communities culminating in the annihilation of Sepphoris and the recent sacking of the Holy City.

It was no wonder, JeanLuc supposed, that it was beginning to look as if the only Kingdom attainable would indeed be the Kingdom of Heaven—a fantasy originally perpetuated by the eggheads at Sekhakha. Clever people like his uncle James and probably his Father as well, must have realised early on that they were reaching for an unattainable goal against the all-powerful Romans. So the only way forward was to change the nature of the goal, take the battle onto another plane of existence. This way, maybe they could wrest a psychological advantage, hold a moral Golan Heights against the hedonistic multi-theistic Romans.

There could be no defeats in the realms of the mind.

To this end, some of the leaders of the Hellenist Movement had already begun the process of mythologizing his Father's story—an exercise in history making and pesher which had occupied his Father, Paul and Luke John Mark for over thirty years now—ever since the Big Argument before he was born. In spite of the exalted loins from whom he had sprung and Paul's long-time tutelage he sided with his Mother and took the simple soldier's view of life— that military victory against one's enemies was vastly preferable to moral victory rewarded in some mystical Heaven. He knew which side would be having its eyes pecked out by vultures, no matter how righteous the cause.

Carrion birds do not compile the many names of Yahweh.

JeanLuc Jesus Justus, sighed and went to look for his belongings. He was unpacking, when he was found by Eleazar who was now alone. "Cousin, don't unpack. We must complete our task and then you must go soon. We've heard word from our spies that the tenth Legion under Flavius Silva is marching from Caesarea. It is rumoured that they may be headed this way. I have sent a messenger to your Mother and sister to make haste while it is still possible."

"What about my mission?" asked JeanLuc "Your mission is to proceed as planned." "What will you do?"

Eleazar shrugged. "We'll hold out as long as possible of course. We have plenty of water and provisions. Masada is easy to defend, as you know. Militarily it will be a difficult job for the Kittim and I can't see why they would want to bother. They might leave us alone, they have until now. But you never know with Kittim, we can't take the risk." He continued soberly." You must leave tonight under cover of darkness. We think it would be best to head across the desert to the Dead Sea and then take the caravan trail south to Alexandria where your uncle Jude is. There is a flourishing community of Jewish Exiles on the Isle of Elephants on the River Nile, so I suppose you could go there as well. I remember we sent the Ark of the Covenant there for safe keeping after the time of Manasseh. You'll have to play it by ear. I'm afraid it may be a long time before you can return.

"Well, exile is nothing new for us Jews, I suppose." JeanLuc said. "Don't worry, my friend! Alexandria is a fun city, I'm told." "What about my Mother, sister and brother? Will they be safe?"

"We will look after and honour them. They'll be safer here than Qumran ... as long as the Kittim don't attack on the Sabbath!" He said after slight pause.

At this last remark, JeanLuc looked carefully at Eleazar to see if he was joking. He wasn't and shiver of foreboding ran down his spine.

"Come, we will go now to a secret place where I have hidden the things of your Father's that he wanted saving."

JeanLuc followed the short sturdy figure of Eleazar, accompanied by two Sicarii Daggermen, through the noisy streets and back down the hill to the Fortress and the Well of Masada. They stopped at the raised wall surrounding the well and Eleazar looked over. He turned and grinned at JeanLuc. "Can you swim, cousin?"

"If absolutely necessary," JeanLuc replied cautiously and looked down at the circle of pale blue water staring up at him like a blank cataract eye, twenty feet below.

Eleazar removed his tunic and weapons and gestured to JeanLuc to do the same. "Okay. This is what we do," he said." Take this stone; hold it to your chest and jump in feet first. Don't forget to hold your breath! When you get to the bottom—it's not very deep; maybe the height of three men—you'll find a hole in the wall. Go through, let go of the stone and float upwards. There is a dry antechamber there where I'll meet you."

"I thought this was supposed to be a secret chamber, Eleazar," said JeanLuc looking meaningfully at the two bodyguards and the queue of women waiting patiently to fill their earthen water vessels.

"Oh. Don't worry about them. This is just the start! We have a long complicated way to go yet," said his cousin laughing. "Only I know the route and I keep the map up here." He tapped his head with its full beard and long black hair oiled and combed back into a thick ponytail. "This is the bit I enjoy!" yelled Eleazar cheerfully and he jumped off the parapet landing with a loud splash. He disappeared quickly below the water surface, leaving a target ring of white bubbles for JeanLuc to aim at.

"Oowah, Ah!" The water was icy cold! JeanLuc nearly lost his breath with the shock of it. He sank clutching the heavy round stone to his chest. Looking up he could see the rapidly diminishing ring of bright water at the surface and then his feet bumped on the bottom of the well. Constriction growing in his chest, he looked around for the entrance to the tunnel. Seeing a darker area within the watery gloom, he waded towards it through the bottom silt, which clutched at his ankles like the soft rotted hands of the decomposing dead. Feeling that his lungs might burst under the strain, he lunged forward and downward through the low tunnel entrance.

Dropping the stone, he expected now to float upwards. But no! The tunnel kept on going. Desperately now, about to black out from lack of air, he swam furiously forward, kicking his legs. It was pitch black in the tunnel, which seemed to be getting narrower and narrower, bruising his arms and legs on the rough stone sides. His mind started to spin and sparks of retinal light flickered behind his eyes. He was not going to make it! A terrible panic gripped him and he thrashed out blindly.

Suddenly, he was through. There was a steady pale yellow light above him and he rose towards it closing his eyes in pure unalloyed relief.

*

Gasping and heaving for breath, he levered himself up only to be firmly pushed back into the soft pillows of a bed! He opened his eyes.

"Sophia! Wha—what are you doing here!" he gaped in amazement.

Seeing that they were alone, JeanLuc reached up and folded her into a fierce embrace. Her face came down close to his. "I dreamed," he whispered, gazing up into her wide fathomless eyes, pupils the colour of agate, like the lioness that kills. Third row down, centre position between the turquoise and the amethyst—a flash of precognition.

"I dreamed I was in God's Holy Place! I dreamed of my Father, the King of Heaven!"

He pulled her face down onto his. Lips touched softly; triggering the solenoid of desire, completing the circuit of love.

Eyes half-closed in drowsy repleteness, Sophia reached over to the bedside table for her crumpled pack of Camels. She lit up and lay on her back pressed against JeanLuc's side. He had fallen into unconsciousness again, eyelids fluttering in synchrony with dreaming alpha waves.

Sophia disentangled herself gently from the dreaming form of the man beside her. Pulling a robe about herself, she walked away from the bed to the door. Hesitating, she looked back at the pale naked form lying on the bed. She shivered—the room was getting cold. Turning back, she sat down on a chair by the bed looking at JeanLuc, wondering, remembering.

Never had she given herself to anyone like this and in her parents' house! It was as if something, some instinct, had told her that there was no time. There was no time for preliminaries; for courtship; for dinners for two; for cinema gropings, for dressing up; for theatre; for cheek-to-cheek dancing. No time for long silent walks, arm in arm, beside the frozen river; for agonised midnight phone calls; for tearful partings at railway stations. No time to show him off to her friends, slyly watching, measuring his worth against their reactions.

By the light of the moon, she let her gaze follow the contours of his strong face and muscled body. Now that she was no longer held in the

59

gaze of those fierce hawk- like eyes or in physical rapture by his body, she could look at him in wonder and not without an element of fear. Like any sophisticated Muscovite she had known many men and, on the whole, they were easy to understand. Always, she had dictated the pace to suit herself and her own desires. But this one! Here was an elemental force, a maleness that would not be denied, that could not be denied. He had not been violent, not insistent, had just taken possession of her body and soul as if by royal command. She hadn't been able to help herself. Tears welled in her eyes and she began to weep, as a child might, uncontrolled sobbing, clutching the robe to herself, rocking back and forth. She was crying for herself—in precognition of what was to come.

The man on the bed slept on regardless.

There would be no comfort here she knew—only certitude and the arrival of destiny. If that was called love, so be it—but it was a terrible love, a love for angels, not for humans. He consumed her; he stripped the insulation off the wires of her soul. When they were close, sparks flew and she burned inside. Oh! She burned, and tears would not quench this cold starfire.

Tomorrow or the day after, they would go to Pokrovskoye. Tomorrow they would begin the search in earnest. Nothing else mattered. She had a feeling that they wouldn't have long for each other. Looking at JeanLuc, she thought this one was an arrow, flighted to its target; a cruise missile snaking its way through Baghdad streets.

CHAPTER 8

"Took your time, didn't you?" said Eleazar ben Ja'ir who was squatting on the ledge beside the water and using a flint to send sparks into a torch of reeds and pitch.

JeanLuc 'Jesus Justus', crawled out of the pool gasping and heaving. He coughed out a lungful of spit and water onto the Commander's sandaled feet. They were in a cave hewn out of solid rock. Leading out was the entrance to another narrow tunnel. Eleazar took the lead, holding the torch in front of him. It spluttered and spat sparks back into their faces. The air in the tunnel was cool and dry apart from the resinous smoke from the torch, which was blown in their faces by a current of air coming from ahead of them.

Reaching a junction, Eleazar took the right fork and continued on a steep winding downward path. "Where does that other path lead?" asked JeanLuc.

"It comes out about halfway up the cliff face. We sometimes use it to get scouts out of Masada unseen and quickly, but you need very long ropes to get down."

As they continued, JeanLuc quickly lost sense of direction in the warren of tunnels beneath Masada. He marvelled at the immense amount of labour that must have been needed to hew these catacombs out of solid rock during the long centuries of occupation by the Maccabees prior to Herod. Eleazar seemed to know his way. JeanLuc's neck ached from the stooping walk they were forced to adopt.

After a while, Eleazar stopped and looked back. His expression in the flickering torchlight was deadly serious. "We are here, cousin," he whispered. "This is the secret place known only to High Priests of Israel. Even the beast Herod knew nothing of its existence. When I die, the secret will pass into history unless I find a worthy successor. Here are kept documents, scrolls, treasures and artefacts too valuable to leave in Jerusalem. Here, until recently, we kept the Ark of the Covenant. Here are original dynastic records of our forefathers dating back to Abraham, the father of our people. Your father and grandmother came here and took copies of these before they left for

Rome eleven years ago.

"Hold my hand now, cousin. I will extinguish this torch and guide you to the sacred treasure house of Masada and Israel!"

Eleazar inverted the torch and stubbed it out on the dry stone floor, scattering hot embers that glowed and died like fireflies. In the dark and deathly quiet, JeanLuc could hear only the beating of his heart, his own quick shallow breathing and Eleazar's shuffling activity in front of him. He imagined the Egyptian Pharoah's concubines must experience the same terrible hush when the heavy lid dropped on the golden sarcophagus of the Exalted One and they were sealed in, forever screaming beneath a million tons of pyramidal rock. Some reward for a lifetime of devoted servitude!

Suddenly, there was a groaning screeching noise as a heavy slab of the tunnel wall revolved around a central hinge. Holding tightly to Eleazar's hot hand, JeanLuc followed him into another space, which smelled of the acrid vinegar of tanned hides and of wax. Other strange exotic odours that might have come from the inside of Pandora's box also assaulted his senses. If JeanLuc had been claustrophobic, he would have been reduced to gibbering madness by now. Nevertheless, it would have only taken the soft fluttering swipe of a bat's wing to push him into an abyss of terror.

"How will we see without the torch?" asked JeanLuc nervously.

"Don't worry. Hold on a second while I fix it up." Eleazar let go of JeanLuc's hand and could be heard nearby winding some kind of mechanism, which groaned with obvious disuse. The cave suddenly filled with blinding white light. JeanLuc exclaimed in pain and shock, shielding his eyes with his hands.

"Clever, isn't it!" said Eleazar calmly beside him. "I'm told it is all done with mirrors. Anyway, we're here. Behold the safety deposit box of God!"

The cave was stacked high with the ultimate cookie jars of history; large brown earthenware pots sealed with wax which Eleazar said contained scrolls made of hide, parchment, reed and beaten copper. The pale gleam of gold was everywhere. In one corner there stood a magnificent life-sized figure of a calf. The gold surface was pitted and smoke-blackened. Leaning against it was a large wooden pole with an intricately patterned bronze snake entwined around it.

"Is that...?" asked JeanLuc in awed wonder.

"Yes. That's the Golden Calf. When Moses had finished ranting and raving he ordered the priests to save it from the fire. The gold would be needed and was too valuable to throw away." Eleazar went over to one of the innumerable acacia wood chests banded and studded with copper. He threw open the lid and pulled out a small carved ivory box followed by a garment in whose folds precious jewels gleamed. "These are my favourite pieces," he said.

" Look at this!" Opening the ivory box, he took out a large gold ring. Set into it, JeanLuc could see a huge flawless diamond, crudely cut, that flashed and sparkled with ice-cold ferocity.

"King Solomon's Ring! Nice, isn't it? Many, many people have died seeking to possess this." Eleazar passed it over to JeanLuc who proceeded to place it on his finger and lift it with wonder up into the beam of white light that drilled into the cave. The ring glowed with starfire. This ring held a Stone of Power, a Key to unlock the mystery of the universe .

But it's time was not now. JeanLuc understood this with absolute stone cold certainty. Its appointment with human destiny lay far far in the future. He had a sudden vision of a time when a diffuse red sun loomed huge and menacing over a bleak landscape of cold desolation...

While JeanLuc was held entranced by the vision of Solomon's Ring, Eleazar had gone to another of the chests and had selected three bronze tubes, two feet in length and an inch in diameter. Each tube fitted into a pocket of soft-tooled goatskin leather. He opened one of the tubes by unscrewing the capped end and pulled out the contents. This was a thin cloth material wound tightly around a spine of ivory. Holding the ends up, Eleazar let the soft filmy material unwind like a flag. He laid and smoothed it out over a table of acacia wood inlaid with gold with four large gold rings at each corner. JeanLuc went over and peered at the pattern.

"Hey! That's Father and Mother!" he gasped. "What is this!? You realise this is an Anathema, don't you?" JeanLuc was shocked to the core by this blasphemy so close, so intensely personal to him. He reached for it angrily. Eleazar pushed his hand away hastily.

63

"For God's sake be careful! These are irreplaceable" he cried. "I promise you, on my life, these were commissioned by your father. Anyway, read this authorisation."

JeanLuc snatched the proffered papyrus from Eleazar's fingers and scanned carefully down the page of Aramaic symbols. "Even so, why? I don't understand." He looked at the picture laid out, anger collapsing within him. The familiar much-loved features stared up at him. Tears welled in his eyes and the old wound of grief opened its dark petals in his heart. The picture depicted his Father and Mother standing next to his uncle Jude and Aunt Martha. Each woman was shown cradling an infant. "That must be me and Simeon!" he whispered.

"Yes, that is you with your parents. They are very good likenesses, don't you think?" JeanLuc nodded mutely. Eleazar took another of the bronze tubes and shook out the contents.

"They were painted by a Phoenician sailor who also had a business painting Egyptian Mummy portraits. Your father secretly hired him when he was visiting Tyre on the coast. The material is woven from the excretions of large caterpillars cultivated in a country far to the East beyond India. It's called silk, I believe. Amazing stuff. Feel it. See how light and strong it is. This was taken from a bolt of the precious material given to your grandparents by the Persian Mage, Melchior, when your father was born in Sepphoris. The Magi gave other stuff as well—I think there is still some myrrh around here somewhere. I'll take it with me, the women use it for preventing wounds from going bad."

Eleazar spread out another painting on the fine beige coloured silk. JeanLuc gazed with awe at the skilfully rendered image picked out in delicate brush strokes. This one depicted his Father standing next to his brother Jude, their arms about each other's shoulders. Both smiled out at him. There was no doubt that they were twins—they were painted as mirror images.

The last of the pictures was unrolled. Eleazar smoothed over the wrinkles and stepped back to let JeanLuc look them over. JeanLuc gripped the edge of the table to steady himself against the emotional flood that coursed through him. This last picture was larger but more crudely done. It was obviously older and by another, not so skilful, artistic hand. It showed a family group instantly recognisable as the

Davidic Royal Family of Israel—the King's family. The Messiah's father Joseph son of Jacob, seated Mary with the twins, Jesus and Jude as six-year-olds. Dandled on her knee was the baby James.

JeanLuc stared for long minutes at the three pictures. Memories and images of the happier past flooded his mind. "These are beautiful. They must be saved," he muttered and turned around to look for Eleazar. This was his task. It was his mission to preserve these holy images for posterity despite the fact they were forbidden by Law. Mosaic Law, after all, was only an advisory accretion on God's Commandments, often contradictory and open to interpretation by High Priests. Had not the Maccabees changed the rules about fighting on the Sabbath or during the Passover to avoid annihilation by enemies who chose these times to attack? God clearly allowed His Chosen People some leeway in matters not central to the core of His religion.

These were potent symbols of Israel. From his own fierce reaction he realised their undeniable emotional power. Pictures were worth a thousand repetitious words from the rabbi. They could ignite a Messianic Zeal—he would charge into battle behind a banner such as these. Such thoughts must have been in his Father's mind when he had them done. The fact that they were locked away here in Masada meant that His Father had changed his mind or that the Essene Brotherhood felt they could not be used effectively except in the initiation, education and consolidation of a select priesthood, or his stepmother, Lydia might have objected to them.

While JeanLuc was pondering these thoughts, the Commander of Masada had donned the jewelled garment, a breast piece. His chest now glittered and glowed with spots of colour. "What to you think, cousin? Does it suit me? All I need now is an Urim or Thummin and according to Holy Scripture I should be able to talk to God!" he grinned. "Do you know what they are—Urim and Thummin? If only I knew what they were I could probably find them here."

JeanLuc shook his head—the play and flash of light on the rows of jewels was intensely hypnotic. Wrong movie, he thought irrelevantly. He turned back to the silk pictures on the golden table and began to roll them up carefully around the smooth spine of ivory for re-packing into the bronze storage tubes.

Eleazar took off the jewelled breastpiece and folded it neatly and reverently back into its chest, closing the lid. Ah well, the chat with the Almighty would have to wait, he thought.

"We will take the pictures now, cousin. The tubes need filling with dry sand to exclude air and prevent mildew. They also need sealing with wax, but we'll do that when we reach the outside. Put them in this bag which will keep them waterproof until we reach the outside," Eleazar commanded, holding out a sack, which had been tied to his loincloth. "We have to get out of here before the light fades or else the lock mechanism will not activate properly. Don't ask me how it works. Believe me, you wouldn't want to spend the night down here without any light or ventilation. Too many dybbuks!" He grinned maliciously at JeanLuc who shivered at the thought and handed over the three precious tubes in their leather pouches.

"Okay, let's close up and go get a drink," he said. And they did.

It seemed no time at all and JeanLuc was back on his miserable hump of a ride, the cliffs of Masada looming high behind him, a black craggy cut-out silhouette against a sunset streaked the colour of blood. Like Lot's wife, he turned in the saddle and looked back. A grim foreboding caused salty tears to well in his eyes as he brought to mind the face of his doomed friend and cousin, Eleazar, whom he would never see again in this life and to whose care was entrusted the lives of his aged mother, elder sister and younger brother. They were due to arrive any time.

"Gee up, you son of a bitch!" he cried and the camel, groaning and farting in protest, loped off towards the silvery sea in the east.

CHAPTER 9

"Did you know, Sergei," said FSB Major-General Anatole Sweridenko," what they found when they did an autopsy on the exhumed body of Vladimir Illich Lenin, ten years after his death?"

"No, Comrade Major-General. What did they find?"

The other man tapped the end of his pencil on his desk in time to the refrain of some half remembered tune that had been bothering him lately. *Oobla di, oobla da. Life goes on. Da,da dada da da* ...

"Maraschino cherries. Four of them. In his gut. I read about it in a decadent American novel that I confiscated a few years ago."

"Is that confirmed officially, sir?"

"For God's sake, Sergei, I don't know, do I! I'm just telling you an interesting fact—what the American barbarians call a factoid."

"Yes, sir. I see, sir. Can I get you something, Major-General? Some coffee perhaps or tea?" Sergei Yemeljan was used to the Major-General's moodiness.

"Bright lipstick-red maraschino cherries. Completely whole, undigested or affected by being in Comrade Lenin's gut all that time. It makes you wonder doesn't it? Yes indeed," said the Major-General. "What do they put Maraschino cherries into, Sergei? Normally, that is."

"I believe they go into vodka cocktails and on top of little red sponge cakes called fancies. Sold in patisseries. Sir."

"Exactly!" said the Major-General with an air of satisfaction. " An icon of rampant decadent Capitalism lurking in the secret bowels of the Revolution!"

"Do you think the cherries had something to do with the Great Leader's death, sir? I mean they must have been nearly the last thing he ate ..."

"And why were they whole?" continued the Major -General. "You'd think they would be chewed or something, wouldn't you? Did he have his teeth at the end? I wonder."

"They are quite big and ..."

"They would be quite difficult to swallow whole. Yes, you're right, Sergei. It's a mystery!"

"Maybe he was poisoned by the CIA! With the cherries!"

"Well, I wouldn't go so far as to say that, Sergei. Anyway, it was the OSS in those days, but you do have a point. The Mystery of the Maraschinos. It does sound like a good plot, doesn't it!"

"Shall I start a file on it, Sir?"

"Why not. Maybe we can sell it as a script idea for the X Files on American television!" Anatole grimaced and swung his feet off the desk. "So! What's next, Sergei?"

"Usual stuff, I'm afraid, Major-General. Oh, this one might be of interest to you." Sergei handed over a scene of crime report. "Four of Leonid Zafod's crew got killed yesterday evening. Burned up in a petrol explosion—black market operation without doubt."

"We've been watching this bunch, haven't we?"

"Yes, sir. Our man escaped with his life, but is in hospital now with third-degree burns. Says he didn't see much but apparently some lunatic dropped a cigarette and after that everything went up in flames."

"Tell me about Zafod's gang. What do we know so far?" "Shall I call in Ilya Bearski, Sir? It's his case."

"Yes. See if he's in his office and get him to report to me immediately. There may be something here for us ..." His voice trailed away and lost in thought he swivelled around in his chair. Looking out of the window, metal-framed and painted FSB grey like everything else in the building, he could see the exotic minarets of the Kremlin glinting yellow in the morning sun. Circling around them he could see pixel clouds of pigeons, doing their morning flight before settling down as a moving, pecking grey carpet—the flying rats of Red Square.

It was rumoured that the enigmatic Stalin kept doves—a pure white strain. He had had special wooden dovecotes made and had even assigned bird fanciers amongst the Red Guards to look after them; somewhere hidden in the many steep rooftops of the Kremlin. Anatole wondered if they were still there. It would be nice to think that there remained a symbol of the old Communist ideals and hopes—there still circling; a core of purity within the rotted heart of what the world had come to label the Evil Empire. Anatole had his doubts. More than likely, the doves had been captured and sold long ago in Izmayolovo Park—along with everything else. Or eaten.

He swivelled in his chair to face the man who had just been ushered into the office by the young Sergei.

"Sit down, Comrade Bearski. I understand you have been watching the Zafod gang. Maybe you can bring me up to date with what's happening?"

"Yes, sir. Thank you, sir," said Lieutenant Ilya Bearski, a vast hulk of a man, with a wide slab of an Asiatic face, small pencil-point eyes and a mouth full of crooked teeth; like a young child's crayoned portrayal of the boy-eating Giant at the top of the beanstalk. His breath came hoarsely. The Major- General wondered briefly where the Lieutenant got the food to sustain such a huge frame and went on to ask ."The explosion in the east of the city? What do you know?"

"Nicholai Slovena was assigned to buy gasoline from the black marketeers who are organised by Zafod in that part of the city. We are collecting evidence and trying to ascertain the extent of the gang's operations. Comrade Slovena is now in hospital for his pains. It appears that he may not live long. The doctor says the fire got into his lungs."

"Yes, yes. Most unfortunate," the Major-General said impatiently. "Did you manage to get a report from him?"

Ilya gazed at the Major-General. It was impossible to fathom what was going on behind that impassive moonlike face. Give him a pair of drooping moustaches and he would look like Genghis Khan. "He said he came up behind a small van that was loading drums of gasoline from Zafod's trucks. Then there was some sort of argument about payment between Zafod's men and a woman. A man got out of the van, threw down a cigarette and everything went boom!" Lieutenant Bearski lifted his fat hands expressively.

"Did he describe the man or woman?" asked the Major-General. "It was dark in the underpass, he said."

"Do we have enough on Leonid Zafod to make any arrests? Is it worthwhile busting these greedy bastards?" The Major-General thought he detected a very slight flicker in Bearski's eyes in their slits behind the rolls of fat, as he answered. His expression and voice remained the usual junior officer monotone.

"Not at this time, Major-General. I believe we need maybe another month and preferably a live witness who is willing to testify in the

People's Court against Leonid Zafod himself. This is very difficult, as people tend to disappear these days."

Although he was expecting this answer, Anatole's years of experience told him that Bearski was probably holding back on him. It would not be surprising if Zafod were paying off Bearski. Looking silently across at the fat Lieutenant, he reviewed in his mind what he already knew about Leonid Zafod. A minor member of the Politburo, a popular crony of Yeltsin in the early days. Not favoured politically by Putin, so presumably had turned to crime in anticipation of the new democratic capitalism that was supposed to be sweeping the land. Definitely an evil man. The very worst that the old Communist regime had spawned—trying to hang onto power and completely corrupted and unprincipled in the way they did.

The Major- General hated men like that more than he hated the former enemies of the Soviet—the barbarous Americans. He resolved at that moment that he would see personally to the destruction of this gang of thievery; nip it in the bud ... for the honour of Mother Russia.

CHAPTER 10

Sophia and Igor walked down the steps of the apartment block into a cold bright sunny morning. Sophia unlocked and opened the rear doors of the van and Igor began to unload the drums of gasoline, rolling them down the side alleyway around to the back of the block. He stacked nine of them in the rear yard and Sophia threw a tarpaulin over them. After screwing in a drum tap, Igor propped the sides of the remaining drum with wooden planks to stop it rolling sideways and Sophia placed a jerrycan under the drum tap. She filled it with gasoline and then transferred the contents into the van's tank. This activity took them the best part of an hour. There was no sign of JeanLuc, who had yet to emerge. Although Sophia and Igor had exchanged only a few words, there was no emnity between them. Each seemed to accept the other's presence. The shared events of the night had created a bond of comradeship that required no verbal expression.

Igor suggested that they should check on his truck and pick up their luggage and other equipment. They had decided the previous evening that they should use the Yemeljan residence as a base of operations.

Sophia went inside and upstairs to look in on JeanLuc. Carefully opening the door to the bedroom carefully, she peered into the dimly lit room stuffy with the musky odours of the night's activity. He was still unconscious, breathing quietly, lying spread-eagled across the bed. She closed the door and went back downstairs into the kitchen parlour where her parents were sitting around the table, drinking coffee. Her father was reading the Izvestia newspaper. As she walked in, he folded the paper carefully—rolled up in bundles they made good logs for the fire—took off his steel rimmed half moon reading glasses and looked up smilingly at his daughter.

"So! What do you want to do, Sophia? No pictures to sell today," he said jovially. "We should prepare a feast!"

"I am going with Igor to pick up some things from their truck. It's in the Lyublino district in a warehouse by the river, not too far. We'll be about two hours, I think." She poured herself a cup of coffee from the jug on the stove. "Is there anything in the paper about last night,

Papa?"

"No, my dear. There may be something in a later edition."

"Oh, well. I just hope they don't link us to it. We don't want police attention or the revenge of the black marketeers."

"It's very unlikely though, isn't it?" asked Saskia. "From what you said, they were probably all killed in the fire. They deserved it, the devils. Criminal exploitation by our own people. Things are indeed in a bad way." Saskia got up from the table and went to the front door. "Igor!" she shouted. "Come and get some coffee."

Igor was standing by the van fending off the attentions of a group of children who were pestering him for money. He waved in acknowledgement and started up the steps. "Where is your son Sergei?" he asked as he came into the kitchen.

Sophia's father shrugged. "He stays in the FSB barracks in Dzerzhinsky prison during the week and comes home only at weekends."

"He is FSB?" asked Igor surprised and concerned.

"The FSB has many departments and responsibilities. Sergei is with the Moscow Crime Division that supports the city police. Most major crime investigations are carried out by the FSB; like the FBI in America. They are not just spies and secret police, you know! Most of what they do is maintenance of law and order. Though God knows, they are failing dismally in that. Sometimes, I thing we were better off under Khrushchev. Our people are paying a heavy price for glasnost and perestroika—whatever that is!" concluded Jean with a current popular lament.

Igor sipped carefully at the hot black coffee—it was surprisingly good. He was in no hurry to go chasing about the dangerous Moscow city streets. He would sit here and watch the large robust figure of Saskia bustle about the kitchen. Looking at the slim pale body of Sophia, back in tight blue jeans and plain woollen jumper, you'd never suspect there was family resemblance with her mother. It must all have come from her father who now sat in the easy chair by the stove, rooting around with blunt peasant fingers in the bottom of a jar of preserved apricots.

In Russia, it was either feast or famine as far as produce is concerned. Like the trolley buses which never come except in threes. This meant that every Russian household spent many hours making homemade preserves. Everything possible was preserved. In a famous scandal, a batch of "Glowberry Jam" made from the extra juicy glowingly radioactive blackberries from the desolated Chernobyl region, found its way surreptitiously onto the sumptuous breakfast buffet of the Moscow Holiday Inn for several months; it possibly accounted for the leukaemic deaths of several American tourists and businessmen. The story broke under a headline "Jam spreads death!", when an obese woman hairdresser on a routine post operative check-up after previous treatment for thyroid cancer, was found to have a startlingly high thyroid radioactivity count. Her New York physician, thinking he'd made a horrible mistake with dosage, and with visions of a malpractice suit, made further analyses and got the shock of his career when the gamma wavelength checked in at the Strontium 90 racetrack and not the iodine 131 boulevard. His patient died soon after. The doctor tipped off the newspapers anonymously, and cancelled his participation at the next International Medical Congress in Moscow.

*

The Yemeljan household was like all the others. Every nook and cranny, every shelf was stacked high with pickles and preserves. Even in this household that would be considered intellectual, there was a large glass jar of dried bananas sandwiched between thick volumes of art history and a tome on religion. Episodes in recent history were still defined among the general populace by whatever produce was in glut at the time. Phrases beginning," It was in the time of the Georgian tomatoes ..." clearly defined for Muscovites a period around the kidnap of Secretary Gorbachev. Igor could see this particular episode of Russian history preserved in sweet red chutney, in jars found on the top shelf above the kitchen door.

Saskia was chopping up cabbage for soup. Her thick muscular arms worked rhythmically. She turned towards them. "Well, get going then! Stop hanging around here, I've a busy morning. I have to queue for bread and Ivanova Petulengra tells me there are chestnuts in at the store. Imagine! Sweet chestnuts. What a treat!"

Igor and Sophia drained their mugs and stood up to leave. There was still no sign of movement from JeanLuc, so the two of them went out to the van. The kids had gone, leaving a graffiti scrawl in the sooty grime on the side of the van. It read 'Dynamo Moscow rules OK!

"Vermin!" spat Sophia and getting a cloth from behind the seat, she rubbed off the words.

Going through the routine of re-assembling the ignition, and putting back the windscreen wipers, Sophia got the van going and they set off towards the Lyublino District. It took them half an hour to arrive at the warehouse. Their way was blocked by large graffiti-sprayed corrugated iron gates topped with barbed wire. Sophia sounded the horn and a small elderly man emerged from a door set into one of the larger ones. He walked over to the van and looked in at them. Recognising Igor, he grunted and went to open the big swing doors. Sophia drove through into a large busy yard. There were several large articulated lorries being loaded or unloaded. The big DAF was parked to one side. There was a pile of tractor tyres heaped up alongside it and a forklift moving between the truck's interior and the pile. Igor jumped down from the van and walked over to a tall thin Russian, wearing an ill-fitting stove-black suit, who was jotting down the inventory on the clipboard he carried.

"Ah, Golemov! So you've appeared. And with a beautiful companion. That's quick work!" Karasamov leaned his lined cadaverous face over Igor and winked horribly. His breath smelled strongly of peppermint—part of his usual fee was a parcel of Trebor Extra Strong mints from England. "Not your usual sort, though, Igor. Must be losing your touch. Eh?" Igor suffered this impassively.

"How's it going, Mr Karasamov?"

"Well, you can see for yourself, the shipment is nearly offloaded except for that small crate which we've been instructed to leave alone. Everything else seems in order. I'll fax a confirmation through to the Germans tonight."

"What's the situation on the return?"

"I'm not expecting a shipment for another week, maybe two, so don't hold your breath. Go and enjoy yourself, my boy! You always do!"

"Okay. But I need to get my things from the cab." Igor held up the

74

infrared key for Karasamov to look at.

"Fine. Fine. Go ahead. But I shall need to know where you're staying so we can contact you when the load is ready." Ivan Karasamov walked away, a dark sinister figure enveloped in an aura of shadow. Igor breathed more easily. That man gives me the creeps, he thought. He had no quarrel with Karasamov; their relationship was strictly business, apart from the occasional leering comment about Igor's imagined sex life.

Going over to the cab of the DAF, he punched the pass code into the keypad on the door and pressed the switch on the infrared key fob. The door clicked open and he clambered in. Checking around, he saw everything was as JeanLuc and he had left it. He got out the two holdalls from behind the driver's seat and found his machine pistol under the mattress of the bunk bed. Twisting around he put the gun into its soft leather holster. He felt better. Much better. He dropped the bags down to Sophia and climbed back out of the cab clutching JeanLuc's anonymous-looking briefcase. He slammed the cab door and activated all the alarms and locks with the key fob. A high-pitched beep lasting several seconds informed Igor that all was secured.

Sophia was watching a long black showroom shiny Mercedes 280 saloon, which had just driven into the yard and pulled up at the foot of the metal staircase that led to Karasamov's site offices on the top floor of the warehouse. Karasamov lived on the premises and he liked to look down into the yard from the high vantage point that his office gave him. Mounted on the metal frame of the staircase, beside floodlights sufficient to light a sports arena, there was a heavy machine gun, normally hidden under a tarpaulin, which could rake the yard with heavy-calibre rapid fire if the occasion arose. Such weaponry was easy to come by from the Black Sea ports to which many of the trucks travelled on legitimate business. Karasamov secretly waited for an opportunity to use this gun—he liked the smell of it—the oiled odour of death. As he cleaned and swung it around on its gimbals, it took a conscious effort of will to prevent himself from pulling the trigger and unleashing a hailstorm of bullets onto the unsuspecting workers below in the yard.

There were not many who would care to cross swords with Ivan

Karasamov. He had lived too long, knew too much and paid for serious protection.

"Who is that?" asked Sophia as the driver opened the rear door of the Merc to let out a small man wearing an expensive-looking fur-collared black overcoat and a Homburg hat pulled down over dark glasses. He strutted impatiently about beside the car with the small bouncy steps of a Napoleonic budgie.

"I've no idea." Igor said. "Come on, Sophia, it's none of our business. Let's get out of here. The less you see, the longer you live around here—surely you know that."

Karasamov had come out of his office and was hurrying down the metal stairs to meet the new arrival. Anyone who can make ol' snake eyes hurry up must be deep trouble, thought Igor. He tugged at Sophia's arm and hissed. "C'mon, we should leave!" She got into the driver's seat and Igor hurried around to get in the other side. Suddenly, Karasamov, who had been deep in conversation with the other man, waved at them to stop and the two men began to walk over. Oh, shit! thought Igor.

Sophia switched off the engine of the van and they waited for the men to approach.

"You were going to tell me where you are staying, Igor," said Karasmov nastily. He stared at Sophia unblinkingly. She looked away at her hands on the steering wheel.

"Sorry, Mr.Karasamov. I forgot. I thought you were busy."

"Who are these people, Ivan?" asked the small man who came up beside Karasamov, took off his shades and stared up at Sophia with curious bird-bright eyes from under the brim of his hat.

"Leonid. This is Igor Golemov, one of our drivers and his whore," he said. "I am nobody's fucking whore! You slimy creep!" flared Sophia angrily.

"No. Of course not, my dear. I could see that at once. You'll have to excuse Mr. Karasamov's bad manners. Stuck down here in the Volga docklands, all he ever meets are the brutes and Moscow low-lifes. My name is Leonid Zafod. I am pleased to meet you." He grinned showing a perfect set of capped teeth flanked by two solid gold incisors. Sophia and Igor were much impressed. A man who carried that much obvious gold in his teeth was powerful indeed. Nobody in their right mind risked having a jaw broken with a hammer and molars heaved out by muggers using a pair of rusty pliers, for the sake of a gold filling or two.

"Ah. I see you have a source of good Army gasoline, Mr.Golemov!" Zafod's sharp eyes were directed at the half-empty drum strapped down in the rear of the van. "You must let me know where you get it. I can always give you a good price in US dollars; cash on the nail."

Igor cursed inwardly. He didn't trust these men. He should pretend ignorance. "I don't know, sir" he said. "I have rented this van and the gasoline was part of the deal."

"Oh, well. Let the owner contact me then. It will be worth his while. Tell him to come to Karasamov's yard and to ask for Ivan Slobodka."

"Slobodka ..." Igor repeated. "Okay, I'll tell them." "Where are you staying, Igor?" asked Karasamov.

"In an hotel in the Kalinin District," lied Igor quickly. "I'll phone through with the details."

"Fine. Just make sure you do that," Karasamov answered stonily. The two men backed away from the van and walked away engaged in animated conversation. Sophia started the van and they drove out of the yard and towards the City centre along Varshavskoye Shosse.

Igor breathed a sigh of relief.

"Nice company you keep, Igor!" yelled Sophia above the noisy rattle of the engine.

"It's not my fault. I have to work for these people. Everything is controlled by gangsters," he said bitterly. "I have to earn a living and they pay very well."

"I can imagine!" Sophia said with a note of sarcasm in her voice. "Have we got everything from the truck?"

"I think so. We'll go back to your house now and pick up JeanLuc. He needs this briefcase to make contact with his controllers."

CHAPTER 11

Jean de Sigor picked up the crystal ball from his desk and hefted it. The size and weight of an orange, smooth with a dull flat finish, he held it in a beam of late afternoon sunlight that was slanting in over his thin bony shoulder through the arrowslit window of his fortress home in Castle Sigor. Sunlight, any light, seemed to slip around the glassy surface neither penetrating or reflecting from within the uniform milky greyness. Even as a child, he'd noticed that it never glittered or shone— lifeless and dull, it could have been a large pebble picked at random off the nearby Normandy beaches for all the visual interest it held. And yet. And yet, it seemed to capture the attention, draw one's gaze. It had always been there on the desk, as long as he could remember. His father, his grandfather, all the way back to his Crusader forebears had had the same desk, in the same secret room in the West Tower of the Castle Sigor—nothing in the room was allowed to change and it was rarely disturbed for cleaning. The only concession to modernity and the present was the addition of a phone extension.

From this room he could see, just a few hundred yards away, the site of where it had all begun—the Dream, the Plan, the Root of the Vine, the Head of the Serpent. Soon it would end. Soon.

The phone on his desk rang shrilly. Sighing inwardly, Jean de Sigor, Comte de St.Clair, Nautonnier of the Priory Arcadia, picked up the receiver. He placed the crystal ball, retrieved from the grave of the Merovian King Childeric I, back onto its solid gold pedestal where it sat like a cataract in the eye of the universe.

"A call from London, sir. Sir John Redcliff. Says it's urgent." "Bien sur. Put him through. Oh, and Charles ...?"

"Yes, sir?"

"Get the Lear Jet ready, I want to be in Brussels this evening. Make the usual arrangements, will you?" He pushed the button on the other line. "Hello, Sir John. What's the problem?"

"Are you going to the G7 summit, Jean?"

"Well, I had thought of going. Why?"

"Could you definitely plan on being there? I've had a call from

Russian President Lebed and he wants clarification about certain matters that concern our deal with him."

"What matters? We've been through this endlessly!"

"He wouldn't say precisely. He wants to meet with you personally."

"It's out of the question. Who does he think he is?"

"I think it might be wise, Jean. We don't want anything disturbing our Russian friends, do we, at this time anyway."

"Lebed knows nothing about JeanLuc."

"I know, but it could be catastrophic if he were to find out," came the quiet reply.

"I'll think about it. I'm having dinner this evening with my cousin, Pierre de Loire. Ring me there in Brussels and you'll have your answer. Bye. A bientôt."

*

In London, Sir John Redcliff, Private Secretary to the Treasury, Seneschal of the Priory Arcadia replaced the receiver. He mopped a florid brow with a silk handkerchief monogrammed in one corner with his initials entwined with a tiny embroidered red rose. He knew where his loyalty lay but things were getting very stretched. Pressure from every side was weighing on him. He felt like a collar under a Chinese laundress's steam iron—hot and flattened. Somewhere inside his chest a Scottish boiler room engineer out of an old World War I ship movie was tapping at corroded plumbing with a spanner and muttering Glaswegian curses as large arrow-tipped needles wobbled in and out of the red on the dials of his triple by-passed heart. Half a century of strong liquor, boarding-school food and spotted dick for pud had taken a heavy toll on his health. Gone were the days when he could mount a thoroughbred or even a maidservant, with a clear eye and protuberant loins. Nowadays he spluttered and wheezed like his wife's podgy pugdog.

Thankfully, it would not be for much longer. He was sure of that. Sure of relinquishing his Earthly cares with a glad heart he looked forward to sending his soul spinning and soaring free forever from this mortal plane; from this degenerating and decomposing body he was trapped in and the Byzantine plotting he was enmeshed in. Screw a few angels, he thought lewdly. That would be nice. Every time he thought about sex these days the rise in blood pressure gave him a headache. Anyway, his body repulsed him and he couldn't bear to inflict it on women, even women who were paid.

He heaved himself up from his desk and waddled over to the mirror set into the wall panelling of his office. Gloomily, he stared at his reflection, the heavy leonine head, the tired eyes, whites buck-shotted with blood spots, the purple veined creepers climbing up the fleshy part of his bulbous nose and fanning out across his white stubbled poorly shaved cheeks. The anti-coagulant rat poison they made him take made it murder to shave properly. Some days his jowls and neck were swathed in blood that refused to clot. He had considered growing a beard but he had a lifelong aversion to bearded people. Anyway he'd look a proper Captain Haddock. He sighed. He was looking more like Horace Rumpole every day.

What did he have to do now? he thought as he walked back to his large untidy Government desk. May as well get on with it. Number 1, sort out the bloody Russian. Number 2, make arrangements for JeanLuc's wedding to Giselle de Sigor and Number 3, continue with plans for the Summit. Oh and then there was his bloody job for the stupid British government. Well, that would have to go by the board. He wasn't going to piss around any more with the pettifogging bureaucracy and unbelievably insular concerns of the British— not when a new World Order was emerging from its thousand-year-old chrysalis under the guidance of the Priory Arcadia. For all that he needed sustenance. He pushed the intercom button.

"Margery? Send out to Harrod's for tea will you? I want the works; crumpets, muffins, scones, Cornish clotted cream and that special strawberry jam they have. I want fresh Assam orange pico tea, not the Ceylon. And hot buttered toast; mounds of it." He remembered his schooldays when all he seemed to do was make endless rounds of toast for himself and for all those nasal-voiced faggots he now saw slumped over decanters of whiskey in the dim leathery recesses of the Carlton Club.

"Things are serious then are they, Sir John?" Margery Lemmings had worked for him for more than fifteen years and knew him better than anyone on earth.

"Not more than usual, my dear. I feel a bit down in the dumps and need cheering up."

"It will be about an hour, Sir. Will that be all?"

"No. Cancel all calls and appointments for the rest of the week. If the Prime Minister calls tell her to go and get knotted. Put a call through to President Lebed in Moscow. If anyone wants to know where I am, tell them I'm having a heart transplant or something."

"Yes, sir. I'll deal with it. Can I have one of those iced-lemon sponge fancies from Harrods?" She asked brightly.

"The ones with the candied lemon peel?"

"Yes, that's the kind. They're lovely aren't they?" she said enthusiastically.

"All right, Margery. But do get a move on, all this talk is making me hungry!" Sir John took his finger off the intercom button and absent-mindedly started toying with the heavy solid gold bee that he used as a paperweight. I wonder where the others are, he thought as he turned it over in his hand. There were more than three hundred found in Childeric I's grave. Sauniére must have sold them, bloody crook! He pushed the intercom button again.

"Oh and Margery? I'll have a couple of those fancies too if you don't mind. No maraschino cherries though. Remember what we did to Lenin!"

Margery, in the outer office, smiled grimly to herself. The ugly bastard is killing himself, she thought.

CHAPTER 12

There is a call for you, mademoiselle. Shall I bring the phone out to you?"

"Who is it, Charles?" asked Giselle, Comptesse de Sigor, daughter of Jean de Sigor.

"Sir John Redcliff in London."

"Oh God, I suppose so," she sighed. She took the proffered cordless phone from Charles Duvain, her father's secretary, and walked across the wide terrace to lean decoratively, wrapped in an Angora wool shawl, against the cold stone balustrade. It was evening and her father had just left for Brussels after having spent all afternoon overseeing in the courtyard the unloading of large truck, that, from the much-travelled dusty look of it, had come a long distance. She could see the faint streaks the jets left against the purple darkening sky and the bright winking wing-lights as the LearJet climbed steeply and turned eastward. It was a clear night but looking west Giselle could see black fists of thunderclouds bunched up along the red-streaked skyline.

"Sir John! Sorry to keep you waiting. I was watching to see if Papa had taken off safely."

"That's all right, my dear. I'll get straight to the point, if you don't mind, Giselle," he said.

A tremor of anxiety made Giselle grip the handset tightly. With a manicured hand, she brushed the long blond hair away from her face. "Has the time come, Sir John?" she asked.

"I believe so, yes. But you must not be afraid. Please Giselle, you must have no fear. There is nothing to be alarmed about. We are organising it all very carefully. That is why we must arrange to meet. There are final fittings and procedures that you must begin to learn by heart."

"Where do you want to meet? I have been staying at the Castle. I don't want to leave for a few days yet and I have friends coming. Can you come here, Sir John?" There was silence on the line. Giselle listened tightly closing her eyes— startling green eyes flecked with gold to those that ever got close enough to see them.

"Giselle, I haven't been very well recently and travelling is a strain in addition to all my duties here. But you know, I haven't been to see you for quite a while, so I suppose I should make the effort. However, I should warn you that you must make a few medical arrangements. Please hire a heart specialist and the necessary equipment while I am there."

"Thank you, Sir John. I'll get everything ready for you. I'll even ask Chef Pierre to cook all your favourite English food. He'll do his nut!" Giselle heard Sir John chuckle at this.

"All right Giselle. I've left the chopper at my estate in the country, so I'll pick it up and fly over on Tuesday of next week. I look forward to seeing you again. But remember you must start to prepare yourself. Things we have planned are happening and cannot now be stopped. You and JeanLuc are a key element. I know you have never met and it is all an arrangement, but please remember that you are making a dynastic marriage and we must all do our duty. Our Lord expects it."

"His Will be done," responded Giselle mechanically.

"I'll see you next week then, m'dear. And try not to worry, the man is not an ogre, you know!" The line went dead.

Not an ogre! She thought wildly. I am Giselle de Sigor. I can have anything or anybody I want. My father is one of the wealthiest and most powerful men in the world. I am a real Princess of the Blood. Fierce rage boiled in her and she threw the phone over the parapet out into the evening air scented by the early spring roses just starting to bloom in the formal gardens below. Red, red roses. Crimson, blood red arteries of rose borders marching out across the lawns and coagulating in a pool at the solitary elm tree in the distance near the private airstrip. The fragrance of roses always pervades Castle Sigor—permeates and saturates the air, the furnishings, the very stone itself. On hot summer nights, before thunder, such as the one when Giselle was told the news of her forthcoming marriage, the scent can be intoxicating, can induce dreams, trances and fantastic imaginings ...

Oh and the thorns! Giselle thought as she paced the terrace in a frenzy of frustration and anger. Her mother's paintings, shortly before she died when Giselle was only a baby of two, were all of thorns. Rose tendrils and stems with thorns—no flowers. Intertwined twisted branches and sharp, barbed thorns. Papa kept them in a map-drawer bureau in his office. Giselle had only seen them once, when she was eighteen, five years ago. Her father had come back from a trip to Argentina and had locked himself away for what seemed like months in his room in the tower. It had been a time of great stress; there were armed bodyguards everywhere and fierce dogs silently roaming the grounds and courtyards. They had few visitors and those that came, swooped in low and fast out of black moonless nights in anonymous helicopters. Papa's normally gaunt features became skeletal, eyes shining with the bright fever of inner turmoil.

It was a fearful time, but one fine autumn day, it suddenly seemed to get better, as if a deathly curse had been lifted. Papa had called her into his room— the Rose room.

"Giselle my child, my only love. It is time I told you certain things about yourself, about your mother and about me. What I am going to tell you can only be known by very few people and is a very big secret.

"We are special people, Giselle. Not only are we very rich but also we are born to an ancient Royal Bloodline. This blesses us with fabulous gifts but also imposes arduous duties and tasks whose scope cannot be comprehended by most people." At this point, Jean de Sigor had paused and gone over to a large antique bureau. He pulled open one of the drawers, withdrew some sheets of watercolour paper and laid them out on his desk. "These duties are sometimes very onerous and can cause great grief. It is important that you now know that your mother, whom I loved dearly, was not able to bear the strain and she took her own life. However, our beliefs tell us that this is not a sin and her soul is with God. These are the paintings she did before she went from us. As you can see they reflect her state of mind. I cannot bear to look at them and yet I cannot throw them away. I grieve for her still." After short spell of staring in silence out of the window, he continued, "Giselle, we have some very powerful and dangerous enemies. Lately we have been in danger of losing the war against these people. But now

I am happy to say that we are back on track and the Plan is in operation once more. I feel hopeful, and you are free once more to leave Sigor and pursue your interests and life."

Here he collected up the paintings and locked them away once more in the bureau. He continued staring at her with an unblinking gaze. She had never seen him like this; so intense, so commanding. "Giselle, you are a Princess of ancient Royal Blood. The Blood of Merovee and Dagobert. These names will mean nothing to you or to most people. Although we do not have a kingdom as such, nevertheless our Family has power and influence and riches beyond the dreams of most present heads of state."

Giselle could not deny the truth of that. The Castle itself, the Chateau in Avignon, the Villas in Cap Ferrat and Rome, the Island on Lac Leman were a fraction of the properties owned by the family. She had unlimited accounts in banks controlled by her father all around the world. The family possessed a fleet of Lear Jets and helicopters standing ready in every major airport and several motor yachts and sailboats. There was even a service company, 'Vaincre SA', whose exclusive task was administration of family trusts and affairs.

"But there is a price to pay and grave responsibilities too; for me and for you in the future," continued the Count. "I cannot tell you everything, my dearest daughter, but we are bound by history, fate and our beliefs to a certain Path we have to follow. In the years to come we will be choosing for you a husband and will want you to bear children. No, no don't protest. There are no choices in these matters. Nevertheless, you have and will continue to have complete freedom in other things. Freedom to come and go as you please, see whomever you want; even to take lovers. But please, Giselle, it is your duty to continue the Bloodline and preserve our heritage—your duty to me and to the world."

The Count ended this speech by going over to his daughter and hugging her to him. He smoothed her long fair hair with his hand and she had leaned her head against his chest, as she hadn't done since she was a child.

Giselle brought herself back to the present. She loved her father but lately the cares, absences and troubles had worn him to a ghostly shadow of his former self. She felt he had been deliberately distancing himself from her, perhaps preparing her for her own life out of his protection and tutelage.

The strategy had succeeded; she was no longer a child. She would obey the family and keep the Faith—but she would do it her way on her terms. Philippe was arriving tonight from Paris. She would plan something with her clever lover, something that would make Sir John need that medical team in a hurry. She smiled to herself feeling a thrill of excitement at the thought of asserting her authority; of drawing to herself the reins of power. How would it be? Would it be like getting astride Philippe's powerful Norton motorbike as it rumbled and throbbed roughly between her legs ready to roar and buck wildly at the twist of her delicate wrist?

The scent of roses wafted in drifts across the terrace. It was intense and intoxicating. In the distance, she could hear a rumble of thunder. She felt electric; a lizard on hot tin. She wanted to scream at the heavens and send blue sparks zipping through her outstretched fingers. Her breasts felt hard and painful and she groaned with a frustrated sexual desire that nearly bent her double. She wanted to fuck; she needed to fuck ...

From an upstairs window, partially hidden behind curtains, Charles Duvain looked down with hooded grey eyes at the restless beauty of Giselle on the terrace. He had bided his time well.

Now he would strike. Now would be the fulfilment of the Atbash Plan. Father Moloc would reward him well. He could return to the contemplative life and strict disciplines of the Monastery ... Forgiven.

Later that night, the leather-clad figure of Philippe Dujon arrived with a muffled roar in the cobbled entrance courtyard of Castle Sigor on his race-tuned Norton NightHawk. He cut the engine and dismounted stiffly—it had been a long hard ride from Paris.

Giselle awaited him, framed in light under the arched stonework entrance to her private living quarters. She wore a kimono of pale yellow silk and her blonde hair was tied back with a black gauze ribbon. God, she is beautiful! thought Philippe, as he approached. A beautiful rich princess for him to carry off—but you ain't no Knight in Shining Armour! snickered a sinister whispery voice in his head. She led him in and came into his arms at once. "Thank God you've arrived, Philippe. I need you ... I have plans ... something is going to happen..." the words spilled out hardly giving him time to remove his jacket. To his consternation and surprise, she was already kissing him passionately. He fell back onto a sofa.

"Wait, Giselle. Wait! I have to get out of these leathers. I am hot and uncomfortable and I need a shower." He pushed her gently away but this only served to increase her ardour and she pulled him by the hand into her huge mirrored bedroom and started to claw at his clothing.

Sighing inwardly, Philippe stepped out of the motorcycle leathers. He stood in front of Giselle dressed only in a black silk thong which was now strained to bursting point with its hardened contents. Giselle nuzzled close to him, a glazed faraway look in her eyes. She licked her lips and her hand went out to stroke and release his captive cock.

Dutifully, Philippe turned and posed professionally under the lights, flexing his beautifully muscled body in front of the mirrors and Giselle's hungry gaze. Feeling her warm lips cover him and her mouth start to suck and lick in long hard insistent pulses, he closed his eyes and standing there, gave himself to the pleasure of her warm slippery mouth.

Philippe fell back onto the bed with a gasp; his organ wilting while Giselle walked to the bathroom where he heard the sound of taps running.

Giselle came back from the bathroom naked apart from white silk stockings and climbed into the bed looking at him demurely from under the cool silk sheets. Philippe groaned inwardly. I shall be earning my keep tonight. Thank God I scored before I set off, he thought. "I'll be back soon, sweetheart," he said and went to take a shower. He took his clothes into the bathroom with him—the coke was in the lining of his belt.

Once closeted behind the locked door, he pulled the wide leather belt off his trousers and prised open the Velcro sealed pocket. He pulled out one of the small clip seal polythene bags filled with white powder. He pushed a saliva-coated finger into the bag and rubbed his gums vigorously with the powder. He felt the tension and tiredness begin to ease from his mind. He would snort later with Charles; but now he needed all his concentration for the job ahead.

He showered quickly and dried himself on the fluffy monogrammed towels embroidered with roses. Jesus, they must be a hundred dollars each, these towels; he mused. Going over to the full-length mirror, he examined his body critically. On the scales, he saw that he'd lost weight—again. He frowned as nagging worry lifted a small corner of the cocaine blanket that cocooned his mind. That was five kilos in a month in spite of the high-energy food he ate to maintain his musculature. He was also tiring easily these days. Maybe he should cut down on the white stuff—it was so expensive too. But he didn't want to think about that!

He examined his features in the long mirror over the gold tapped washbasin. The harsh light stung his eyes and made them water. His hair was still lush and black; tied back in a ponytail—but he'd noticed the odd white hair and had taken to oiling it to give it an illusion of condition. Tongue all right but he'd been plagued recently with a rash of small white blisters in the soft inside of his cheeks; the gums of his teeth were inflamed and receding—but that was the coke again, he suspected. Christ! His incisors were looking positively Dracula-like—they wobbled in their sockets too.

Definitely tomorrow, he would cut out the coke. He would take Giselle to a health farm where he could recover. Christ, he was only twenty-four— sometimes he felt eighty-four, like tonight. He looked down at his flaccid penis with growing dread.

"Cherie, come on. I am impatient for more loving!" called Giselle from the bedroom.

In desperation, Philippe tapped out the rest of the contents of the baggy onto the back of his hand and snorted it up into the far recesses of his sinuses. The cold icicle of drug hammered into his brain—for an instant, he couldn't breathe and he sucked in his stomach. In his constricted chest, his heart skipped a beat and re-started lumpily at a slow slow rate. He gripped the edge of the basin, head hung low and waited. Thankfully, like fog burning away in the morning sun, his mind began to clear and his heart revved up a few notches. He felt better. A few more seconds and he felt wonderful—good enough to screw the socks off that rich bitch in the next room. He was a professional. It was Showtime! Once more into the breach.

He opened the bathroom door and went back into the perfumed bedroom. Led Zeppelin was on the stereo ready to drive them to ecstasy—up the stairway to heaven.

CHAPTER 13

So! Now he knew for sure. The traitor was Murphy in New York; the ambitious Irishman. Pope John XXIV stared down at the two sheets of paper lying on his desk. The letter had come in that morning's diplomatic pouch from America marked for his personal attention. On the envelope was a hand-written covering note from Cardinal Murphy emphasising the importance and urgency of the letter within.

The letter consisted of an invitation and a list of names. An invitation to a 3-day Summit Meeting for 17 January—a date that was six months in the future— at Sigor Castle in France. Topic for discussion: 'The Millennial Agenda'. With increasing bewilderment and shock, His Holiness read through the list of named participants. Although he'd never heard of most of them, he was astonished to learn that US President Dillon, Russian President Lebed, EEC Commissioner Pierre de Loire and the political leaders of most European countries had already consented to attend, according to the list. The letter was signed Jean de Sigor and written underneath the scrawled signature was the phrase 'on behalf of the Desposyni'.

Who the hell were the Desposyni? He racked his brain. It sounded vaguely familiar but he couldn't place it.

The letter ended with the statement that he would be contacted again in due course to confirm his reply which they were sure was going to be in the affirmative. They must be joking. His agenda was already fixed for three years in advance. Every minute of his time was taken up and already planned and these Desposyni or whoever they were wanted three days! It was clearly impossible. Out of the question.

The letterhead gave no address but was printed with a logo that he had seen before but only very rarely in material passed to him by the Rome station of the CIA in their weekly reports. It was the official device of the Priory Arcadia! Emilio wanted to tear it up into small pieces. He felt rage and anxiety boiling up within him at this betrayal by Joseph Murphy. How else would such a letter get through to the Pope bypassing the normal channels of the Curia, except through mediation of a Prince of the Church? And if Murphy was acting as a channel for the Priory Arcadia, then it was certain he was their chosen candidate for the next Papacy. This then was a gauntlet thrown down at the feet of Roman Orthodoxy; at his feet, the legitimate Pope and occupant of the Throne of St.Peter.

He looked again at the list of names. In spite of his rage, he knew that this would be a most serious event and he would have to consider his response very carefully. There were powerful and influential moves afoot and the holy church could not afford to make the mistake of ignoring the Priory Arcadia. Action must be taken if this cancer sent by Satan was to be rooted out once and for all. It had taken a Crusade in the 1300s, three Civil Wars, a bloody Inquisition, countless excommunications, firm imposition of doctrine and constant vigilance to suppress the heresies that the Priory Arcadia espoused. But still it survived.

Emilio thought of the Priory as the appendix of the Body of the Church—a primordial useless organ that flared up from time to time when it went sour from collecting the residues of failed or disaffected churchmen. Primordial in the sense that it has always been there right from the birth of the Church; a consequence of the rift between St.James and St.Paul and the hidden facts of Jesus' life. A bile-filled pocket of heresies and discarded doctrine now turned cancerous and malignant; a threat to the ageing body of a Roman Church weakened by lack of faith and loss of trust.

Occasionally, he had wondered why he didn't join them as had, he suspected, one or two of his immediate predecessors. After all, he knew most of the true facts about the origins of the Church and the life of Jesus. He was acutely aware of the malaise within the Roman Catholic Church: the loss of revenue, of doctrinal relevance and of flocks of believers that supported the whole vast edifice. He had played the game, held the levers of power within the Vatican. So why not? Maybe they had solutions to what seemed the impossible problems that faced him.

Perhaps, it was because he was a pragmatist, suspicious of Faith. He knew that there were fundamental psychological reasons why the Church was still here and continued to exist with all its faults and its foundation of myth and confusion. The Papacy itself had always been corrupt and inefficient, a battleground of vicious, sometimes murderous, internal feuding. The only new factor was that this whole mess was now the subject of investigative journalism and widespread dissemination by the hysterical media. That had eroded one of the archetypal planks on which a religion is built—ritualised secrecy and the cultivation of mystery. God speaks to priests and priests hand this information over, suitably edited, to the common people. If God were understandable by ordinary men and women or spoke via the Oprah Winfrey Show or tabloid newspaper, where would this leave the Church?

Emilio knew that the problem was soluble, but the situation was dangerous. TV evangelism was not the way forward—for all their slick professionalism and wealth, a small financial or moral mistake and it took only seconds to destroy them. They didn't have the centuries of the momentum that the Catholic Church had behind it, they were not part of the social fabric. Mistakes by men of the Church were viewed by the faithful as signs of human frailty to be wrestled with and forgiven through Christ's mercy—the religion itself was incorruptible, men were not. That was why new sects could always be allowed to come and go like evangelising comets but the main world religions would remain forever in the bedrock of the human psyche. Christianity could not be destroyed but the institutions of the Church were increasingly vulnerable.

The Priory was dangerous because they knew how to keep secrets and how to generate mystery—they'd been doing it since the Crusades. They also understood that the Church operated hierarchically through the Curia with the Pope at the top wielding absolute power. Evangelising reformers always start at the bottom of the pyramid with the mass of people who have no power or organisation and who have only a transient attention span. Only someone with the stature of Jesus could hope to succeed by that means.

In computer terms, the Priory aims to replace the operating system – Windows with Linux. Put their man in the Seat of St.Peter, as they had done before. Nevertheless, reasoned Emilio, even if he were to become a creature of the Priory, he still had to contend with the same machinery of power. The hard disk-drive, the printer and the VDU work within their own constraints whatever operating system is driving them. It is the same with the Church.

When all is said and done, the Priory was still only a cult or cabal; it must wield its power in secret and through indirect means—always hidden. Emilio preferred the relative honesty inherent in the direct exercise of power and influence for all to see and all to worship. But with that came huge responsibilities and that in the final analysis, more than anything, is what separated the Chair of St.Peter from the Grand Mastership of the Priory Arcadia. The Pope and Church still held sway over the souls of millions and were welded inextricably into the fabric of society—he had real power. Why relinquish it or share it with other ruthless powerful men who only existed in the labyrinthine shadows?

Nonetheless, Emilio knew and experienced hourly the God- like loneliness of the Papacy. It was terribly tempting to pick up the phone and pay the price of power sharing. But something always stopped him—his Spanish obstinacy, his arrogance, and his rage at people who had never known hardship and poverty, who had acquired power by birthright, his refusal to acknowledge the painful truths of history. Most of all, as he grew older and approached death, there was his totally irrational but increasing fear of the Devil and everlasting hellfire. If all of human history was right then the Pope, of all people, would be among the first to ascend to Heaven when he died and his name would be recorded on the side of the angels, sins forgiven by a merciful Christ Saviour; whilst the Nautonnier would suffer everlasting torment in the flames of the innermost circle of Hell with the mocking laughter of Satan ringing forever in his ears, testimony to the hollowness of earthly ambition and vanity. That was the choice.

Both groups were essentially Christian, both believed in the same God and shared many doctrines, both were experienced and knew the nature and psychology of Man. However, the physical reality was plain to see—the Church was here in bricks and mortar and priestly pensions dedicated to God, while the Priory was not. And yet why the doubts, torments and temptations? Why the sleepless nights in what should be a haven of holiness? Why even bother to think about them when there was more than sufficient workload to drive a normal person insane? Would it really ease his mind to talk through some dark night with Jean de Sigor or would it be tantamount to an informal chat with the Devil?

Pope John XXIV sat at his desk wearily rubbing his eyes. There was a decision to make. A decision that would affect the fate of the Church. A decision, the ramifications of which would impact on the future of the whole of mankind.

Should he or should he not accept the invitation?

For the first time in his long and eventful life; for the very first time, Emilio D'Ascriba, Pope John XXIV, occupier of the Throne of St.Peter, Head of the Holy Roman Catholic Church, focus of the worship of millions, wished there really was a God to pray to and who would offer guidance. But all he could think of ... was that terrible prophesy of the monk Malachi. Another cursed Irishman! Was it really his fate to reap the whirlwind?

He switched on the PC and it glowed into life. He put his hand on the mouse and smoothly clicked onto the Veronica icon. The soothing bouncy tune started, the strange flat, brilliantly coloured, landscape appeared with the familiar figure strolling and rolling along with a cheery grimace. Sonic would give him the answer. Yes. He would let God inform Sonic of the decision. If he got past the Boss on the fourth level, then he would go to the summit; if he didn't he wouldn't. He would leave it in the lap of the Game Gods.

No one else seemed inclined to help.

CHAPTER 14

"Ah, Alexei. So you are awake now. Please join us for something to eat. What would you like? I have some hot borscht and I have baked some bread fresh this morning." Saskia pulled out a chair at the long scrubbed wooden table and JeanLuc sat opposite Sophia's father, Dmitri Yemeljan. JeanLuc was still wearing the white robe, now rather crumpled, that Sophia had given him. His bare feet were cold on the flagged stone floor.

"Please excuse my dress, I have clothes in my suitcase. Oh and please call me JeanLuc—that is my real name " he said.

"No matter. No matter. Sophia and your friend Igor have gone to pick up your suitcase and other things. We are expecting them back any time. Now eat, you look weary and hungry, didn't you sleep well?" asked Saskia earnestly. "Is the bed uncomfortable?"

JeanLuc looked up at her warily, looking for signs of knowledge of what had gone on between himself and Sophia in the earlier hours. "No. Everything is fine. I was dreaming a lot that's all. Sometimes it takes a lot out of me ..." his voice trailed away.

Saskia went to the stove and ladled out a bowl full of red soup. Dropping a large dollop of yoghurt into it, she placed it in front of JeanLuc. He tore off a chunk of warm dark bread and started eating, dunking the bread into the soup which was sharp and delicious—full of nutmeg. He felt his head clear instantly. Dmitri watched him amiably from across the table. He was nibbling at some nuts from the bowl in front of him, beside which was a large leather-bound book. "When you are ready, we can start our discussion," he said.

"Sure. I'm ready anytime, go ahead Dmitri. If you don't mind me eating while you talk. This is truly excellent; I feel better already. Thank you." Saskia beamed and refilled his bowl.

Dmitri cleared his throat. "Let me start by telling you a little about myself and then I will tell you what led me to the discovery which has brought you here," he continued. "Until five years ago, I worked as a curator at the Tretyakov Gallery under the great Antonov who was the director. My job as one of the curators was to catalogue, clean and look after the huge collection. I also had a teaching job in art history at Moscow University. I have always been interested in religious art from my youth, but as you can imagine, in the heartland of Communism, this was hardly a politically correct speciality to have!" he smiled grimly. "No, my outward speciality was in factory art—the art of depicting tractors and machinery! Art of the working man or proletariat." He cracked open a peanut shell and tossed the contents into his mouth.

"However, this speciality allowed me to travel extensively, visiting collectives and factories throughout the Soviet Union on a mission to collect and encourage artistic activity in the service of the State."

"So this gave you the ideal opportunity to secretly look for icons?"

"That's right. Even better, my job was to seek out and denounce religious artwork as symbols of social degeneracy, intellectualism, capitalism, Royalism and any other ism that was in the firing line. My mission was to destroy these opiates of the people and replace them with strong strutting imagery of Soviet Pride. Pictures showing vast legions of high-stepping military against a phallic landscape of missiles and tanks were particularly favoured. Any icon or holy picture I found I confiscated in the name of the State and had sent back to the Gallery."

"I was told that the Tretyakov Gallery holds a collection of some of the finest icons in existence," said JeanLuc.

"It was true. Many of those are ones I collected over the years," said Dmitri. "But alas, in the last three or four years most have disappeared to the West: Germany, Japan, USA—who knows," Dmitri shrugged. "We who were on the staff of the Tretyakov have handled some spectacular treasures; a Goya, a Dürer even a Caravaggio. They were never displayed and most have gone now to secret private collectors or are being hoarded by ex-politicians of the Soviet State. It is heartbreaking to an historian and artist such as myself. I love Russia and this cynical pillage of our God-given heritage can never be forgiven. Never!" Dmitri banged his fist on the table.

JeanLuc could sense the whip flick of temper and fanatical zeal that must have driven the man in his younger days and maintained his religious faith against the numbing weight of State indifference or persecution throughout the Communist era.

"Tell me more about icons, Dmitri. I know they are images of holy

Christian people painted on wooden panels, but how did it all come about?"

Dmitri smiled at JeanLuc. "You are asking for a long lecture," he said.

"Well, I don't want all the details of course, but I am curious about the origins of icons. Above all, I'd like to know why you think you've gotten wind of some very old ones. That's why I'm here after all."

"All right, but you'll have to forgive the lecturing—it is a complicated subject." He reached over to the stove and refilled their mugs with fresh coffee.

"I've heard it all before, so I shall leave you two to it while I go and queue at the GUM store," said Saskia, pulling on a heavy woollen coat, grabbing a basket and heading for the door. "I hope there are some chestnuts left," she said as she went out.

Dmitri took a sip of coffee. "The first Christians were Jews and fanatically opposed to painted images and image worship," he began. "They would have regarded icons as idols, graven images banned by the Old Testament books of Exodus and Deuteronomy. Nevertheless, if you read the relevant passages carefully, the ban is actually against making images of God. There are plenty of examples in the Old Testament where Jews were allowed to decorate the Temple with various figures, sculptures and embroideries. In fact, specific instructions are given for decorating the Ark of the Covenant, the Tabernacle and the Holy of Holies."

"So does that mean Jews were originally allowed to and did do painting and decorations within the Temple but were only forbidden to construct false idols?"

"Yes, that's right. However, around the time of the Maccabees, this aspect of Mosaic Law was re-interpreted by the High Priests of the time and became much stricter. The ban on images was extended to virtually every form of artistic or pictorial representation. In fact, much of what was done earlier was destroyed at this time, including many statues of early Jewish kings."

"So, if Jesus was a mortal king of the Jews, then theoretically there would be no ban against making a statue or image of him for posterity?"

"Again you are right. At that time, most Jews including his disciples would not have considered Jesus to be a deity. A Messiah certainly: but a Messiah was not considered to be the Jewish God. A Messiah was a teacher of righteousness, a war leader and as a prophet, the voice of God. It is only many years after Jesus lived, some think nearly a century, that he became generally accepted as the Son of God and hence a deity in his own right and thus making it sacrilegious for a devout Jew to make images of him. But by this time, Christianity as a religion had become Hellenised, Romanised and Paulinised, adopting many gentile concepts and pagan customs as its own in order to become the successful worldwide religion it is today.

"Around the beginning of the Christian era, if we exclude the geographically small area of Israel, people lived in a world of imagery and it was an accepted and integral part of religious life. Christianity came into existence in a world that looked kindly on religious imagery and as Christians by then were mostly gentile it was only natural for them to incorporate images in their worship and use pictorial art to help propagate the holy message. Nevertheless, this was frowned on in the very early Church.

"I suppose, also, that Jews, unlike the rest of mankind, believed that the end of the world or Armageddon was almost upon them, so there would not be much point in making pictorial records for subsequent generations if there weren't going to be any."

"That's a good point, JeanLuc. You would make a fine student! On the other hand, this didn't stop Jewish sects, like the Essenes, from making voluminous written records and commentaries."

"You mean like the Dead Sea and Nag Hammadi Scrolls?"

"Yes, among others. Anyway, as I was saying, the earliest Christian Fathers were, on the whole, against the use of iconography especially charakteres or portraits. It smacked too much of idolatry and reversion to paganism. Pictures with a narrative content, the so-called historiai, were viewed with less hostility and so were the symbola or symbolic pictures. There are examples of these preserved in the Roman Catacombs."

"That's very interesting, Dmitri. I didn't know that the Catacombs had icons. They must be the earliest Christian art then?"

98

"Possibly. However, there is doubt about the true age of some of the better-known burial chapel decorations since the Catacombs must have been accessible to Christians and others for many centuries. I went to Rome as part of a large trade mission to Italy in the sixties when the Vatican bought a number of paintings from us in exchange for hard currency. In fact, that was when I first met Father Mirphy. He was not yet a cardinal and was assigned, as a representative of the Vatican, to look after us. He took me on a tour of the Catacombs. I was shocked and horrified at the naked commercialism and exploitation of the pilgrims. I understand that Lourdes is even worse. They can hardly be called holy places. At least here in Russia we still venerate our sacred places; even Lenin's Tomb remains more or less intact." Dmitri continued. "It is not until the second or third century after Jesus that we begin to see any writing about the subject of religious imagery or icons and then it is usually a critical commentary or a complaint in a letter. For example, Origen of Irenaeus, Bishops Eusebius, Clement and Epiphanius were all opposed to the idea of images and their worship. At the start of the fourth century the Synod of Elvira banned painting on church walls of objects intended for veneration and worship."

"I don't understand why they were so against it."

"Well, Bishop Eusebius said that ordinary people, especially women, were prone to idolatrous worship of images and this led to reversion to paganism. Even Constantia, the sister of Emperor Constantine, apparently thought it reasonable to ask Bishop Eusebius for an accurate portrait of Christ. Of course her request was turned down." Dmitri continued with his discourse fortified by a fresh jar of preserves dating from the time of the taking of the 'White House' Parliamentary building and fall of the reactionary old guard people's deputies in the autumn of 1993.

"Most Christian leaders stood out against religious images until the fifth century. But this same conflict against devotional images shows us at the same time how firmly rooted they had become in the soil of popular piety. Within the context of the paganisation of Christianity, I believe that assimilation of pagan, universal or archetypal religious sentiment played a vital role in the final victory of the Church as we know and love it. The veneration of saints, the martyr and relic cults also encouraged the manufacture of images by Christians and paved the way for image worship."

"The halo of Christian imagery dates from Constantine. Is that right?"

"Yes. Emperor Constantine was a sun worshipper, a follower of Mithras, all his life. His accommodation with and tolerance of Christianity resulted in a synthesis where you see early icons, especially Coptic icons, painted with the sun aura, a symbol of Mithras. Only later did this become the ring halo familiar to Western art and the Renaissance. Most Icons of the Orthodox Russian Church even up to the 16th or 17th century maintain the sun form of halo. Are you sure you want to hear all this? It is pretty specialised, you know."

"Yes, yes, go on. I find it fascinating. What happened after 400AD to make icons acceptable to the Church? Did they just bow to popular pressure from the congregation?"

Dmitri got up from the table and refilled their mugs with fresh coffee. "Would you like some of this dried fruit? I still have some dried bananas."

"Thank you, that would be very nice," JeanLuc chewed on a banana slice. It was hard and brittle but had a terrific flavour.

Dmitri continued: "Where was I? Oh yes. The Church adapted itself to the various trends existing in the community such as icon worship, in spite of powerful objections to this materialisation of the Faith. However, there were increasing numbers of eminent Church Fathers such as Basil the Great, to whom the cathedral in Red Square is dedicated and John Chrysostom, the Patriarch of Constantinople, who were in favour of imagery but only for decoration, educational purposes for those who could not read and to encourage piety by example.

"The first icons, paintings of the Madonna, Apostles and Saints on wooden panels were first described by Pope Gregory I but only in a cautionary letter to the Hermit Secundinius warning him not to let them be worshipped. From the fifth century onwards we can begin to see serious attempts to depict the true likeness of Christ and it is around this time that the first accounts of acheiropoetic images of Christ appear at Edessa and at Camulia."

"Hold on Dmitri! What is acheiropoetic?"

"Oh sorry. Yes. Acheiropoetic means 'not created by human hands'. It is a miraculous imprinting of Jesus' face or crucified body on cloth. The Turin Shroud is acheiropoetic as is the Veronica kept in St.Peter's basilica in the Vatican."

"But the Turin Shroud is a fake. Scientific carbon dating supposedly gives it a date in the fourteenth century. They showed me back in New York, this article in New Scientist or Nature; some such specialist science magazine."

"Is this the article?" asked Dmitri after briefly disappearing into his book and manuscript- littered study.

JeanLuc looked the photocopied sheets over. "It looks like it, yes."

"Well, the Shroud probably is a fake although there are still some, the Englishman Ian Wilson for one, who think the carbon dating may be wrong. Not on technical grounds but there is an argument that the samples used for analysis were taken from the much handled edge of the cloth, so human sweat, tears, incense smoke, fire damage and recent atmospheric pollutants could have made the age come out wrong. To counter this, the scientists state that the cloth fibres were detergent-treated before carbonising and, in any case, the weave of the cloth is typical thirteenth-fourteenth century material. Also, we shouldn't ignore the Conspiracy theory of the Germans Kersten and Gruber who maintain that the Vatican deliberately gave the scientists the wrong test samples so that the Shroud could be declared a fake officially in the eyes of science."

"Why would they want to do that?" asked JeanLuc

"Well, the reasoning is quite interesting. If the Shroud was actually genuine then the forensic evidence points to the likelihood of Jesus being alive, not dead, when he was wrapped in the cloth. It is conceivable then that the lotions of aloe and myrrh in which he was anointed made a vapour imprint on the cloth and a living Jesus would have bled from his wounds. Now, as everyone knows, the absolute core of Christian Faith and Catholic Dogma insists that Jesus had to have died on the Cross and then have been resurrected three days later. Therefore, it is argued that a genuine Shroud whose image could only have been produced by a still living Christ, might be highly embarrassing to Christian Doctrine—more dangerous to the Faith than having a genuine Shroud declared a fake."

"But that's incredible! That would mean conspiracy at the highest levels of the Vatican, involving even the Pope himself."

"Well, it may be so. Myself, I think it is probably a clever fake. The incentive for making fakes in the eleventh to the twelfth century was enormous—relic hunting was at its peak then. Also, from an art historian's point of view, I find it more disturbing that Albrecht Dürer made an engraving in the sixteenth century which has facial features almost identical to those only revealed in the photographic negative done for the first time in the nineteenth century. I find this truly mystifying.

"So what can you say? It is a matter of Faith like all such things. Who knows what is true and what has actually happened in over a thousand years of turbulent history? Look at you Americans who are now claiming to have won the Vietnam War! History is re-written even in the same generation."

"As far as I'm concerned, if you really, really believe you have one of the nails of the True Cross then you do and I am not going to waste my breath telling you it was freshly minted in Sicily only last week. Experience has taught me that faith has the power to imbue a tawdry copy, even a dog- eared postcard, with some element of the mystical original—this is the entire foundation on which iconography is based."

"Some would argue that this is the fundamental flaw in the human psyche— given the right circumstances and presentation, people will believe anything, even the most outrageous things—completely against logic! Koestler wrote well on this subject, if I remember correctly."

"I agree, but without this so-called flaw then religious faith would not exist and one of the prime movers of human evolution would not be there. Where would be the motivation behind the lives of the Saints? We would all be like Mr. Mulder in that TV series in America, what do you call it? "

" X Files?"

"Yes. X Files. Sergei took us to see the film. I enjoyed it. Excuse me, JeanLuc, but I need to go to the toilet. I will be back in a few minutes." He left the room.

"Now look at this JeanLuc!" said Dmitri as he came back into the room. He laid a small carved wooden box on the table. Producing a tiny silver key, he opened and lifted the lid, which was inlaid with mother of pearl. With infinite care, he lifted out what looked like a small sports trophy made in a ceramic or plaster material. It was clearly very old. The composition was of a small Buddha-like figure squatting on a fluted pillar. Crosses were carved at intervals into the surface in a helix from base to the top pedestal. Faint vestiges of paint or gilt work clung to its surface. "Can you guess what this is?" Dmitri asked, a note of reverence in his voice.

"I don't know. An old trophy of some sort perhaps?"

Dmitri laughed. "Well, it's certainly a trophy in one sense. But it is a prize for many years of seeking and study in ancient history. It is my most prized possession," he said. He placed it down tenderly on the table. "This is a statuette of St.Simeon the Stylite; a pilgrim's souvenir from the sixth century."

JeanLuc made no attempt to touch it. It certainly looked old and he could only take Dmitri's word for its authenticity. Yes, it was a matter of faith.

"He was a pillar saint or Stylite. An holy ascetic who spent thirty years on top of a pillar. People went on pilgrimages to see them and as souvenirs they would take little clay statuettes like this or small plaques home with them. They were widely believed to be endowed with the power of the Saint who would protect them from calamity."

"A sort of St.Christopher's medal?"

"Not exactly, but close enough. However, these objects have great historical significance because they represent the acceptance by the Church of the inspirational potency of images and relics. This had in any case become a fact of life amongst ordinary people."

"From these little souvenirs." he picked up the statuette, " it is only a small step to belief in miracle-working images; to the idea that divine forces operating within the image could grant a supplicant help and protection; to the idea that you could be healed by touching or seeing the holy image or making a pilgrimage to the place where it was kept."

He continued: "One interesting property of icons, especially ones

103

revered for their Divine power, is that God appears to the visionary in the form depicted in their favourite icon. For example, God appeared to Rasputin in the form of the Virgin of Kazan; to Bernadette as the Blessed Virgin of Lourdes. If he ever appeared to me it might be as Sophia Divine Wisdom, or to my son Sergei as Elvis Presley!"

JeanLuc laughed: "How would he appear to me? That's a good question! I don't have any favourite icon."

"Well, it could be the burning bush that Moses saw or the blinding light that set St.Paul on his way, whatever would bring the mystic revelation or do the trick."

"Yes, I take your point but we are entering the realm of fantasy here. If we just assume that some icons were more influential than others, what characteristics distinguish them? Is it age? The artist? The source? The technical skill?"

"To be honest I don't really know. It certainly isn't skill because the most famous are often rendered in the crudest, least artistic, fashion. I think that age, fame and the accretions of history associated with it, are probably the most significant factors and of course worth—not worth to the Faith but worth in terms of its decoration, jewels and precious metal content bestowed upon it by grateful worshippers.

It probably came about like this: If you happened to take an icon into battle as a good luck charm or mascot and you survived to be on the winning side and if this happened frequently enough, and you were promoted to General, then you might come to believe that God, as made manifest by the icon, was on your side. This icon would then be seen as a potent one to be carried as a standard in battle and decorated with gold and precious gems.

The downside of all this is that it is a well-known battle strategy to try to demoralise your opponent by striking directly at their standard bearers. The Mongols knew this and would invariably send their crack riders only at the Russian troops bearing their precious icons. Incidentally, this habit of carrying icons to war led to their being constructed in an easily transportable form, like a hinged box protected by metal facings to ward off arrows.

The problem with increased portability was that icons could be captured in war, stolen, pillaged, smuggled or even traded as currency."

"This brings us to the present practice of international trading in icons as wooden roubles?" asked Jean Luc.

"Alas yes. It is very sad. But I justify my own activity in this by the fact that it has been going on for centuries. It's certainly no worse than the selling of indulgences—at least you get something tangible for your money!"

Dmitri paused and drank the rest of his coffee. "Here, have a dried apricot—they are especially good. Go on try one!"

"We're back, Papa!" called Sophia cheerily as she and Igor came in the door. "Ah, you're up, JeanLuc. How are you feeling? I hope my father hasn't been boring you with all that ancient history. We've got all your stuff. Where's Mama?"

"She went to the shops. You know how it is with the queues, it'll be a while before she gets back," said Dmitri.

"I'll go and collect her with the van, then. Give her a hand."

Igor placed the briefcase on the table in front of JeanLuc. "Do you want me to come, Sophia?" he asked.

"No. I'll be all right. You sit down and get yourself something to eat. Bye, everyone." She dashed out.

"Whew! She's full of beans this morning. What happened at the yard?"

Dmitri placed a bowl of soup in front of Igor who said: "We had no trouble. But we were seen by someone who noticed the gasoline drum in the back of the van. I am a bit concerned about that."

"Who saw you?"

"A small but important-looking fellow called Zafod. Leonid Zafod. Do you know him, Dmitri?"

"Doesn't ring a bell. Maybe my son Sergei will know of him. Do you want me to call him and find out?"

"If it's no trouble, it will put my mind at rest. Is that okay with you?" Igor looked at JeanLuc for confirmation. JeanLuc nodded, drew the briefcase towards him, opened it up and plugged a lead into the nearby wall socket. Dmitri went out of the kitchen to the large living room at the rear of the house where the phone was.

JeanLuc got out the aerial and stuck it to the kitchen window pointing skywards. He booted up the CPU and soon a mass of jumbled code began to scroll across the screen beamed down from the Biophar Drugs comsat in the dark heavens above. A few seconds later this was decoded and messages appeared on the screen in plain English. JeanLuc scanned the contents of the files as they downloaded. Hmm. Quite a lot was happening back home in the US. Maybe he should risk a voice call? No, they were too easy to intercept. He typed in a brief progress report to Joel Maniato and left it at that. After all he'd only just arrived and nothing had been achieved yet.

He had no idea of what to do next. Dmitri would have to guide him and the rest he would leave in the hands of God. JeanLuc was quite fatalistic about these things. He'd understood from an early age that he was some sort of human catalyst of events. Wherever he was things seemed to happen. He was reminded of that hapless Cherokee family that always managed to pitch their tents in an oilfield. Vulture-like, the oil companies would rush in and erect a drilling rig and sure enough they would strike oil. The Indians got kicked off the land and the whole cycle would begin again. Of course there was also that other fellow, Frank in the 'Some Mothers Do 'Ave 'Em' TV show. Things happened around him too—disastrous things!

Dmitri came back into the room: "I left a message for Sergei to call me. He is in a meeting."

"Okay, Pop," said Igor continuing to slurp up his soup. "This is good soup!" he said.

"Help yourself, Igor. There's plenty more. With the dollars JeanLuc has given us, we are rich!" He smiled benignly at JeanLuc who was closing up the electronic briefcase.

"Tell me about your icon searches, Dmitri. What do you have for us?" He indicated towards the briefcase. "They are pestering me for progress."

Dmitri sat down. "Hmmm. Where to start? Yes. It is very complicated … it has taken me many years, nearly thirty to be precise, but the first clue that started me on the track was an old letter."

"An old letter? Something with a puzzle?" asked JeanLuc.

Dmitri regarded him unblinkingly across the table with his pale blue gem-like eyes. "Please let me tell this without interruption in my own way. I know you have pressures, but I am an old man and this is my life's work we're talking about. I am happy to help Father Joseph and yourself since I believe we are doing God's work but it is difficult for me to give up secrets which I have had locked away in my heart for decades and which not even my children know about."

"I apologise for my impatience, Dmitri. Please continue as you see fit. If you'd prefer to talk direct with Cardinal Joseph Mirphy ..." JeanLuc pointed at the briefcase "... that can be arranged right now, pronto."

"No, no. I have an instinct for people and God tells me that you are the right one. I knew it from the moment you stepped in the door. But please indulge me, I am old and you are young and represent the future. It is difficult to let go or to trust anyone these days."

"I understand, Dmitri, but how will we know that we are doing the right thing? How does anyone know? You know I am here on His Eminence's' orders, but I am also sure that this is where Fate or God has directed me. I can't explain how I know this ..."

"There is a way to find out. We must pray and we must hold a Meeting tonight."

"A meeting? A meeting with whom?"

"The Brotherhood. If I tell you who they are, you must swear never to tell anyone—there are many risks involved. You must swear too, Igor."

"I swear in Christ's name," said JeanLuc seriously.

"Me too," mumbled Igor, his mouth full of the dark bread with which he was mopping up the remains of his soup.

"Wait here. I'll return in a few moments." When Dmitri returned he was carrying a large old book manuscript with wooden covers and bound with leather straps. "I am an elect of the Brotherhood of the Khlysty. This is the Dove Book," he said sonorously. "In this book are the Sayings and Teachings of our sect as revealed by God to Daniel Philipov, one of the Chosen Ones." He laid the book reverentially on the table and undid the straps. "This book was left to the family by my father shortly before he was killed in the October Revolution. I lived with my mother and older sister in Ekaterinburg, which is now called Sverdlovsk, until they were both shot by Stalin's militia in one of the purges of the twenties for the usual excuse of 'Tsarist tendencies'. My sister's eyesight had been restored by God through the healing hands of the Holy man Rasputin; so she refused to renounce religion even in the face of death. She is one of many Khlysty martyrs."

Dmitri looked at the two men sombrely. "I escaped death only because, by then, I was in the Army here in Moscow. I am not proud of what I did to stay alive in those times but the Brotherhood helped me when it could, because I am descended from a Chosen One. They even got me my job in the Tretyakov. Chosen ones are the avatars of our sect, re-incarnations of Jesus Christ living amongst us."

This is getting pretty weird, thought Igor. He looked up at the old man. By rights, I should be in some grimy hotel room just waking up with a blinding hangover, next to a perfumed beached whale of a whore snoring beside me; not having this white-bearded geriatric religious freak ranting on, or his skinny daughter getting us into trouble with gangsters and the goddamn FSB. Still, JeanLuc had paid him well, he'd collected his gun and he would go along with it—for now. Things weren't all bad—the food was terrific and he was sure he'd seen that Saskia woman eyeing him speculatively. The old man didn't look capable of adequately servicing a good-looking, solid woman like her. Now there was a passionate woman! Igor smacked his lips appreciatively and let his mind wander off in erotic thought—letting any further conversation flow past his ears unheeded.

JeanLuc was saying: "This book must be very rare, Dmitri. Can I take a look? Is it in Russian? I promise to take the greatest of care."

Dmitri gently lifted off the wooden covers that held yellowed sheets of thick manuscript paper pressed together. He pushed it across to JeanLuc, who started to leaf carefully through the hand-written pages. "Do you have any objection if I scan these pages electronically? It will preserve an accurate record which I can study at leisure."

"Will it damage the pages?"

"Not in any way. Look, I will show you." He lifted his briefcase, opened it and took out a small hand-scanner attached to a thin lead. Booting up the CPU, he accessed the correct directory and loaded the scanning software. He unfolded wing-like projections on the hand-scanner and ran it over the first page of the Dove Book. The ornate hand-written Cyrillic letters reproduced themselves in miniature on the

108

screen and were saved instantly to a flash memory card that JeanLuc pushed into the slot in the CPU.

Dmitri put his spectacles on and peered short-sightedly at the screen. "Amazing!" he said with complete lack of conviction. "You go ahead and do what you want. I'll go and phone the members of the Khlysty Brotherhood about a Prayer Meeting for tonight." He went out.

JeanLuc scanned the hundred or so pages of the Dove Book into memory and then set an OCR program to work on the file contents. OCR of that complexity is a tough job and would use a lot of computer time, so he left it on one side to get on with it. He picked up one of the wooden covers and studied the picture painted on its varnished inner surface. "Who is this, Dmitri?" he asked when the old man returned once more to the kitchen.

"Ah! Beautiful, isn't she? That's a copy of a seventeenth century icon of the Stroganov school. It is Sophia Divine Wisdom. The original is in the Recklinghausen Icon Museum in Germany. Fellow named Strobucha acquired it—if I remember correctly." He stared at JeanLuc with a peculiar expression and said, "I named my daughter after her—though I don't see much sign of wisdom there!" he laughed.

The phone rang and Dmitri went to take the call. After some minutes he returned, his face shadowed with concern. He went over to Igor. "Igor, that was Sergei. I asked him about that Zafod fellow you told me about. Sergei says he is some kind of top-level crime boss and that we should be very careful. The FSB have him in their sights apparently but he is very powerful and they can't touch him for the moment."

"Did you tell him about us and what happened with the gasoline?" Igor asked.

"No. No, of course not. I just said that some friends of Sophia had run across him recently. He seemed very concerned that we should be careful of this man."

"Well, there's nothing we can do about it now. We can only hope they aren't the people involved in the black-market gasoline operation that we blew up. Logically, there must be several such outfits in Moscow. Zafod is probably backing Karasamov in military hardware or drugs. I don't think we should worry." JeanLuc couldn't quite understand why he'd said that with such confidence. He shook his head and turned back to his examination of the screen on which translated pages of the Dove Book were slowly beginning to appear. He felt disturbed however; as if there was something here he'd missed, that he needed to know more about. He was about to query Dmitri some more, but Saskia and Sophia returned at that moment carrying a vast quantity of shopping. The thought and the niggling worry went out of his head.

"Clear the table, then. Get rid of those dusty old things, Papa!" said Sophia brightly. "We are going to prepare a feast for this evening. Those dollars are truly miracle workers. We bought things we thought only the Politburo and Police could get! Look. Salami, fresh vegetables, sweet chestnuts, olive oil, cream, pistachio nuts for you, Papa. Go on, get out of here, we have work to do!"

Dmitri had taken Saskia by the arm to one side. He told her about his plan for a meeting of the Khlysty that night. At first, she looked startled, but then a big grin of pleasure came over her large chubby features and she looked back at JeanLuc and Igor, especially Igor, with a wicked glint in her eye. She guffawed loudly and clapped her hands; then the two women got caught up in their culinary preparations and the men went into the back room. Through the gap in the door, JeanLuc could see that Sophia and her mother were huddled close to each other whispering and clutching themselves in fits of giggling .

Nonplussed, JeanLuc looked over at Dmitri who was nibbling happily on pistachio nuts, eyes unfocused, savouring the taste. "God, these nuts are wonderful" he said." I am in heaven!"

"Okay, Dmitri. So what's next?" JeanLuc asked impatiently. "Ah. Yes. The history of icons. Where was I?"

"We'd got to the fifth century and you said that the Church's ban on icons was lifted leading to an explosion of picture-making and image-worship."

"Yes. But soon after, there was a reactionary backlash resulting in what is known as the Iconoclast Controversy which lasted more than a century until 843 and the seventh Ecumenical Council."

"So what really is an Iconoclast? An artistic barbarian?"

"Technically, it is someone who is totally opposed, on religious

110

principle, to the making of religious imagery. The iconoclasts were exemplified by the Byzantine Emperors Leo III and his son Constantine V who banned icons and any form of image worship by imperial decree. Sadly, it is from this period that we have lost most of the religious art that might have dated from the earliest times. The iconoclasts, particularly Emperor Theophilus, launched a vicious campaign of persecution and destruction against the monasteries which were the main repositories of icons. It was not until the seventh Ecumenical Council convened by Empress Irene, that we see a formal lifting of the ban on iconography. It was another woman, Empress Theodora, who finally confirmed the practice of image worship as a mainstream activity. The synod that confirmed this is still celebrated here in Russia as the Sunday of Orthodoxy.

"It is after this time that we begin to see a separation in the development between Eastern and Western forms of religious imagery. In the Christian West, pictures were to edify and educate the faithful and to adorn churches, while in the Orthodox East, images were used primarily as objects of and focus for worship. Therefore, in the West there were fewer constraints on artistic licence and imaginative expression. In the East, however, the tradition was to imprint or copy some Byzantine prototype, like Luke's Mother of God or the acheiropoetic Camulian image of Christ or the Eddessa Mandillion. It was believed that a copy made in good faith by an artist of good reputation, like André Rublev, would have whatever mystical or miracle-working qualities there were in the original, transferred to it by the power of God. This copying tradition explains the iconographical consistency spanning centuries of the iconography of Orthodox or Coptic religion—any deviations or artistic licence was virtually ruled out for fear of losing the sanctity of the icon. Also, because of this, artists and schools of icon painters like the famous Stroganov or Novgorod schools were always on the look-out for reliable source material and originals to copy. Those which revealed the true appearance of Jesus or the Saints were, and still are, the most sought after."

Dmitri fell silent after this long discourse. He looked at JeanLuc with steady eyes.

111

"So you too were looking for original-source icons?" asked JeanLuc. "And I think I found one. But it is not here," he added hastily. "And I am here to help you get it back from wherever it is. Right?"

"You are correct, JeanLuc. It has taken me many years and to many places but I now believe I know where the ultimate icon lies. I think it will be a portrait of Jesus, but I have no idea what it looks like and only cryptic clues to its present location; although I believe I am correct in my guesses," he added emphatically.

Dmitri went to the bureau in the room and took out several large-scale maps of Russia, the Baltic and Middle East. He smoothed them out onto the table. JeanLuc and Igor went to look. The maps were covered in lines, notes and symbols. Dmitri handed them photocopies that showed maps of Russia with various dots and symbols representing the location of monasteries or holy sites as well as the main cities and towns printed by name.

"Look, see. I have been all over Russia in my searches from the Siski monastery near Archangel in the far North to the Percherski monastery near Kiev.

"My first clue to the existence of an undiscovered secret icon came not from my travels but when my mother left the documents and Books of the Khlysty to me. As well as the Dove Book, certain old manuscripts, letters and membership lists have been kept by the Khlysty."

Dmitri bent down and lifted a corner of the carpet and then prised up one of the floorboards. Reaching down, he fished out a large screw-top tin. The tin contained bundles of letters and sheets of yellowing paper all neatly wrapped in protective polythene. There was a layer of crystallised silica in the bottom of the tin and a naphtha mothball. Dmitri selected the bundle of letters he was after and laid it out on the table under the sharp light of an anglepoise lamp. The text was hand-written in spiky Cyrillic letters.

"Let me read some passages to you, Gentlemen."

"Can I scan the letters afterwards, Dmitri?" asked JeanLuc.

"Of course" he replied. " These letters are a secret correspondence between Grigory Efimovich Rasputin and Father Makary who was a hermit who lived near the Verkhoture monastery in Siberia. The first few letters are about the difficulties that Rasputin encountered in St.Petersburg before his adoption by the Tsarina. This would be around 1910. Makary the Hermit is believed to have died in 1913, just before the Great War."

Dmitri selected one of the letters from the small pile. "This is an interesting letter. It describes, in Rasputin's own words, his vision of the Virgin of Kazan, a famous icon which is important to the Khlysty as well. Maria, Rasputin's daughter believes that it was this vision that set Rasputin off, from his previous existence as a well-to-do farmer, on his travels and to his destiny and eventual murder at the court of the Tsar. "

Dmitri picked up another letter. "But it is this letter written in 1913 that contains the clue that I was seeking." He adjusted his spectacles and started to read aloud. "It says: 'Beloved Teacher. The inheritance from the Carpocratians must be preserved at all costs. Sadly, the World is not yet ready for Our Lord's secret face, beautiful though it is. The time is not now ...'

"At first reading, I thought this was just the usual religious metaphor but then I played with the idea that it was a straightforward statement. Said in other words, 'the world is not ready to see the Lord's face which has been preserved by some group called the Carpocratians'.

"I tried then to look up the Carpocratians but could find no reference to them anywhere; so for some years I forgot about the letter. Then, last year, in a book that Cardinal Mirphy sent to me titled The Secret Gospel by a professor called Morton Smith at Columbia university, I suddenly found a reference staring up at me."

Sophia came into the room. Standing behind her father, hands resting lightly on his shoulders, she looked across at JeanLuc. Their eyes met. She blew him the faintest of kisses. He smiled at her.

Dmitri continued. "To cut a long and amazing story short, my research tells me that the Khlysty are the direct descendants of the followers of the early Christian visionary teachings of Carpocrates and Nestor. According to Bishop Clement of Alexandria, the Carpocratians were a libertarian sect who had many unorthodox beliefs and practices that needed suppressing, and indeed this purge seemed to have been successful because the sect died out very early. However, I believe they continued in another guise or merged with Coptic or Nestorian Christianity. Anyway, the crucial point is …" Dmitri paused dramatically,"… is that they were said to possess actual true to life pictures of Jesus and his family!"

"Good God! So you think that pictures of Jesus were passed down to the Khlysty who are descended from the Carpocratians? And you know where these are?" JeanLuc stood up in excitement.

"I think so, yes."

"And Joe Mirphy knows about this too?" "Yes," said Dmitri simply.

"Christ, no wonder he has moved heaven and earth to set this up. It could get him the Papacy!"

"Thoroughly deserved too, in my humble opinion. From a selfish point of view, revealing this to the world will bring legitimacy to the Khlysty in the eyes of the Orthodox Church who still regard us as heretics. That is my life's work and God's Will, I believe."

JeanLuc started to pace the room feverishly. The others watched him curiously. Connections were snapping into place as if he'd found a corner piece of a huge mental jigsaw. He felt fantastic energy flow into his limbs, his mind suddenly seemed to fast forward through the flickering frames of old strange dreams and visions flashed across a mental screen behind his tightly closed eyes, bringing him to the verge of some blinding revelation ...

But as quickly as it came the moment went, and he collapsed in an armchair, face in his hands.

Dmitri went to him and put an arm around his shoulder. He whispered in his ear. "I know, my friend. I understand. God is trying to speak to you, but you are not yet ready. The Khlysty will help you to free your mind so you can become a vessel filled with the light of the truth! If we did it for Rasputin we can do the same for you. It is even possible that you are one of the Chosen Ones, a Son of Light—an avatar of the Faith. But we'll know for sure after you worship with us tonight."

CHAPTER 15

After a truly memorable meal, towards midnight, as JeanLuc was beginning to wonder if he could decently go up to bed, there was a knock on the front door. Saskia went to open it and two men came in. Taking their coats, she ushered them into the living room where they sat down in silence and bowed their heads as in prayer. Dmitri made no effort to introduce them. More and more people arrived in quick succession. They also sat down, some on cushions that Saskia had placed on the carpeted floor; all with heads bowed and arms folded across each other with hands spread upwards in the old Coptic fashion of prayer.

Now the living room was crowded—JeanLuc counted twenty people. Dmitri came back into the room carrying the Dove Book. He had put on some kind of priest's cassock of white linen edged with gold trim. On it, there was a dove embroidered in an Egyptian design. Saskia came in behind him, carrying a large shallow-draught copper bowl containing a few inches of rose-scented water. This she proceeded to place on a wooden stand against the wall.

Dmitri raised his arms, the dove appeared to stretch its wings. This was the signal for everyone to fall on their knees. Feeling somewhat uncomfortable, JeanLuc and Igor followed suit. Dmitri chanted aloud from several pages of the Book. The congregation murmured Amen at suitable pauses and crossed themselves.

Suddenly there was a loud piercing shriek. JeanLuc, who had begun to nod off, woke with a start, his hair standing on end. Sophia had been jolted to her feet and was swaying back and forth, eyes wide and staring, tears running down her cheeks, the curtain of her black hair flying wildly. She chanted something incomprehensible and repetitive and then the possession dropped her back to the floor, abandoning her to wail and beat her forehead against the carpet. Immediately, another girl was caught in the emotional swirl and she too leapt to her feet with a strange growling cry, only the whites of her eyes showing, the pupils having fled upwards into their sockets.

As if on cue, the other worshippers began a rhythmic chant, beating their heads in time and clapping their hands. The girl began a sinuous slow-motion dance with others starting to join in and follow her around the room, bent double, their knuckles almost touching the floor in ape-like fashion.

Dmitri and Sophia were leading the clapping in a primitive rhythm that began to increase in tempo. For the first time, JeanLuc felt an electric excitement which made him want to join in; obeying the irresistible impulse he did so, jerking and convulsing in a manner over which he had lost all control.

On and on they danced and time seemed to lose all meaning. The wild strange spirit that filled the room with its feverish energy now possessed all in the room.

One of the men broke away from the group snake and, in the centre of the room, started to spin on one foot like a dervish. As one man fell in exhaustion another took his place; spinning, spinning, faster and faster. People were now shrieking and wailing; women were writhing on the floor, hair loose, bodies arching in epileptic convulsions.

JeanLuc suddenly felt himself gripped by the same power as it moved from person to person. He started to spin. To his vision, the room became a blur of flashing light as the spirit pushed him, driving him to spin faster and faster. Like gas bubbles rising from his gut, words burst from his mouth—strange unearthly words, each seemingly charged with meaning, each screamed loud in a cry of triumph!

Someone grabbed at him and he collapsed on the floor; a woman grasped his shirt and tore it from his body. Panting, he got to his knees and saw that most of the people in the room were now naked, bodies slippery and glistening with sweat from their exertions. Looking over, he could see that the water in the copper bowl seemed to be boiling, giving off a gold-coloured steam and flickering with an unearthly St.Elmo's -fire light. He recognised the form of Dmitri, now nude, his white beard and stringy body giving him the appearance of some Old Testament prophet, standing by the bowl dipping his fingers in the steaming water and throwing drops over the bodies around him. When some of these drops of baptismal water fell on JeanLuc he was immediately wracked by fierce juddering seizures; where the drops hit him it felt as if he'd been sprinkled with hot embers. Looking down in horror, blisters were rising on his body in burning red weals. He opened his mouth to scream but suddenly Sophia was beside him and she was kissing him in the places where it hurt. Her soft lips were a cooling salve and he felt an instant relief from the burning pinpricks of pain.

All around, people had paired off and were grappling and groping at each other in orgiastic frenzy. Then the lights dimmed and went out almost at the same moment.

JeanLuc felt himself writhing on the floor in a tangle of bodies; his flesh tingling, jumping off his bones. Sophia's arms closed around him, naked warm slippery flesh pressed against his in urgent unmistakable need. An immense sexual desire surged through them, obliterating all conscious thought. Sophia rode him rodeo fashion, pelvis bucking and driving violently, her back arched, crying out with ecstasy.

JeanLuc's own climax was like nothing he'd ever experienced before—the very marrow of his being had been sucked into a black vortex; a long tortured moment of infinite pain and exquisite pleasure, which left him an enfeebled quivering shell, in this state, he passed out among the others.

CHAPTER 16

King Dollar money had gotten Dmitri, JeanLuc and Igor first-class seats together up front on the next internal flight from Moscow to Sverdlovsk.

They took off in a blizzard but eventually the old Aeroflot airliner climbed wearily through the dark layers of wintry cloud into the sunlit blue, heading East.

"It took Grigory Efimovich Rasputin more than a month of hard travelling to get to Moscow from his home, but it will take us only about three hours," remarked Dmitri as they settled into the flight. Moscow Airport Security had put them through half-an-hour's grilling after JeanLuc's briefcase was picked up on the security scanners. It had taken two hundred dollars to smooth its passage on to the plane where it now lay beneath his seat.

The contents of the Dove Book, the Khlysty documents and letters had already been microwaved to the Biophar Drugs comsat and then onward to Joel Maniato and Cardinal Mirphy in the US. This'll keep him quiet! thought JeanLuc as he hit the send key.

The original plan had been to use the Yemeljan's van to drive to Sverdlovsk, but this was dropped in favour of flying because the weather was taking a turn for the worse. According to Moscow Radio, the roads into Siberia were getting blocked by snow.

JeanLuc's body ached all over from the night's exertions. In the window seat, Igor had already dozed off, an unlit Camel drooping from his fingers. From JeanLuc's confused recollection, Igor had certainly been there in the thick of things last night as well himself. They'd all been at it, he smiled to himself ruefully. There were certainly interesting aspects to belonging to a libertarian sect. Maybe he should get religion!

"So. What do you think, Dmitri? What route did this icon we're after, if it is an icon, take to get where it is now?"

Dmitri stroked his beard meditatively. The niet smoking light went out and he knocked out a Marlboro and lit up, taking a deep lung full of the acrid smoke. "Saskia forbids me to smoke. She says they'll kill me and she refuses to sleep with me if I smell of tobacco." He looked at JeanLuc and winked lecherously. "Women!" he said.

"To answer your question, the most likely place it would come from would be Alexandria; after Jerusalem that is. There were many Christian sects in Alexandria, including the followers of Carpocrates. It was a hotbed for many religions, not just Christianity. My theory is they were then taken either to Edessa in Turkey or to the strange eyrie-like monastery at Kermanshah in the Zagros mountains.

"In favour of Edessa is that we already know that King Abgar V of Edessa had specifically asked Jesus for a likeness imprinted or painted on cloth in the belief that it would have miracle-cure properties. Throughout early Christian history, Edessa has figured either as the source of acheiropoetic images or of non-orthodoxy like the Nestorians from whom I believe the Khlysty are originated.

"On the other hand, there are many strange tales attached to the monastery at Kermanshah. For one thing, it served many times as a neutral meeting point between warring forces. For example, it was here that secret deals were struck between the Crusaders and the Saracens. A special troop of the Knights Templar controlled this monastery for several hundred years, using it as a training school and retreat for an elite known as the Soldiers of Ormus. It has a tradition of scholarship and a library dating back to the dawn of the Christian era. Therefore, it would be a logical place to keep the Carpocratian Legacy. The Knights Templar have always had a divergent history from mainstream Christianity. Perhaps possession of these treasures influenced their peculiar traditions and differences with Catholic dogma," Dmitri mused.

"Sounds like just the sort of place to look for the Holy Grail!" said JeanLuc.

"You better believe it! Thousands of people over the ages have taken that place apart stone by stone! Always zilch. The reason is simple. There is nothing there any more; nothing of any importance. I would take you there myself if I really believed anything could be gained by going. No, it is in Russia that we must seek."

Dmitri lit another cigarette from the glowing stub of the last, drawing in thick lungfulls of smoke. JeanLuc took sips of vodka from the plastic cup the hirsute Russian air stewardess had given him. He

119

topped up with some weird tasting cola—probably dandelion and burdock.

The plane would touch down at Kazan, Perm and then Sverdlovsk, their destination. They would hire a car for the final leg to Pokrovskoye.

Dmitri resumed. "I think the Carpocratian Legacy reached Russia sometime between the ninth and eleventh centuries. The first millennium was a time of great turmoil in Christianity with many end-of-the-world, Armageddon and Doomsday cults springing up—rather like our own times in fact."

"Only now we have the technical capability to make Armageddon a reality," remarked JeanLuc caustically.

"Quite. But to all intents and purposes the Legacy was lost at this time. I could find no traces and clues anywhere until the mid-seventeenth century. During the Thirty Years War, an extraordinary meeting occurred between Daniel Philipov and a powerful group of Frenchmen known as the Compagnie du St.Sacrement who included a man called Robert Fludd. According to the Khlysty, at this meeting precious relics and treasures were shown to the members of the Compagnie du St.Sacrement to cement a secret treaty of co-operation and accord. I am making a guess that the Legacy was amongst these treasures. How they got into the hands of Daniel Philipov is a mystery. Unfortunately, both groups went on to get involved in losing wars, one against the Mongols and the other in the French uprising known as the Fronde. This unusual French interest in Russian affairs can be traced to the cryptic writings of Nostradamus—a much misunderstood visionary of the sixteenth century."

After half an hour more of this, JeanLuc felt bubbles of irritation rise within him as he listened with increasing bewilderment to the wizened white-bearded old fart beside him. His balls ached, he had an incipient headache not helped by the cheap airline vodka, the seat was worn and uncomfortable and Igor was snoring like a pig in his ear.

"Christ, Dmitri," he eventually burst out angrily, "what are you trying to say? That every fucking fruitcase, like Nostradamus and every bloody revolutionary group in history were members of some sort of fucking international conspiracy? My God! You've dragged in Anti-Popes, Cathars, Nostradamus, Cardinal Richlieu, the Knights Templar,

Rosicrucians, Rasputin; what next? Soon you'll be telling me that Adolf Hitler and Saddam Hussein were misunderstood, that Anthony Blunt was the Fifth man because he was a Poussin freak, that Kennedy was assassinated by a gay J.Edgar Hoover, that the pyramidal eye in the dollar bill is a symbol of the cabala, that Pope John Paul I was assassinated with a cup of tea by a Vatican cardinal dressed up as a nun, that General De Gaulle and all EEC commissioners since 1950 were Freemasons and that the Eiffel Tower is really a huge mystic radio beacon to make contact with an alien master-race, that history is bunk and we are all pawns in some vast panoramic glass-bead game of chess played by superheroic grandmasters of secret societies!"

"You have summarised well! Yes." Dmitri said unperturbed by the outburst. JeanLuc started to laugh hysterically. "I was joking, you old bastard!"

"But I was not," said Dmitri calmly.

JeanLuc continued to laugh, tears running freely down his cheeks. "You really believe all this conspiracy shit? Jesus! I've come all this way to this fucking freezing madhouse of a country on a crazy wild-goose chase."

"Hey! What's going on?" grunted Igor." What are you laughing at, JeanLuc? Is he all right, Dmitri? Damn it, cut it out will you? You woke me up."

JeanLuc coughed abruptly into his hands and relapsed into silence, interspersed with fits of giggling. He leaned over and offered the remaining vodka to the other two. Dmitri declined huffily, got up out of his seat and walked down the aisle towards the toilets in the rear of the plane.

The niet smoking and fasten-seat-belts signs flashed on and the plane started on a steep dive in towards Kazan, their first stop. Dmitri had found an empty seat further back and they didn't see him again until after they had landed and deplaned at Sverdlovsk. He was standing at the end of the rollered ramp along which the suitcases and luggage were to emerge. JeanLuc went up to him.

"I'm sorry, Dmitri. I don't know what came over me. Please accept my apologies."

Following an impulse, he gripped the old man and folded him in a fierce bearhug embrace. Emotional bastards these Russians, he thought as he saw the tears in Dmitri's eyes when he let go of him.

He looked at him squarely. "Promise me, Dmitri, you won't tell me any more goddamned history. It was never my strong suit at school. We've got a job to do, the Cardinal sent me and I must follow through—no matter what craziness may turn up. I know the world may be a weird place but please let's stick to the rational if at all possible! Sweet Jesus, its cold here! Let's go find us a cab. What a dump this place is!"

Retrieving their luggage, they headed towards the entrance and a line of battered Lada and Motzgreich taxis.

"Pokrovskoye? You want to go to Pokrovskoye?" "That's what I said."

"Which one? Near Nizhni Tagil or past Tyumen?"

"Which one? Are there more than one? Hey, Dmitri! This comrade says there's more than one Pokrovwhatsit."

Dmitri came over. "Pokrovskoye on the road to Tobolsk."

"That's past Tyumen; nearly a three-hundred- kilometre drive. It'll cost you!" The driver looked at them suspiciously. "Don't waste my time, comrade" he added.

"What's your daily rate?" The driver mentioned an astronomical sum of roubles.

"Will fifty US dollars be OK?" JeanLuc fanned the bills in front of the driver's nose. The man's blunt Slav features beamed and he jumped enthusiastically out of the Motzgreich flinging open the rear doors and the boot for their bags.

Tyres spinning in the wet mushy snow, they hit a road that was cut through deep soot- blackened drifts by a constant convoy of snowploughs.

"The road will be bad, I warn you, comrades" said the driver. "We have had another snowstorm in the last two days. I will stop for gasoline before we leave Sverdlovsk."

They took the main highway East and moved at an insect crawl through the nightmarish landscape of industrial Siberia. Vast windowless black factories massed smoke stacks prodding grimy fingers into a lowering snow- laden slate-grey sky in a horror panorama that would tax the descriptive power of H.P.Lovecraft. The freezing wind, howling directly out of the Arctic , buffeted the car on exposed stretches and strained the heating system to its limit. They were stuck in a nose-to-tail traffic jam for virtually the entire journey.

The driver, "Call me Mule—everyone does", seemed happy enough singing along with the radio which gave out a ghastly concoction of static, CB interference and Russianised versions of western popular music. JeanLuc, Dmitri and Igor spent most of the journey withdrawn into a silent huddled stupor—it seemed a very very long way from the relative civilisation of Moscow. If I hear another Russian rendition of "Love me tender", I shall scream, thought JeanLuc; but the radio was a reassuring contact with humanity as they journeyed onward through the desolation and towering snow drifts.

Eventually, after eight hours' driving, they came into Tyumen. The streets were uncleared and the snow-covered pavements deserted, and only a few cars moved about on chained tyres.

"We'll hole out here for the night and then go on to Pokrovskoye in the morning", JeanLuc decided for them. "Mule? Do you know of anywhere to stay here?"

"Sorry, Boss. This is way out of my territory. Tell you what, I'll cruise the streets till we find someone to ask. Okay?"

Before long, they were cosily installed in rooms of a dilapidated but welcoming working- man's hotel. After a hot shower and change of clothes they came down to the cheerfully crowded dining room. Two bottles of Stolichnaya stood smartly at attention next to a stack of blinis on the clean red-and-white checked tablecloth.

JeanLuc filled four shot glasses to the brim with the vodka—they each took one. "A toast, gentlemen." Igor, Dmitri and the Mule all looked at JeanLuc.

"To our Quest," he cried loudly and drained his glass in a gulp. "The Quest!" they chorused.

In the Russian winter, vodka is the antifreeze of the soul.

CHAPTER 17

JeanLuc closed his eyes tight against the fiercely bright glare off the snow and breathed shallow lungfuls of the frosty air. He tried not to let nausea overcome him as the sleigh swayed and slithered along behind the horse. He concentrated on the rhythmic jingle of the silvery bells attached to the harness, the trotting clop clop of the hooves and the hissing of the sleigh rails on the ice—maybe this would help soothe his thumping hangover.

Mule and Igor, apparently immune to the ill effects of vodka, were happily geeing the horse along at a fast clip on the frozen river to Rasputin's family farm a few miles down river from the village of Pokrovskoye where they had left the car after an early-morning start from Tyumen. "Sleigh is the only way to get about now. Everywhere is snowed in," had slurred one of their newfound companions amongst the hotel residents, in last night's drunken camaraderie funded by JeanLuc. "I have family in Pokrovskoye, I will ring my brother to lend you the family sledge and a horse," offered the hotel manager." Any friend of the Khlysty is a friend of mine," he whispered knowingly.

Dmitri sat beside JeanLuc sharing the huge fur blanket, his diamond-bright eyes gleaming out from behind his frosted over spectacles.

They had stepped back in time, it seemed. Advanced technology and civilised sensibilities were not much use out here in the Siberian hinterland where the wolves had a hunger fiercer than an addict's for crack cocaine for red bloodied flesh. And the cold was truly terrible. In these parts, brass monkeys had become extinct long ago for lack of vital reproductive parts. Even under the thick furs, JeanLuc felt chilled to the bone. Instant numbing rewarded any exposure of bare flesh followed by a painful tingling as the affected area was rubbed warm. He was supremely thankful for the thermos flasks of coffee that the hotel cook had made up for them.

They stopped to drink the coffee when they'd travelled about ten kilometres from Pokrovskoye, on a sheltered frozen pool in a bend of the river surrounded by tall snow-laden conifers. The noonday sky was a clear intense blue with a tracery of mackerel-patterned cloud high in the stratosphere. It was deathly quiet apart from the snorting of the horse and the creaking of its leather harness. The wind had died down completely and it was still and utterly peaceful as the men drank their hot coffee in companionable silence.

Suddenly, they heard a high-pitched beeping noise. JeanLuc frowned in irritation; he was just beginning to feel a little better. It must be the bloody phone in his briefcase. He reached behind him to the rear of the sleigh and rummaged about until he found the briefcase with the phone inside still beeping insistently. He flicked open the catches and lifted out the slim phone. He snapped open the mouthpiece and barked "Yes! What is it?" into it. "Oh. Your Eminence! It's you."

"Yes, JeanLuc. It's me. What is going on? I haven't had a peep out of you for weeks, apart from pages and pages of some unbelievable crap you sent over to Maniato. What is this? What are you up to? Where are you?" JeanLuc grimaced at the others and held the phone away from his ear. The Cardinal of New York sounded somewhat pissed off judging by the non-ecclesiastical language streaming from the earpiece. JeanLuc waited for the abuse to subside. The reception was pretty good here; that satellite must be almost overhead, he thought.

"We're in Siberia, Your Eminence."

"I know that!" came the shouted reply. "This satellite can pick up the infra-red of your shit in the snow. What I want to know is why? Is Yemeljan with you?"

"Yes, he is, and the reason we're here is to look for the Carpocratian Legacy. Dmitri Yemeljan thinks it is to be found near Pokrovskoye a small village about ten miles from here. Because of the snow we're travelling by Dr.Zhivago."

"By what? What in God's name is that?"

"Oh, sorry. I mean by horse-drawn sleigh. You know, jingle, jingle, cue violins Rachmaninov, close-up on Julie Christie all wrapped in sexy furs ..." JeanLuc laughed. Igor and the others grinned back at him not understanding a single word of the English. The horse stamped its feet and steamed gently; impatient to get moving again.

"Listen, don't get smart with me. If you ever want to get out of that freezing hellhole you better wise up and get that load you picked up

125

back to France. Never mind this other stuff that is not important." The Cardinal now sounded Irish which meant he was genuinely angry.

"Yes, Boss! Don't worry, we're on a hot trail here."

"Of course I'm worried. The proverbial is about to hit the fan and you are pissing your time away taking sleigh rides in Santa country! Those bastards in Rome are breathing down my neck and that fat creep Von Helsinger is due in tomorrow from Argentina for an urgent meeting." Joseph Mirphy's voice suddenly became lower and more conciliatory. "Listen, JeanLuc. Von Helsinger is old-style Inquisition and he smells something—I can feel it. Just get a move on will you, son. Give my kindest regards to Dmitri." The phone went dead.

With a resigned shrug, JeanLuc folded the phone and put it away in his coat pocket. "OK, boys. Let's move it. The Boss wants progress!" They climbed back onto the sleigh and Mule heehawed them onward along the frozen river through the still silent forest.

*

Igor shovelled away the last of the snow, emerged from the tunnel that he and Mule had dug and blinked owlishly in the lantern light. "We've got to some kind of a door and cleared it, JeanLuc." he said panting. The fog of his breath spiralled up into the dusk. JeanLuc tore his gaze away from the pulsing iridescence of the Aurora Borealis in the star-sequinned sky and climbed down from the sleigh. He'd been thinking that it must have been close by here that Rasputin's mother saw that display of shooting stars that had blazed in the heavens as she was giving birth to her infamous son.

Dmitri poked his nose out of the fur pile and emerged creakily. He was shivering with suppressed excitement and cold. "So! Is it done?" he asked.

"I guess so," said JeanLuc as they approached the entrance to Rasputin's chapel. The mass of cows moved uneasily and the occasional protesting moo disturbed the silence of the night. Maybe it was the horse that disturbed them— more likely it was the digging in the snow under their pen.

Crouching down, he entered the short tunnel under the snow and came to a dark, rotted wooden door. He kicked at it and the wood crumbled and splintered beneath his foot, leaving the rusted old padlock attached to the doorjamb. Stooping to avoid hitting his head on the threshold, he penetrated the dark musty space beyond. To JeanLuc's surprise, it felt reasonably warm and dry in there—it must be the layers of cattle manure composting down, he thought. Keeps the place warmer.

Dmitri followed him in with the lantern.

The room was still neat and tidy. There was a line of benches and a crude altarpiece covered in a moth-eaten yellowed cloth. A brass tube-framed iconostasis screen still remained intact although the icon panels had been removed. JeanLuc held the lantern high, throwing yellow rays into corners that had not seen light for several decades.

"Okay, Dmitri, where is it? Where is the Carpocratian Legacy?" JeanLuc asked tonelessly as he viewed the emptiness of the room with disappointment. The room was a simple earth cellar under a winter paddock for cows—hardly a repository for fabulous treasure! JeanLuc felt the first stirrings of doubt and anxiety. Had he been wrong to trust his instincts; to trust Dmitri to drag him to the depths of Siberia on the basis of some cock-and-bull story about Rasputin? He wasn't even certain that the passage in the letter shown him by Dmitri really said what Dmitri said it did—it looked almost unreadable to him. He didn't want to have to contact the US and have it re translated. Not now—it would be too humiliating.

Well, there was only one thing for it; they would have to check the place out for hidden cavities or compartments, using the micro- SIR. It would take some time even in this relatively small room. He handed the kerosene lantern to Igor and crouching low, made his way back out to fetch his bag of tricks from the sleigh.

"What's that you're setting up, JeanLuc?" asked Dmitri curiously as JeanLuc brought out yet another gadget from his briefcase.

JeanLuc booted up the CPU under battery power and looked up at Dmitri."It's a miniaturised subsurface interface radar or SIR. Latest thing in archaeology. Robert Eisenman has been using it to locate new scroll caves at Qumran. It detects cavities in a solid surface using a combination of radar and ultrasound. It is rather a tedious process, I'm afraid, but if there are any secret chambers in the floor or walls of this place, SIR will find them."

"Is it rather like knocking on wooden panels to find the hollow parts?" asked Dmitri.

JeanLuc blinked. "I guess so. Anyway it is supposed to work very well. It was invented by the Russian military for studying the shockwave patterns of nuclear explosions. I saw on TV the other day that someone is even using it to trace the network of secret tunnels under the Kremlin."

"Well, I'm glad it's found a proper peaceful use. Show me what happens. I can see this is an incredibly useful tool to have. Just think! Secret burial chambers in Egyptian pyramids, lost cities under the Sahara sands ...!"

JeanLuc stared at Dmitri in surprise. This was the first time Dmitri had shown any interest at all in his or any kind of technology. He was somewhat taken aback. "Wait a minute, Dmitri! I've never done it before myself. Let's see now. You're supposed to place this rod in contact with the soil and start the software running—the computer will do the rest. Yeah, look at this."

Dmitri peered down at the backlit LCD screen that was now patterned with spike graphs and contour maps in varying shades of grey. JeanLuc pressed on a function key and a message with some tabulated figures appeared on the screen. "Basically, it is telling us there are no cavities in the floor within a two metre radius of where I have placed the probe; down to about ten metres in this soil. So we move it along bit by bit until we've covered the whole area. Okay?"

An hour later, they had found nothing apart from numerous mouse and rat holes where the walls joined the floor. JeanLuc and Dmitri sat down with their backs to the wall and stared gloomily at the flickering lantern. Suddenly the pale blue square of the VDU winked out; only a couple of small LEDs remained glowing—like demonic rat's eyes.

"Dammit. We've lost battery power now," cried JeanLuc. "You got any ideas, Dmitri? Are we in the right place?"

"Yes, I'm sure it's the right place. Look there's the plain altar, the iconostasis screen where they hung the icons, the benches, the cows on top. It's all exactly as described to me by his daughter, Matriona. This is definitely Rasputin's chapel."

"What makes you think the Khlysty kept the Carpocratian Legacy here? It could be anywhere. With Father Makary in the Verkhoture monastery. Or buried with Rasputin at the Imperial Park at Tsarskoye Telo. Anywhere!"

"No, I'm sure it is here. I'm not surprised it is not on the iconostasis. That was where they displayed the Virgin of Kazan, amongst others. Anyway it would be too visible and vulnerable. My mother told me that the Khlysty used to meet here regularly before and after Rasputin's death, at least until Stalin's Purges. And although she left me the Dove Book and the Khlysty papers, I'm ashamed to say that she would not or could not trust me with what she called the ultimate secret of the Khlysty. You will know when the time comes, she told me. God will guide you, was all she would say. God has brought me here and I have faith that we will succeed," he said. "I'm exhausted. I don't know about you, but I think I will try to get some sleep. Maybe inspiration will come."

"Yeah, I suppose," said JeanLuc morosely. After a while, his eyelids drooped and soon the hypnotic flicker of the lantern flame caused him to drift off. The fresh air and exertions of the day had caught up with them.

*

In his dream ...

he was a cat.

A fat black glossy cat, black as coal crouching down by the mouse hole.

Watching, waiting for the telltale rustle, the little pink whiskery nose, the anxious pause, then the scurrying dash along the wall ... the warm sweet taste of blood.

"Alexey?

Here you are, then!" says a voice. He was being stroked by the boy with the dark eyes ... dark fathomless eyes—like empty mouse holes.

He felt his fur bristle with static as the boy stroked him; stroked him. As a cat he arched his back and rubbed his temples against the rough corduroy of the boy's trousers.

The boy put his face down close; their eyes met and ... locked. The boy smiled, but then his mouth suddenly snapped open, lips pealing back to reveal sharp pointy dragon teeth! He felt a ring of strong hands

129

grip his furry throat and pure terror knifed through him as he heard
deeply crazed laughter echoing in a well of darkness ... !

*

JeanLuc jolted awake, sweating with fright, Dr. Adrenaline busily
pumping hot iron into his juddering heart muscle. Roughly, he pushed
Dmitri off his shoulder where he'd been resting his sleeping head. He
got to his feet and paced about the small room.

Dmitri awoke, rubbing his eyes. "What's the matter, JeanLuc?
What's got into you? Are you okay?" he asked in puzzlement.

"Nothing, Dmitri. It's nothing. Just a dream, a horrible dream."

"About what, my son? A dream in this strange place is a message—
a ign. You must tell me!" urged Dmitri.

"Stop it, Dmitri. Don't ask! I can't remember" JeanLuc covered his
ears with his hands as he thought he heard a faint echo of that demonic
laughter ...

Dmitri looked at him and would have pressed him further, but just
then they heard the jingling of the sleigh bells and the raucous drunken
laughter of Igor and the Mule. "Any luck?" called out Igor as the two
of them squeezed through the broken doorway. He was grinning like
an idiot as he held out to them a half-empty bottle of vodka.

JeanLuc and Dmitri stared in sober disgust as the two men staggered
about the cellar chapel in a drunken imitation of a Cossack dance.
Suddenly, Igor tripped and fell heavily against the iconostasis, which
toppled and crashed to the floor under his weight. It broke apart at the
corners and lay on the floor in a twisted heap.

Dmitri jumped as if he'd been shot.

"Look! Look!" he cried. "We've found it!" He rushed to the
crumpled iconostasis pulling the broken pieces of tubing apart in a
fever of excitement. Igor and Mule untangled themselves and watched
bemusedly, as Dmitri and JeanLuc tore away at the brass piping,
levering it apart.

"Yes. Yes! These must be it! We've found it!" Dmitri held aloft three
long slim metal tubes that he'd pushed out from one of the hollow
crosspieces. He carried them over to the lantern and laid them gently
on the floor. They were each about a quarter of a metre in length and
the thickness of a fat cigar. Black and grey in colour, with flecks of

coppery green. Strands of rotted leather were stuck to the surface in places.

JeanLuc picked one up and looked at it closely—it seemed vaguely familiar to him.

Dmitri collected the three tubes. "There will be something rolled up tight in these. We cannot do anything more here—we must return to Moscow as soon as possible" he said decisively." I am sure this is the Legacy!"

The others looked at him. "Return now? This minute?" asked Igor and shot a questioning glance at JeanLuc.

JeanLuc glared back at him. "Yeah, now. It's not our problem you went and got pissed again. Come on, let's get out of here," he commanded.

*

Leaving the chapel, they propped the smashed door in place and backfilled the tunnel with snow. They climbed into the sleigh and Mule whipped the horse, which dutifully set off at a quick trot back the way they'd come.

JeanLuc sat hunched on the back seat reflecting that, in most modern adventures, heroes leave the scene of the treasure-find in a hail of stones, arrows, spears, bullets, lasers or rockets, chased across the movie frames by the usual assorted baddies and screeching automobile tyres. But here, it was past midnight and any potential enemies amongst the inhabitants of Pokrovskoye were shuttered up tight against the winter world and ravening wolves.

It all seemed a bit anti-climactic and he felt strangely unelated by the apparent success of their mission and the ending of his long Quest. He felt empty somehow, as if he'd suffered a loss rather than enjoyed a gain. Maybe it was that horrible dream and that terrible evil laughter.

Although the jury was still out on whether they'd really got the Carpocratian Legacy, he felt somehow sure that they had.

He was cold and shivery again. He tried to turn his thoughts to Sophia; to the woman who, in such a short space of time and with such little effort, had captured his heart. They had resonated on the same psychic waveband as if they were meant for each other. Maybe this was love, maybe not. But, strangely, at that moment, he had difficulty conjuring up the memory of her features. It was as if she was a presence rather than a physical being—a presence that for some reason he couldn't locate just now; that was just out of reach, not there, not tuned in. Absent, leaving him incomplete and uneasy.

He dozed off.

It is still relatively light in Arctic regions during the winter night, so they could see their way back plainly and made good time. In spite of Mule's tendency to fall asleep at the reins, the horse knew its way home and kept at a steady pace.

They reached the outskirts of Tyumen just as dawn was breaking over their shoulders. Lowrey stick figures trudged the white streets on their way to work or to another queue. Arriving at the hotel, the four men walked in rubbing their bleary eyes and frozen faces. The manager came rushing out of his office. "Yemeljan? Dmitri Yemeljan?" he cried. "There's an urgent message for you, comrade. Very urgent. You must ring Moscow at once!"

"What about? Who called?" asked Dmitri worriedly.

"Your wife, I think. But she sounded hysterical. You must call. Here, you can use the phone in my office."

Dmitri went with him whilst the others went on into the dining room to order breakfast.

"When did she call?"

"Last night about eleven. We had no way of contacting you. I'm terribly sorry." The manager wrung his hands in apologetic sympathy.

Dmitri dialled the Moscow code and his home number with a shaky hand and a rapidly escalating anxiety in the pit of his stomach. Saskia answered the phone immediately. "Where have you been?" she wailed.

"What's happened, Saskia?" snapped Dmitri down the phone. "Don't get hysterical, just tell me!"

"It's Sophia!" she sobbed . "She's gone. She's been kidnapped! They dragged her away from me. My baby!"

Dmitri white-knuckled the phone and forced himself to speak calmly. "Saskia? Have you called Sergei? You must tell him."

"Yes, yes, of course I've told him. Where were you?" she cried accusingly. "Chasing about after your bloody stupid relics and getting the family involved with criminals. Where were you?" she screamed down the phone.

Dmitri waited for the hysterical tirade to subside. "Listen to me, Saskia. Who has taken your daughter? Who?"

"It was those gasoline crooks," she wept. "When will you be home? I can't take much more of this."

After further difficult questioning of Saskia and getting few coherent answers, Dmitri ended the phone call and went through to the dining room. He slumped down in a chair at their table. The others looked at his aged and horror-struck features with increasing concern.

"Zafod's gang has kidnapped Sophia," he said chokingly. "They want to negotiate some kind of a deal to compensate them for the gasoline explosion and loss of their men."

"But ... but how did they find out it was us?" cried Igor. "They couldn't have known."

"I don't know. Saskia is in a terrible state. We must get back at once."

In the clear blue flame of rage ignited at this news, JeanLuc understood then that it was not over. Good had not triumphed over Evil. There was still a long hard pilgrim's progress ahead. He realised that destiny has to be lived through; had to be cut and shaped. Even if the outcome was known, was prophesied, and was fated, he still couldn't avoid the psychic damage of living through it.

CHAPTER 18

Police Captain Anatole Sweridenko looked up at the uniformed young FSB man who stood smartly at attention before him. "You wanted to see me, Sergeant Yemeljan?" he said softly.

"Yes, Sir. Personal matter, sir!" Sergei said through gritted teeth.

"What's the trouble, my boy? Sit down and tell me." Anatole forgot his own troubles and turbulent thoughts for awhile and gazed with concern at his junior. He had grown fond of Sergei. He did as he was told in a willing manner without moaning or questioning. He was always closely shaved and well turned out in his uniform, and had no known vices apart from a devotion to the music of Western rock'n'roll stars which verged on idolatrous. Still there was not much the Captain could do about that—one had to have something. There was precious little motivation in working for the State these days—only an old fashioned sense of duty kept them all at their desks. He was grateful Sergei had stuck with him these past five years.

"My sister ... It's my sister, sir! She's been kidnapped by the Zafod gang, sir." Sergei blurted out on the verge of tears.

"This is terrible! Sit down. Tell me what has happened. We must get the whole department on to this. We can't let these bastards destroy one of our own," retorted Anatole angrily.

"Do you remember that petrol explosion last week, sir? My sister was involved—I have seen the drums of gasoline at home. When I asked where they came from, she admitted to me in confidence, that she had taken two of her friends to buy them but things had gone horribly wrong. Apparently, Zafod's men tried to hold them up and threatened them with machine guns, but in order to escape one of her friends blew them up and they escaped."

Good for them! thought Anatole. "Go on, Corporal. But how would Zafod know your sister was involved and where to find her to extract his revenge? I thought all his men had been killed in the explosion."

"That's the terrible part, sir! I first of all went to look for Lt.Bearski because it his case but neither I nor anybody else can locate him. He has disappeared too. His assistant, Alexei Dimyozic, told me he'd gone to locate the owners of the vehicles that were involved in the petrol explosion. It turns out that Nicholai Slovena always noted the registration marks of suspect vehicles in his pocketbook. The Lieutenant was checking out the last entry in it. I immediately contacted Vehicle Records and they said Bearski had earlier requested a computer search for details on this van." Sergei handed over a slip of paper.

The Captain looked at the printout description of a Moskgreich van registered to 'Icon Services' and an address in east Moscow.

"This, I presume, is the vehicle your sister was driving and your home address?"

"Yes, sir."

"I imagine Comrade Slovena's pocketbook is missing as well?"

"Yes, sir."

"Are you accusing Lt.Ilya Bearski of this department of collaborating with these criminals? That's a very serious charge, Sergei," intoned the Captain sternly.

"I know, sir. That is why I am coming to you. I need your help, sir. There is no other way that Zafod could have known of my sister's involvement."

"Exactly when was your sister kidnapped?" continued the Captain.

"Two hours ago. A car came to the house and two men dragged her away from the arms of her mother!" he sobbed.

This Zafod creep had gone too far, thought Anatole furiously. He'd always been suspicious of that fat idle slob, Bearski, and now it appeared to be justified. "Your sister's friends, how are they involved in this and where are they now?" he asked.

"I don't know, sir. They spent two nights and then they left on a trip with my father. Mother doesn't know where and she hasn't heard from them for two days."

"Do you have any ideas about where we should look for your sister, Sergei?" "No, sir. But if I find Zafod, I'll shoot the bastard!"

The Captain sat back in his chair and considered the situation: Yemeljan's sister had taken two men to buy a substantial quantity of petrol from Leonid Zafod's black marketeers. In an ensuing disagreement, four of Zafod's men were burned to death witnessed by their own FSB undercover man Slovena— now dead also—who arrived on the scene only to be caught up in the conflagration, but who had taken the time to note the registration of vehicles. Lt.Bearski as a routine task followed up the last entry in Slovena's charred pocketbook and saw a chance to curry favour and earn further pay-offs by informing Zafod, suppressing the evidence of the pocketbook and dragging out his own official enquiry into a meaningless charade. Zafod then took his revenge by kidnapping the woman. Meanwhile, the two mystery men and Sergei's father Dmitri have disappeared.

"Sergeant. In view of the serious charge you are alleging against Lt.Bearski accusing him of complicity in the violent kidnapping of your sister, I shall look into this myself. Unfortunately, because of your personal involvement I cannot allow you to assist me in your official capacity. But I think you know me well enough by now to know that the Department will pull out all the stops on this one," said the Captain. "And for God's sake, Sergei. Don't do anything foolish. Zafod and his cronies are dangerous and I want you and your sister to come out of this alive. It would be best if you go home and look after your mother."

"Yes, sir. And thank you, sir! If I can do anything ... anything at all. I am in your debt for ever," cried Sergei with emotion.

"Yes, you will be!" said the Captain soberly. He was under no illusion about the difficulties and political flak that lay ahead of him. "Before you go. Did the kidnappers leave a note or say what they wanted in return for your sister?"

"No, we don't know yet."

"Ah well, no doubt they'll contact your mother soon enough."

After Sergei had left, the Captain allowed himself a grim smile. Zafod had at last made a serious mistake. He must have gone ahead with the kidnapping before his crooked poodle had cottoned on to the link within the FSB. It was even possible that Bearski still believed he was undetected—after all he'd not been back to the office and there was no way he could know that Icon Services was owned by the Yemeljans and Sergei.

Anatole sat forward in his chair. With a sense of growing excitement, a plan of action began to form in his mind. A plan that, if successful, would destroy Zafod forever.

136

CHAPTER 19

Saskia Yemeljan met JeanLuc, Dmitri and Igor at the airport with the van. As they drove back to the Moscow apartment, she harangued the trio between fits of weeping. As a result of this, when they were stuck in the inevitable traffic jam where Mozhayskoye Shosse joins the outer ring road, Dmitri lost his temper shouting at her violently, "Shut up, woman!" He followed this up by clouting her in the face with an open-handed slap. They drove the rest of the trip in grim silence interspersed with the occasional sob from Saskia as she fingered the swelling on her cheekbone.

"So what do we do, JeanLuc?" asked Dmitri as they sat at the table with the Stolichnaya in front of them. JeanLuc knocked back his vodka—it burned its way down to his gut and lit the blue touch paper. His stomach was constricted in tension and anger. Saskia had rushed to her bedroom on a tidal wave of tears, slamming the door behind her.

"We have to find out what the bastards want" JeanLuc said. "So, Igor, you ring Karasamov now and tell him we want to talk."

"OK. But it means I'm fucked as far as my job is concerned."

"You're fucked anyway, Igor," snapped JeanLuc. "If they snatched Sophia, they sure as hell know by now that you were involved."

"Yeah, I guess you're right. I'll phone." He drained his glass as Dmitri brought the phone in and plugged it into the kitchen extension. Stolidly he dialled the number.

"Get me Karasamov. It's Golemov here." He listened to the reply and then barked angrily, "he knows what it's about—now put me through and get off the fucking line!" After listening for several minutes he put the 'phone down and looked across at the other two. "Okay. So this is what they want. They want the gasoline brought back to the yard. They want me to bring it back personally and then they have a special job for me which should clear the account and ... then they'll let the girl go."

"What special job?"

"I don't know. My guess is they'll want a shipment of drugs run through to the West—that's the usual."

137

"Did he say anything about me or Dmitri?"

"No. It's possible they believe it's entirely my own operation along with Sophia, of course; because they saw us together when we picked the stuff up from the lorry," Igor said.

"But why would you concede to their demand? I mean holding the girl to ransom wouldn't necessarily have any effect on you—as far as they know she is just one of your casual pick-ups," said JeanLuc.

"Maybe they took Sophia on the spur of the moment or it was done by some of Karasamov's men who didn't know the connection between us. They must figure that snatching her would cause someone to come out of the woodwork. Anyway, Karasamov knows I can forget the truck and the job, unless I did this for them."

"We have to get Sophia back, Igor" JeanLuc looked at Igor who shifted uncomfortably under JeanLuc's burning gaze.

"Yeah, Boss. Yeah, no problem. I'm with you no matter what." What the hell, he thought, he was as good as dead anyway if he started running drugs for Karasamov. Nobody lasted long on that trail of death. Anyway he quite liked Sophia—she had spirit and guts even if she was skinny. Also, he was fed up with Karasamov and the crooks that controlled him. It was not right for a patriotic ex-soldier to be pushed around like this with no direction. JeanLuc had been fair with him and in some strange way he'd fallen under his spell. It now felt natural to him to be around JeanLuc and it felt right to obey his commands, even if this meant taking on powerful enemies like Karasamov, which in Moscow usually meant probable death in some grimy litter-strewn back alley doing the kickdance of the piano wire garrotte. He'd also been profoundly moved by the night of worship with the Khlysty—it had caused a tectonic shift, touched some deep nerve in his being which he hadn't yet come to grips with.

"Shouldn't we contact my son Sergei before we do anything?" asked Dmitri, looking up at JeanLuc who had opened his briefcase preparatory to sending a message to the US.

"Let's try it our way first, Dmitri. The police are as corrupt as hell and you can be guaranteed that Zafod will find out somehow or other. I still can't figure out how they cottoned on to us in the first place. I'm not accusing Sergei, you understand. It's just we should try on our own first. I think it is time we paid Karasamov a visit. Go get your pistol, Igor—you left it here in your room, didn't you?"

"But Zafod will be making the decisions and there's no way he'll be there at the yard or Sophia either," objected Dmitri. "Someone like Zafod is not going to associate directly with Karasamov on this. He'll be in a dacha somewhere surrounded by henchmen."

"I agree. That's why I'm calling in some favours." JeanLuc pointed at the briefcase. "We have done our part of the mission. We have the load and we have the Carpocratian Legacy. If New York wants them they'll have to help us get Sophia back," he said.

"Good. That's a better plan," said Dmitri. "I have an old but serviceable weapon too. You want me to dig it out, JeanLuc?" "Yes, go find it Dmitri. I'll contact the US."

*

As the cab screeched to halt at the corner of 50th and Broadway, Joel Maniato flung a ten spot at the driver and hit the pavement running. The old soot-blackened greystone offices of New York's Roman Catholic Church loomed above him. He ran up the steps, into the lobby and over to a reception desk.

"I have to speak with Monsignor Mirphy at once. My name is Maniato—he knows me," he said to the receptionist nun behind the desk.

"I'm sorry, but he only sees people by appointment. Perhaps I can make one for you, sir?"

"No, no it's very urgent. Please ring up and ask if he'll see me."

"Well, its very irregular, sir. But hold on, I'll talk to his secretary." She lifted the phone and punched in the number; as she waited for a reply she blew a pink bubblegum bubble that burst wetly on her pale lipstickless lips. Joel forced himself to be calm and took several deep breaths. "What was your name again, sir?" queried the bubblenun.

"Maniato. Joel Maniato," he said loudly. You ugly bitch he thought to himself.

"His Eminence's secretary says the Holy Father is saying Mass at the moment, but if you'd care to wait you're welcome to go up to his office and wait there." She held the phone and looked at him expectantly.

"Yes, yes. I'll wait. Where is his office?" he said.

The bubblegum-nun said a few further words down the phone and then turned to him and said "His Eminence's secretary, Sister Mary will come down for you and show you the way, Mr.Maniato. Can you please sign your name in the book please—it's over there. And here is a visitor's badge. May God be with you." She turned away, blew another pink bubble for Jesus and picked up the Mills and Boon where she'd paused at the scene of another bodice ripped.

Seated in the Cardinal's outer office, Joel flicked through back numbers of

The Tablet, Catholic Herald and National Catholic Reporter until he found the latest issue of Bass & Trout at the bottom of the pile. He leafed through it idly while he waited. He was perusing the full-page ad exhorting him to join the NRA when Cardinal Mirphy appeared. He was dressed in the vestments for a Catholic Mass.

"This'd better be good, Maniato. Come through," he said brusquely, sweeping through on a waft of incense into his inner sanctum; past the fat bland gaze of the secretary- nun who must have consumed at least ten Dunkin' Donuts while Joel was waiting. That's quite a habit at eighty donuts per diem, Joel reflected.

"JeanLuc says he's got the icons!"

"Fantastic! That's incredible news," nodded the Cardinal delightedly. "But ..."

"But what?" asked the Cardinal, his smile fading.

"But there's been a hitch. He says he needs our help before he's willing to come out of Russia with them."

"Help with what? He's got all he needs, hasn't he? Has he run out of money?"

"No." Joel took a deep breath and handed across the page of type with JeanLuc's email. The Cardinal snatched it from his grasp and quickly read it.

"I see ... Well, I suppose we'll have to accommodate him. He has the Legacy and the crate from General Morelin, so we can afford to take a few risks now. Contact Fritz König in Berlin and tell him to put some muscle on to Leonid Zafod and this Karasamov character. Tell him that we will pull out from all further business unless they get Zafod to meet JeanLuc and give the girl back. That should do the trick. Do it now from downstairs in the street. No faxes, no cellphones, just use the payphone. Remember to be careful."

Sixty-odd dollars in change later, Joel hung up the payphone receiver, hailed a cab and headed back uptown to the Biophar Drugs Corporation Offices. There were five Japanese execs and a whole bunch of lawyers waiting for him there to deal with the sale of the Corporation.

Ah, fuck'em, he thought and leaned forward to talk to the cab driver. "I changed my mind. Take me to Romano's Sandwich bar—you know it?"

"Yeah," said the driver laconically "No problem." The yellow cab jerked forward in the traffic. Joel sat back on the seat. He needed to eat and he would murder a beef and horseradish hero, a double side order of fries and a frosty Kronenbourg. His mouth watered in anticipation.

*

"Here they come, sir" said Sergei Yemeljan. He nudged the snoring figure beside him. "Here they come," he repeated.

Captain Anatole Swerdilenko pulled down his thick woollen scarf and peered out blearily. He leaned forward and wiped some of the condensation off the windshield. "Right you are, Sergeant. You know what to do."

"Yes, sir. Follow them at a discreet distance and don't interfere."

"Right, my boy. This is the best way for now, believe me, son. I know it's your sister that's been kidnapped. I haven't forgotten that." He lit a cigarette, took a deep drag and coughed harshly several times. After the spasm, he took another deep drag and his lungs resigned themselves to their polluted fate. "Ah, that's better" he breathed. "Okay, start her up, they're off!"

They shadowed the Yemeljan van as it set off towards the city centre. "Have you seen those two before, Sergei? Are they friends of your sister's?" asked the Captain.

"No, I don't think so. That tall one looked vaguely familiar though—Its possible I've seen him before. I'd like to get a closer look."

"Not yet. Just stick to following them. Turn the heater up will you, it's still bloody cold in here. Don't they have better cars in the motor pool than this pile of rusted shit?" The Captain twisted around in his

141

seat to find the thermos of coffee he'd brought. He located it wedged in the back seat next to the Kalashnikov machine guns that were hidden under a blanket.

"It looks like they're headed south towards Lyublino, sir."

"Right. Stay close. I don't think they know they're being followed, no signs of evasive action." He poured himself a generous cupful of coffee.

Igor drove. JeanLuc hefted the ancient large-bore pistol that Dmitri had dug up from under the floorboards. It was a museum piece; a German Infantry Lüger from the Second World War. JeanLuc hoped the ammunition would work after all this time. He cracked the gun open, spilled out the bullets and dry fired it several times. The firing mechanism seemed to function. Well, he'd have to risk it.

The drums of gasoline in the back of the van rattled noisily as they drove over the corrugated roads.

Dmitri had wanted to come but JeanLuc had ordered him to stay to look after Saskia and to get the Carpocratian Legacy repacked for travel to the States. They'd had a call from Karasamov in the afternoon—a curt message that Zafod would meet with them at the yard; no tricks, no police or the girl would get it and they'd be next. It seemed that the US pressure was working. Maybe they could resolve this and get Sophia back.

The gates of the yard were already open and they were waved through at once. Igor stopped the van behind the Mercedes with its darkened windows, parked by the metal staircase leading up to the offices. He looked across the yard for the DAF. It was still there—he hoped his stash was still undetected. He was determined to get it back even if he had to fight his way through the lot of them.

Several men were hanging around in the yard apparently doing nothing, just watching impassively. Igor sized them up with his pale grey-blue assassin's gaze. He recognised Gronowski, another Pole, and one or two others with whom he had been on drinking sprees in the past. Riff -raff, he thought; not a real soldier amongst them—he would take them out, no problem. He flicked off the safety on his Uzi and followed JeanLuc up the stairs to Karasamov's office, at the end of a short corridor.

"Ah, Comrade Golemov, you're here. And who is your friend?" Karasamov called out.

"My name is Alexei Fedorov," said JeanLuc tightly. "Who are these people?"

"Let me introduce you. At the desk, Comrade Leonid Zafod, over there his assistant Ilya Bearski, and I am Ivan Karasamov. I'll leave you now to your discussion. If you need anything just call." Karasamov walked out of the room. They didn't attempt to shake hands, which would have meant putting away the weapons they all held.

"You have influential friends, Mr Fedorov. I congratulate you!" began Zafod.

"Let's cut the bullshit. I am a busy man. Where's the girl, Mr. Zafod?" said JeanLuc.

"So! You're a busy man, eh! Why? What's the hurry? Here in Russia we like to observe the social niceties." Zafod pulled open a drawer in the desk and took out a bottle of vodka. "Let us discuss our little problem like gentlemen," he said.

JeanLuc ignored this gesture. "We've brought the gasoline back, so where is the girl? My principals have obviously told you of the consequences of messing me about," he said quietly.

"But it is not so obvious, my friend. This is my territory. I rule here," snapped Zafod. "The girl is in the car and you can have her—she is not important. But you have killed four of my men. On principle, I cannot allow that to go uncompensated. Where would be my credibility?"

"That's not my problem, Mr.Zafod. Your thugs were going to kill us and take our money. You know it and I know it." JeanLuc suddenly sensed that Zafod was going to be difficult. He felt a surge of anger and fear sweep through him. "Look, Mr Zafod," he grated." We can either stop and resolve this right now or I cannot answer for the consequences. You know I have powerful friends and you know I will use them. Believe me I can have you destroyed; swatted like a fly."

"No-one, no-one threatens me!" The infuriated Zafod jumped to his feet shouting "Ilya ...!"

JeanLuc could see the time for discussion was over as Ilya Bearski turned ponderously towards Igor, tightening a chubby forefinger on the trigger of his automatic. Shell casing jumped and gleamed as he fired. Igor had seen the big man turn and dived to the floor. Holes punched through the plasterboard panels just above him. Plaster dust sprinkled down into his hair. The revolver in Igor's hand crashed.

"Oh, Mama! " Bearski screamed in a strangled breathy voice. It was a wonder he could scream at all with his chest caved in as if punched by a sledgehammer. On his white shirt bloomed dark Rorshach poppies. "Oh, Mama. Oh, Ma ...!"

Two of the framed pictures on Karasamov's office wall crashed down. One showed friend Ivan shaking hands with First Secretary Putin; it fell on to Bearski's head, shattering glass onto his slumped shoulders. "Oh, Mama!" he wheezed in a fading whisper as blood foamed in bubbles from his mouth.

Gronowski and one of the other men who had been waiting outside burst into the room ducking and weaving. Gronowski had an automatic in each hand, the other man a shotgun sawed off as short and as black as the muzzle of a rottweiler. Ivan Slobodka, Zafod's driver, appeared behind them both, carrying the very latest Red Army issue rapid-fire assault weapon. All the best-dressed terrorists were wearing them this year; a crucial piece of equipment for young upwardly mobile mass-murderers to match the Hannibal Lecter lambswool jumper in knives-and-forks pattern designed exclusively by Frederick of Elm St.

"Where's my comrade, you fucking foreigner" Gronowski screamed. "What'd you do to him?" Without waiting for an answer, he let fly with both pistols from the hip like a cowboy in a Western movie.

I've had it! JeanLuc thought but then Igor fired. Gronowski propelled backwards, a spray of blood spurting from his throat in another fine display from the Fountain of Carotid. The automatics dropped from his enfeebled hands and thumped onto the threadbare carpet.

"Kill them!" Leonid Zafod was shrieking. "Kill the bastards. Blow them away!" He aimed and fired his 0.357mm Magnum at JeanLuc. Zeppelin-calibre bullets smashed gaping jagged holes in the wood panels either side of JeanLuc's head, causing yellow light from the bathroom to shine through in ragged rays. This sure is getting to be Dirty Harry Country, JeanLuc thought in semi-panic. JeanLuc raised his own gun for the first time and pulled the trigger.

The crash was so loud in the confined space that for a moment he thought Dmitri's ancient gun had blown up in his hand. The recoil snapped his arm up in a savage arc. He saw part of Zafod's shoulder disintegrate in a crimson spray; heard Zafod's wounded hyena screech and he yelled, "You bastards! What have you done with my girl? Give her back or we'll finish this for good!"

There was a boom like a crack of thunder as the man fired his sawn off. JeanLuc rolled to one side as the blast ripped through the walls and the bathroom door. He was seared by shot in several places. If he'd been where the shot pattern was tight, he would've been shredded. He tried his gun but it had jammed. He worked furiously to free it. Hell, I'm dead, he thought, watching in desperation as the man worked the pump of the sawn off, jacking in more cartridges . The son of a bitch made a shit-eating grin as his eyes narrowed for the aim. Christ! I'm going to get killed by some sadistic Russian fuckhead, JeanLuc thought helplessly. At least I put one into Zafod. At least I did that much for Sophia. He looked around desperately for Igor. Where was the stupid fuck?

"He's mine. I have him! " Slobodka yelled cheerfully from the doorway. "Gimme a clear field!" But before the man with the shotgun could give him a clear field, Slobodka opened up with the Red Army Special. The thunderous chatter of the machine-rifle fire filled Zafod's office. The first result of this barrage of bullets helped to save JeanLuc's life. The man with the rottweiler had drawn a bead on him but just before he could pull the double triggers, Slobodka's runaway Special cut him in half.

"Stop it! You crazy idiot!" Zafod screamed. But Ivan Slobodka either didn't hear, couldn't stop or wouldn't stop. Fat lips pulled back from crooked stumpy teeth bared in a huge shark's grin, he raked the room from one wall to the other, turning the wooden partitions into riddled colanders, framed pictures into fragmented shards of glass and exploding the frosted glass panel in the bathroom door. The brass ornamental urn by the fireplace bonged like a bell as bullets ricocheted off it.

For a moment JeanLuc was stunned by the racket and incapable of doing anything more constructive than crouching in horror. Then he saw other men crowding at the door behind Slobodka, so he raised the old Luger again.

"I musta got him!" Slobodka was screaming with the abandoned hysteria of a Bungalow Bill who equates the juddering of a hot gun in his hands with the climactic jerking of his sexpistol. "Got him. I got him. I go—!

JeanLuc pulled the trigger and the top of Slobodka's head flew away leaving a grey splatter of brains dripping lumpily off the patterned wallpaper. There was a loud kaboom from JeanLuc's left. Something tore a hot gouge in his side just above his left kidney. He saw Leonid Zafod pointing the smoking Magnum at him from behind the corner of his desk. JeanLuc ducked as Ol'Harry's dirty muzzle spoke authoritatively once more.

Calling on all his old training, Igor adopted a stance. Arm extended, he aimed at the first of the men coming in through the door and squeezed the trigger. The gun roared, jumping in his sweat slippery hand like a live frog. One of the opposition spun aside, the handgun he'd been holding falling from his dying fingers. Igor saw the others duck behind the doorjamb and then he was crawling through splinters of wood and glass that littered the floor. He retrieved one of the automatics that Gronowski had dropped.

"What are the rest of you waiting for?" screamed Zafod. "There are only two of them, for Christ's sake!"

Igor crawled to the corner of the desk. JeanLuc aimed towards the door. Zafod rose up suddenly, his nerve broken. He'd not noticed that Igor had now appeared on his flank. Zafod was thinking now of only one thing; finally putting an end to the goddamned bastards who had brought this ruin on his head.

"Hey, creep!" Igor shouted to distract him. Zafod, in spite of his ruined shoulder, twisted around viciously.

"Fuck you," he exclaimed and hefted the 0.357mm 'Call me Mister Eastwood' for the final time. Igor pumped four shots into him in rapid succession. Leonid Zafod collapsed and died with an expression of terminal fury on what remained of his smashed face.

"Come and get it, motherfuckers," JeanLuc yelled and pulled the trigger. That satisfying boom came again. One of the opposition got

146

off a wild shot, but JeanLuc's bullet drove him back into the corridor, bowling him over. His heels did a dying ratatattat-tap-dance on the floorboards and then remained still. An irrational but utterly persuasive feeling had come over him; a feeling that the gun held some magical talismanic power of protection; as if he held King Arthur's Excalibur of shooters. As long as he held it, he was invincible, couldn't be hurt, and the Ol'Grim Reaper would scythe his enemies as sure as shit will spatter from the spinning fan.

Silence fell, a silence in which JeanLuc could hear only a man in the corridor moaning and a high ringing in his ears. He wondered if he would ever hear right again.

Karasamov's office was no longer recognisable. It had been totally wrecked. The wall between the bathroom and the office was collapsing. Broken glass was everywhere. Ceiling panels that had been shredded by the lurching machine-gun fireworks hung down like torn paper.

JeanLuc coughed dryly. Now he could hear other sounds—a babble of whispered conversation at the far end of the corridor and voices shouting outside in the yard below. "Is it over?" Igor asked JeanLuc. "Can we have got all of them?"

"I don't know. Hang on in there."

Suddenly, a voice yelled from the doorway. "I got something precious for you, scumbag. You'll want this to remind you of us when you burn in hell!" Swinging it by the long black hair, he lobbed a freshly severed head through the open doorway. It landed at JeanLuc's feet. The momentum of the throw caused it to roll over so that the bloodied features, grimaced in death agony, lips still quivering, faced up at him.

It was Sophia.

JeanLuc screamed in horror and anguish. He leaped up and lurched suicidally towards the door, heedless of the danger. Splinters of glass and wood punched into his shoes as he stumbled blindly towards his tormentor. "No, JeanLuc! No!" Igor yelled, but JeanLuc did not hear. He was way beyond mere rationality. He was aware of nothing but the fact that Sophia was dead. They had cut off her precious head! Some cocksucking Russian pervert had cut off Sophia's head and that son of a bitch was going to die for it. Now!

He stumbled towards the door, firing blindly again and again,

147

oblivious to anything except the growing python of rage and despair that coiled around his heart and squeezed with ever increasing intensity.

It was Karasamov who stepped out of the corridor to meet him, a 0.38mm automatic steady in his fist. He smiled bleakly, eyes narrowed like the slits of an armoured car.

When he saw JeanLuc leap up into the open, Igor quickly rose to his knees and steadied his gun on the edge of the desk, grimly concentrating. He thought he would have one chance only to save JeanLuc. Then, as Karasamov stepped up smiling his tight Russian smile, Igor fired into it and suddenly Karasamov was lying against the wall of the corridor with his eyes wide-open and a ragged hole drilled through his grin. JeanLuc was standing over him, screaming and sobbing, dry firing his empty gun again and again as if the man could never be dead enough.

Igor knew then it was over. If there had been other soldiers, they had taken to their heels when Karasamov had bought his ticket for the ride across the Styx. He got wearily to his feet, reeled and then walked slowly over to where JeanLuc stood.

"Cut it out!" he said sharply. JeanLuc ignored him and continued dry firing the big revolver at the dead Karasamov. "Stop it, JeanLuc. He's dead. They're all dead."

Igor reached for the gun, but JeanLuc turned on him and before Igor was entirely sure what was happening, JeanLuc struck him on the side of the head. Igor felt a warm gush of blood in his ear and collapsed against the wall. He was out for no more than a couple of minutes, but when he managed to get things back into focus and back onto his feet, JeanLuc was no longer in the corridor. Igor bent, fighting off a wave of dizziness, picked up his weapon and pushed it back into its holster.

"JeanLuc?" he croaked. His throat was sore and throbbing even worse than the swollen place on the side of his head where JeanLuc had struck him.

JeanLuc didn't notice him approach. He found JeanLuc sitting on the floor with Sophia's head cradled in his arms. He was shuddering all over and crying. Igor reached for him but JeanLuc shrank away, still weeping. "Don't touch me," he whimpered.

"JeanLuc, it's all over. They are all dead. Sophia too."

"Leave Sophia out of this!" JeanLuc shrieked and another fit of shuddering went through him. He hugged the grisly severed head to his chest and rocked it. His blood streaked hand tried to stroke and smooth the twisted knotted hair. He lifted his streaming eyes to Igor's face. "The only woman I ever loved!"

He sobbed so hard, Igor could barely understand him. "Why? Oh! Why couldn't I have taken care of her just this once? God is so cruel!"

"We have to go, JeanLuc," Igor said sadly. "Go? I'm not going anywhere."

"Do you want to stay here and explain this mess?" asked Igor with some urgency.

"I don't care!" JeanLuc cried. "Without Sophia, it doesn't matter. Nothing does."

Igor shrugged resignedly. He squatted down on his haunches and waited. Oh shit. What have I ever done to deserve this, he thought wearily.

PART II

On God's steed, with Cross ablaze
I destroy the Demon Guardian at Time's Gate. Blue Apples.

Anon

CHAPTER 20

He was sorry about the girl. But his plan had worked and he took a measure of satisfaction from that. Zafod was dead and the two strangers had done the killing for him—as he predicted might happen. He had an instinct for such things.

He and his department were in the clear; none of his men had died apart from Bearski who was a corrupt traitor. The whole thing would blow over in a couple of days—until the next time. Sergei would get over it. Boys of that age always did. The parents were another matter, but hell, life was one long tragedy these days.

FSB Captain Anatole Sweridenko steepled his fingers and leaned back in his chair. It was only right to let them go, he thought. He had given them a FSB escort back to the Yemeljan apartment to change out of their bloodstained clothes, pick up some things and then the younger one, the American, went straight to the airport onto the first scheduled evening flight out. The other, the Pole, had insisted on collecting his truck and was now on his way back to Europe. To keep his mind off recent events the Captain had insisted that Sergei should accompany the truck back to the border. Golemov had raised no objection.

The Captain smiled. They were a strange pair, but then many things in Russia are strange these days. Moscow was swarming with foreign businessmen, investment bankers, politicians and, of course, legions of network marketeers and pyramid sellers, out for a fast rouble from his poor naive countrymen still relatively innocent of the devious ways of Capitalists.

He'd done his stint in Chile, Cuba and El Salvador and he knew that morally the West was worse off than they were. He felt in his bones that his people would not go the same route as the corrupt West—they had a stronger sense of what was right and what was wrong. They were closer to the subliminal pulse of human moral evolution; who else would have had a bloody Revolution based solely on the humanist ideas of Marx and Lenin? Without scum like Zafod and Bearski he felt more optimistic that things could improve.

He lit a cigarette and blew the smoke across his desk. The ancient central-heating pipes and radiators in his office creaked and banged intermittently as they did throughout the decrepit building; but at least they were warm.

He picked up the object on his desk: a triangular box made of some hard material, asbestos or something ceramic, he surmised. As he'd been shown, he pushed one end and an inner compartment slid out from its outer sleeve. Inside there were thick tightly rolled bundles of dollar notes. His fat fee!

He went to the door and locked it before commencing to count. Close to three thousand US dollars! That Polish Golemov character had looked as if he was being disembowelled alive when it was handed over by the tall zombie one. Anatole chuckled out loud at the memory of it. But he'd kept his side of the bargain. He'd gotten the American on the plane, no questions asked, past Airport Security with that hi-tech briefcase and a length of plastic drainpipe capped at both ends that looked as if it might hold posters or maps or something. Let the New York Customs worry about that! And if it was a bomb? Well, the American would be committing suicide and Anatole didn't think he'd do that; not after the bloodbath they'd caused. They weren't the suicidal or plane-bombing type.

That was a clever hiding place, he thought. He'd tell the Drugs Squad to pass the word to look in the exhaust manifolds of the big trucks in future. It was a nice piece of workmanship—the triangular wedge shape allowed the hot exhaust gases to flow around the box without impeding the flow too much. He folded the bills back into rolls, wedged them carefully back into the container and locked it in the top drawer of his desk.

He lit another cigarette, lifted his shiny black boots onto the desk and contentedly began to consider how to debauch the loot. Maybe now was the time to move to Prague, his favourite city. Set himself up with a little restaurant business.

Yes, it was a fine day and it was going to be a terrific evening. He started to hum the tune that had been bothering him. "*Ob-la-Di, Ob-la-Da, life goes on …*"

*

From Moscow Igor Golemov went through four national borders, and several random checkpoints and searches by police, to arrive back in Normandy. His passage through the numerous checkpoints in Russia had been greatly smoothed by the young Sergeant Yemeljan who'd spent most of the trip slumped against the side-door window staring sightlessly out. Igor had dropped him off at the Polish border where he saw him climb into an Army staff car that seemed to have been waiting for him. They had hardly exchanged a word.

Igor was exhausted. He pulled the DAF off the highway and into the lorry-parking area of the Routier café just outside of Beauvais to wait for further directions. They had given him an approximate destination but now he was due to get final instructions by fax.

He switched on the in-cabin fax machine and climbed into the rear sleeping cabin to rest. He lit one of the last of his strong Russian-made Sobranie cigarettes and stared unseeingly at the cabin roof reviewing past events in his mind. He'd known all along that this was a dodgy trip – you didn't get paid this much for a routine delivery of agricultural machinery. The small anonymous-looking crate they had picked up from the Russian military on the outward journey was all the proof Igor needed to confirm that he was on a highly risky mission. And then there was all the mayhem in Russia culminating in the handover of his precious stash to that policeman to get JeanLuc out of the country and to get his truck back. That was the worst part. He still felt resentful about this, even though JeanLuc had promised him treble the amount if he could complete the delivery back to France. He believed JeanLuc; after all the horror they had been through together in such a short period. But he wasn't so sure about his employers. Would they come through? He would have to wait and see. After all, he didn't really have much choice.

He fell asleep.

A couple of hours later Igor awoke. A tongue of paper was now hanging out of the fax with printed directions on it. He tore it off, pulled out a map of Northern France from the pile on the seat beside him and went to get a meal and a wash in the Routier.

The weapon would be here shortly. The confirming fax to the lorry had been sent and a suitable forklift truck would be on hand to unload it. They had decided to store it at Castle Sigor in one of the old cellblocks underneath the Grand Hall that had been built on the remains of the ancient central Keep, a structure that dated back to the eleventh century. As the 'Guardian to Normandy', Castle Sigor had been damaged and rebuilt several times over the centuries. The most recent damage caused by American shelling during the Normandy landings of World War II. The Western Tower in which the Compte, Jean de Sigor, had his offices was part of the old defensive wall that surrounded the central Keep. It was built in the twelfth century, for Geoffroi D'Anjou, one of the earliest Grand Masters of the Priory Arcadia. Jean de Sigor, the last in a long and illustrious but secretive line, could see from his window the courtyard below and across the formal rose garden to the solitary elm tree in the Champ Sacre with the chimneys and church spires of the town of Sigor in the distance. He watched as the long-expected truck arrived up the long straight drive exclamation-marked with poplar trees; the truck from Russia with its darkly ominous payload on a February wind from the cold dangerous East.

Shivering slightly, because it was always cold in the Tower in spite of the modern heating, he turned away from the window. It would be here shortly. His staff would handle the unloading and storage of the device in the cells. He had instructed them earlier and his secretary, Charles Duvain, would handle it.

Levers. That's what it was all about. Levers of power. Throughout its history, the Priory Arcadia had collected holy relics, instruments, documents, weapons, books, material evidence, love letters, tapes; anything that could perpetuate their tight hold on the secret levers of power.

To the Grand Master, Jean, Compte de Sigor, adding a nuclear weapon to their collection was no different in principle from the acquisition of a holy relic that millions of people, and of course their leaders, would venerate. This activity was the source of their power. Not their vast wealth or property holdings, but those sometimes subtle things that would bend a King, a Tyrant, a General, an Ayatollah or an Emperor to their will and their purposes which were to perpetuate the Bloodline and thus survive the Ages ... until the Prophecy could be fulfilled.

Archimedes maintained that with a long enough lever you could move the Earth, but you needed a fulcrum. He was right. But levers could take many forms, both physical and in the mind of those being levered. A nuclear warhead was a significant and potent fulcrum on which to lever power but it was almost impossible to think of a context in which it could be used and the unimaginable consequences managed. It was nothing like as potent a force these days as people imagined. Everyone of consequence had these weapons and of course nobody would dare to use it—apart from the obvious candidates amongst the suicidal Terrorist fraternity. Even they would probably think carefully about letting one of those off. Terrorist fear- vampires prefer an audience of weeping mothers and widows to witness a TV spectacular show like 9/11—even they understood there was no glory in nuking everything.

Jean de Sigor stared at the objects on his large ancient desk and picked up the jewel-handled dagger, with a blade jagged and black with age that he used as a letter opener. This was the dagger of Godfroi de Bouillon that had last been used twisted into the heart of a Saracen somewhere in the tunnels below the Temple Mount in Jerusalem at the end of the First Crusade. Yes, that had been an earlier mission to acquire a lever of power – the Ark of the Covenant. This had been sold to the then all-powerful Venetians in return for the protection and survival of the Bloodline.

Jean de Sigor still wasn't sure why he'd decided to get the warhead at this particular time. It had seemed the opportune thing to do, a culmination of the activities and acquisitions of the past five years, a precautionary response to the dangers ahead: International Terrorism and the advent of the World of the fifth Sun prefigured in the Mayan Calendars.

The five years leading up to the Millennium had been a constant struggle against powerful enemies who used to be allies, such as the Hospitallers and the Catholic Curia. The years since the war had been spent in retrieving their wealth, and building their power- base in Europe. Until recently, he had found no male successor to marry his daughter Giselle. The whole process had aged him. He felt tired and mentally exhausted. It was becoming increasingly difficult to see clearly into the future. He felt powerless, in the grip of something that was driving them all to a destination, an objective he only half understood. He suspected that it must be the long-prophesied, long- awaited, and long- dreaded Fulfilment. Something was happening beyond his or even his enemies' control and it seemed to have started, crystallised, when Jean Luc was identified by Rosa Roncalli as the Chosen One, God be praised; in America of all places.

Only two others knew of his new purchase: his Seneschal, Sir John Redcliff, and Cardinal Joseph Mirphy one of his Commandeurs of the Rose Croix. Joseph had arranged everything from New York.

The trigger for Project Maraschino, the original excuse to go to Russia, risking resources and their most precious people like Jean Luc, was mainly the desire of the Cardinal to confirm a rumour from one of his contacts that there might be valuable icons to be found. This might help in his attempt at the Papacy and might also bolster the American Catholic Church whose reputation and effectiveness had been shattered by the Boston pederasts, leaving a power vacuum that was being filled by Mormons, and far-right Fundamentalist sects.

The Priory Arcadia was Joseph Mirphy's sponsor for his bid to become Pope. Yes, it was all about levers and killing two birds with one cliché.

Jean de Sigor sighed and turned to the window to watch as a small crate was unloaded from the truck now parked on the ancient cobbled courtyard below.

It did not look much for 30 million dollar cash and 10 million carat dollars in diamonds. Still it was only money and the Priory Arcadia was awash with money these days. This was one of the benefits of having a senior member of the Order as EEC Commissioner, dipping his beak into the Brussels gravy train on their behalf. Through ingenuous creative accounting, a small island owned by the Priory located off the coast of Jersey had been classed as a Principality, like Monaco, and was thus eligible and in receipt of huge development funds normally reserved for an entire country the size of Poland or the Czech Republic. Access to this tiny island, basically a rocky outcropping, was strictly prohibited because it was the only migratory stopping-off point for the nearly extinct Great Icelandic Whooping Crane on its way to the Land of Godknowswhere—at least that was what was on official documents. The Priory maintained a small monastic group of accountants and convalescing members there, whose task was to look after a row of bomb-proof filing cabinets filled with share certificates, bonds and other documentation.

Yes, it was all about leverage! But Jean de Sigor increasingly felt the counter-weight of events and history exerting its own leverage on him personally and on the Priory Arcadia. Ach! Let it come!

Not for the first time, he felt afraid of the impending future. Afraid of the Fulfilment. He was now an instrument of Fate.

There was only one other man who could possibly understand how he felt and that was Moloc. Father Moloc. His one time comrade-in-arms, best friend and even mentor.

Outside, the forklift truck with its load disappeared into the tunnel beneath the Grand Hall towards its final resting place in the cells, a place of ancient tortures and tribulations.

As the nuclear warhead disappeared from view, Jean de Sigor turned his thoughts once more towards the recurrent battle with the Hospitallers, an Order of which Father Moloc was a 'Turcopolier' in the French 'Langue' and a key strategist. The Hospitallers, the Order of the Hospital of St. John of Jerusalem, are the more public, well-known survivors of the original Knights Templar that split from the Priory Arcadia in 1188 at the site of the elm tree, which he could see, with its flush of new spring leaves, from his window. According to history, the Templars disappeared from general view in 1307 after the massacre of most of the Knights and the fiery immolation of their Grand Master Jacque de Molay by King Philip the Fair.

He wished Moloc was here, like the old days, as a comrade. But no, that was not to be. Moloc had had his own agenda all along, which did not include the Priory Arcadia who, in the view of his Order, were the perpetrators of an ancient Heresy. He still remembered the sadness in the older man's eyes when they separated at the Liberation of Paris in 1945.

'Go now, mon cher. We must prepare now for our separate destinies. What is prophesied must be made to come true. Adieu. We will never see each other again." With that he had disappeared into the

159

beret-waving cheering crowds that lined the boulevards as the Allies rolled into the City in their tanks and jeeps, bringing their new ways, filter cigarettes and awesome technologies.

Ah yes the technologies! The sciences, the computers, the cars, the internet, the cruise missiles, the space stations, the nuclear weaponry. Where did all this come from? Where did it all fit in? Who controlled it? Initially, his European sensibilities were completely bewildered and befuddled by this onslaught of brash American ways. The world changed in 1945, as it did again twenty years later, and again at the end of the Eighties, in a series that would end with the Fulfilment. This was the only certainty.

It had taken the older men of the Priory many decades to adjust to the relatively sudden emergence of America as a world super power and the Priory, at least until Joseph Mirphy joined, did not have any real understanding of the American psyche or control over what happened there. However, the Priory Arcadia was immensely wealthy and Americans certainly understood the power of the dollar and the balance sheet. And, of course, since most Americans came from immigrant European stock, there was still an understanding and contact, even if increasingly tenuous as the importance of Family was eroded by computer video games, television, global communication, federated government and corporate ideology.

This was now truly the Information Age and secrets were harder to keep— everything was now a fair game subject for a documentary for the History Channel, a movie for the masses, or a digitalvideogame for the delinquent. And of course there was the 'net. He had only to type in the phrase 'Priory Arcadia' into the Google search engine to have thousands of links to thousands of web sites with enough information to fill an encyclopaedia. Most of it was rubbish but there was also some serious detail and quite intelligent theoretical speculation in the form of fiction. All that was hitherto the preserve of learned Initiates and Scholars of Esoteric Arcana was now available to anyone at the touch of a keyboard in a cyber café with a double-shot cappuccino. Ah! But only if they knew what to look for and had the knowledge to recognise it if they found it. Jean de Sigor took comfort from the thought that the Priory and its predecessors dated back to the Jewish Essenes, and had practically invented the concept of disinformation. The internet was a perfect vehicle for disseminating this. For example, look at the huge industry that had grown around Gabriel Knight and Dan Brown. He smiled to himself … now that was entertainment! No, they hadn't lost the art. That was ticking along nicely, thank you. Roll on St.George and the Schattenjägers!

So, of course, they needed JeanLuc. A young man steeped in Americana, practiced in the new ways, the new technologies. Their very own Gabriel Knight! Their very own Indiana Jones! Welcome to Sigor, Mr.Bond! Hah!

Jean de Sigor almost laughed out loud at these thoughts. Turning away from the window, he walked from his office through the narrow stone arch and down the steep winding stairway of the Western Tower, to oversee the unpacking of his latest holy relic – a relic of the Cold War, holy in the sense of 'Holy Terror'. Forget the mythic Seal and the Key of St.George, forget the Ark of the Covenant, forget the Sandal of Allah, forget the Essene Scrolls, forget the Holy Grail, all you needed were the two little silver keys, that should, even now, be hanging, next to his dog tags, on a chain around JeanLuc's neck. Now turning those keys would initiate a real wake-up call for mankind.

The Compte felt again the thrill of fear, of mortal dread, gripping his stomach as he let his mind's eye raise the curtain ever so slightly on a Vision of the Future that was rapidly coalescing into existence.

CHAPTER 21

'But Nemi's woods are still green, and as the sunset fades above them in the West, there comes to us, borne on the swell of the wind, the sound of the church bells of Rome ringing the Angelus. Ave Maria! Sweet and solemn they chime out from the distant city and die lingeringly away across the wide Campagnian marshes.

Le Roi est mort, vive le Roi!'

Frazer certainly knew his stuff, thought Sir John Redcliff. He closed the huge last volume of the Golden Bough and laid it on the bedside table. He lay back on the pillows for a while and nursed the glass containing its finger of golden Glenfiddich. Yes, a man of learning and insight. They could do with such men in the Priory. Oh, they'd had their fair share of literati; Victor Hugo, Jean Cocteau, Debussy amongst others … but recently? Well, nobody of equivalent stature certainly in the English-speaking world, unless you counted Anthony Burgess who was well-regarded by some, but not to his taste. Sir John was more of a Trollopian himself but then he couldn't entirely escape his upbringing. The world, nowadays, seemed to be full of politicians or scientists; the latter being a breed he couldn't understand or cope with and had actively tried to keep out of the membership. They had no soul! Why they were put up for membership in the first place he couldn't imagine—it was mainly down to the tedious American faction who still couldn't fully grasp the significance of what Frazer had meant by 'Le Roi est mort, vive le Roi!' and thus what the Priory truly stood for. The Priory Arcadia was not a funny-handshake brigade, an exclusive bloody golf club or a fraternity house with quaint Olde Worlde initiation ceremonies. They would be happier in Opus Dei.

Most of them would go screaming wet-trousered to their apple pied mommas if they knew what really went on, what was being planned by Jean and the higher echelons of the Order. He felt like doing that himself some days; only his dear Mummy was twenty years in her grave, tossing and turning in the family vault and the wet trousers would be more to do with his atrophied prostate.

He sipped at the whiskey and stared meditatively at the twin peaks his feet made in the richly patterned bed cover. Ah, yes, he thought.

The Americans with their fancy toys. He would lay any odds that those expensive electronic gewgaws they'd fitted JeanLuc out with for his trip into Russia would prove to be useless. Give him plenty of hard currency—that had been Sir John's only contribution to the discussions. In his opinion, it was a wild-goose chase, but if Mirphy wanted to do it, it was fine with him. It would keep him occupied until they could manoeuvre him into the Chair of St. Peter. It would be good exercise for JeanLuc too—toughen him up mentally for the ordeals ahead and knock some of the playboy out of his character. It would also serve as part of JeanLuc's 'peregrinatio'; his mystic journey of the mandala.

If they found something of value, so much the better. As long as they brought back the nuke which was the other purpose of the trip.

Personally, what he'd been shown at Sigor by Jean at his own Initiation, all those years ago, was quite enough to convince him forever about the legitimacy of the Priory's activities in the 'shardic' realms of religion and world politics. He shivered at the memory and knocked back the remaining whisky.

He didn't need convincing, but he understood why the others might need extra props for their faith or a sign from heaven. May God spare him another sign from heaven! Oh the folly of mankind; they should leave well enough alone!

Anyway now they were back unscathed and had apparently accomplished their mission. He'd arranged for Jean Luc to be picked up after his flight from Moscow. He'd then stayed for a week in a London hotel until Golemov the driver had made his delivery. They had both flown out from Heathrow that morning for New York.

He wished he could have a refill but the night nurse only let him have the one drink. As he grew older and more decrepit his life became more and more like his boarding prep-school days. Matron hovering anxiously over him, tucking him up in bed, smoothing his forehead, clucking now now Johnny-boy, the huge mantelpiece of bosom heaving in starched blue uniform ... Sir John tottered into the domain of sleep and began to snore gently.

A nurse tiptoed into the room, turned down the bedside lamp and removed the glass from his limp hand. Jobs done, she returned to her desk outside the door and picked up her knitting. A large black tomcat approached her. Round and round, back and forth it threaded between her blue stockinged legs, purring loudly. "Enough Alexey, enough of that, you randy little sod. Go catch a rat or something!" she whispered.

The pendulum grandfather clock downstairs in the hallway of the ancient house started to chime musically. Twelve o'clock, midnight. Alexey looked up at the nurse, one last time, out of those strange mismatched eyes of his, one blue, one brown, and ran purposefully down the corridor. She heard the faint clatter of the cat flap in the kitchen below. Jesus! It was creepy here sometimes, she thought; and put down the knitting to light a Silk Cut. Some winter nights, it was like participating in a ghost story, especially when it was windy and raining. The old timbers of the house would groan and creak ominously and the branches of trees would bang scratchingly against the leaded windowpanes, causing her heart to jump into her mouth and cower there until she chased it back with a gulp of medicinal brandy. But the money was good; she had an emergency mobile phone and Sir John was no trouble really; always on the phone he was, and often away in London.

The display of the electrocardiograph machine that monitored Sir John's heart blinked rhythmically. All was well. She picked up her knitting; more baby clothes for her sister's new child. She wished she could have a baby too. She wished she could cuddle a milky newborn like her sister. She wished she could kill her sister's child. She wished she could kill her sister. The clicking of the duelling needles grew to a fever pitch. It was just as well, Alexey the cat had taken off in a huff, otherwise he might have been spitted from bum to furry whiskers, the mood she was in tonight.

*

Philippe awoke with a sudden jerk, eyes immediately open. He was itching, his flesh tingling and goose pimpled. There was an aching cold feeling in the marrow of his bones. My God! He thought. How could I need to fix again so soon? In the bathroom, he'd snorted a whole bag full—three times his normal dose. But he was definitely craving with a need worse than he'd ever experienced before. What was wrong with him? Maybe it was bad dope; cut with angel dust or something. He was

164

in a literal cold sweat—freezing and yet the perspiration was pouring from him in malarial rivers, soaking the sheets under him.

Shivering uncontrollably, he pushed his legs over the edge of the bed and sat up. His vision was blurred and he couldn't focus properly. Gritting his teeth, he put his head into his hands to massage his temples with his fingers. Then he got up and stumbled over to the dresser where he knew the chocoholic Giselle kept a stash of candy bars. Ripping the covering off, he crammed a Galaxy chocolate bar into his mouth, chewing and gulping it down. He needed the sugar desperately, but even more he needed to fix, so that this pain and shivering would go away and his mind could clear. But he felt so weird. Oh my God! He wept inwardly; this is the worst I've ever been. I must've gone mad, what have I done? Hardly bearing to look he turned his gaze back to the bed.

Giselle lay crumpled foetally on the huge bed. Philippe edged closer and examined her face. It was puffy and bruised and her bottom lip was split open. A thin trickle of blood mixed with saliva dribbled from her mouth onto the silk sheet. But she was breathing. Thank God! She's alive, he thought.

Philippe couldn't remember what they'd done—what he had done. But Giselle was clearly unconscious and looked badly beaten up. Her nude body looked blotchy with red marks and scratches; there were strands of semen still glistening stickily in her tangled hair and on her buttocks. Dear God, I must've raped here, he realised with a flood of confusion and despair.

The shivering was getting so bad he could hardly control himself— he would have to see Charles now. Charlie'd got him into this mess and he would fucking well get him out of it. Holding onto this bright warm flame of rage, Philippe grabbed a dressing gown from one of the wardrobes to cover his nakedness and went to the door of the apartment that led to the rest of Castle Sigor.

He opened the door carefully and peered out into the dimly lit corridor— nobody about. The corridor, richly carpeted, with priceless paintings—he ignored a Picasso Blue Period—hanging on the walls, led to a stone staircase. From previous visits, he knew that Charles Duvain's suite of rooms was at the top of this staircase. There was still no-one about, so Philippe came out of Giselle's rooms and closed the door behind him with a soft click. Looking about nervously, he made his way at a quick walk, almost a run. As he approached Charles Duvain's rooms, he saw that the door was slightly ajar and yellow light streamed through the narrow gap. Philippe ghosted up to the door and tapped gently on it.

"Come in, my boy," chuckled Charles. "I've been waiting for you. Surely Giselle can't have kept you, of all people, occupied for this length of time?" Charles was sitting at his desk, on which there was an open leather briefcase and a notebook computer switched on; he'd been working.

He swivelled around in his chair and looked at Philippe with a knowing grin on his face. He regarded the dishevelled figure of the desperate Philippe with the dull flat eyes of a shark. Satisfaction gleamed briefly in him. The Plan is working, he thought and now he could reward himself with some pleasure.

"Close the door will you, Philippe. Thank you," he said softly. The other man complied. "Now come over here and have some of this. By the looks of you, I think you need it!" From the top drawer of his desk, Charles took out a thin flat tin. With a mixture of repulsion and need, Philippe saw two syringes lying neatly side- by-side in the tin. Wordlessly, he approached the desk. Charles held out a small, oval capsule to him and pulled him down on his knees in front of him.

"Here, Philippe, lover boy. I want you to take this just before you come," he said throatily. Charles parted the robe he was wearing to reveal his one-eyed purple fungus standing stiffly attentive. "Now you must fix me here. I want it here—but after you." He closed one hand over his cock and stroked it. With his other hand, he passed one of the syringes over to Philippe who immediately popped a vein on his muscled forearm, sliding the needle in with delicious ease. He squeezed the plunger and sweet blissful peace soothed his aching needful body. A curtain came down on the hurricane of fear and despair in his mind.

He turned his grateful attention to Charles who was holding out the remaining syringe, and now breathing in harsh gasps. "In here ... Do it here!" he grated urgently indicating towards his cock. More than anxious to please, Philippe, with a hand that was now rock steady,

166

carefully inserted the needle into the large pulsing vein in Charles's cock and squeezed the plunger. The vein bulged briefly as the liquid went in. Above him, Charles gasped. Philippe withdrew the needle and a thin jet of blood sprayed in his face from the torn flesh. Charles suddenly moaned and a thick stream of yellowish semen spurted from his penis. Philippe put his mouth on and sucked in the fresh jets of semen and blood that came pulsing out. As he felt himself begin to orgasm, he popped the capsule that Charles had given him, under his nose. All hell broke loose in his head as the fumes of amyl nitrate hit his brain. The intensity of the orgasm was multiplied a thousand fold and he felt himself spurt repeatedly like a machine gun. In frenzy, he bit down hard and ground away with his teeth on the soft flesh in his mouth. He barely heard Charles' agonised scream as his gullet ballooned with hot salty blood. Charles bucked suddenly with epileptic violence; fell forward in his chair and then lay quivering and still.

His spine had snapped.

Philippe pushed the heavy body off his back onto the floor and staggered to his feet. With growing horror and disgust he regarded the blood spattered murder scene in front of him. He projectile vomited a ghastly mess onto the carpet. His heart was hammering at an unbelievable rate causing the veins on his forehead to stand out, knotted under the pressure. A tidal wave of fear and hopelessness washed over him. This is the end, he thought in despair. I cannot live after this. How could it have got like this so quickly? He was a decent guy— his mother loved him; Giselle loved him; he had many friends. Tears of self-pity cleared a path down his blood- soaked cheeks.

Revved up to cardiac redline by the amyl nitrate and high on the crack, Philippe ran from the room, down the staircase and back to Giselle's suite. He threw open the door and grabbed around for his clothes, pulling them on with desperate fumbling haste.

Giselle sat up suddenly on the bed. When she saw the gruesome apparition he had become, she started to scream with an intensity beyond hysteria, into the realms of black insanity. Philippe ignored her, grabbed his leather jacket and ran for his motorcycle.

Wristing the throttle full circle wide, he sent the NightHawk howling away into the night, leaving a smeared exclamation mark of black rubber on the courtyard cobbles.

For an hour, he rode the night with a wild exhilaration and then ... screaming with the joy of release, clenched defiant fist held high, he merged in flame and thunder with the turbo inter-cooled heart of an oncoming DAF-Leyland 450 heavy articulated truck.

With those headlights coming down the hill ... *between the stars.*

CHAPTER 22

The phone on the night nurse's desk buzzed insistently. She put down her knitting, cursing at the dropped stitches, and picked up the receiver. This must be urgent, she thought. There were strict instructions never to disturb Sir John's rest. "Hello, this is Sir Redcliff's medical unit here. Nurse Boyle speaking, can I help you?"

"Wake him up and get him on the phone," came the terse reply.

"Who is it? Who shall I say is calling?" she said tartly.

"This is Jean de Sigor in Brussels. Get him ready for travel at once. Do whatever is necessary, understand?"

"Yes, sir. But he is not well. It will be a shock for him."

"I don't care, just do it, Madame. It is an emergency. Now I would like to speak with him, please."

Carrying the cordless phone, she opened the heavy panelled oak door to Sir John's bedroom and went in. Toad of Toad Hall, Ratty your master calls, she thought.

"Wake up, sir!" She gently shook his shoulder. The man grunted and then slowly opened up his heavy-lidded eyes. Consciousness swam up from the depths and his eyes focused on the trimly uniformed form of Nurse Boyle holding out the phone to him. He heaved himself up, buttons of his blue-and-white striped pyjamas straining to hold the flesh within.

"What is it?" he growled into the receiver. "Do you realise what time it is?"

"John? It's Jean. I'm still with Pierre De Loire in Brussels. I've just had the most appalling news from Sigor. Giselle has been attacked and raped!" Jean's voice sounded strained and high pitched.

"What! This is monstrous! How could it be? The security there is the best in the world!"

"It was that new lover of hers, Philippe something. But that's not all, John. He killed my secretary too. I don't know all the details but I am flying back immediately. I want you there, I can only think this may be an attack on the Priory."

"I'll come at once, Jean. Of course. Have you called the police?"

169

"No, I don't want them involved yet. I've told my staff to go on full red alert, nobody in or out, and not to touch anything till you or I arrive."

Sir John took a deep breath. "Jean? Is Giselle ...?"

"All right? I don't know. She's alive and unharmed physically, that's all I know."

"I should be there in about an hour and a half. I'll get my chopper-pilot up at once."

"My bloody jet is at the airport and it will take me at least three hours to get a flight plan—that is, if I can find my pilot at this time of night. When you get there, find out what you can and call me on the mobile. Sergeant Nollet is my Chief of Security at Sigor, he will assist you. Oh, and John?"

"Jean?"

"Do what you can for Giselle! She must be devastated."

"Yes of course, my friend. Have they caught the man?" asked Sir John.

"He got away." The receiver in Sir John's hand suddenly felt icy cold to the touch. "But that man will be dead; wherever he is, whoever he is," came the flat statement down the line. The phone went dead.

Sir John heaved himself off the bed, tore off the wires that were attached to his chest and began to dress. He handed the phone back to the nurse. "Call Fred and get the chopper going for emergency take-off. Tell him we're headed for France."

"Yes, Sir John. I'll get onto it right away. But sir, please take this if you're going now." She handed him a small box that contained the drugs he needed to remain alive.

A couple of hours later, Sir John Redcliff's helicopter plummeted out of the dawning sky and landed on the wide lawn in front of Castle Sigor. A security man rushed over to open the helicopter door and guide Sir John into the Castle.

"So what has happened, Sergeant?" asked Sir John as he walked wearily up the steps. The man wrung his hands, obviously in mortal terror. "It is not our fault, Sir John. He was booked in, past security, by Mademoiselle and okayed by Monsieur Duvain," he wailed.

"Yes, yes. Where is the body? Have you touched it? "

170

"No. We left it exactly as it is. I must warn you it is a pretty horrible sight in there."

"Where is Mademoiselle Giselle?"

"In her rooms, sir. She is under sedation."

"Good. Now take me straight to Monsieur Duvain's room and then call the police. Do we know the local Inspector?"

"Yes, sir. He is a good man. He won't cause any trouble."

"Nobody must leave or enter the Castle until the Comte says so. He should be here shortly."

"I understand. All the staff are accounted for. They know nothing of what has happened. Most are still in bed."

Sir John approached the murder scene. Duvain's body lay where it had fallen, in a pool of blood that had soaked into the Chinese carpet. His features were set into a rictal grin. As a very young man, Sir John had fought with the French Resistance during the War and had faced and seen much death, but it had been many years since he'd had to view such a scene as this. Immediately, he felt nauseated; it was the smell, the smell of blood and excrement. He held a handkerchief to his nose and walked in.

"Get a video camera, Sergeant. I want everything video-archived on tape down to the last detail. But don't touch anything."

"Yes, sir. I have one in the guardroom. I'll go and get it." He left, leaving Sir John alone in the room.

Beside the body, Sir John spotted two empty syringes and a squeezed capsule. A drug murder, he thought. Duvain and this other chap must've been in a collusion of some sort—it was not looking good. He went over to the desk. There was a pile of papers that looked to do with Jean de Sigor correspondence next to the Dictaphone. The notebook PC on-light still glowed but it had reverted to sleep mode. Sir John rested his buttocks on the edge of the desk and hit the spacebar. The screen lit up with a text sentence written across. He peered down at it.

What he read caused him enormous alarm. Bending down with difficulty, he traced the lead from the PC to the telephone socket in the wall. Clapping a hand to his forehead, he hurried out into the corridor, shouting "Nollet! Get back here quick."

171

The Sergeant appeared at the top of the staircase carrying a camcorder. "Do you log all calls going out of here?" demanded Sir John.

"Yes, sir. They are all logged at the mini-exchange."

"Get me a listing as soon as possible; as soon as you have filmed in here. Whatever you do, don't touch that small computer on the desk. Leave it on. Who on the staff knows about computers?"

"I think one of the aircraft-maintenance people is au fait with that sort of thing, sir."

"Get him in here, quick."

"Yes, sir." Nollet spoke rapid French into his walkie-talkie. "He'll be fetched at once."

The Chief of Security got busy videotaping the scene. Sir John pulled a chair up to the desk and taking a biro, scribbled down the sentence on the screen that read:

'Attention: Father Moloc. Re: Atbash Target visited tonight by PD'

Duvain must have been interrupted in the middle of writing this note. The highly disturbing fact was that someone of his position shouldn't have known Father Moloc and even worse, the word Atbash had a secret significance that only a Senechal or higher in the Priory Arcadia could know. This was a serious security crisis—more than just a sex attack, he worried. Who really was Charles Duvain and why was he was sending modem messages to Father Moloc, a known sworn enemy of the Priory? There were many questions that needed answering.

A short time later, Emil the young curly-haired engineer looked up at Sir John. "We were lucky this PC wasn't switched off," he said. "The contents are automatically protected by an unbreakable password and all the files would have been saved encrypted." He looked sideways towards the body on the floor now thankfully covered with a blanket. "I can access all the directories and files while the PC remains on, but if it ever gets switched off it will be impossible to get back in."

"What was he doing?" asked Sir John. Computers were a fact of life these days, but that still didn't mean he had to understand them. He left all that to Margery and the whizz kids in the Treasury Department.

"It looks like he was going to send a message to someone, because it is written in a communications software program and placed in an outbox folder ready for sending down the phone line." He tapped a few keys. "If you look here I have brought up the directory tree, a list of directories. Do any of these mean anything to you?"

"Sir John scanned the list. "Under which directory would he have filed any previous messages he sent?" he demanded.

"I'm not sure, sir. If they were long documents or letters they might be in a sub-directory of a word-processing programme but short messages may have been stored directly in a communications sub-directory."

"Well, look there then," said Sir John.

Emil moved the mouse to highlight the ProTalk directory and hit the return button. A list of twenty files came up on the screen all prefixed with the letters ATB. Bingo! thought Sir John. Caught the bugger with his files undone. "Dump all those files to a printer and let me have a transcript. Then do the same for the rest of the files. Make back-ups onto disc," he ordered. "Don't mess this up; it is vitally important." Emil nodded.

There was a commotion outside the door and the Comte de Sigor appeared ashen-faced as he took in the scene.

"What's the damage, John?" he asked anxiously. "Let's go somewhere private to discuss this, Jean."

"Okay. Come with me to the Rose Room. It's nearby." Jean de Sigor turned on his heel and led the way. Sir John followed, his mind spinning. It was a disaster, all right. A Vatican spy in the heart of the Priory. He wasn't sure how he was going to break this news to the Nautonnier—it would surely weaken his position; the Yanks would see to that. They would have to re-organise.

How much had this Duvain known? How much had Jean taken him into his confidence? How had he been planted? What did Atbash mean to the Vatican? Was Giselle the intended target? Did he know about the bomb? These questions would have to be answered.

Sir John's heart was thumping painfully from all the unaccustomed exercise and stress. Did they do quadruple bypasses? he wondered, or would this episode see him off—he half-hoped it would.

The two men sat down facing each other. Outside, dawn's rosy light haloed the distant treetops shrouded in thick cobwebs of early morning mist.

"How's Pierre?" asked Sir John as he massaged the numb bloodless fingers of his left hand. Bad sign, he thought. Must take a pill. He fished with his right hand in his coat for the pillbox.

"Fuck Pierre. What's your preliminary assessment of what went on here?"

Sir John sighed. He would have to be blunt and brutal. He handed over the slip of paper on to which he had copied the text from Duvain's computer screen. "I think Charles Duvain must have been a spy planted on you by Father Moloc. We know from the past how dangerous he is to us. If true, this means you have been telling things directly to the Vatican and the Inquisition!"

If Jean could have paled even more, he would have. "Moloc!" he hissed. "That devious cock-sucking cleric."

"How long has Duvain been your secretary?" "Two, maybe three years, I can't recall exactly."

"How knowledgeable would he be about your affairs?"

"He'd know all my political and financial correspondence and my movements."

"And the Priory?"

"It's difficult to say. As you know, we very very rarely meet or put anything on paper. I have never myself divulged anything to him about the Priory or its members; that's not to say that he hasn't overheard things or listened to my phone calls. Is it possible he was only recently corrupted or recruited by Moloc, so would know very little of what to look for?"

"I doubt that. Why did you hire him in the first place?"

"Well, he came with impeccable references and we did thorough checks through the Sureté and Interpol. He was recommended very highly to me."

"We shall have to check all that again. Who it was that recommended him and why?"

There was a knock on the door. "Come in," shouted the Comte. Sergeant Nollet appeared holding a printout in his hand.

"This is the list of outgoing calls made from Sigor over the past

174

couple of days, sir."

"Thank you, Sergeant. Have the police come?" "Yes, sir. They are dealing with the body now."

"Please show them every courtesy. I'll be down in a few minutes." The sergeant nodded and went out closing the door behind him. Jean scanned through the blizzard of calls that had been made from such a busy organisation as the Castle Sigor. "It'll be impossible to find anything in this!" He dropped the listing on the desk.

Privately, Sir John agreed. "Well, we can always get someone to ring all the numbers and see who they are. But if it's an email or a modem attached to a PC, it'll be difficult to identify. In any case, I can't imagine Duvain would contact Moloc very often and we already know he was interrupted last night, before sending anything. Our only hope is that the number is stored in Duvain's computer communications files. Emil is working on that right now." Sir John continued relentlessly. "Who is Philippe Dupont? And why did he kill Duvain, do you think?"

"He is Giselle's current lover. I allow her that as you know, as long as it's within reason. We checked up on him, too!"

"Is it possible that Duvain introduced the two?" "I don't know; we'll have to ask Giselle." "Duvain was a drug addict," said Sir John flatly.

"How do you know that?" Jean de Sigor groaned and put his head in his hands.

"There were syringes around the body. It looked as though he normally used his scrotum for fixing. In this case, Philippe and Charles must have been engaged in some sort of shared fix that went horribly wrong. Charles's penis was chewed to a shred."

"Dear God, is there no end to this perversity!" moaned the Comte. "All our hopes, the Plan ... Is it all worth it?" he exclaimed.

Sir John stared at him with sympathy. He remembered their war days together. Life didn't get any easier, he thought. No matter what they tell you. "It may not be so bad, Jean. Maybe we can turn it to our advantage. After all, Moloc can hardly have planned for Duvain to be murdered, at least not yet. He won't know we have access to his computer, so he won't know what we've discovered. I think we should plan accordingly."

"You're right John. I must not panic. You are a valuable friend.

Come, let us go and see how Giselle is and what is being done to find the murderous bastard who did all this."

Unnoticed by the two highest-ranked men of the Priory Arcadia, the Nautonnier and one of the three Senechals, a small hairline crack had appeared in the smooth, hitherto featureless, surface of the ball of crystal from Childeric's grave which had nestled for a thousand years in its golden chalice on the desk between them. But who would explain the momentous significance of this to them? Who indeed? Who could tell them of the unravelling of sub-atomic vortices whose momentum was slowly but surely changing as the Christian aeon moves from Pisces further into Aquarius; *'luciferi vires accendit aquarius acres!'*

CHAPTER 23

JeanLuc showered and came back into his room at the Carolina Inn. He put on a robe and lay on the bed. Channel surfing on the TV with the remote, he paused on Channel 10—a God- botherer's slot. The screen showed a preacher speaking in a surprisingly civilised manner when compared to the demented ravings of the hyperthyroid crooks and charlatans that usually saturated the religious etherways.

'Send ten dollars now and God will forgive you. Send a hundred now and receive absolutely FREE God's blessing on your family. Allow twenty-eight days for delivery. Four-ninety-five post and packaging.'

JeanLuc turned up the volume slightly and listened with idle curiosity.

"Friends!" the man was saying. "What would JEEESUS have felt if He had returned to Earth and taken a taxi to the Vatican?

"Today, imagine with me for a moment, what would the man who declared 'My Kingdom is not of this Earth' have FELT, if He had been allowed to wander through the departments of the Administration of the Patrimony of the Holy See and the Vatican Bank?

"HOW would He have reacted to the teams of clerical stock-analysts, each with a phone prosthetic instead of a rosary, all worshipping the day-by-day, minute-by-minute fluctuations of the shares, securities and investments owned by the Roman Church? Where prayers are only offered to the Almighty if Virgin Vehicles or Consolidated Copper drops a share point?

"WHAT would He make of the banked layers of flickering computer consoles and the chattering printers that dominate the trading rooms of these Holy Institutions only a stone's throw from the last resting place of the Apostle Peter?

"I ASK YOU, what would the man, who compared the difficulty of a Karshoggi entering into the Kingdom of Heaven with that of a laden camel trying to pass through the eye of a needle, have said about the latest stock-market transactions that flush twenty-four hours a day, non-stop, through the TOILET BOWL OF SIN that is the Vatican today? YEA! By 'phone, by modem, by satellite, by microwave and by ultrasecret fibre optic networks!

"From evil Wall Street, from Godless Tokyo, Zurich, London, Hong Kong and NOW, may God forgive us, even Moscow!

"I ask you, Brothers and Sisters, to REFLECT on HOW He who said 'Blessed are the poor' would have reacted to Peter's Pence being used as Papal Pocket Money!"

The TV preacher paused and leaned forward to look more closely into the camera. His moon face filling the screen, he continued quietly. "Of course, my friends, Jesus would NEVER get very far today. Oh, no!

"As to turning over the tables of the moneychangers: there are no tables to turn over. If He had gained entry into the LOFTY cool marbled foyers of the Vatican Bank, He would be instantly videotaped from every angle by security cameras and LO! The high blue wail of armed PO-LEEECE would be upon him in a neeenar, neenar."

The Preacher winked confidentially at the camera and raised a blunt stubby forefinger to his lips. "So, how would he do it, Brothers and Sisters?

"Dear Friends. LISTEN closely and I'll tell you," he continued. "To have ANY impact whatsoever on the financial dealings of these new Temples to Mammon, Jesus would have to hack his way into the main Vatican computer by modem. BUT, this poses digital difficulties that would certainly require DEE-VINE intervention. Upon access, he could then introduce a software VIRUS. Yea! a HOLY VIRUS, a Virus, that would destroy the satanic computer, Hallelujah!" The preacher paused briefly for breath.

"That's one thing He could do. On the other hand, he could BUY up equity on the open market. YES, he could! He could become a majority shareholder, call an extraordinary General Meeting and attempt to oust the Board of Directors and its Chairman, the Pope!

"These, my friends, would TRULY be MIRACLES worthy of videotaping for posterity. These would TRULY merit Jesus the awed respect of a techno-cynical world!

"And now this...

'Heaven is THE soft soap. Let Heaven soothe your troubles and your cares

... Nothing is better for your skin than the Touch of Heaven ... You too can be sent to Heaven for only a dollar ninety-nine at all good stores near you ...

ONLY a dollar ninety-nine takes you to Heaven! '"

The phone beside the bed rang. JeanLuc zapped off the TV, reached over and picked it up. "Yeah, who is it?" he said.

"It's me."

"Ah, yes. Monsignor. Are we ready?"

"Yep, I'll pick you up in the lobby in half an hour. Bring that gorilla with you. I guess he's earned it."

*

Earlier, JeanLuc had been met at La Guardia by a phalanx of Biophar Drugs employees and security people and whisked through Customs and Immigration straight on to the next Piedmont flight to Raleigh-Durham.

About an hour before they landed at New York, JeanLuc had phoned from the plane to Maniato's New York apartment. "We have the Legacy. Landing in an hour's time. Just get us through without hassle." On receiving an affirmative, he'd handed the phone back to the stewardess and resumed his blank stare out at the black sky beyond the winking winglight. Beside him, Igor had drunk himself into a stupor on a succession of champagne cocktails. On the plastic foldaway table in front of him, there was a football team of uneaten Maraschino cherries and a logjam of toothpicks.

The muted roar of the jets matched the roar of mental static in JeanLuc's mind. He didn't know how he felt; he didn't want to know. He knew only that, to survive, he had to continue like this; closed down emotionally, operating only on intellect—in zombie mode. Maybe one day this would change, maybe not; but his life would continue. He had to continue, otherwise there would be no reason for Sophia's martyrdom; no meaning to the Fulfilment—at least for him.

He tried to forget the anguish of loss on Dmitri's face and the hysterical grief of Saskia . There was nothing he could do; no comfort he could give; it was a burden of guilt not even Job could shoulder.

He must submit once again to his Fate—any other road led to madness and disaster.

179

Joel Maniato put the phone down and rolled off the bed. He picked up the pink furry dice from the floor and used the attached key to unlock the steel Krieg handcuffs that held Shelley Lang to the bedrail. She groaned and stretched with relief, curling up on the bed, thumb in mouth. He threw the cover over her naked body and went to shower and dress. He had a lot to do. His tongue ached from the amount of oral dictation that Shelley had required of him the previous evening. He popped a Bennie and breezed out into the street to catch a cab to the Biophar Drugs HQ.

At the office, he made the arrangements for JeanLuc and his companion to be picked up and transferred directly onto a flight to Raleigh-Durham and then booked the Company jet for himself and the Cardinal to fly out the next day.

Later in the morning, he called Duke University in North Carolina. "Dr.Spikel, please. Dept of Antiquities." He was put through at once. "Dr.Spikel? This is Joel Maniato of Biophar Drugs."

"The pharmaceutical company in the Research Triangle park?"
"Yes, sir. RTP, that's right."

"What can I do for you, Mr.Maniato?"

"We have acquired a rare and valuable icon from Russia and we would like you to have a look at it with a possible view to expert restoration. Cardinal Joseph Mirphy of New York recommended that we get in touch with you as being the best in the field."

"Well, I have a very busy teaching schedule at the moment and I don't normally accept outside work," demurred the Professor.

"Believe me, sir. This is an extremely important and rare find and of course you and the University would be suitably compensated."

"In what way?"

"We would naturally feel obliged to make a contribution to the University funds and a one thousand dollar advance fee to yourself. Thereafter you will be paid pro rata at a rate of $1000 per day of your time."

"I want the advance as a banker's draft. Anything else?"

Joel sighed. "Two tickets to the Duke-Chapel Hill basketball game on Friday?" Dammit, it had taken him months of wheeling and dealing to get those tickets.

"Done. Give me a call when you have the money and let me have the tickets as soon as possible. Can you give me any clue of what I'll be working on?"

"I'm afraid not, Professor. I don't know myself, to be honest. Oh, and do you have any objection to signing a secrecy agreement between us?"

"No, I suppose not—if you insist. But if it is an important find, I would like to publish in technical journals."

"I suspect that might be allowed in due course, with our written agreement."

"Fine. I look forward to working with you, Maniato. Don't forget the banker's draft!"

Joel put the phone down. Whatever happened to all those nice doddering old professor-types who did things for free or the academic interest? They're as bad as the rest of us, he thought.

His next call was to Technical Services. He ordered the Biophar Drugs communications satellite to be returned to its old position above the Canary Islands and the Eastern Atlantic. He wondered if there was a way of making it disappear before the new Japanese owners moved in. Maybe he could sell it to someone before it was listed in the assets.

He dialled the Cardinal's private number. It was picked up immediately. "Monsignor? It's Joel Maniato here. Good news!"

"Spit it out then, Maniato."

"JeanLuc just called from the plane. He has the goods and is due in at La Guardia very shortly. I've made arrangements for him to be picked up and put on a flight to Raleigh. We can follow in the Company jet tomorrow."

"That's good news, Joel. I'm pleased. Have you contacted Dr.Spikel yet?"

"Yes, sir. He's agreed to our terms and is awaiting our call."

"Good, good. Joel, since we'll be in Raleigh tomorrow any chance of tickets to the basketball on Friday?"

"Sorry, Your Eminence. I had to throw in my last pair to swing the deal with Professor Spikel."

"Oh well, in that case maybe it is time I made an impromptu visit to the Raleigh-Durham diocese—that might flush out a couple by

Friday."

"If you manage to get a spare, can I have it, sir? asked Joel tentatively. "I'm not that bloody holy," snarled the Cardinal, ending the conversation.

Joel replaced the receiver and gave it the finger. "Up yours, Your Shittyness," he muttered. He felt tired and hungry. Maybe he would go out for a hamburger—just an ordinary non-whopper plain burger and a Coke not coke. Take a breather from the vampiric sexual excesses of Shelley and the monotony of the robotic Japanese and their legal team who were pressing him for their attention. No sushi, no fancy white wine; just a fix of boring old cheeseburger with its slice of pale limp acidic gherkin. His mouth started to water. Boy, he loved junk food!

So! Project Maraschino was coming to a head. A culmination of nearly thirty years' work, and like all things it had started from such few beginnings. Cardinal Mirphy paced his room in a fever of excitement. The Papacy was within his grasp. He had an edge! If he could only hold off Von Helsinger and Paliato, the Papal rottweilers, he would be home and dry. It would be difficult but possible. Reports back from his contacts in the Curia suggested that the Holy Father was getting more and more bizarre in his behaviour and was now sometimes found at his desk in a catatonic state. The jostling and whisperings that always preceded a change in the Papacy had already begun—the Church could not function with a Leader who was non compos mentis; not with the the Four Apocalyptic Horsemen snorting in the offing. Mirphy could recognise the psychic prefigurations, he could see the future and he wanted to be he who dipped his toe into this particular vortex of destiny.

The meeting with Von Helsinger, that autumn, had been a guarded psychic boxing match between two heavyweights. The suspicious Von Helsinger launched into a flurry of jabbing questions as soon as he stepped into the New York Legate's room. His first were about the invitation to the Pope to attend that Summit in January. But Mirphy was ready for him; parrying with a defence of overwhelming financial detail, accountants' meetings and a detailed presentation on the proposed sale of Biophar Drugs and other assets. To keep him further off guard and deflect him from his true purpose, which was to bend

Mirphy to his will, Mirphy had also arranged an intensive social agenda and Special Masses with all the trimmings to which he'd invited the Kennedy family and other luminaries of the New York Catholic world.

At one point, as they were kneeling together side by side in full purple-and-gold regalia in New York Cathedral, the massed voice of the choir soaring into the rafters, Otto Von Helsinger turned his mitred head towards him and in a low furious voice spoke in his ear. "Don't think I don't know what you're up to, Mirphy—it won't work with me. You're getting too big for your boots, and I will recommend that the Holy Father recall you for other duties. Opus Dei is looking for good new incardinations in Iraq and Argentina."

Mirphy stared coolly back into Von Helsinger's angry button-black eyes as the notes of the Te Deum reverberated gloriously through the Cathedral's acoustic pleroma. "Up yours, Fatso" he said smilingly and rose from his knees to glorify God once more.

Mirphy smiled at this memory. But his strategy was not without serious risk. Von Helsinger and his Italian poodle Paliato were powerful and dangerous. Nevertheless, short of having him 'suicided' they couldn't touch him—at the moment. And now he had the Carpocratian Legacy he could really insert the pussy amongst the peckers; or is it the other way around.

Jean would be pleased and he, Joe Mirphy, would be vindicated against that supercilious Brit, John Redcliff, who'd thought Project Maraschino was a time-wasting exercise.

It was time for another strategy meeting—they would want to see the icons and he hadn't yet heard of the outcome of the raid on the Ecole Biblique or the status of the marriage arrangements to be made between JeanLuc and Jean's daughter. Also they needed to assess the damage done to their operations orchestrated by the Machiavellian figure of Father Moloc, whom he'd never met—very few people had. Apparently, he lived in hidden seclusion in Paris and by all accounts was a fanatical upholder of pre-Vatican II orthodoxy. Now there was a real enemy that Mirphy feared; an enemy subtle, intelligent and lethal who understood where the real wellsprings of power lay and could strike at the core of things. If he was going to nominate anyone for a satanic role, then Father Moloc would be the choice; played by Robert

183

de Niro, thought Mirphy irrelevantly. Nor would it surprise him if Von Helsinger was colluding with him. The whole nasty affair smacked of the hand of the Inquisition or possibly P2.

"Sister Mary?" he called out. "Pack my bags for me, will you. We're off to North Carolina on a visit. Three days probably—not much more."

"Yes, Father Joseph. When are we leaving?"

"Tomorrow morning, Sister. Oh and it is possible I may have to fly to France next week."

"The Lord's work is never done," she said blandly. Father Moloc would want to know of these new developments, she thought.

From Durham, she would send him a nice postcard of the Blue Ridge Mountains.

CHAPTER 24

"What's this three-day Summit Meeting in France you've marked me down for in January? I never authorised this!" United States President Robert 'Popeye' Dillon glanced inquiringly from his official diary to his secretary, Madeleine Feroc.

"Mr.Folditch asked me to put that in, sir."

"Since when do the CIA fix my schedule for me, Madeleine?"

"He said he would discuss it with you, Mr. President. Shall I cancel it?"

"Yes. But I want to know what the hell is going on. Get Langley on the phone, I want to speak with that slippery son of a bitch."

'Popeye' Dillon looked down at the entry and frowned. He always took a holiday in that week. The family would be at Camp David. There was no way, short of nuclear confrontation, he was going to change this fixture—his wife would give him hell. It was part of their secret contract, drawn up when he was running for office; he could do his President thing as long as he agreed to a set of family priorities, one of which was this week to themselves in January.

His wife was quite capable of ruining him politically. Like his predecessors, he'd been no angel as far as other women were concerned, but more importantly it was she who had gotten him what he thought of as the 'Rapture' vote. This voting block had been a decisive factor in the election. It was his wife, Colleen Fraser Spiggot, a fundamentalist 'born-again' Christian who had convinced the Mormons, the TV evangelists and all the other loony tunes to endorse his candidature. If he was honest with himself, those people scared him shitless, but once his wife started motoring the Jesus theme with hyperthyroid intensity they all fell into line and all he had to do was mouth Amen. They treated her like the Virgin Mary or Margaret Thatcher. Politically, therefore, she was a godsend, but hell on earth for a normal man to live with, which was one of the primary motivations for running for the Presidency—he could get away from her!

As penance, he had to endure that whole week in January in the bosom of his family, 'to refresh his spirit' and 'talk to the children' as

Colleen would say. Their awful children, all five of them, that cost him a fortune in upkeep and ran to their dragon mother at the slightest upset. Blame Daddy had become the recurrent motif of their family life. If they fell in the park, blame Daddy; if someone teased them at school, blame Daddy. Sometimes he despaired; he was the goddamned President of America, the most powerful man on the planet, akin to a god and yet his eldest daughter still fucked all her security guards no matter how ugly and his wife still ranted on that he should repent his sins and read the goddamned Book of Mormon.

His secretary handed him the phone. "Mr.Folditch for you, sir."

"Thank you, Madeleine. That'll be all for now. Oh and make an appointment for Rosa Roncalli, please. And don't look at me like that, she is important to me!" She nodded and left the Oval Office.

"Ah, Michael. How are you? Still in business, ha, ha! Listen, what's this thing you want me to go to in January?"

Deep in the metal and concrete heart of the Pentagon, Mike Folditch, CIA Chief, grimaced as he held the glacé cherry red phone to his ear. Oh, shit! he thought. Here we go.

"It is an important meeting of world and European leaders, Mr.President. We think you should go. We were going to brief you a little nearer the time." He sucked a deep puff from the Havana Gold Castro Special that smouldered aromatically in the cut -glass ashtray next to the photo-portrait of his wife and kids on one side, and the picture of himself in Navy uniform shaking hands with J.Edgar on the other. He'd had the polished brass spittoons removed from his office as an anachronism. Those few Senators from the sticks who still chewed, kept missing and getting brown gobs of tobacco juice all over the Star Spangled Banner that stood beside his desk. He was proud of his flag. Let them spit in the White House, but not here!

"Well, it's not on," said the President." Any other time of the year perhaps, but not that week. And I don't want you to put things in my diary without proper warning and discussion in future. Got that?" The phone went dead before Folditch could answer. Folditch looked at it with disgust as if it were a dead fish and placed it back on its hook. Probably the fucking stars were not right, he thought bitterly. He had nothing but contempt for the President's unhealthy reliance on the

186

astrological forecasts of Rosa Roncalli.

Sometime in the 1980s, during Queen Nancy's reign, the CIA had done a study of astrology using the big Cray mainframe in the Pentagon War Room. They'd fed the computer with every planetary and zodiacal detail; movements, orbits, conjunctions; the lot, including all the additional scientific data from NASA and the Observatories—stuff which was not available to any astrologer. Then they asked the computer to compile astrological charts for all the famous or infamous names they could think of—including 'Popeye' Dillon of course. The result was pure baloney, hogwash, rubbish, whatever you wanted to call it. Careful statistical analysis of all the possible points of concurrence between the computer predictions and the President's actual life revealed only random correlations of absolutely no significance. If the President was not important enough to be of astrologically significant, then who the hell was? Folditch had asked himself. They'd even gone on to analysing the President's life and character by palmistry. They'd needed his palm print anyway for the nuclear trigger mechanism. But there was nothing in the lines of his hand that might denote a life of significance—no star lines under the forefinger or any other signs. According to their analyses, President Bob Dillon could have been any old plain Joe out there in the great mass of American consumers.

The only charts that had borne any retroactive resemblance to what the CIA had in their files about their lives were the Dalai Lama, a Brit physicist named William Thomson, some Indian weirdo Sri Sathya Sai Baba, and an obscure French aristocrat Jean de Sigor. These positives had irritated Folditch so much that he'd ordered an immediate investigation of these men as well as a re-run on the computer. A peculiar feature of computer runs on these particular astrological profiles was that they had absorbed minutes of the massive Cray artificial-intelligence time compared with the usual split second it took for most analyses. Invariably the computer would ask for more detail like a more accurate birth-time.

Once, Folditch asked the computer to do his own chart which duly came back after a microsecond of computation. He was a Scorpio with a rising sign in Pisces. He didn't bother to read the rest and shredded the printout immediately so no one else could see it; especially the computer staff who were the nosiest and most superstitious people he knew, apart from actors and politicians— always worried about glitches and viruses. And then he'd had a couple of them cashiered from the Service when he found out that they were authoring the syndicated astrological forecasts that appeared in many of the daily newspapers.

On reflection, he should have had them 'terminated with extreme prejudice' because they were now in Hollywood doing a lucrative 'Stars for the Stars' service using a variation of the same software the Pentagon had used in their own study. It was still rubbish though—by every conceivable yardstick.

Folditch took another meditative toke off the Cuban. He would have to figure out another way of getting Popeye to go to that Summit. He picked up one of the other phones and dialled a number. When the answer machine gave its beep, he said, "This is for Cornelius. We need to meet," and hung up.

"Mr.President! It's so nice to see you again!" Rosa Roncalli, self-styled Astrologer to the Stars, swept dramatically into the Oval Office like a mezzo-soprano hitting the stage at La Scala.

Madeleine followed in her exuberant wake. "Can I get you any refreshment, Mrs.Roncalli?" she asked charmingly. A cup of hemlock perhaps, she thought churlishly.

"Noo, noo. To see our beloved Leader is refreshment itself!" gushed Rosa Roncalli as she settled her bulky figure on the sofa that had embraced the well-dressed tight-assed buttocks of all the rich and famous of the day. The sofa took Rosa's weight and gave thanks to J.C.Penney that few, since Nixon, dared anymore to fart into its fabric. Maybe it should consider writing its memoir—

'Bums in the Oval Office' sounded quite a catchy title. Maybe Joe Esterhaz would do the screenplay.

Rosa silently regarded the President with shrewd dark gypsy eyes until Madeleine Feroc had left them. "So, what's the trouble, Popsicle. Tell Mama," she said.

"I wish you wouldn't do this, Rosa." "Do what, honeybunch?"

"Play the gypsy astrologer role to such an outrageous extent. I mean, look at you! That red dress and all those rings in your ears and that flashy vulgar jewellery. They all think you're an evil witch!"

"But it's fun, sweetiepie. I love dressing for the role."

"Yeah, but they think you're a joke and I'm getting a hard time in the Senate. My wife would have you burned at the stake if she knew. You know that, don't you? I'm serious, there's no limit to what these fundamentalists will do!"

"Ah, fuck 'em. I can look after myself. Don't worry cupcake! So, shall we do it then?" she said coyly.

The President sighed, went across to the drinks cabinet and poured himself a stiff slug of Kentucky sourmash. "The CIA have booked me into some kind of a Summit in Europe. I'd like to go but it coincides with my week with the family at Camp David. You know how my wife feels about that. I would need to have a hell of a good excuse for going. So, give me a reading, Rosa. Is it worth me breaking that date with my family?"

"When is it exactly?" "January seventeenth."

Jean was right! She thought to herself. The fool will make the decision whether to attend, based on her advice. She felt a huge thrill of power pass through her and the shudder this generated was no act. My God, I have control over the President of the US, she thought. But then sense quickly prevailed; compared to Jean de Sigor, Robert Dillon was a powerless peasant. No way was she prepared to break from Jean for this jerk; the consequences would be too awful in this and the next world. Oh well, back to business!

Expertly Rosa shuffled a pack of Tarot cards, tapped the edges straight and placed them face down on the coffee table. "Don't worry about these, sugarlips" she said. "They're just to help me concentrate; they don't mean anything!" She took the top card and flipped it.

The Raven! That was a shock! Damn, she hadn't expected that one—in fact she'd carefully sequenced the cards beforehand. She turned over the next one: The Lovers reversed. And the next; Queen of Cups. And the next: The Grim Reaper!

Rosa stared at the four cards with bewilderment. She'd removed the Grim Reaper card beforehand; she always did that—no one liked to see it turn up during a reading. She swept the cards together back into the pile and started again from the top, hurriedly flipping through the pack.

"So Rosa, what do you think? You look a bit disturbed!"

Hastily recovering a semblance of composure, Rosa looked at the President and regurgitated mechanically what Jean had told her to say. "It is a time of great changes and you must be a part of them, shaping them, or there will be a disastrous rift. You must go, Mr.President, I feel it is most important that you go."

Rosa felt completely exhausted and her good humour had deserted her. She found it difficult even to come up with the usual banter that was part of the interplay between her and the President. She wanted to get home, curl up in a ball in her bed and try not to think about the meaning of those dreadful cards.

"I will give it some thought, Rosa," said the President. She knew he would go. He always did as she told him. Staggering slightly, she got up to go. "So soon, my dear? I thought we could have some lunch. I'm not due in the Senate until this afternoon."

"No, I really must go, chickadee. I don't feel so well. Maybe I'm coming down with something. White House flu, probably," she said wanly.

"All right, I'll see you again soon. Promise?"

What has the old fart done to her! Madeleine wondered with amazement as Rosa tottered out a bundle of rags compared to the galleon in full sail that had been the metaphor of her arrival. Rosa dived into the dark welcoming recesses of a limo that smoothly moved off past that famous green lawn on which Frank Zappa had wanted to 'do it'. Or was it Lou Reed or the Doors? Rosa could no longer remember.

She stared unseeingly out of the darkened bulletproof window. It was not just the sequence of cards that had startled her; it was the fact that she'd removed the Grim Reaper cards before setting off. She always did that without fail. The gut-wrenching feeling of teetering on the brink of a psychic abyss still remained with her. She'd not felt such confusion and fear since her Initiation all those years ago in the Sixties. Reality was cracking up, dimensions were being unzipped and she was afraid! She was terrified that if she closed her eyes, just the once, she might see straight through into the cold starless heart of the universe and her spirit would be sucked into a void of nothingness; extinguished like the flare of a match in a hurricane. She cursed all those past acid trips! She was far too old for this. No more flashes, please God. No more visions! She started to weep in terror as she felt the tingling in the base of her spine; the melting feeling; the sparkles of sensation that rocketed up her spinal column bursting like fireworks in her brain. ... The watoosi!

"Are you all right, Madame?" The limo driver had lowered the connecting screen after stopping the vehicle on the emergency hard shoulder of the Beltway.

Rosa Roncalli, Astrologer to the Stars, Croisé of the Priory Arcadia, was lying collapsed on the back seat. Her eyes were staring open in a face gone blotchy and blue with death. In the throes of her torment, she had swallowed her tongue.

Number nine, number nine, number nine ...

CHAPTER 25

JeanLuc and Igor found their way to the lobby and met there. Igor dropped the briefcase and the plastic tube containing the Legacy onto the sofa beside JeanLuc and went to the hotel shop. He bought himself a comic to read, thinking that he might as well try to learn American while he was here. JeanLuc ordered latté coffee and two chocolate donuts from the waitress, and the men sat in silence waiting for Cardinal Mirphy to pick them up. Igor flicked through the pages of his comic.

Shortly after they had sat down, a young man approached holding out a religious pamphlet. He was a clean-cut crew cut Preppy type uniformed in chinos, weejuns and branded sports- shirt. Mouth full of chocolate donut, Igor stared at him in disbelief; he'd only seen such pretty youths in the pages of magazines lusted over by the homosexuals among Polish long-distance drivers and in old posters of the Hitler Youth.

"Can I tell you about Jesus, gents?" He thrust the pamphlet forward as if warding off the evil eye. JeanLuc put down his cup of coffee and stood up. The kid, slightly nervous of the two battered-looking men, backed away a few steps. "Are you ready to be saved? There's not much time, you know," he went on determinedly. "This will tell you all you need to know; all about the conspiracies that are undermining the lives of good decent Americans. Are you on our side, sirs?"

"Okay, young man. I got five minutes. Give me your sales pitch. I don't want no leaflet. I want to hear what you have to say to me, boy."

The boy's face brightened and he immediately started his well-rehearsed peroration. "Brother in Jesus. I speak the plain truth. I speak of the fundamental truth as revealed in the Bible by Ezekiel and St. John the Evangelist.

"Beware my friend! The Antichrist is now amongst us. The World has entered the Last Days!

"There will be a time of terrible tribulation and God will avenge Himself against the wicked.

"The World will be utterly destroyed. But do not despair, my friend.

192

The second coming is at hand.

"Jesus will descend in glory, the Dead will rise from their graves and a new kingdom of heaven be established.

"But you must REPENT, because only the ELECT and the SAVED will be allowed in."

"And who do you think is the Antichrist?" asked JeanLuc amused.

"The Antichrist of the Book of Revelation is the ten-crowned Beast of the European Economic Community. It is predicted that the nations of the EEC will wage war against us and will defeat us and enslave us in sorrow. The Bible says this war will last for two and half years and cost two thirds of the population of Britain and America.

"The war will start without warning with the nuclear annihilation of all major cities and end with the Battle of Armageddon to be fought at Megiddo in Israel. The Antichrist will be defeated and Jesus will TRIUMPH!"

The boy's eyes had glazed over with the effort of remembering all this guff but with ever-increasing zeal, sensing a possible convert, he continued dramatically. "But! If you REPENT now, allow yourself to be SAVED and make a small CONTRIBUTION to the funds of our Church, you will be spared the carnage to come and be RAPTURED to a place of SAFETY!" He waxed the lyric.

"At the LAST TRUMP, all TRUE believers will suddenly disappear, dematerialise, evaporate in the flicker of an eyelid from their homes, their offices, their golf courses, and their cars, and will rocket upwards to be with Big J himself. From a position of shelter, amidst the celestial choir of angels, you will have a grandstand view of the unfolding of the Battle of Armageddon! Jesus guarantees it! JESUS LOVES US!"

Igor looked up at JeanLuc, who looked at the zealous Preppy, who, in turn, looked back at JeanLuc, hope of a possible convert shining through his pink un-lined Southern-fried features. JeanLuc smiled benignly at him and said, "I love you too, brother." He took a step closer, bunched his fist and punched the guy hard in the solar plexus. The boy went down and lay writhing on the lobby floor. JeanLuc bent over him and shouted in his ear. "You're full of SHIT, you hear? Full of shit. If you ever come near me again, I'll rapture your BALLS into HELL, you hear?"

The manager of the Inn came rushing out of his office, together with the receptionist. "What's the trouble? What have you done? What's going on?" he bleeted.

JeanLuc turned towards them. "This man made HOMOSEXUAL advances to me!" he shouted accusingly. "This man was soliciting money from me for his AIDS treatment!" he yelled at the top of his voice. "He has AIDS!" he screamed.

Everybody in the lobby, including the manager suddenly seemed to disappear. Maybe they've been 'raptured' thought JeanLuc.

The Preppy staggered to his feet, clutching his stomach, his face a mask of tears and bewilderment. "Why?" he gasped hoarsely, "why did you do that?"

"It is a Time of Tribulation, sport. A Time of Tribulation" said JeanLuc, much cheered by his violence. Igor shrugged and picked up the comic he was trying to decipher. Yanks! He'd never understand them.

A big old long Lincoln Continental Mk I slid to a smooth halt outside and the rear doors opened. Cardinal Mirphy emerged blinking in the harsh Carolina sunlight. A younger man in a sharp business suit cleared the way before him, as his eminence strode commandingly into the lobby. Seeing JeanLuc, the Cardinal went to him and embraced him like a favourite son. Igor braced himself for another possible fight— the business-type looked dissipated and weak, so he foresaw no problem from that quarter. He relaxed further when JeanLuc responded positively to this engulfment by the tall priest.

As they both headed back out together, they ignored the whipped dog of a Preppy that preceded them out of the glass exit doors clutching his guts, muttering fascist racist insults under his breath. He was from Greenville, and by God they knew what to do with cocksucking motherfucking niggerloving Jewboy Papists in Greenville, North Carolina. Yes, sirree! The Grand Dragon would hear about this. A flaming rubber necklace was too good for them.

Igor collected the briefcase and the plastic tube and followed them out to the ancient gas-guzzler that grumbled quietly by the kerb adding about a thousand ppm of carbon dioxide to the Greenhouse Effect every second. Wow! This is macho Americano! he thought, admiring

194

the high polish, the white-walled tyres and the acres of glass and chrome. This was more like the America of the old propaganda films—the motif of America they all secretly admired back in the Eastern Bloc.

'Back in the USSR. You don't know how lucky you are, boy!'

The antique Continental rolled smoothly to the security barrier at the entrance gate of the Biophar Drugs Corporation R&D facility in the RTP. The barrier went up immediately and the chauffeur drove them through, down the long winding driveway between the pines, either side of which stood a tall electrified fence, topped with the latest computer-optimised designer barbed-wire.

"What did he say?" asked Joel Maniato.

"He says those fences look better than those on the old Berlin Wall and what are you trying to keep out?"

"Yeah, Igor is right. Security is tight here. It is the animal experimentation and testing that Biophar Drugs has to do on its products. The animal-rights fanatics are quite persistent and determined. " He looked at them blandly. "And of course some of the transgenics can get a bit wild!"

The car approached an uncompromisingly futuristic glass-and-steel building like something Ayn Rand's architect might have designed for Margaret Thatcher—all the sharp angles and multi-levels of a Mondian. They stopped at an imposing entrance canopy flanked by several flagpoles sporting the Biophar Drugs flag or the Stars and Stripes. In front of the entrance was a manicured green lawn sloping gently down to a mirror-tiled pool whose crystal waters reflected the Carolina blue sky above. Narcissistic Koi carp drifted like multicoloured Zeppelins amongst the reflections of clouds.

They went into a lobby as tall, cool and marbled as any big city bank's. The receptionist came forward immediately. "Welcome to Biophar Drugs, gentlemen. Please follow me and I'll take you straight to the Board Room."

"Hi, Josie! We'll skip the Board Room bit and go straight down to the labs, if you don't mind. You're looking fantastic honey, as always!" Joel winked lecherously at her.

"Thank you, Mr.Maniato. Good to see yo'all again," said the receptionist demurely and she turned on high-heeled shoes, shapely

195

stockinged legs to lead the way. They followed her blonde bobbed hair, tight black-skirted wiggle down to the underground levels. Here, the hushed carpeted executive corridors were replaced by brightly lit tunnels crowded with white-coated scientists and technicians moving between laboratories filled with computer screens, winking multicoloured lights and whirring, humming equipment. Hazard signs everywhere proclaimed the lurking presence of radioisotopes, inflammables, biohazards and toxic chemicals.

"Is Dr.Spikel here yet, Josie?" asked Joel as they arrived at the door of the ultra-clean aseptic pharmaceutical packing-room that had been set aside for them.

"No, sir. He said he'd be here this afternoon after lunch."

"When he arrives, show him up to the Hospitality Suite until we're ready to see him."

"Okay. Here we are sirs. Please get changed in that shower room in there. There are special paper suits available for you to wear. Is this to go in?" Josie pointed at the plastic tube carried by Igor.

Igor looked questioningly at JeanLuc who asked "What happens to it?"

"It will go through this slot here into a sterilised Perspex box, fitted internally with whole arm latex gloves for you to use when you get inside." JeanLuc indicated to Igor to give her the tube and she pushed it through the slot in the wall. "It will be waiting for you when you get in. I'll leave you now if you don't mind. I'll see yo'all later." She smiled cheerily at them and went back the way they'd come; followed all the way by the hooded envious rat eyes of the male scientists. She was an untouchable. She was an angel from the daylight regions of the Executive high above them. They would have to remain content to E-mail obscene suggestions to the white coated mustachio'd witch-dykes that inhabited their strange fevered world of scientific fantasy, biochemical magic, designer drugs and rodent torture.

Whilst he was changing, Joe Mirphy wondered if they were making a mistake. It seemed somehow sacrilegious to reveal the Legacy, an icon of possibly incomparable sanctity and religious value, in this aseptic temple to Atheism through which a daily Holocaust of God's little furry creatures passed away, bombarded with carcinogens, ad libitum PCB, irradiated, flash frozen, dissected, and operated on; looted for cloning cells, for DNA, for blood, for still-twitching organs, for lymph, for seminal fluid , for subdivisions of everything. All sacrificed in the cause of a non-generic variant of aspirin, a food flavouring like FlavAdd or a cosmetic liposome lotion. Forget the big problems and the fancy stuff like AIDS, cancer, or Alzheimer's—leave that to the NIH at Bethesda. These boy and girl PhDs were here to make Biophar Drugs money-spinning products.

If they didn't like it they could try up the Cornwallis yellow brick road at Glaxo Wellcome where they'd find exactly the same situation; the same Fisher or Sigma chemical catalogue, the same Sprague-Dawley rats staring out through the same cage bars at them with their cute trusting pink eyes and immaculately groomed white fur, as the scientists reach into the sawdust, grab their scaly tails, lift them up and swing them down with an audible thwack against the edge of a stainless steel basin unit. They could watch with the same impassivity as the rats kick their legs in a final spasm of death agony in the ether gas chamber, before being laid out neatly on a white aseptically clean paper towel, blood seeping from their cute little noses and bright yellow urine from their death-discharged bladders, ready for snipping open with the bright stainless-steel scissors and scalpels that glitter under the merciless fluorescents.

Cardinal Mirphy shook off this horrific vision of what scientists did in their rodent, monkey and doggy Dachau. He couldn't believe it. Nobody sane could do work like that, he thought. He came out of his cubicle dressed in the blue paper suit. No more ridiculous than some of my church vestments, he supposed. The others, similarly dressed, were waiting for him in the anteroom to the clean room beyond.

They were all keyed up and jittery. The environment was so alien to Igor that he felt as if he'd been beamed up into the orbiting space station. But it was better than being stuck in a motorway jam up at Smolensk in a blizzard or being chased around Moscow streets by the FSB or worse. However, he could certainly use a shot of good vodka. That pale piss of American beer gave him a headache and had gotten him up several times in the night to urinate in the hand basin.

JeanLuc pushed his way through the rubber flapdoors, followed by the others. The Carpocratian Legacy lay ahead of them, in a Perspex box on a stainless steel table lit from above by a high- wattage floodlight. Beside the set- up stood a couple of gas cylinders whose valves and hoses were attached to the Perspex chamber.

"Okay," said JeanLuc. "Everything seems to be here. Shall I start, Monsignor?" He looked at Mirphy. Mirphy nodded but was distinctly nervous—maybe he should say a prayer.

The others watched as JeanLuc turned on the valve at the cylinder to flood the chamber with nitrogen gas. "The nitrogen gas passes through these blue crystals of drying agent," he remarked, "the nitrogen is inert and dry, that way we prevent water-vapour and oxygen spoiling the contents." He pushed his arms into the long latex gloves that protruded into the chamber and took hold of the sturdy grey plastic tube that had travelled with him from Russia. He untwisted the caps on the ends and gently shook out the polystyrene packing chips that Dmitri had managed to find.

His eyesight blurred briefly with tears as he recalled the circumstances surrounding the getting of this artefact—he hoped it was going to be worth it. Laying the tube down, JeanLuc extracted his arms from the gloves and took a tissue from the box nearby to wipe his face. "Joel, can you handle the videocamera? We should take a record of everything we do."

"Sure thing, JeanLuc. I have it right here. There's plenty of light. You go ahead and don't mind me." Joel brought the videocamera on its tripod close to the chamber, focused it on the package inside and set it rolling while JeanLuc stuck his arms back into the gloves. Joseph Mirphy and Igor stood by looking on.

JeanLuc extracted from the plastic tube, the three rods comprising the Carpocratian Legacy. Each was wrapped tightly in old Izvestia newspaper and tightly bound with tape. He laid the three packets on the floor of the chamber and taking a scalpel from the supply that lay ready, he cut away the newspaper wrapping revealing the metallic rods they'd found hidden in the brass frame of the iconostasis in Rasputin's dark snowbound underground chapel.

"Your Eminence. This is how we found the Legacy in their original state. You will note that there are three hollow rods or tubes made of ancient copper or bronze metal. Although corroded, they appear to be intact. At one point, they might have been sheathed in leather as you can see traces of skin attached here." JeanLuc held up each rod and turned it around slowly so that the videocamera could get everything in shot. "I'm now going to attempt to open the first rod. It looks as though it is sealed at either end with wax or animal glue." JeanLuc took a rod and started to cut away at the seals. He pulled away from one end a plug of hardened wax about an inch in length. A reddish-coloured sand started to trickle out; upending the tube allowed a substantial volume of sand to fall out.

They all stared at this pyramid of sand. Was that it? Was that all that was left of the Carpocratian Legacy after two thousand years? Only dust?! Joseph Mirphy felt the ravening wolves of panic circling the campfire of his composure. His dreams and hopes began to evaporate like so much mist. He bit his lip. Igor looked on stolidly—he hoped it would be time for lunch soon.

JeanLuc took up the rod again and tapped it gently on the still sealed end. Suddenly, a stick-like object fell out of the tube. They all cried out in excitement, pressing forward to look at what now lay on the floor of the chamber. Carefully, JeanLuc picked it up and turned it around in front of the camera.

"It looks as though we have something at last, gentlemen. Something of great antiquity and highly unusual." Suddenly, for a second, he had a vision of a dark bearded Jewish face grinning out at him. Collecting himself with an effort, he cleared a space in the chamber. "It appears to be a stick of bone or ivory around which has been wrapped some very thin cloth material, cotton maybe even silk. Before I start to unwind it , we ought to consider whether to mount it on something, a board or plate. It may be so fragile that we'll never be able to rewind it."

"How about between sheet glass, JeanLuc," said the Cardinal.

"Yes, that's good. We'll do that. Can you get that, Joel? They need to measure one metre by two metres and we'll want six sheets brought in. Make sure they clean it well. Spotless."

"I'll get it done at once." Joel picked up the internal phone and gave the necessary orders. "It'll be about an hour JeanLuc. Anything else you think we'll need?"

"Yeah. I want three more boxes like this for the other scrolls, and for this one without the packing material." He paused to consider. "I think I'll unpack them in this box, then transfer them to the new ones and unroll them directly onto the glass sheet. Okay?"

"That sounds good to me, JeanLuc" said Joel and dialled out again with the new instructions.

They all sat down to wait. JeanLuc's eyes kept drifting over to the scrolls. He was sure he'd seen something like that before—maybe in a dream.

CHAPTER 26

"You want me to clean and restore a portrait which is two thousand years old?" he asked incredulously. "You gotta be kidding. Who is it of? Jesus Christ?"

This joking remark did not elicit any laughter or smile from any of the assembled group in the Board Room. All looked at him with the utmost solemnity and seriousness.

"You are quite correct, Dr.Spikel. We have here the banker's draft that you requested as a condition of your services. We want you to start at once."

Joel Maniato handed over the money. Josef Spikel glanced at it to check the amount, folded and put it away in the pocket of his shirt. He looked slightly startled. "So what is it? Some kind of icon or what?" he blurted excitedly. "Where is it?"

"They are waiting for your attention below in one of our laboratories. But please, before we start you must sign this secrecy agreement. Because of the important nature of this, it is imperative that no word gets out until the right time—after suitable preparations have been made."

Having looked at the faces around him, which seemed to be glowing with an inner light and tension, Spikel quickly read the document, grabbed the proffered pen and scrawled his signature on the bottom.

"Now that you have signed this document, we can disclose to you what we have found. But I give you fair warning, Dr.Spikel. If you break your word to us, I cannot answer for the consequences to you personally. This is a standard legal secrecy agreement; but believe me, if word gets out then what will be done to you and yours will be strictly non-standard and illegal. You have now stepped beyond the bounds of normal existence and no amount of paper will protect either you or us, if things go wrong."

Josef Spikel listened open-mouthed to this. What the hell were they talking about? What was going on? "Come on, don't give me this bullshit! I have an international reputation. I am consulted by ..."

"We know all that, but as you will see, things are different in this

201

case. The stakes are truly immense," interrupted Joel. "Please, let me introduce you to these other gentlemen. This is His Eminence Joseph Mirphy, Cardinal of New York; this is JeanLuc Kuovic and Igor Golemov who located the icons. If you will sit down, His Eminence has agreed to summarise the situation and then we will show you what we have found."

Cardinal Mirphy began. "Thank you for coming, Professor. I'm sorry about all the formalities but I know you'll come to understand, with me, that this is the beginning of a tremendously exciting time for all of us. I think we are all privileged and blessed by God to live at this critical time in history." He paused to take a sip of water from the glass in front of him. Igor nibbled from the bowl of salted peanuts as the Cardinal continued.

"Some years ago, when I was working in Rome at the Vatican, I met a Russian art historian who was attached to a delegation of Soviets visiting on some secret business which I won't go into. It was my job to act as a guide and I got to know Dmitri Yemeljan quite well in the week he was with me."

"I think I've heard of him," said Spikel. "Wasn't he with the Tretyakov Gallery in Moscow?"

"That's right. Do you know him?"

"No, but Professor Gerhardt, with whom I did my early research in Germany, occasionally did some business with him; collecting for the Recklingshausen Icon Museum."

"Well, I have corresponded secretly with Dmitri for some years now, because he was and is a committed Christian. Such people were rare in Soviet Russia in the sixties and I felt it my mission to let him know that we in the West sympathised and supported him in his faith, even though I understand his beliefs are somewhat unorthodox."

JeanLuc laughed abruptly at this. Mirphy looked at him queerly and continued. "Anyway, about six months ago, he wrote to me telling that he was on the trail of a very old icon of incalculable holiness, and asking if I could help, because things in Russia, as you may be aware, are pretty chaotic at the moment and he no longer had the financial or other resources to pursue it.

"I therefore agreed to send JeanLuc Kuovic here, who speaks

Russian, on a mission to help Dmitri and bring back the icons to the US if at all possible. We decided to do it with the utmost secrecy, through our contacts in Poland and Germany,and I'm glad we did. This mission has been incredibly successful, despite some terrible setbacks, and JeanLuc and Igor here brought back three items from Russia which I believe will shake the very foundations of Christianity and the world!" The Cardinal paused dramatically.

"So what did Yemeljan dig up? The Edessa Mandillion? Another Veronica?" demanded Spikel, now extremely interested despite his early reservations and cynicism.

"Professor Spikel, we believe we have nothing less than original paintings of our Lord Jesus Christ and his close immediate family done while they were still living 2000 years ago!"

"Good Lord! That's some claim. If it is true, you're right; it will be mind blowing in it's importance!"

"You are here to authenticate our claim, using whatever scientific tests need to be done; carbon dating and such like. We want you also to help restore them so that they can be shown to the world in due course."

"Are they badly damaged? What are they painted on?" asked Spikel anxiously.

"Considering their age, they are remarkably well preserved as you will see. The portraits were painted on what we think is silk which has now become very fragile indeed. This morning, before you came, we had them pressed between glass plates under a dry inert atmosphere."

"Good, good. Well done! That is what I would have done. When can I see them?" He jumped up with impatience and excitement.

The Cardinal smiled at him. "I think we would all like to see them again, so let's go. Joel can you lead the way please?" They all rose. Igor took JeanLuc to one side.

"JeanLuc, what about lunch? And can you get me someone to teach me American—a big blonde American woman, huh? I'm tired of not understanding a word of what is being said. Don't get me wrong, but I think also you should try to contact Dmitri and Saskia to see if they are all right and to tell them what we got."

"Forgive me, Igor. You're right! I apologise. Joel?" he called. "Can you fix Igor up with an English teacher, someone on the staff, maybe? And we need to make some calls."

"Sure thing, JeanLuc. Just ask Josie to get you anything you need. Anything at all. There is just one thing I ought to mention to you all. We have less than one week left before the new Japanese owners move in, so everything has to be out soon—especially the Jesus Icons. After that, I will no longer have any authority here."

"But some of the scientific tests may take several months, especially the carbon dating," objected the Professor. "Also, if we have to chemically stabilise the cloth; that also takes weeks, sometimes months, of capillary permeation."

"In that case, we shall have to consider moving the icons to a safe place. Do you have any suggestions?"

"They could come to my Department at Duke University," offered the Professor. "The security is good because we have so many rare manuscripts and works of art."

"That might be a good idea," said the Cardinal. "Can you arrange that, Joel? But remember, absolute secrecy!"

"Yeah, no problem. Let's go. I'll take His Eminence and the Professor to see the icons and JeanLuc, if you and Igor remain here in the Board Room, Josie will see to whatever it is that you want, okay?"

"Behold, the Jesus Icons!" cried the Cardinal his voice cracking with emotion. Professor Spikel almost ran to the four Perspex chambers in the clean packing room. He stared in at each of the pictures in turn. Despite himself, he was moved. He had not been prepared for the incredible realism of the images that now confronted him; the sheer artistry of them.

Sandwiched between glass plates were banners of thin material on which he could see the painted heads of various people, the men, robed in white, had dark beards, long uncut hair and Jewish features; the women and children in costume characteristic of the time and region. Underneath and along the sides he could see the distinctive symbols of Aramaic lettering.

The panels were almost intact, apart from a few tears and small holes. As the Cardinal had said, they were incredibly well preserved, considering their presumed antiquity. The colours of the paint had faded, leaving predominantly dark and light-brown hues rather like the sepia tones of an old faded photograph. But Spikel could see traces of other colours; red, green, even blue in the dramatically painted eyes— a typically Phoenician touch.

"They came rolled up around a spine of ivory in those copper tubes, packed with dry sand." Mirphy told the Professor and he pointed this out.

"We will need to take photographs immediately in case of disaster!" he exclaimed.

"We have a high-quality videotape already."

The Professor turned to the Cardinal, grabbed his hand and pumped it enthusiastically. "Your Eminence, You and your colleagues have to be congratulated. If everything checks out in the scientific tests, you have here the find of the century—no doubt about it. I cannot even begin to contemplate the impact this could have."

"I agree! Biblical scholarship is one thing but this, this could reach the hearts of millions!" said the Cardinal simply.

"The Aramaic writing must be translated at once. I have a colleague at Duke who is an expert at that," he said.

"Do what you have to do then, Professor. I leave them in your care. But I think you begin to understand how important it is we keep this secret. If they were found to be fake or a hoax, premature disclosure would be devastating to us all."

"Yes, of course. You can count on me."

Cardinal Mirphy went to the Professor and, placing his face close up so that their noses were almost touching, his eyes searched the other man's into the depths of his soul. "I know I can count on you. I believe with my whole heart that this is the Lord's work we are doing and that it was meant to be," he whispered fiercely. Pulling back, he walked towards the doors, but turning, he said: "I am taking this videotape with me to Europe. When I return, I want as complete a restoration as possible and all the test results to be completed. Joel here will help you to move them to your laboratory in the university. They'll get you anything you need. Finance is no object. If you have to consult anybody, do it on a need-to-know basis and if possible show them only fragments of the whole in photographs. Remember, I want this whole thing sewn up by December of this year. Maniato, let's go!" With this the two men left.

*

The Professor returned to his study of the panels, his mind whirling with possibilities and plans. The first thing would be to scan the images into the computer for storage and later enhancement of the digital images. Then, he would have to think about what to use to stabilise the cloth without affecting the colours—but this was his life's work and expertise and he foresaw no difficulty there. Also, he needed to take samples for carbon-dating by NMR. So many technical thoughts were going through his mind that he never, at that time or subsequently, really looked at the panels as pictures, but only as an artefact to be picked over and analysed. In the end, Professor Spikel must have known more about the Jesus Icons than any living being but, sadly, he seemed to miss the simple visual message that they would convey to everyone else. It was case of not seeing the trees for the wood—a common failing of the technical specialist or scientist.

"I am calling a full meeting of the Ruling Council for next Wednesday" said Jean De Sigor.

"That's a serious step, Jean. We haven't had one for more than fifty years. What's sparked this off? Is it necessary?" asked Sir John Redcliff.

"I've had word from Joseph Mirphy in New York. JeanLuc's Quest has located something of vital importance, he says. He won't divulge exactly what it is except at a full meeting of the fourteen."

"Do you believe him?"

"I've no reason to doubt him and we are, after all, trying to make him Pope. All he would say is that JeanLuc has brought back from Russia artefacts concerning Jesus that would prove of vital importance in our efforts to restore our way of thinking in the world. He is flying over on the weekend to talk with me first," observed Redcliff.

"It will be very difficult to get everyone together at such short notice." "Just do it, John. We'll book a private function room at the La Tipia brasserrie in Paris; like before."

"All right, if that's what you want, I'll get on it, Jean. If we're holding a meeting it will be a good time to discuss and inform the Commandeurs individually of our plan for January and their roles in it.

We also need to elect a replacement for Rosa Roncalli."

"I agree. But we'll have to be extra careful. So many famous people in Paris at one time is bound to cause comment."

"Not easy, I know. But most of us are pretty experienced in dodging the Press and other nosy bastards like the Sureté."

"It's not the Press I'm worried about, it's that Father Moloc whom we still haven't located. Von Helsinger must be keeping him hidden away in a monastery somewhere. Much as I hate to suggest it, we may have to use a P2 terminator again and risk another Pecorelli debacle. Unfortunate but maybe necessary—anyway Pierre will handle all that."

"Good. How is JeanLuc, by the way? How was the trip?"

"Joseph didn't say much but they had some trouble apparently. He had to burn some of our influence in that area to get them out." He took a sip from his brandy balloon.

The conversation turned to the arrangement for Giselle's wedding, which could proceed as planned now that JeanLuc had extricated himself from Russia and the nuclear warhead had been delivered to Castle Sigors. This would be their first marriage in the sequence of betrothal, first then second marriage held when pregnancy had advanced to the third month. They had already been formally betrothed at a meeting of lawyers nearly two years previously. The two would not meet until their first marriage. These were the Jewish customs followed by the Order to avoid the sort of Royal legitimacy problems encountered by Jesus because he was conceived out of wedlock between betrothal and first marriage. Until such time as their second marriage, Giselle would technically remain a 'Virgin'. Not a physical virgin, although this had been desired and insisted on in earlier times, but a virgin according to the religious doctrine of the Order.

"How is Giselle, these days?" asked Sir John cautiously. "Is she recovering from you-know-what?"

"I suppose so. She seems very withdrawn and she left the Castle to go and stay in my old Chateau in the South. To be honest I am a little concerned about her."

"It must have been a hell of a shock, what with Philippe's suicide and everything. You never told her about Duvain?"

"No. We kept that from her. She imagines that Philippe killed himself because of what they did together that night. Unfortunate, but I felt it would be too much to let her know the full story."

"So she thinks Philippe's death is her fault!"

"In a way, I suppose she does and it is probably preying on her mind. I'm sure she'll get over it in time."

"Well, I hope so. You can't tell with women, though. She might brood about it. Have you engaged any medical help—a psychologist or something?"

"Give me a break, John. Why the hell would I want to do that? What bloody trick cyclist could help someone like Giselle? She's got to get over it herself. You know that worse things are in store for her than the death of that cursed junkie muscleman faggot."

"You're right, Jean. I just wish I could help."

"Thanks for the sentiments, John. Maybe JeanLuc will snap her out of it when they meet."

"Do you have a schedule for that yet?"

"Well, I thought maybe in a couple of weeks after the meeting of the Council and when we've had time to digest what Joe Mirphy has dug up."

"I hope we can use it whatever it is. Ideally, we need something to capture the imagination of the masses when we make the Big Move in January."

"It might help, yes, but even if it doesn't, nothing can now change the Plan—we are committed."

"I understand that, Jean. I agree." Both men sat in the deep leather armchairs and sipped their drinks. They stared into the glowing coals of the fire that warmed their feet.

"Not a bad club, this," remarked Jean. "At least you can get your feet warm. Is this one of the benefits of being a British aristocrat?"

"Well, there are others, but precious few since the loss of the Empire." "But you still have a monarchy—that is a singular achievement."

"I suppose so, if you can call it that."

"Oh, but I do! That is the only thing that saves you English from the evils of Republicanism and Democracy! Everything we are fighting against and which demeans the highest ideals of mankind!"

"I don't want to debate with you, Jean. I know what the Priory stands for; you don't have to convince me again. Let's just stick to the basics, right? Get Giselle and JeanLuc married to perpetuate the Bloodline, hold the Summit, and then God's Will will have been done. We can do no more," Sir John said tiredly. He didn't think he could last much longer and the issue of his successor was something that he had been thinking a lot about lately.

Who should it be? Of course, he had no vote but his wishes would be taken into consideration when the time came. The choice of one of the Elohim of the Order was always a difficult business. Of the three Seneschals, himself, Cardinal Mirphy and EEC Commissioner Pierre De Loire, he was the oldest and closest to death. He was resigned to the fact that he would never make it to Grand Master now. His choice of successor would have been Jean Luc but it couldn't be, for the obvious reasons of separation of Church and State; an Essene doctrine at the core of the constitution of the Priory. The High Priest ruled, the King lived to pay the price and God interpenetrated all.

On only one occasion had this Rule been broken and that was when Jesus himself had merged the role of High Priest with that of Royal King of the David Line, way back in AD34. In the process, he supplanted the positions of Jonathon Annas and Simon Magus and caused the final schism within the Essenes out of which eventually grew Christianity.

Members of the same family, even brothers, could be King and High Priest, as had happened many times in history, but the roles themselves could not be embodied in the same man unless they aspired to be another Messiah. A similar doctrine was at the heart of modern Roman Catholicism—except that their Pope High Priest could be anyone, from anywhere; another aspect of the democracy that the Priory despised.

CHAPTER 27

Every morning, after early morning mass with the other monks, Father Moloc went to his letterbox to collect mail before retiring to his cell in the monastery to work, meditate or pray. He rarely left the monastery physically but this didn't prevent his mind being everywhere at the forefront of the battle against heresy and Satan's evil presence in the world. The Abbé was happy to leave him alone to do as he wished because, when Moloc had joined, the monastery's longstanding debts had been suddenly and mysteriously cleared, causing the expressions of the local shopkeepers and traders to change from scowls to beaming welcome. The repairs to the ancient buildings had been done by teams of professional workmen who had appeared out of nowhere, to fix the leaking roofs, repair the toilets and to install a modern institutional kitchen. These were sufficient miracles to keep the Abbé happy for the rest of his mortal life, so he didn't interfere. As far as he was concerned, Moloc was a blessing from heaven and he cheerfully paid the enormous quarterly phone bill without flinching.

One glorious day last summer, the monastery, dedicated to St.John of Jerusalem, had even had a real live Vatican Cardinal, Cardinal Von Helsinger, visit to lead them in prayer and to bless their efforts. This was honour indeed and the respectfulness and dedication of the Abbé's flock of fifty or so inmates had increased markedly since that day.

Father Moloc, or Brother Maurice as he was known, had the largest mailbox and it was always full every day. In contrast, the other brothers had maybe one or hallelujah, even two letters each a month. Brother Maurice's post-box was filled with airmail letters from exotic places like Jerusalem and Sao Paulo, and many with glossy looking envelopes with Vatican City stamps. He received many technical journals and foreign newspapers mostly in English, like the Wall St Journal. Oh he was an important man, no doubt about it. But he seemed friendly enough and did his chores like the rest of them and never missed a service.

In his cell, lined with modern steel filing cabinets and floor-to-ceiling shelves groaning with papers and books, he sifted through the new day's mail; postcards in one pile, letters another, magazines and journals in a another. Brother Maurice always received many many postcards. It was an integral part of his system. He liked the colourful pictures and the choice of subject often gave him a clue about the state of mind of the sender. He also enjoyed the mental discipline of deciphering the cryptic messages in plain view on the back.

Ah! This one he'd been waiting for! A lovely panorama of the Blue Ridge Mountains in all their glorious Fall colours. Sister Emmanuel had such good taste, God Bless her! He turned it around and read what she had to report.

Hmmm. So! Mirphy was on the move was he? A lot of coming and going. Biophar Drugs being sold. Well, he knew that already from Von Helsinger— Mirphy was just doing as he was told. But why the sudden unscheduled trip to North Carolina and now secretly to Paris? Could this be linked in some way to the satanic doings of the Priory Arcadia? And what was happening at Duke University?

He turned to the window, lost in thought. Yes, he felt that things were on the move; he felt it in his old and brittle bones. He was nearly seventy and thin as a rake—he hoped God would call him to his rest soon. All those years in the Middle Eastern sun struggling against the sinful Arab, the devious Jew and the remorseless advance of Islam had taken their toll. Although his tan had long since faded, his thin face was deeply lined and leathery like the old Biblical parchments he used to study. He'd lost his hair and the skin of his skull was blotched with liver spots, but God had blessed him with a still-keen mind and a strong constitution bolstered by the simple food and disciplined routine of the monastery.

Abstractedly, he played with the smooth milky white stone he'd picked up back in 1961 at the excavations of Qumran and kept ever since. It was a stone from the River Jordan, identical to those used as receipts given to Jews of the Diaspora under the Herodian system of raising revenue. Normally these stones would have had the name of the owner scratched into its surface but this one had no name, only the Hebrew letter Tau. Father Moloc's long bony fingers had rubbed the surface of this talismanic stone even smoother with the passing years— it was an aid to concentration as a rosary is to prayer.

His access to information on the activities of the Priory had been sharply curtailed with the death of Charles Duvain. This part of the operation codenamed Atbash had ceased to function. He was still uncertain what had happened, he'd been unable to get much information—as far as anyone could tell both Charles Duvain and Philippe Dupont had suddenly disappeared off the face of the earth. That last message he'd received via the bureau service that took his electronic mail had been a puzzle. He would have liked to know if they'd accomplished their mission before the Priory had got to them, as he suspected might have happened.

The Parisian low-life Dupont was dispensable, just another tool to be discarded, but Duvain he'd known for many years in Jerusalem. He'd had to extricate the young novice out of several awkward situations before the final straw which came when Duvain was caught raving incoherently on hashish and naked with a couple of Palestinian Arab boys in his sleeping quarters. The monks had chucked him out after that. Father Moloc then used him occasionally as a researcher or a negotiator with the Bedouin for the odd scraps of parchment or scroll that they turned up. There was no denying his scholarship, intellect or religious zeal; it was his little satyrical habits that let him down. This made him the perfect person for the job of infiltrating into the Priory Arcadia. When he succeeded in doing this, he opened up a rich vein of information for Father Moloc and Cardinal Von Helsinger, enabling them to identify most of the people within the Order. They then proceeded to put their own people close to them. For example, Sister Emmanuel now shadowed Cardinal Mirphy, and sure enough here was her postcard right on cue.

Of course in emergency there were other channels of communication but for routine use, postcards were fine. But this particular card had taken four days to reach him, which meant the Cardinal would be due in Paris this weekend at the latest. He would need to act fast and get some men to the airport to identify Mirphy on one of the flights in from Atlanta and then try to tail him to wherever he was going in Paris.

If he could send in a hit squad, there was a fair chance, just a chance, they might get more than one, maybe even the Grand Master Jean de Sigor, whose security was normally impenetrable. But to assemble the hit squad, he would first have to square it with Von Helsinger. They didn't come cheap in Paris; a team from Marseilles would be better— they could come up by train with less chance of being noticed. Yes, he would arrange it this afternoon.

He didn't think of it as arranging a killing, God forbid! No, this was an exorcism of demons, the succubae of Satan. No mercy could be shown to those who worship and serve the Devil, they had to be eradicated, and it was his sad duty to lead this holy fight. Cardinal Mirphy would bless him for releasing him from their foul and fiendish clutches so that his soul could eventually be redeemed by Jesus Christ, Amen. His was the most difficult of jobs; to save men from themselves and from Satan, for there was no doubt in his mind that people like Mirphy had been possessed by the Devil himself.

The Monastery bell tolled. It was again time for prayer and then some menial work in the new kitchen. Father Moloc adjusted his brown cassock of coarse material, came out of his cell and joined the other monks as they walked serenely to the chapel for another round in the prayer continuum.

*

Joseph Mirphy tensed in his seat, as the Priory of Arcadia corporate jet dropped flaps causing the sleek bird of flight to dip its sharp beak into the dark wintry shroud of cloud that wrapped Northern France. After some sharp turns and a steep dive, the aircraft's fat wheels kissed the rain-slicked runway at Orly. Mirphy breathed more easily and loosened his seatbelt. He was more used to the sedate lumbering progress of the 747 Jumbos, not this jet-fighter champagne-drenched dash across the Atlantic. Such a small plane, such sumptuousness! He could get used to this! Carrying only his briefcase and a small leather suitcase, he emerged blinking from the warm VIP Customs and Immigration, to face the cold rainy late afternoon.

Straightaway, a man came up to him. "Taxi, monsieur? I take your bag. Follow me this way please!" Mirphy shrugged his shoulders and followed obediently. Other passengers were being similarly accosted so it was probably normal, he surmised. He followed the man through the crowds to a taxi rank and to a black Citroen Xantia parked fourth in line. "Here we are, monsieur," said the man as he opened the rear door for Mirphy to get in. "Where to, monsieur? I am at your service."

Mirphy thought quickly. "Gard du Nord, please." This would enable him to lose himself in another crowd and then catch a different cab to the small exclusive hotel on the Left Bank he had been told to book into when he arrived. "You can't be too careful. Just take a few sensible precautions to avoid being followed," were Jean's parting words to him on the phone from the Concorde.

As the Xantia pulled away from the kerb, the driver of the identical taxi behind, picked up and pressed the send button on his radio-microphone. "Tell the Father that the Target has been picked up by one of ours and is on his way. Will follow. Over." Leaving an irate family of four standing by the kerb, he pulled the car out into the traffic, and closed in behind the tail lights of the car carrying the Cardinal into Paris. With his free hand, he lit up another Gaulloise from the soft crumpled pack on the dashboard.

It was a surprisingly long trip into Paris from the airport—the meter clicked away unremittingly. B'Jesus, it's as expensive as the ride in from O'Hare to downtown Chicago, thought Mirphy as they passed the 50 euro mark. He held the briefcase with the videotape in it on his lap the whole trip.

Mirphy paid off the unsmiling driver at the Gard du Nord rail station and plunged into the grey mausoleum-like building amidst a crowd of evening rush hour commuters. He went to the toilets and emerged about fifteen minutes later to hail another Citroen cab.

"Hotel Barbusa, Rue Honore le Corbusier," he shouted at the driver who smiled cynically to himself, stubbed out his foul-smelling Gaulloise into the overflowing ashtray and said "Oui, monsieur, tout suite!" He picked up the microphone, sent the destination and his call sign into control and started the car off towards the Seine. Amateurs! He thought to himself. They never learn, it's so easy! Nevertheless, he was relieved; Father Moloc was not sympathetic to mistakes and he needed this job—he didn't fancy joining the AIDS terminals and the drunks under the river bridges or the dreadful syringe-city park adjacent to the station they'd just left behind. He shivered even though the car heater was on full blast. He'd never understood why people imagined Hell was a hot place!

Outside the rain had turned to sleet driven by a freezing east wind out of Germany and continental Russia. Like the song says, I'd prefer Paris in the Spring, thought Mirphy as the taxi threaded its way jerkily through the insanity of Parisian traffic.

"Ah yes! Monsieur Mirphy of New York. Your suite is ready for you. Oh and there is a message for you. Enjoy your stay with us, sir."

Mirphy followed the bellboy to the lift and up to his suite on the top floor of the hotel. The Garden Suite had its own roof garden attached and a view from the windows across the River Seine towards the City centre in the distance. The Eiffel Tower was a dim blur of pale light obscured by the driving rain. He paid off the bellboy with a ten-euro note and went to the bar to get himself a stiff shot of Irish. He tore open the message envelope and read the contents: 'Will meet for dinner tonight, await my call.J.'

"Should we take them out now? It'll be easy, the hotel is in a quiet street, over."

" No, no. The word is to wait for the Marseilles team to arrive."

"Why? What's so special about those cochons from the South? We can do the job as well as them. Over."

"There might be more targets arriving and we need to get them all. Any action now will be premature; so don't fly off the handle, okay? Keep a lid on this radio chatter, too. Over and out!" grated the radio voice.

Ricardo Suzo reluctantly put the radio-microphone on its hook and lit another Gaulloise. He hoped he wouldn't have to wait too long. His skin was starting to itchy crawl , his legs were fidgety and he drummed his fingers on the steering wheel. He needed to fix soon; he also needed to score for the next few days. His mouth was dry and his tongue felt like a stick of wood. He prayed that the Father would soon make him well.

To distract himself, he took a handgun from the cubbyhole and played with it; aiming it at random at the few pedestrians as they hurried along the dark wet side streets, coat collars up, ignoring the Citroen taxi parked with its lights out and the dark hunched figure within. Many Parisian taxi drivers live their entire existence in their vehicles so this was not an uncommon or alarming sight.

Mirphy took a shower and came back into the luxurious bedroom. He switched on the TV—it had everything; the usual fifty or so channels; arcade games, cableporno; and satellite. He tuned into the CNN satellite channel to listen to the news. There was an item about new GAT trade talks starting in Paris attended by EEC Commisioner Pierre De Loire. Pierre is looking old, thought Mirphy. European power-politics were taking their toll. It was the opposite in America where the power juice seemed to rejuvenate the Presidents and they got younger and younger until they became infantile.

At eight o'clock sharp, a black Rolls Royce Mistral swooped into the narrow street leading to the Barbusa Hotel, preceded by a black Volvo estate car. Four men emerged from the Volvo and stood covering the entrance to the Hotel. All had their right hands in their jackets ready to draw a weapon. The engines of both cars remained running, chauffeurs primed for instant getaway. Another black Volvo pulled in behind the Rolls, from which a man got out and went into the hotel.

The phone beside Mirphy's bed rang and he leaned over to pick it up. "Your car has arrived, sir," said the receptionist—he sounded slightly nervous.

"Right, I'll be straight down." He put down the phone and pulled on his dinner jacket, putting the videotape in a side pocket. Emerging from the lift into the lobby, he was met by a tall Frenchman in full evening dress like himself. "This way, please, sir" and after giving a hand signal to the men outside, he escorted the Cardinal to the door of the Rolls, which swung open as he approached.

Inside, he saw the Comte de Sigor waiting for him, wearing a wide grin of pleasure. He climbed in and the two men embraced clumsily, kissing each other on the cheek. The convoy set off at a swift pace.

"Joe, mon cher. It is good to see you again. Sorry about all the cloak and dagger, but Paris is a dangerous place for me these days." He tapped the windows with a bony knuckle. "See! Bulletproof glass, it cost me a fortune! Even the floor of the car is bomb-proofed. It never used to be like this; the streets of Paris were my home during the War and when De Gaulle was in power, but now!" He gave an expressive shrug. "It is like a war zone, drugs, bandits and muggers have taken over."

216

"It'll soon be like New York then," said Mirphy regretfully.

"Anyway, enough of this depressing subject, we have something to celebrate, do we not? I am taking you to La Fronde, a restaurant I sometimes go to. You will like it and we can talk."

The phone beside the Comte buzzed and he picked it up. He listened briefly and frowned as he put it down. "We're being followed, Joseph. We've monitored a radio-call from a Citroen taxi just behind us. Are you sure you weren't followed from the airport?"

"I can't be sure, Jean. I changed cabs at the Gard du Nord just in case."

"Well, my security men think we're being followed so we'll have to deal with the situation." He picked up the phone and spoke some rapid orders into it. The car suddenly accelerated sharply, pushing Mirphy back into his seat. "Hang on to that strap, Joe. Things may get exciting for a few minutes." commented Jean blandly. For several hectic minutes the Rolls and her escort of Volvos drove swiftly through the traffic, swerving and dodging between the cars with total disregard for other drivers. Then they dived down a deserted unlit side street and screeched to a halt. Security men spilled from the Volvos holding automatic weapons. They ran back up the street and waited, backs against the brick, for the following vehicle.

Ricardo was sweating buckets as he drove like a fiend trying to keep up with the Rolls and her escort. They'd gone crazy just after he'd put in that radio-call for back up. The bastards must've monitored him! Where the fuck had they gone? He'd lost them. Shit they must've gone down that back street!

In a panic he slewed the car around on a handbrake turn and drove back to the street down which the Rolls must have gone. As he turned into the street, Ricardo the taxi driver, drug addict and father of four daughters, died in a maelstrom of bullets that ripped through the car windows shredding his body into a bloody pulp.

"Was that really necessary, Jean?" asked the Cardinal shaken by the suddenness and brutality of the execution.

"I'm afraid so, Joseph" said the Comte sadly as the Rolls set off once more at a more sedate pace ... towards the bright lights of the City.

"I wasn't joking when I said that Paris is a dangerous place for me;

but I also make it a bad place for my enemies. I think the Mafia have a saying about going to the mattresses. In Paris we are now on the mattresses against Father Moloc and his killers—it is war, and has been since Giselle was raped by that drug-crazed golem."

"I thought that was all over and done with?"

"I'm afraid not. It's personal now. If I find Moloc, I will kill him!" cried Jean with a fevered light in his eye.

"I hope this will not interfere with the Priory. You cannot let a thousand years of survival and planning be jeopardised because of a personal vendetta!"

"Don't worry, I won't but you must realise that Moloc is intent on destroying the Priory as well as myself and my family. The Priory must stop him and I have committed the Order to his destruction!"

Joseph Mirphy sat the rest of the journey in worried silence. It was just as well he'd asked for a meeting of the Council. This was another vital topic to discuss. It would be terrible if, after all this time, the Priory self-destructed in a war against the all-powerful Church of which he was a senior member. They'd screwed up several times in the past, and it was unfortunate that they were going to a restaurant named after one of the biggest of those failures: the Fronde uprising of the 1650s.

CHAPTER 28

What would be the worst nightmare of a conscientious go-getting paparazzi? Not to be there at the unveiling of Madonna's latest sexual preference? To miss Michael Jackson's opening of the Moroccan branch of Mothercare? To run out of film at Cherie Blair's gym club? Possibly, but a true professional, a dedicated follower of fashion, a big game Hemingway of the glitterati, would have sold his eternal soul, by-line and photocredit to Paris-Match or Stern to have been at La Tipia brasserie on the Rue de Rome; to catch in wide-angled close focus, in stark coarse-grained high-contrast black and white, in the harsh flare of sudden flash, the startled furious expressions of the rich, the famous and the infamous who came by that dark rainy Wednesday in March and hurried upstairs to the private room at the rear.

In the anteroom, each of the Commandeurs of the Priory Arcadia donned his white robe of cotton (Article 8) to cover their clothing and a hood with mouth and eye slits to cover their heads before going in and sitting down around the long conference table.

With some pride and satisfaction, Comte Jean de Sigor surveyed the assorted people sitting quietly waiting for him, the Nautonnier, to start the proceedings. On his right was Sir John Redcliff; on his left Pierre de Loire; and at the other end of the table was Joseph Mirphy. Jean de Sigor and his three Croisé were the only unhooded people in the room. The Nautonnier wore a very old rabbinical robe of cotton rubbed white with frankincense. The hems of the sleeves were stained blue with the dye from the crushed shells of an unique species of mollusc only found at the Temple of Jerusalem, scraping an existence within the cracks between the stones of the Wailing Wall and feeding on the holy tears and spittle provided by the frenzied penitents who rend their garments at its footings. Around his waist was a rope woven from strands of purest gold.

Each person laid before him on the table, the insignia of membership, a gold bee from the grave of Childeric I and a round white stone from the River Jordan with their secret names scratched into its smooth surface.

On the table before each of them, there was a crystal wine glass and a small flat loaf of unleavened bread. In the middle of the table there was a carafe of red wine and a large shallow copper bowl half filled with water and with a mass of red rose petals floating within, perfuming the air with their oh-so-sweet essence.

Jean led them through the words of a brief communion in which the bread was broken and the wine sipped. He then started the Council without further ado.

"Brothers, I have acceded to the wishes of Brother Joseph here to call a Council of the Rose Croix. Thank you all for coming at what I know is very short notice and some considerable danger to you all. However, I know that God is among us and he will bless this first meeting of the Order in nearly fifty years. Since the war in fact."

He continued. "All of you are Chosen Ones, Sons of Light put here to lead mankind towards the one True God and the Path of Light. I have called this Council, because we need to discuss and guard against certain imminent dangers and also to prepare for the Fulfilment. To end the meeting, Brother Joseph has some astoundingly good news that will cheer us all and send us on our way until we meet again in full session at Castle Sigor in January." The Nautonnier sat down and waved a languid hand at John Redcliff who stood up leaning forward as he spoke in a gravelly voice.

"You all know me. From me you get the hard truth. We are having a lot of pressure from the Vatican in the shape of Cardinal Otto Von Helsinger and his henchman Father Moloc. Moloc, who operates out of Paris here, although we haven't located him as yet, is extremely dangerous. He managed to place an informer into Castle Sigor as the secretary to the Nautonnier!" There were many gasps of horror at this.

"Yes, right at the heart of our Order there was a spy! Fortunately, he was discovered and has now been dealt with. However, there have been unfortunate consequences. One of these is the state of war that exists between ourselves, Father Moloc of the Hospitallers and the Catholic Curia in the guise of the Congregation of the Doctrine of Faith. This is not what we want. We do not want war with the Church. Brother Joseph here is our choice for the Papacy and this warfare could lose us votes in the next Conclave. It must cease and peace be made

220

between us. Does anyone have a suggestion?"

There was silence around the table. Then one of the nine hooded Commandeurs—a woman's voice—spoke. "Can we not get rid of Father Moloc? Can he not be liquidated?"

"We have tried. Believe me, we have tried. It is not so simple though. Moloc is not a gangster in the usual sense; he is a fanatical believer of Catholic Doctrine and is supported by an Order that evolved out of the same antecedents to ourselves. There is no way we can get at him by normal means, by trolling through the underworld, because such a man is incorruptible. He probably believes we are agents of the Devil!"

Another voice spoke up. "What about Von Helsinger? Can he brought around?"

"The man is impossible. He is committed to Emilio D'Ascriba and both are sworn enemies of Brother Joseph." "But is he vulnerable? Can we buy time until the Fulfilment? I suggest we try to isolate Father Moloc by cutting off his support from the Vatican."

At this point, Jean de Sigor spoke."My decision is that we concentrate on Von Helsinger and make him an offer that cannot be refused!" This comment was greeted with a trickle of laughter around the table. "We shall just have to deal with Moloc as and when he poses a new problem. I agree that getting Von Helsinger to withdraw support will isolate him and reduce his effectiveness." He stared coldly over at Joseph Murphy at the other end of the table. "Brother Joseph. You are to make the peace with Cardinal Von Helsinger." Murphy grimaced: "That is an onerous task you have given me, Nautonnier, but God's Will be done," and he bowed his head in acceptance.

"Pierre, we have not heard from you in a long while. Would you give us an assessment of the current situation from your perspective?" Pierre de Loire, cousin of the Nautonnier and of the same Bloodline, was a short fat man with the wide jolly red face of a meat-fed butcher. Tonight though, the bags under his eyes were bruised purple from tiredness and too much reading of small Europrint. He stood up wearily.

"Okay, you know who I am. You know I am a wonderful negotiator. I can get mountains of butter converted to mountains of wine. I am a genius. Let me tell you, just in case you'd forgotten, that I am charged by the Order with the federalisation of Europe. From the end of the War, we have been aiming for a United States of Europe. The way we have done this is through Pan Europa and then the EEC. Where the money goes, goes the power and we are the power brokers. In fifty years, we have had reasonable success considering the wreckage of European nations we started with; but now we have a more or less effective EEC which more are clamouring to join. Looking in, the US and the East now view Europe as a formidable trading bloc rather than as separate nations. So we have succeeded. We have put in place a framework and an identity. But as we in this room know, that is not our hidden agenda. This is only the groundwork for what is to come."

"Pierre, can we skip the history lesson and the Eurospeak and get to the point. We only have two hours, you know, before we have to disperse from here," interrupted the Nautonnier.

"Sorry, Jean. But we meet so rarely that I thought you might want an update."

"No!" said the Nautonnier abruptly.

"Well, I do!" said one of the hooded Commandeurs. "I would like to hear some more from Brother Pierre. It seems to me he is the only person here who hasn't made an almighty cock up of things in the past few months!"

All heads turned to look at the speaker, who nonchalantly continued to crumble bread between his long aristocratic fingers. Jean de Sigor glared at him

furiously. He recognised the voice as that belonging to a famous English novelist. "Well, what do you want to know, Brother? And I don't like your goddamn insinuations."

"Come on, Nautonnier, you said we only had a short time. Remember it was you that called this meeting presumably for our advice and input. It seems to me that the problems we are facing are self-inflicted. We have been shooting ourselves in the foot!"

"Bullshit!" shouted Joseph Mirphy as he leaped to his feet. "You have no idea of what we've been through these past few months and what we are facing. I for one don't want a goddamn recap of the collapse of the ERM or the German Unification problem or the damage Tony Blair has done. With respect to Pierre, that is past history and not what we're about."

"Well fuck me with a broomstick! Just because we've got you marked down for Pope doesn't mean we have to listen to you, you Irish troublemaker!" yelled the Commandeur.

Jean de Sigor sighed. It was not a good idea for this vital meeting to degenerate to a slanging match—he would have to act. "Brothers and Sisters!" he held up his hand. "Please don't let us bicker. None of us is perfect as has been amply demonstrated—we are unworthy vessels for the Light of the Shining Path!"

He glared at them. The nine Commandeurs of the Priory Arcadia were each of them successful, famous men and women, strong willed, opinionated and used to power—that's why they had been elected. But, they had to be bent to His Will. He stood up to his full height and concentrated his mind. As he let the Spirit enter him his eyes rolled upwards into their sockets, only the whites showing. All in the room groaned aloud as they felt the mortal dread that had been a part of their Initiation, fall again on their minds like a psychic vampire. The bowl of rose petals began to steam and the rose perfume intensified to intoxicating levels.

The Nautonnier stood with his arms outstretched over them in a Biblical stance and silently he mouthed indecipherable words. Then he shook himself out of the trance and fell back into his seat, panting. The others were instantly released from his mental grip and relaxed with relief. Some hastily lit a cigarette; others popped pills or gulped at a glass of water.

"Now, where were we?" Jean said. "I would like to discuss two points before we move onto other matters and to Brother Joseph's important presentation. "First of all, the Merovingian Bloodline must be preserved. To this end, we have betrothed my daughter Giselle to JeanLuc Kuovic. Kuovic is the last male descendent of Hugues de Payen through a branch of the Habsburg-Lorraine family. "This marriage is a symbolic re-unification of the Knights Templars and the Priory Arcadia to repair forever the rift that occurred at the 'splitting of the elm' at Sigor in 1188," he continued. "Their marriage is set for June of this year at Rennes Le Chateau. I'm sure you would all like to be there. We are hoping that a child will be conceived in time for their second marriage to coincide with the Fulfilment in January.

"For the second point; final plans for the Fulfilment are being drawn up. The nuclear weapon that we are using to emphasise our position, has been purchased from the Russian Military and is installed at Castle Sigor. Each of you has a specific role to play and we will soon be sending you coded tapes and papers, which will allow you to learn the ceremonial words and actions. You have all done well in getting non-initiated participants for the Summit. Our list is almost complete. Emilio D'Ascriba is the only one of importance who is still holding out. We shall work on him in the next few months. That is all I have to say for now. Brother John, I hand over to you for the membership issues that have arisen."

Sir John got wheezingly to his feet. "Thank you, Nautonnier. I'm sure all here are grateful to you for all you've done, and for your Leadership over these difficult years. We are all looking forward to the Fulfilment, which will be the dawning of a new epoch in human history." All around the room nodded and applauded with enthusiasm.

"It has been my sad duty to record the deaths of several Brothers over the years. May their souls rest in peace. Rosa Roncalli, one of our long time Chavaliers, is the most recent to have died and I would like to use this meeting to take a vote on the admission of a new senior member." He handed out slips of paper on which there were five printed names. "Under Article 14, please register your preference in the usual way; fold the paper and put it in this bowl here."

After the bowl was returned to him, he tipped the contents out and recorded the votes.

The choice didn't surprise him in the least. He exchanged looks with the Nautonnier and gave him a barely discernible wink. "The choice has been made. A new member will be elected according to the Community Rule. The only people who will know this person's identity for sure are the Nautonnier and the three Croisé. You will be able to make a good guess but you still won't know for sure. These are the Rules, Brothers, which have governed us for centuries. They are for our protection. I suggest the Initiation Ceremony be carried out at Rennes le Chateau at the time of the marriage of Giselle de Sigor."

All nodded their agreement. "I also recommend that this person be made a Chevalier to fill Rosa's vacant place in view of their importance and rank in the outside world. All agree?" Again all nodded. Sir John struck a match and set fire to the little pile of voting slips, which flared up and burned in a few seconds. Well, it was a good choice really. The English Prince would certainly be more in tune with their thinking than Margaret Thatcher or the others. He'd worked with Thatcher in cabinet and admired her steely will. But they already had a Nautonnier and she'd probably cause more trouble than it would be worth. The Catholic Irishman Murphy would have found it hard to swallow. No, God had guided them to make the right choice. There was now a good likelihood of a proper dynastic link-up in the future to consolidate Britain's place back in the European mainstream. He would like that, yes he would! It gave him a sense of comfort, a sense of belonging and hope for the future of his country. God knows it needed something!

The Council of the Arche of the Rose Croix went on for another two hours as various local issues were raised by the Commandeurs and discussed. The acrimony of the first part of the meeting seemed to have subsided as they concentrated on the details of who would do what and when. They had to work as a team from now onwards—there was no time for infighting or manoeuvring for higher rank. They would all go into the Fulfilment as they were, barring accidents.

One of the Commandeurs spoke up. "Nautonnier, I would like to know more about this Kuovic character in whom we seem to be investing so much. I mean, what do we really know about him?" Jean recognised the voice of the German, Von Moltke.

"I have been expecting this question," said the Nautonnier calmly. "You can be assured that I have thoroughly investigated JeanLuc Kuovic and he is of the Bloodline that we say he is." Like you did Charles Duvain? Thought Sir John wryly. "Of course, he has emerged from a very troubled past which has made it hard to check everything but his parents certainly appear in the correct genealogy."

"Where did they come from, and what is his history?"

"Well, I have relied mainly on the genealogies drawn up by our Brothers in the Order of the Temple and given to me by their Grand Master. Kuovic is descended from Hugues de Payen and as far as we

225

can determine his Bloodline is as legitimate as my own, leading back to the Merovingians and thence to Our Lord Jesus. In fact, we share most of our ancestors. Early in the nineteen twenties, his grandfather, a Habsburg-Lorraine, married into the Russian Romanovs but was killed in the October Revolution. His Grandmother and Father, who was a child of four at the time, escaped to America where they've been ever since. After the war, his father married a New York Jewess but both parents died tragically in the nineteen fifties leaving the baby JeanLuc to be brought up in a succession of orphanages."

"Does he have the birthmark?" asked one of the hoods.

"Yes, he does, on the right shoulder where it should be. Using her remarkable psychic talents, Rosa Roncalli finally located him. He'd been drafted into the Military and had returned from his first tour of duty in Vietnam. We pulled some strings, got him out of the Army and into a job at Biophar Drugs Corporation where he has been ever since, under the watchful tutelage of Brother Joseph."

"Okay, so he's got some kind of a pedigree, but is he the Chosen One?" asked another hood. Jean recognised the whiskey-and-cigarette coarsened voice of the Hollywood actress Shirley Mackie.

"I don't know. Rosa thought so, but we cannot know for sure until God's Hand is placed upon him. That may not happen until the Fulfilment."

"Talking of the Fulfilment, what if we are wrong about the date; what if all this planning and effort is a waste of time? Look what happened to the Baptist when he got it wrong and all that fiddling with calendars of those who also got it wrong—even Jesus Himself!"

"We are not wrong. The Prophesies will come to pass!" said the Nautonnier with conviction. We hope! thought Sir John darkly.

"Can we have a report on what was found at the Ecole Biblique?" interrupted Cardinal Mirphy.

One of the hooded Commandeurs spoke up in a very thick Middle Eastern accent. "It went very smoothly and we got what we wanted," he said.

"And what was that?" someone asked.

"Go ahead," said the Nautonnier when the hood turned questioningly towards him.

226

"As most of us know, much of what people call the Dead Sea Scrolls has been hidden away by the Vatican with the understandable excuse that misinterpretation by laymen would be counterproductive and cause doctrinal chaos in Catholic theology. This means that virtually all the Essene Commentaries and Sectarian writings are still unpublished. Although these scrolls were our main objective it didn't surprise us that none of this was at the Ecole Biblique when we raided. What was of interest was the new material laid out in the Scrollery. Our experts tell us, from the photos we took, that it is probably fairly recent material retrieved from the Yigael Yadin excavations at Masada and others near Mar Saba."

"But I don't understand why we are still chasing after all this ancient history? I mean what is there to be gained, what is there in the Q4 scrolls that we don't already have in our own vaults or know about?"

"It is still important for us to have as complete documentation as possible to substantiate and cross-reference our own material about the time of Jesus," chipped in Sir John. "You have all been shown the Dynastic Scroll which the Order has kept preserved for nearly two thousand years. This is our sole remaining document from that period. It is important that we get more corroborative evidence from such sources as Q4, Nag Hammadi, Bar Saba, Masada and the new sites that are being explored right now, using the new technologies like SIR."

"What's that?"

"Surface Interface Radar. I won't go into details about how it works. Suffice to say that Robert Eisenmann, the famous archaeologist, is using it in the Holy Land to locate caves and secret underground passages."

"My God! You don't think some bloody treasure-hunter will find our Shrine at Rennes le Chateau with this thing, SIR or what do you call it? You know what the place is like; they're swarming all over the place these days—ever since that dreadful Lincoln chappie published that rot in the Eighties."

"It is possible, but SIR is extremely expensive technology and well beyond the means of most amateur investigators. Anyway, Rennes le Chateau is riddled with mine shafts and old tunnels and it will take decades to locate our secret place unless you knew how, or had the map," he paused. "And of course there's nothing in the Shrine and hasn't been for hundreds of years. All our Treasures are of the Mind, in our Hearts, in our Membership and ... in our Swiss banks." There was a ripple of laughter at this. "The Dynastic Scroll has come down to us as the Order's oldest and most cherished possession; it is our Legacy and Birthright. Without it we couldn't prove the Bloodline. It is also a key document that unlocks many secret meanings hidden within the pesher of the Qumran Scrolls and the Christian Gospels."

"Where is it now?" asked one of the hoods.

"In a safe place!" parried Sir John. "The raid on the Ecole Biblique was to get access to more scroll material that has been suppressed by the Catholic fanatics who work there. We already know they have been trying to suggest that the Dead Sea Scrolls are not contemporaneous with the Jesus era, but predate them by about a hundred years. This is supposed to differentiate Jesus from the Essenes in the mind of the layman and confuse the critics. But of course, we know better because of our own Scroll handed down to us by Mary the Mother of Jesus and by Jesus Himself—God be praised!" The others bowed their heads and murmured an Amen.

"But ancient scrolls are not enough!!" cried Cardinal Mirphy who jumped to his feet and threw down his videotape onto the table. The others looked at it in silence. "Brothers in Jesus, Sons of Light; what I have here will astound and amaze! What I have here is a vindication of what the Order has striven for over all these centuries! What I have here will fulfil the Fulfilment!"

CHAPTER 29

The Cessna aircraft skimmed in low over the spring greening trees and drifted down onto the narrow airstrip and bumped along across the weed-choked gaps between the concrete blocks. JeanLuc taxied the aircraft to the timber shack that served as an airport building in this Carolina hinterland.

JeanLuc and Igor had flown up from Durham following the grey car-beetled thread of Interstate 15 north to Clarksville where they turned Northwest along the shit- brown trail of the Roanoke River section of Kerr Reservoir, to where the Dan River joins at the Staunton River State Park.

Hunched down patiently waiting on the stoop of the shack at the airstrip, was Walter Jonas of Clarksville, their fishing-guide hired for that day. As the Cessna's engine spluttered to a halt and JeanLuc and Igor climbed out, Walt stood up, pulled an old tractor cap over his crew cut, spat out a jet of toxic tobacco juice that drowned an unfortunate crawling insect, and walked over to meet them.

"Hi!" he said "I'm Walter Jonas, yo' fishing-guide. You folks have a pleasant flight?" he drawled.

"Yep," said JeanLuc."How's the water? It looks pretty high."

"Oh, it's brown all right, but we've had a dry spring so far and there's little or no wind to bother us. If you'll follow me we'll go get the boat."

Walt turned on his heel and headed down the dirt road towards the Aaron's Creek boat landing stage. JeanLuc and Igor followed the denimed figure whose jacket was a walking billboard for BASS, NRA and other redneck sports organisations.

The April sunshine was hot, and the air smelled of the warming earth. Grey green buds were beginning to burst on the bare-branched larches and the dogwood was in full bridal blossom.

A rush of excitement and anticipation coursed through JeanLuc's veins as they came down the hill and saw the sleek black fibreglass bass boat riding menacingly, like a Neanderthal flint arrowhead, on the sun-glittered water.

Walter Jonas pulled the boat in tight to the jetty and they climbed aboard. JeanLuc and Igor each strapped themselves into a swivel chair and Walt sat in the back, next to the massive hump of a 500HP Evinrude outboard.

"If you're ready, gentlemen," he said, "let's go fishin'!" He stabbed the red start button on the steering console and the big engine gurgled throatily into life. Walt cast off and pulled away slowly from the jetty, heading out into the Dan River. As the boat got into the mainstream, Walt pushed the throttle knob hard forward. The engine banshee howled and the boat's predatory prow lifted thirty degrees in the air as the propeller bit off large chunks of brown water and chewed them into cappuccino foam. They rooster-tailed it east at high speed towards Nelson's Island at the mouth of the Little River, where the big striped bass were supposed to be this time of the year.

The restoration of the Jesus Icons was going well, reflected JeanLuc as half an hour or so later they drifted slowly across the wide lake powered only by the silent electric motor. He carefully paid out another ten metres of line of braided 100lb test line and locked the star drag on his reel. His short stiff Kevlar rod was attached solidly to the boat's gunwale in its special trolling clamp. They only had to wait now. To wait for his Tao and the fate of a striper to synchronise.

After Cardinal Mirphy had left for Europe, JeanLuc and Igor moved from the hotel into a condominium-type apartment on the South Side of Chapel Hill. Igor spent most mornings learning American English with tutors of varying skill and bosom dimension, while JeanLuc commuted to Durham to assist Professor Spikel with the intricate and careful restoration of the silk paintings of Jesus and his family. For transport, JeanLuc had bought an anonymous-looking brown Ford LTD for himself and a 1965 black Cadillac Eldorado two-door for Igor who spent hours polishing the cars and fiddling with their V8s. JeanLuc spent many solitary afternoons and evenings fishing on University Lake, joining Igor at night in Rico's bar in downtown Chapel Hill.

Suddenly JeanLuc's rod bent double and there was a short agonised screech from his reel before a juddering twang signified that the line had snapped.

"Shit!" exclaimed JeanLuc." What the hell was that?"

Walt looked up from the depth-finder sonar, his lined brown face expressionless. "Sorry, folks," he said, "that was a submerged log. There's quite a few of them floating around these parts—specially in the north shore over yonder."

JeanLuc wound in the remainder of his slack line and unclamped the rod. Walt opened one of the side compartments and pulled out another of his speciality rigs for striped bass trolling - a complicated tangle of lead weights, swivels, feathers and the business end of a foot-long, shining polished silvery spoon with its big barbed trebles. No live mackerel bait for Walter Jonas who liked to give the fish a sporting chance. He methodically tied his rig to JeanLuc's line and dropped it back over the side. For a moment, he watched its glittering wobble in the boat's wake and then paid out an exact thirty metres of line before placing the rod back in the trolling clamp.

JeanLuc smoked a Kent and watched as Walt set out the tackle once more. Igor puffed on his cigar and seemed to be dozing. It was a wonderfully calm morning, hardly any wind; just the occasional balmy gust carrying the smell of the shore and its sweet odour of spring blossoms.

JeanLuc resumed his reflections. After supervising the transfer of the Legacy to Spikel's laboratory at Duke University, Joel Maniato had returned to New York. Biophar Drugs Corporation had now been transferred to Japanese ownership and he was apparently looking for another job. There had been a subtle change in Joel's behaviour. He'd been reluctant to leave for New York and even when he'd returned he didn't go back to his old haunts. He seemed to have dropped out of sight—JeanLuc hadn't heard from him for several weeks.

The paintings were powerfully empathic—it was impossible to forget them. Always they remained imprinted on his mind's eye. Always at any moment, he could conjure up the images, whatever he was doing. They filled him with a sense of awe and wonderment. Professor Spikel had become a man possessed, cancelling all his lectures and courses to work full time on the restoration and the authenticity tests. The laboratory was sealed off and new security measures added at vast expense. Students were turned away and Fiona, his secretary, had orders to say he was ill and couldn't be contacted. When JeanLuc arrived in the mornings to act as an assistant, Spikel had already started, or often hadn't finished from the previous night.

By mid- April of that year most of the scientific tests for authenticity were completed; the NMR carbon dating gave an age for the silk cloth of 50-100BC; the pigment analyses, the spectrophotometric patterns, the X-ray ultraviolet infra red scans had all been done. To their surprise, they had even found the faint outlines of fingerprints. Incredibly, the computer matched some of these, the faintest, to JeanLuc's own prints. Professor Spikel immediately accused JeanLuc of unwarranted tampering with the material, but JeanLuc swore he had never touched the cloth at any time from their discovery in Russia to being annealed between the glass plates. The issue could not be resolved and was a source of friction and puzzlement between the two men. However, the prints were very faint indeed and the computer allowed itself only a fifty- percent confidence in the convergence statistics. But it was still strange, and added to their increasing bewilderment over the interpretation of the various symbols and texts that embellished the pictures.

"Stay alert, folks! I think mebbe we're passing over a shoal of 'em." Walter Jonas spat over the side and fixed his pale blue gaze on the FishFinder sonar. He changed direction fractionally. On the chart, the pen flicked erratically as he turned up the gain; small flecks of ink were appearing in the mid-water section of the chart above the solid trace of the bottom contour.

"We're running too deep!" said the guide. "We'll go back through them. Reel in twenty metres of line Mr.Kuovic. Mr Golemov reel in forty, and we'll run it shallow; mebbe we can get one to come up for the lure. Sometimes they'll do that, if it's coming up to spawning season."

Jonas steered the boat in a wide circle and headed back towards the mark. All three men were tense and silent as they watched their rod tips and the lines slicing through the turbid milky brown water.

Stripers are the largest and strongest freshwater fish on the American continent. Only the Maheer of the Himalayan source of the holy Ganges surpassed them in size, strength and sheer fighting quality. The Kerr Lake stripers could exceed forty pounds in weight, exceeding even those found in South Carolina's Santee Cooper Lakes—the only other source of this much-prized land- locked sea fish. They were tough to locate and even harder to catch. A fish over twenty pounds was a lifetime achievement for a striper fisherman. However, most Kerr lake fishermen are content to chase the lunkers and bucketmouths in the creeks and shallow reaches during the summer and autumn months. Striper fishing is a tough proposition requiring sturdy tackle, big lures and intimate knowledge of the water; Walter Jonas was famous for all of that.

Suddenly, Igor's rod bent double. The reel wailed a long howl of pain and the boat veered sharply off course.

"Fish on!" yelled Walt. Igor dived for the rod, lifted it out of the trolling cradle, and held the rod tip high. The taut vibrating line cheese-wired the water in long curving arcs.

"Reel in, Mr.Kuovic. Give the guy some room!" JeanLuc wound furiously on his reel as Walt cut the electric motor. Muscles straining, Igor held the bowed rod against his chest and tried to pump the fish up; but it was still taking line off against the drag in short, sharp screaming pulls.

"It's a darned good fish! Don't lose it now! Give it some space and let it run awhile," ordered Walt, his face now animated with unaccustomed excitement.

JeanLuc sat back in his chair and watched enviously as Igor fought the big fish. Some people have all the luck! he thought as he reached under his seat, brought out a six-pack of Blue Riband and pulled the tab on a can. He tossed one over to Walt.

They would soon have to finish up in the US and get the Jesus Icons to France, he mused. The pictures would be out of the capillary-permeation chambers and into the vacuum-drying process by the end of next week. Then they would be ready for packing up. JeanLuc didn't anticipate too many problems but he was still uncertain how to ship the consignment, and how would he get it out of the country without alerting unwanted nosiness from officialdom. Maybe it was time to alert the Cardinal to make the necessary arrangements at the other end. But that would inevitably start the ball rolling on his marriage to Giselle de Sigor. Was he really ready for that—so soon after Sophia?

JeanLuc crumpled the empty beer can in his fist and watched

through misted, unfocused eyes as Igor and Walt struggled to lift a huge thrashing striper out of the water and into the boat. Finally, it lay there in the bottom of the boat twitching electrically; forty pounds of beautiful black striped iridescent silver treasure of the deep.

Igor sat back in his chair, exhausted. He beamed a wide grin of triumph at JeanLuc. "How I love this fucking country!" he yelled " God Bless America!"

The boat rocked wildly as he stumbled over to Walter Jonas and engulfed him in a clumsy bear hug, kissing him exuberantly on both cheeks. JeanLuc grinned at the shocked redneck: "He is happy! He is Russian!"

Igor went back to his seat and upended his flask of Wild Turkey in celebration. He stared in amazement at the beautiful monster. "Sure is one hell of a fish," said Walt grudgingly.

A grey heron flapped slowly over them, long matchstick legs stuck out behind, heading up- river west to the quieter shallow creeks.

JeanLuc and Igor dropped their shiny lures over the side and paid out line as Walt got the boat under way again. But somehow JeanLuc knew he wouldn't catch a striper that day; the urge had passed—the desire to concentrate on the line and subconsciously will the framework of reality that would make the fish bite on his bait, was no longer there. He was just happy for Igor.

"Goddamn no-good vultures!" muttered Walt. "Why the fuck they don't find their own hotspots?" The submerged Nelson's Island mark and the deep channel of the old Dan River course where they'd caught the fish was now being criss -crossed by numerous other bass boats who'd spotted Igor's long battle with the big striper. Several had cut across their bows already and one was even trolling in their wake. After an hour of this harassment, with no sign of more fish, Walt cut in the Evinrude and they horsed out of there, down river towards Clarksville.

The afternoon was getting to be warm and there was no wind as Walt drove the boat up into the largemouth bass-spawning beds of Bluestone Creek. Once into the flooded tangle of undergrowth and bushes, the guide tilted the big outboard forward and went back to electric power. They glided silently along with hardly a ripple on the smooth still surface. Walt handed each of the other men a stiff carbon-fibre rod rigged out with either a Mudbug deep-diving lure or an eight-inch purple jellyworm.

"Okay, men," he said." Let's see if ol' bucketmouth's in the mood."

JeanLuc cast his worm into the middle of a thicket of flooded bushes. It dropped with a plop into the water and slithered below the surface. For several minutes, he imagined the worm dropping, sinking and sliding off the mud-slimed branches beneath the surface to where a lunker might lie in wait.

It was uncannily silent without the normal wind noise, and it was still too early in the year for the incessant insect chirrup and frog croak. The only noise was the whizzwhirr splash of Igor casting his lure in a systematic fan around the boat and the occasional warning chatter of a bird deep in the thicket. A black water snake swam lazily by, heading for shore.

JeanLuc's gaze was focused intently on his high-visibility yellow monofilament. Was that a twitch? Was that a slow tell-tale sideways movement of the line?

Yes!

He snapped up the rod and instantly felt the heavy throbbing pull that denotes a strike. "Fish on!" he shouted. The rod bent double under the pressure and the drag slipped in short sharp screeches as the fish wrestled for its liberty.

Suddenly, the line went slack.

"Watch it!" cried Walt. "She's gonna jump! Keep a tight line or you'll lose her!" Just as he spoke, the bass rocketed out of the water in a shower of spray, shaking its head from side to side and then flopped back into the water with a mighty splash. Thankfully, JeanLuc felt the pressure on the rod once more—still hooked.

After several tearing runs, the fish was exhausted and he was able to bring it into the boat. Walt dropped a net over it and hauled it on board. "That's a nice fish, sir," he said. "Six, maybe seven pounds. Shall I put her back?" He pointed out the gravid nature of the fish so JeanLuc nodded, consenting to its return. Walter Jonas lifted the silvery green slab up by its huge sharp-toothed jaw and lowered it gently back into the water. She swam slowly off back down into the murky depths of the reservoir.

The mobile phone in JeanLuc's pocket buzzed insistently. "Yeah, " he snapped irritably into it, "what is it?"

"JeanLuc? This is Josef. Where are you? Can you get to the laboratory as quick as you can—we have a serious security problem."

"What sort of problem?" asked JeanLuc.

"There's a sort of student demonstration going on outside here!"

"A demonstration!" cried JeanLuc incredulously. "At Duke University? You must be joking."

"No joke. It is directed at me and my department. They're shouting and carrying banners. Shit! They're even throwing stones at the windows now!" JeanLuc could hear faint background noises of thumps and bangs going on behind the Professor's anxious voice. He asked: "Have you called the police?" "Yes, yes. Of course—they're on their way."

"What are they shouting about? What seems to be their gripe? You've never had this before, have you?"

"No! Of course not," exclaimed the Professor. "It's incredible, but they have got banners with Jesus Lives! Satan Out and Repent printed on them. I'd swear they were going to some kind of a fundamentalist religious revival if they weren't attacking me!"

"Do you think they've got wind of what we're working on?" JeanLuc asked horror struck.

"I don't know and if they did know, why react like this? It makes no sense!"

"We're on our way, Professor. But you'll have to hold the fort for several hours. We're at least three hours away from you. Can the Legacy be packed up in any way or hidden?"

"I have locked and barred the doors so I cannot see them getting in easily, at least not without a determined effort. I've taken the Icons out of the fixing tanks and they're in the drying chamber now. It shouldn't take longer than a few hours to complete the process."

"We'll try and take them out tonight in van," said JeanLuc. If you can find a large wooden box or crate, that would help."

"Okay, I'll stick it out here and get ready for you."

"And whatever you do, don't show the police what we're working on—just pretend ignorance about what is going on."

236

"I don't have to pretend, JeanLuc. I don't have a clue myself what sparked this off. Do you?"

JeanLuc folded the mobile and turned to Walter Jonas and Igor who were watching him curiously. "We have an emergency back in Durham," he said. "Can you get us back quickly to the airstrip please, Walter?"

"Sho'thing, Boss" drawled Walt, a glint of amusement in his deep-set pale blue eyes. He turned to drop the outboard back into the water. With a push on the red start button, the engine growled immediately into life.

"Give that thing all it's got, Mr. Jonas!" exclaimed JeanLuc and he gripped the armrest of his chair.

"Aye, aye, suh!" said Walt and he spat over the side. With a grim smile, he pushed the throttle stick hard forward and the mean machine leaped forward like a greyhound out of the starting cage. The boat streaked back down the creek into the wider lake beyond with a hi-tuned roar that pulverised the delicate eco-silence and churned up a tidal wake worth several years of bank erosion.

Her painted name was 'Bitch'—ain't nothing gonna catch her now. Sheeee Harghh !

*

That goddamn Papist son of a bitch has gotta be here, thought Denzil B. Rutwiler.Jnr. He picked out a rock from the sack full they had brought with them from Greenville in the pick-up and hurled it at one of the second floor windows of Professor Spikel's laboratory. The glass smashed with a satisfying tinkle.

No shit-eating New York kike is gonna humiliate me whilst I'm doin' the Lord's Work! Denzil Rutwiler threw another stone.

Around him, his fellow students from the Bible College chanted ... Satan

Out ... Satan Out ... Jesus lives! ... Jesus Lives ...

They were working themselves up to a good old-fashioned frenzy. There had been too few good excuses recently to string up a nigger or barbecue a sinful heretic on a burning cross. This was too good an opportunity to miss ... Jesus Lives! ... Satan Out! ...

This'll put one up the ass of the high-toned kikes that study here!

237

raved Denzil. Hitler was right, the budget deficit is a Jewish Conspiracy and a plot by the Pope! Another window smashed.

In the distance came the yowl of police-car sirens as they converged on the small but vicious crowd that was demonstrating outside the laboratory of Professor Spikel in the History Department.

"Shit! The pigs are here," shouted Rutwiler. "Disperse. Get outa here. We'll get 'em later as we planned!"

"The police are here," said Josef Spikel over the mobile to JeanLuc "and the demonstrators have run for it."

"Well, that's good news, Professor. We're just getting to the aircraft and will be taking off for Durham in about ten minutes with an ETA of about six this evening."

"There's no hurry now, but we need to meet to decide what to do. The pictures are safe, by the way."

"Good. Don't do anything until I get there. Get rid of the fuzz if you can." JeanLuc folded his mobile and walked the final steps to the Cessna. Igor followed close behind, lugging a sack with his fish in it. Back at the jetty, Walter Jonas folded two crisp one-hundred-dollar bills carefully into his snakeskin wallet. That done, he started up the outboard and drove his bitchin' boat into the channel back towards Clarksville. He fancied a steak and a few cold ones in Fidgety Joe's bar before returning to his mobile home to feed his dogs.

*

"Slow and easy now, motherfuck!" grated Denzil Rutwiler through the mouth of his knitted balaclava.

JeanLuc froze with his hands on the steering wheel as he felt the cold muzzle of the shotgun jam viciously into the side of his neck through the car's side window. "Don't do anything stupid now, y'hear?"

The rear doors of the LTD were flung open and two other men jumped in behind JeanLuc. They breathed a sour mixture of bourbon and coarse tobacco into the humid atmosphere of the car. JeanLuc sat very still, hardly daring to breathe. Shit! Who are these guys? What did they want? This wasn't New York for Christ's sake. It was Hicksville, North Carolina! This sort of thing never happened here! You could bring up your kids in this town.

The shotgun was withdrawn only to be replaced by the sharp prick of a hunting knife blade placed delicately against his Adam's apple from behind.

"Who are you? What do you want?" JeanLuc forced himself to speak calmly. "I got no dope. You can have my money."

"We are not interested in your money, fuckface." said a mask-muffled voice from behind. "You're gonna pay the price! You're gonna bend the knee! No-one, but no-one beats up on a man of Jesus!" The voice continued: "Okay, start her up and drive. We're getting outa here."

JeanLuc started the engine, put the car into drive and they moved off away from the now-empty parking lot outside the History faculty building. The lights still burned in the second floor of the building. The Professor was waiting for his arrival. The Legacy was packed up and ready to go. He would have to do something. But what? JeanLuc felt a rage of frustration begin to boil over within him.

He drove.

"Take the Interstate east, shitheel!' murmured the man beside him, shotgun resting on his thighs, barrel pointing at JeanLuc's kidneys.

Behind them, in the Cadillac Eldorado, Igor's mouth was tight in a thin line. Beside him on the empty seat rode the brand new M16 automatic rifle he'd bought the week before in the hunting-and-fishing store in Southgate Mall.

CHAPTER 30

Giselle lived alone the rest of that spring and summer, in a long disused Chateau, three miles beyond Rennes Les Bains in the French foothills of the Pyrenees. She received no visitors. There was no phone. The hedonistic, languid lifestyle of the nearby Cotes D'Azur held no appeal for her. She felt the need to escape, to lick her wounds, to forget and ride out a recurring nightmare—the stark horrific vision of Philippe Dupont stumbling around her bedroom, wild mad eyes glaring a message of hate from blood-streaked features.

An old caretaker and his wife were the only humans she saw, not too often and merely for necessities. They came by car every day from Rennes Les Bain where they lived. The old man attended to the grounds and the horses, while his wife attended to the house and cooked Giselle's meals. The simple home-cooked food was served with the gracious severity the old woman had learned in the days when Giselle's mother still lived and had presided over the Compte's guests in the immense dining room.

In the evenings, Giselle found her solitary place at the long polished banquet table laid out with the finest cutlery and silverware. A single candle's smoky yellow flame was a protective beacon amid the gloom of gathering darkness within the huge long room, where tall damask-curtained windows loomed over her like a parade of ancestral ghosts. A Venetian crystal vase glittered in the centre of the long table, always filled with fresh red roses, within whose dark folded hearts yellow stamens gleamed like drops of gold.

The old woman served the meals in unobtrusive silence and disappeared from the house soon afterwards, the putt-putting of their battered old Deux Chevaux fading down the driveway, leaving Giselle to the silence of the house and her own thoughts and imagination. When Giselle walked up the stairs to her bedroom, she found the fragile folds of her lace nightgown laid out on the bed. In the mornings, she entered her bathroom and found jasmine scented water in the old-fashioned lion-footed bathtub, the floor polished and shining under her feet, huge snowdrift towels ready to swallow her pale body—yet she heard no steps and felt no living presence in the house.

Giselle had spent so many summers and winters surrounding herself with people in order to feel alone that this experience of actual solitude was a cleansing, healing enchantment. She felt she could do this forever. If it weren't for the dreams, a growing restlessness and a mysterious sense of something impending—that she couldn't precisely define—she would have been entirely happy. Gradually, as the days passed into summer, the numbness of spirit that had enveloped her began to lift. Her body began to come alive. She became aware of physical sensations and desires not felt since childhood; the intoxicating smell of flowers in the garden gone wild with neglect, the shrill calls of birds that shrieked her awake in the dawn; the feel of her clothes against her skin; the sounds of the wind moaning through the roof rafters; the warm smells and feel of the horses that she rode.

The Chateau stood alone amid vast grounds with woods stretching beyond; there were no neighbours for miles; not until the small huddled village of Rennes Les Bain. She took long rides on horseback down long, deserted roads, down hidden paths leading nowhere. Leaves fluttered and twigs snapped in the wake of her flying passage.

On occasion, she would be brought up short by the sudden prescience that something magnificent and deadly lay in wait for her beyond the next turn of the road, the next bend in the path. She tried to avoid thinking about what she was expecting; she couldn't say whether it was a sight, a person or an event. Sometimes, she started on foot from the house and walked for miles in the hills and valleys surrounding the estate, setting herself no destination and no hour of return. It was on one of these walks, seeking shelter from the last of that winter's Mistral high desert-wind, that she found the hidden path leading down to the Sals River.

The path crossed the river at a narrow wooden bridge and then seemed to stop abruptly at the main tarmac road that followed the deep wooded valley from Couiza to Arques. Unsatisfied at this, she pushed her way through the thick undergrowth on the other side of the road and eventually found the faint outline of the old path, overgrown and barely perceptible amongst the tumble of loose rocks from the overhanging cliffs above. She followed its steep and winding progress up the side of the valley, emerging near the summit in a dense coppice of beech trees that grew cocooned within a rocky hollow. It was strangely quiet here; the Mistral roaring its sandblasting fury overhead was muted and distant. Under her feet, the footing was soft and lush green grass, almost moss -like in texture. The harsh metallic glittering grey light that characterised days when the Mistral blew, was softer and misty green. She had entered a natural cathedral; a magical spot; a nexus on a ley line; a holy place. With increasing sense of awe and wonderment, she approached a clearing dominated by the shattered remains of a large stone sepulchre broken at the foot of a huge dark beech. Beyond this, Giselle could see a vista of rocky outcrops on one side and across and up the valley towards Rennes le Chateau on the other side. She picked her way among the ruins of the tomb—there was nothing of interest within. It had obviously been picked over and desecrated many times in the past. But she was enthralled by the sense of place. The spirit of the area was still active, in residence, and watching over her.

For the first time in many years, she felt alive, her body suffused with well-being. In a trance, she removed her clothes and danced naked to the pan-pipe tunes of the overhead wind whistling through sharp rocky teeth. She hugged the trees, pressing her breasts against the rough bark. At last, exhausted, she threw herself down on a soft mossy grass bank and fell into a deep dreamless sleep; legs and arms spread out trustingly—cruciform sacrifice to the pagan gods who abided there.

She never knew how or when she got back to the Chateau. She didn't take that path again—not then.

And next came the letter from her father, the Compte, delivered to her by the old woman as she sat down for breakfast on a warm balmy morning.

CHAPTER 31

As they drove, a sickle moon rose over the horizon ahead of them. JeanLuc felt the unrelenting pressure of the shotgun in his side, jammed against his right kidney. The hooded figure beside him didn't speak. Terse directions came at intervals from a young man's squeaky-with-tension voice behind him. Flicking his eyes over to the side mirror, he could see behind them the steady glare of following headlights from Igor's Cadillac.

The Motorola carphone was out of action, its red LED's dangling crazily from out of its gun-butt -smashed interior. The radio was tuned to FM 104 and the silky insistent voice of the Reverend John B Goode of the First Baptist Church of Fayetteville murmured exhortations to his audience to return to JEE..ZUS—before it was TOOOO LATE!. Send fifty dollars for a genuine plastic crucifix and a 'Heaven is Carolina Blue' sticker.

Amen, brother, thought JeanLuc. Amen.

He was in deep trouble. Deep deep shit, to quote a movie aphorism of Eddie Mirphy's. But that was what Igor was there for; to get him out of the clutches of these maniacs. His fate was in Igor's hands and he would have to think of something—yes, he would. This was crunch time, when he had to earn his burgers and blond, big-bosomed bimbos. The worst of it was that his captors seemed to be irrational amateurs, capable of anything. They hadn't spotted or even cared about the fact that JeanLuc was being shadowed.

They drove onward East on Interstate 90. At Greenville, they turned north around the city and onto back roads.

"Okay, cocksucker, pull in here!" JeanLuc obeyed. It was very dark but he could just make out in the distance off the road, a white- painted wooden slat boarded house with a stoop. "Drive up there and stop," shrilled the vaguely familiar voice in his ear. He drove off the road, up a dirt track driveway and towards the house. There were several Ford and GM pickups already parked outside; men sitting in the cabs, waiting, smoking Marlboro's or Pall Malls through the mouth-slits of their pointy white hoods. "Okay, shitface. This is the Place of

243

Punishment. Get out!" hissed the voice excitedly.

JeanLuc could now smell oily smoke coming from a recently lit gasoline-fueled bonfire in the cornfield beside the house. A sudden gust of wind blew a spray of sparks towards them. He started to sweat. He could see no way out of this. Where was Igor?

"You gotta have a trial first. We do things right around here. American Justice for nigger lovers and Jews!" The gun prodded JeanLuc out of the car and towards the house. Chinks of yellow light could be seen from behind the dark-curtained windows. The door opened for them and JeanLuc was pushed violently in.

They were waiting in the parlour: ten hooded men dressed in the damask of the KKK. The Grand Dragon wore the heavy emblem of his office around his shoulders and sat in judgement at the head of a large scrubbed kitchen table. An unctuous voice of surprising culture and reasonableness issued from the Dragon's mouth. "Ah! At last, Mr.Kuovic. You must be anxious after all that has happened—but don't worry, we are good Americans here and no man goes without a trial. Justice must be seen to be done. Don't you agree, my dear fellow?"

"Well, yes," began JeanLuc hesitantly. "What am I accused of? Why have you brought me here at gun point?" Suddenly, he felt his head explode with pain as the man behind him side took a swipe at his face with a gun butt. Groaning he fell to his knees, tasting the hot trickle of blood that began to ooze wetly from his nose, dripping onto the bare floorboards. Fury and hurt surprise flooded his mind as well as the first knee- weakening stirrings of real fear. His arms were jerked behind his back and he felt the rough bindings of rope being wrapped around his wrists.

"Drop his pants," ordered the Grand Dragon. Hands pulled at his Levis and underwear leaving them tangled around his ankles and exposing his shrivelled privates to the hostile gaze of his tormentors. "Ah, I thought as much. A fucking Jew. A dirty fucking Jew!" said the Grand Dragon quietly. There was a murmur of obscenities from around the room.

The soft cultured voice of the Grand Dragon sounded once again, penetrating through JeanLuc's pain-filled brain. "Let the proceedings begin," he said."Brother George will act as prosecutor, and Brother

Willard has kindly agreed to defend."

At this, Brother George, on the left of the Grand Dragon, stood up and started to read out a long litany of alleged crimes from a piece of paper held in front of him. The list ranged from cannibalism of young white children to undermining the tobacco-growing economy, culminating with: "and not the least of these heinous crimes was a vicious unprovoked attack on our good Evangelist, Brother Denzil, whilst he was engaged in God's holy work in the lobby of the Carolina Inn last month."

Ah! So that was it! This was nothing to do with the Jesus Icons. That little weasel had finally caught up with him. The little prissy preppy shit had friends after all! JeanLuc was beginning to regret his hasty, bad-tempered outburst those few weeks ago after arriving back from Russia. God was punishing him indeed! First of all Sophia was taken away from him; now this farcical but highly dangerous episode.

Prosecuting Brother George ended his recital by shrieking: "This man is an enemy of Jesus, an enemy of God-fearing America, and he deserves to DIE!"

He sat down to whoops of applause from around the assembly. Someone kicked JeanLuc in the side and he fell sideways onto the hard floor. He lay there gritting his teeth against the throbbing pain. These guys were all vicious and crazy as bedbugs.

"And has the Defence Council anything to say before I pass judgement?" asked the Grand Dragon quietly turning sideways to look to his right. The hood shook its head from side to side and remained silent. Terrific defence! Thought JeanLuc caustically.

"Well, in that case, I have no choice in this serious matter," he said with a note of pleased satisfaction. "Stand the no-good bastard up!" The Grand Dragon heaved himself up and waddled over to JeanLuc who was pulled to his feet by the men beside him. The Klansman pushed his hooded face up close. JeanLuc could smell the foul breath of a whiskey-sodden diabetic. Marbled red-veined eyes glittered hotly with gleeful insanity from behind the white mask. "You're gonna die, you son of a bitch!" he screamed in JeanLuc's face. JeanLuc flinched at the vehemence of the hate that oozed from the man. "Take him outside and burn the fucker," the Dragon yelled as JeanLuc was dragged

245

towards the door. "Give Satan back his Jewboy servant!"

Outside in the cool night air, JeanLuc was frog- marched away from the house. With growing horror and panic, he saw ahead of him the grim upright pole to which he was being led. Beside it, the huge bonfire burned fiercely, sending rockets of sparks into the night, tinder-dry wood crackling and cracking loudly as it burned. Several truck tyres lay on the hard ground beside the pole. Oh, God. No! JeanLuc screamed inwardly. His vocal chords had locked tight. They're gonna necklace me! Oh, no! Oh, No!

His legs collapsed under him. The hooded men grabbed his elbows and dragged him bodily towards the post over hard rocky ground.

Then came the rest of the KKK men from the house and from the parked vehicles drunkenly chanting a strange weird hymnal and forming a circle around the bonfire with its death pole beside it. Firelight flickers lit the scene in a hellish yellow-orange glow.

Igor flicked off the safety on his M16. He would have to go in himself. There was no time left. No time to wait for the police who were on their way in choppers but who would be too late. From the cover of the trees, he watched grim-faced as JeanLuc was tied to a thick post and truck tyres lowered over his head one by one until he looked like the Michelin man, with only his head showing. That was good— the rubber tyres would now protect him from stray bullets.

It would have to be now! Now, before the Firestone necklace of death was lit! Igor leaped up and ran forward screaming a war cry taught him during his long hard years in the Russian Military. Firing short staccato bursts, he charged the ring of white hooded figures who fell like pins in a bowling alley, red stitches of death appearing suddenly in their white robes as bullets sprayed among them. Those Klansmen who weren't hit, scattered with no stomach for a fight, running for their trucks and their mommas. It was over in seconds.

Igor went to the post and shone his torch. "Feeling a little tyred, are we?" he grinned wolfishly at JeanLuc. JeanLuc looked at his rescuer from a face that was white and haggard. His expression was unsmilingly grim. "Get me outa here, Igor! And shut the fuck up!" he croaked. Igor shrugged and proceeded to lift off the heavy tyres.

A few seconds later, JeanLuc stood free and Igor cut his bindings.

Immediately, he started towards the white- robed bodies of the fallen, taking Igor's Commando knife with him. He turned over the dead one by one, looking. At last, he found the Grand Dragon who'd been gut shot and lay with his back against the wall of the house, hands clutching at the red stain spreading over his belly. He was moaning with pain, breathing in shallow gasps. JeanLuc stood over him, stooped down to pull off the hood and played the flashlight on the man's ugly sweating features. The Grand Dragon squinted fearfully up at the bright light shining in his eyes. His dying gaze never really saw the hand that held the knife that came out of the light to slash a bloody red grin across his throat. Nor did he really hear the muttered "Go to Jesus, you fascist motherfuck. God have mercy on your soul!"

From the East, JeanLuc heard the thudding clatter of a fast-approaching police helicopter. He wiped the knife blade carefully on a white robe and returned to where Igor stood waiting. "Get to the car. We need to get outta here!" he urged. "I don't want to be hassled by the police. Half of them are probably secret members of the KKK and we can't take any more risks out here in the boondocks."

They ran for the Eldorado parked on the road. Jumping in, Igor started her up, put her in drive and pressed the gas pedal to the floor. The big seven litre roared throatily and the spinning front-wheel drive dragged the heavy chassis off the grass kerb and they arrowed away down the road fishtailing wildly. They drove by faint moonlight for several miles until they hit a main highway. Then Igor switched on the twin beams and filtered into the westbound traffic.

JeanLuc spent this time on the car-phone arranging to buy an aircraft, filing a flight plan out of RDU and arranging for Professor Spikel to meet them at the airport with the shipment.

"Jesus, Igor. What is that awful smell?" JeanLuc put the car-phone back on its hook and looked over at his driver, wrinkling his nose.

"You don't smell so good yourself, Boss. But it will be the fish. You know, the striper I caught this morning—it's in the back." "Oh, yeah. Well get rid of it," he said. "No! Hold on. Pull in here!" They were approaching the neon of a roadside 'barbecue' restaurant. Igor drove in and parked in the empty lot.

"Bring the fish, Igor," ordered JeanLuc. He got out of the car and went inside the restaurant. The dining area was deserted. JeanLuc went to the counter, dug out his wallet and laid fifty bucks fanned out in front of him. An enormously fat Negro attired in a greasy cook's apron came out of the kitchen towards them.

"Can you cook this for us, buddy?" JeanLuc asked the monstrous black man. Igor heaved the heavy sack onto the counter. "You're welcome to join us if you like, there is rather a lot for the two of us," he said ironically.

"Depends," said the cook. "What is it? A pig?"

"No. A striped bass we caught in Kerr Reservoir this morning."

"No kidding! You're a hell of a way from Kerr. That's in Orange County, ain't it?"

"Yeah, I suppose. Will you do it? My friend Igor and I are kinda hungry." JeanLuc peeled back the sacking to reveal the dull silver of the big bass.

"Wow! That's one helluva fish," gasped the huge chef. "Seems a pity to eat it. Maybe you could get it mounted."

"We don't have time unfortunately, and we always like to eat what we catch—it seems the right thing to do, don't you think?"

The big man's banana sized lips spread in a smile. "Okay, boys. If that's what you want. I aint doin' nuthin in particular, any ways." He picked up the bundle of notes from the counter and tucked them into the back pocket of his vast loose trousers. "I'll cook it whole in the barbecue pit—won't take more than an hour or so." Effortlessly, he picked up the fish by the gills. "Help yo'self to a beer. I'll be back in a few minutes." He waddled off back into the kitchen,

JeanLuc walked around the counter, found a clean glass jug and pulled the handle to fill it with draught Stella Artois . They sat at a Formica-topped table. Outside, they heard the whine and saw the flashing cherry red as a posse of smokies whizzed past their window view of the highway. JeanLuc lifted his foam-topped frosty glass and looked at his companion with a serious expression.

"Thanks, Igor. You saved me from a terrible death. I won't forget it!" Igor looked back at him and nodded gravely in acknowledgement. They drank. Nastrovia.

The barbecued fish was delicious.

Shortly after this, they hit the highway for an uneventful drive back to Raleigh. JeanLuc made calls to the Cardinal, and to the university to arrange for them all to meet at the airport to fly out to Europe that same day.

JeanLuc's hands rested lightly on the joystick controls as the monotonous digitised voice in his headset earphones went through the take-off checklist routine. There was nothing to do these days, he mused. Everything was computer-automated. You risked an abrupt computer admonition and electronic sulks if you so much as touched a switch. Not that there were any switches to touch in the cockpit of this brand new state-of -the-art Lear Fanjet he'd just bought for a couple of million bucks, using up, in one fell swoop, the rest of the dollar budget the Cardinal had left him, and leaving behind a Lear Corporation executive slack- jawed with astonishment and delight and ready to go back to the bed he'd been dragged out of at three in the morning.

JeanLuc glanced at the head-up display. The on-board indicators were all green. They were ready to roll.

The full long-range fuel tanks caused the wings to droop and bounce alarmingly as he carefully manoeuvred the delicate insect-like jet through the crowd of small planes towards the main runway. They would need to refuel four times on this long trip to their European destination.

They queued behind the United Airways early morning commuter flight to New York. As the Airbus took off, the tiny plane shook in the backwash of its thundering jets. RDU Tower gave JeanLuc the go-ahead; the yellow GO light glowed on as they turned into the main runway. JeanLuc lined up the nose and touched the take-off control that glowed green under his finger. Under computer control, the FanJet howled behind them and they accelerated, lifting off quickly and smoothly. The wheels came up with a hydraulic whine, the wings swept themselves back thirty degrees and they climbed steeply. Soon they reached a cruising altitude of 18,000ft and 'Flight K209' headed Northeast into a yellow dawning sky.

JeanLuc slid an REM Greatest Hits CD into the stereo caddy and

249

relaxed in his pilot's seat. Behind him in the cramped but luxurious passenger cabin, Igor stared morosely out of the porthole window, a glass tumbler of twenty-year-old Scotch clutched in his large paw. He loved America and he didn't want to leave. The Professor was already busy at work on a notebook PC networked into the plane's on-board computer.

In the luggage hold, in the tail of the aircraft, rested a wooden crate brightly red-labelled 'Urgent Medical Supplies'. Cocooned within polyethylene chippings, sandwiched, preserved between annealed plate glass lay the Jesus Icons now ready for the gaze of the Christian world, for the Fulfilment of a destiny ... dreamed into place two millennia in the past.

CHAPTER 32

Joel Maniato had been dreaming; too many dreams. His nights were one long uninterrupted nightmare from which he awoke sweating, and bleary eyed to face the long uninterrupted disasters that were his days. Ever since his return to New York, he'd been having the dreams. He dreamed he was in an office; an office like old Visorkis had at Biophar Drugs; an office with huge tall windows that reached from floor to ceiling, with a dizzying outlook over the City. They were whispering to him; whispering in his head. He was standing by the windows but there was no solidity to the window, only space, and his hand met no resistance and he could hear the traffic noise suddenly loud in his ears and the blaring of car horns and the ever present sirens of the police and ambulances echoing far below. Again the voices, the whisperings which had a sinister meaning he could never quite decipher. And in the vast black room behind him, there were pictures; many pictures with dark flat faces and huge eyes. Accusing eyes that seemed to bore into him, drill into the raw meat of his soul. Fly! The urging voices seem to say. Fly ... ! It was a very attractive proposition, compared to facing those eyes in the dark room behind him ...

Nothing had gone right for him from the day he arrived back and found his apartment locked and barred with a repossession notice stapled to the door. It had cost him nearly ten thousand bucks in back rent to be allowed back in. The eyes of the doorman and the lift-attendant seemed to slide unseeingly over and past him as if he had become invisible. Jesus! He'd tipped those suckers hundreds over the years, and now the shits wouldn't even give him the time of day!

And when he eventually got in, mail was piled up against the door in a deep drift: all bills; not even a letter from his mother. It took another day and several more thousand dollars to get the utilities reconnected. Even the fucking toilet was electrically flushed so he couldn't even take a shit without it lying there accusingly, smelling the place out. And the fucking bank had sent him another fucking letter and charged him another fucking hundred for telling him what he already knew—that he needed money real bad.

His regular salary cheque from Biophar Drugs had stopped abruptly when the Japs took over. The word was out that he was unemployed. Just the brief weeks he'd been in Durham with the Cardinal had caused them to forget him. For all they cared, he was a total unknown; a has-been. He'd missed the boat. Jesus, he'd even had to send a written CV to an employment agency—a task that took him two whole days to perform without the aid of a secretary. His contacts in the business were always 'in a meeting' or 'out of town on business' when he tried to ring. After a week or two of this, in desperation, he rang the Cardinal's office, only to be told that Cardinal Mirphy was still in Europe and not expected back for some time and would he like to talk with Canon Stentorian, the Cardinal's deputy? He had banged down the phone angrily. His mobile was already disconnected and he'd thrown it into the street where it was crushed flat by a passing taxicab.

Shelley let him back into her soft perfumed arms just once before his lacklustre performance and lack of finance for drugs and rock'n'roll caused her to chuck him out. Standing one night outside her apartment block, he watched in envious fury as a stretch limo pulled up outside and she welcomed effusively, a diminutive elderly Japanese executive. Cocksucking whore! he thought to himself and dispiritedly hailed a cab back to his lonely apartment that was getting dirty and uncared for, since the maid-service had been stopped to save money.

Man, he was bleeding! Money seemed to have been sucked from him by a vampiric vacuum cleaner and there was no more coming in. And he couldn't afford cocaine and he couldn't afford whiskey and he could barely afford taxi fares and his fucking credit cards all disappeared into the machines when he tried to get cash out. But he needed money to stop the dreams, to buy the drugs, the liquor, the women to stop the nightmare whispers and the haunting vision of that Holy Face beaming down on him with unendurably pitying eyes.

The answer came to him as he sat in the bar across from his apartment block, nursing a beer, staring out of the window at the driving April rain and the blurry neon lights, boiling inside with resentment at his predicament. Those Icons must be worth money to someone beside the Cardinal, he thought. The fucking Cardinal had left him in the shit, without a job or any means of support. He didn't owe them anything. They owed him! They sure as hell owed him! It was he that had set everything up for them, run Project Maraschino from the start, got that supercilious Kuovic into and out of Russia and out of trouble with the gangsters. They owed him, and where were they now? Fucking disparu.

Yes: he would find another buyer for those old pictures! Some Texas millionaire eccentric. Some Church Foundation was bound to find good money for Jesus Icons. But how could he convince others of their existence? He cursed himself for not getting pictures or a video whilst he was sorting things in North Carolina. He would have to get some proof; that was the number one priority and then make an approach to someone—preferably someone who would pay to have their existence suppressed, pay to have them destroyed! Yes, that would be better. Who would want such things destroyed? Who? Who would be affected most if the Jesus Icons were shown to the world?

Joel quickly drained his glass of beer and impatiently waved the waitress over. He would have a whiskey to help him think. The girl came over. She looked at him suspiciously; he'd been nursing that drink for over an hour and she divined that he mightn't have any money. As a waitress she'd quickly learned the signs. Maniato dug into his coat pocket and pulled out his last ten dollars. He pushed them across the table at the girl. "Get me a treble whiskey, please Miss. Irish—Jameson's if you have it. No ice, no water. Here's the money." She took up the grubby crumpled notes and went to the bar to get his drink. Cheapskate asshole, she thought cynically. No chance of a tip there.

Joel sipped the fiery liquid and continued his line of thought. Christian Churches presumably would benefit most from a resurgence of interest in religion caused by the Jesus Icons. It would validate and underpin belief in the historical existence of Jesus and the truth of the Bible. Certainly the Catholic Pope would kill for this—look at the revenue brought in by the Shroud of Turin and other Holy Relics trotted out periodically when funds were low. However, this was an avenue he couldn't explore without alerting Mirphy. Damn him! But hold on, maybe not all Christian religions would want this, after all, some were doing okay, thank you very much, especially the evangelical TV-disseminated fundamentalist type. To them, the Icons would be a distraction from an undiluted focus on the Coming of the Lord in the Apocalypse. Maybe their Nielsen's might drop, God forbid! And what about other religions? The Muslims or the Hindus or even the Buddhists? He couldn't imagine they would benefit either one way or the other from the Holy Faces.

He took another sip of whiskey and then an idea came to him. He collected up his meagre change, drained the whiskey and headed out into the cold rain, back to his apartment.

He let himself into the cold cheerless rooms and went straight to the phone. He breathed a sigh of relief when he heard the dial tone that meant they hadn't cut him off yet. He scrolled quickly through the phone numbers on his PDA. Ah, yes! There it was. He punched in the Utah code followed by the number.

"Josiah Smith, here" a voice drawled. "Josiah? This is Joel Maniato."

"Oh, hi! Joel! Long time no see! How are you, you randy son of a bitch! What's new? Are you in town?"

"No, I'm still in New York. Listen Josiah, are you still a director of Physico?"

"Yeah. Doin' good too, pal. Why? You looking for a job?" he continued in a more cautious tone.

"No, nothing like that," said Joel quickly.

"Good, I'm sure glad to hear that. You know what its like nowadays. It seems everyone is looking for work. Biophar Drugs treating you good? That's who you work for if my memory is right?"

"Not any more, Josiah. Biophar Drugs was sold to the Japs. I have my own independent consultancy now."

"Oh," said Smith sceptically, "that sounds pretty good," he continued doubtfully. "So. What can I do for you, Joel?"

"Physico Pharmaceutical is owned by the Mormon Church, am I right?" "Yeah and Moroni has been very good to us lately" laughed Smith gaily.

"Let's consider a proposition, Josiah. What if I had certain information that could lead to the destruction of the Mormon Church?"

"That would be impossible, kiddo. Many people have tried."

"Yeah, I know. But the Mormon Church is based on faith and

254

organisation not on truth. What if belief in the Mormon religion were to be taken away suddenly. You would have nothing, right?"

"I doubt it. Listen Joel, are you wasting my time or what? I don't need to discuss religion with you. You know where I stand. Physico only employs good Mormons."

"Listen, Josiah. If the Mormon Church collapses then Physico Pharmaceuticals goes too. Am I right?"

"I think you're raving, Joel. What's got into you? You been doing too much white stuff lately? Shit, I just got in from work and you're giving me this crap about the Mormon Church collapsing. Listen, it's impossible. The Mormon organisation is worth billions; it has millions of faithful followers including me. We have several Senators and many Congressmen. Shit, we Mormons own the State of Utah!"

"Yeah, I know. But what if I had proof—absolute proof that Mormonism is about to be discredited and destroyed. You'd want to know about it, wouldn't you? You're a Bishop. Surely, you'd want to counter the slightest threat to your Church?"

"Maybe, but I'd have to see it first. You'd have to convince me and then you'd have to convince others higher up in the organisation than me. I don't want to put my ass in the fire for nothing!"

"Listen, Josiah." Joel allowed a note of urgency to creep into his voice. "You know me from the past. I wouldn't bullshit you. I genuinely have information about something that can destroy Mormonism. You owe it to your beliefs to check me out because if you don't I shall have no option but to sell to another bidder and you can take your chances. I don't have much time."

There was a longish pause on the other end of the line. "So, what is this information? What form does it take?" Maniato breathed a sigh of relief. Smith was still on the line. He would listen—maybe he would pay.

"Can you come to New York to meet with me?" "You gotta be kidding!"

"The information I have is on video cassette." Joel took a deep breath. "As a start, I want thirty G's up front for the information and believe me it will be worth every cent to you."

"I doubt that, Maniato. I doubt that very much. You know I've got

255

to have more information than that. And why so little money? That's hardly a month's salary to you. Blackmailers always ask in millions these days!"

"I'm not a goddamn blackmailer. I need ..." Joel suddenly felt hot tears well in his eyes and he began to sob uncontrollably. He dropped the phone on the carpet and then rushed to the bathroom to throw up.

In Salt Lake City, at the other end of the line, Josiah Smith, Vice President of Operations for Physico Corporation, Elder in the Mormon Church, stared in puzzlement at the cordless phone and then pushed in the aerial and put it back down on the coffee table. "Pity about Maniato," he muttered to himself. "Used to be a good man."

He paced for a while up and down the spacious living room dominated by a huge original oil painting depicting Saint Joseph receiving the Plates from the Archangel Moroni, arms uplifted into a blaze of golden light. He then picked up the cordless again and dialled a number from memory. "Jedediah? Sorry to disturb you but I'd like you to drop by my office first thing tomorrow morning and I'll want time on the mainframe." He listened. " Yeah, the new VAX—the one that cost us three million. I shall want you to help me draft some questions and model some scenarios. God bless!"

He dialled another number, this time in New York. "Philip? Hi, this is Josiah Smith here, sorry to call you so late. I need you to make some inquiries for me." He listened." No, No, nothing like Whitewater, nothing like that—at least not yet! Just have a man called Joel Maniato followed. Look up his address and let me know what he's up to." He listened again and sighed. "Yeah, yeah, yeah, I know. Cash as usual. Don't fret. I have to be in DC next week so I'll stop by on my way. We'll meet at La Guardia—usual routine. And for God's sake, don't dress up as a pink Hare Krishna like you did last time. It gives the wrong impression here! Bye." He rang off as his number-eight wife came into the room. He put out his arms and said: "Hi, honey! Everything okay? Is it your turn tonight?" The fourteen-year-old child smiled at him demurely and shed her blue silk gown to reveal her pale, thin, unformed body. Smith's lizard tongue wet thin dry lips framed by his full dark uncut beard. The duties he had to perform for his Church! Oh well. Here we go again.

CHAPTER 33

Out of the reddening westward sky, with a high tail trade wind, came the Lear Jet, making landfall over clouded Scotland in the early evening. Spikel came into the darkened cockpit and handed JeanLuc a note. "It came over the microwave link. It's from Sir John Redcliff. Says welcome and he wants to know our ETA at his place. Oh, and it's raining hard down there."

"Thanks, Prof." JeanLuc keyed some figures into the navigation computer and having looked at the result, he twisted around. "It'll be about another forty-five minutes as long as we don't get tangled with the Glasgow air traffic pattern."

"Okay, I'll tell them. Do you want anything to eat or drink?" he asked. "There's loads back here—enough to feed an army. Even some barbecued fish, though God knows who brought that on board. It wasn't me—I hate fish!"

"No, thanks. I'll be busy until we arrive. The British sky is crowded and kinda tricky to get through. Everything all right back there?"

"Yes, no problems. Your gorilla is still asleep. It's been a smooth trip."

"Have you finished editing the flopticals for showing to Sir John and the Cardinal?"

"Yes."

"And the back-ups are safely locked away?"

"Yes, JeanLuc. Give me some credit for knowing my business."

"Sorry, Prof but you know how it is. There's a lot at stake—more than you can possibly imagine."

They were getting very low on fuel, and the yellow warning light had just lit up, when they flew over the English Northumbrian county border. JeanLuc spoke into the mouthpiece microphone: "Right, boys. We're landing in a few minutes. Get strapped in cos' I'm going in steep."

The navigation computer told him that they had arrived but he couldn't see a damn thing on account of the heavy unbroken cloud layers. For a few minutes, JeanLuc skipped the jet gingerly along the top of the clouds edged with pink sunset reflections and then, making a decision, he slid back the throttle sliders, pushed the joystick hard forward and gave it some hard left rudder. The jet spiral-dived into the dark rain clouds towards the ancient gloomy water sodden landscape below.

They emerged and levelled out at the cloud ceiling of five hundred feet, buffeted by gale-force gusts of wind. Ahead of them was the North Sea coastline outlined in the darkness by the white surf breaking against the bleak Northumbrian cliffs. They flew over a massive building complex beside which JeanLuc could see a line of bright runway lights. He banked the aircraft out to sea, turning to make his landing approach manually. He'd have to watch the up-draught from the cliffs. He'd do what the gulls did. He pitched the nose high, dropped the wheels, the landing lights coming on automatically, and drifted in carefully with pops of thrust to compensate for the viciously gusting wind. The Lear was as light as a feather with most of its fuel load gone and frisky... Boy, was she frisky! JeanLuc's eyes narrowed in concentration as a huge turreted cliff-top castle loomed rapidly out of the dusk with its illuminated landing strip beyond. Shit, it looks like something out of Lovecraft out there. Hell, these were the right co-ordinates and there was the airstrip—this must be it! He cut thrust and dropped the white hi-tech bird, ballerina dainty, down onto the rough rain slippery slicked concrete. Not a bad landing, even if I say so myself, thought JeanLuc with a smirk of satisfaction. Not lost the touch even after a narrow escape from fiery immolation and a ten-hour flight.

The voice of the Air Traffic Controller burst urgently into his earphones. "What's happened to you, Flight K209? Come in please? Flight 209, please acknowledge!"

JeanLuc sighed and worked the send button. "This is K209, Newcastle Tower, over."

"Copy, K209. You suddenly dropped out of our radar net. Why, K209? Are you all right, sir? Over," said the oh-so-British voice.

"We've run low on fuel and had to make an unscheduled stop. Over." JeanLuc gave his co-ordinates and listened patiently to the officious reprimand handed him over the air. Sir John would have to sort it out later. He taxied the plane over towards a rain-swept hangar, in front of which were parked a couple of Range Rover off-road vehicles.

Sir John Redcliff watched from the narrow window of his large comfortable study in the seaward turret of Redcliff Castle, as the plane first headed out to sea and then, turning, came back towards the shore. It looked like a large stormy petrel silhouetted against the dark scudding clouds. Or an albatross, thought Sir John nervously. He took a large gulp of twenty-five-year old Special Reserve Glen Morangie, refilling his glass from a half-empty bottle. His gaze followed the Lear Jet as it dropped out of the sky to touch down on the landing strip. He wiped his sweating brow with a handkerchief and flopped into a leather armchair. Christ! The terrifying risks they took! Why couldn't he have come by scheduled airliner or better still by boat!? Oh, no. He had to blow a small fortune on buying that tiny aircraft and come all the way from America single-handed with history's most precious cargo! Sir John couldn't bear to think what the consequences of the simultaneous loss of the Jesus Icons and of the linchpin of the Fulfilment might be. It was too frightening to contemplate. It would be the End—the triumph of the Anti-Christ! And yet he couldn't interfere. JeanLuc was on his narrow fated Path, he couldn't be touched. Events must unfold as they would. The Priory must stick to its pre-ordained role. He must grit his teeth and have FAITH!

He shuddered as the phone on his desk shrilled impatiently. Heaving his bulk out of the chair, he picked it up. "Sir John? Our foreign guests have arrived. Shall I bring them over at once?"

"No, Hampton. Show them to their quarters in the guest wing. They're probably exhausted and want to get themselves cleaned up. I'll see them in the morning at breakfast."

"Yes, sir."

"And Hampton? That aircraft must be guarded day and night. Get it into the hangar and I want at least ten armed men and dogs in there. No outsider is to go near and issue live ammunition to the men. While our guests are here, the Castle is on Red Alert status. Got that?"

Yes sir. Anything else, sir?"

"Yes, but it'll wait until later." Sir John replaced the phone and picked up his glass. Fuck the doctors, he needed this, he thought and drained it. This is the last stretch. He knew he wouldn't live to see the end but at least he'd have carried his baton to the next stage even if that baton was the stick of metaphysical dynamite, fuse now fizzing, that presaged the End of Things.

He picked up the phone and tapped in a number prefixed with 043. The line was picked up instantly. He engaged the scrambler. "Jean? They're here. Start things rolling."

"All right, John. Mon ami. I understand. I will inform Giselle."

"Fine. I will talk with you tomorrow and let you know when they will be flying."

"Good. Keep your strength up, John. There is still much to be done, but, God willing, this is the last stage in a long road—a culmination of centuries of work!"

"Is Joseph with you?"

"No. He is in Rome. I asked him to make a rapprochement with Emilio D'Ascriba and Von Helsinger—a difficult task."

"Will he tell them what he knows?" "Only in the last resort."

"And Moloc?"

"All quiet at the moment, but with him you never know." "What is our next step, Jean?"

"We must prepare Sigor for the Fulfilment Ceremonies and, of course, Giselle must be married. I think it would best to do this in Rennes le Chateau. I feel that this would have the most historic significance for a Merovingian."

"I hope this line is secure, Jean."

"So do I. However, no one has yet unscrambled the scrambler. I'm told it is impossible. It makes your voice a little squeaky, n'est pas?"

"Where should JeanLuc fly to from here? Sigor?"

"No. We will meet him in Avignon. You should also fly over. Drop what you're doing—this takes precedence over everything."

"But my movements are constantly monitored by my Government and probably others too. Won't this cause problems?"

"Maybe, but you'll have to invent some excuse. Come, my friend, as a politician you are an expert in that. Say your doctors advised immediate sun and rest in Southern France—that's probably pretty close to the truth, isn't it?"

"Fine, I'll say that. But I can only come after the International Match on Saturday, I don't want to miss that. I thought you were going to be there too."

"I had hoped to be, but things are a little difficult at the moment. I will watch our winning team on the TV!"

"Hah, you hope!"

"Eh bien. I'll see you in Avignon then. Sergeant Nollet, my Security Chief, will pick them up. You remember him?"

"Of course, how could I forget?" Sir John still vividly recalled the awful murder of Charles Duvain and the consequences that had flowed from that.

The next morning, Hampton the butler knocked discreetly on JeanLuc's bedroom door and went in carrying fresh clothes and an expensive new dark-coloured suit from Saville Row. JeanLuc was still asleep in the four-poster bed. Hampton picked up the soiled clothes strewn carelessly on the floor, frowning in distaste at what looked like a bloodstain on the sleeve of the shirt and at the strong smell of sweat, rubber and bonfire smoke. The other fellow was as bad, with his peculiar odour of fish and gunfire cordite.

Hampton pulled back the heavy curtains, letting in the pale watery morning light. The window overlooked the central courtyard of the castle, where there were two Range Rovers parked on the brushed yellow gravel alongside Sir John's seventy-year-old Rolls Royce Phantom and his new delivery mileage 220mph Bentley Java. The Redcliff-liveried chopper perched locust-like on its red-crossed pad in the grassy centre—its ever-ready stickjockey reading the latest gruesome offering by Dylan Jones.

JeanLuc stirred on the bed and opened his eyes. His gaze was unfocused and confused. "Where am I? Who are you?" he asked and sat up abruptly, drawing the blankets up around his naked body.

Hampton replied soothingly: "You're quite safe, sir. This is Sir John Redcliff's home and you arrived last night. I have some fresh clothes for you and when you're ready, breakfast will be served downstairs in the dining hall. I'll leave you now, but please ring the bell when you're ready or if you need anything further, sir." He bowed himself out and closed the door softly behind him.

JeanLuc shook himself and rubbed his face with his hands. He'd been dreaming ... but he couldn't remember what it was about ... just this fading vision of flames within smoke and dreadful screams of dying horses and swirling banners with red crosses and forests of spears...

He got out of the large bed and went into the en-suite bathroom. To his relief, he found that this British home did not subscribe to the cold-bath regime with its gold-tapped Jacuzzi and shower facilities. There was serious old money invested in this place—from the genuine antique furniture, to the original paintings by Constable on the walls.

He got dressed in the perfectly fitting new clothes provided by Hampton and admired himself in the mirror. Ignoring the large purple bruise on his cheek, he looked the perfect English gent! He could always maintain that the injury was acquired while fox-hunting! 'What ho, old chap!' JeanLuc laughed aloud at the thought and strode towards the door. After wandering some distance down deserted long carpeted corridors lined with large heavy intense portrait-oils of bygone members of the Redcliff family, JeanLuc found himself in a small private chapel. It was an empty, peaceful, well-lit place and he felt a quiet contentment just sitting there in the front pew. True, it was a somewhat unusual chapel in that he saw no crucifix or other symbols of Christian religion. On one wall, there was a massive oil painting by Poussin. At least that was what was written on the brass plaque. It looked imposingly original in its gilt frame. The other main decoration was provided by wood panels with carved scenes from the Mort d'Arthur; the search for the Holy Grail, the Knights of the Round Table and so on. A ray of morning sun shone through the east- facing window and JeanLuc looked up at it in surprise. The light was shining through a very unusual stained-glass window depicting strange Egyptian figures with curved fan-like helmets similar to those of Tibetan Buddhists, and with pyramids, and the whole was dominated by a many coloured peacock-feather eye. JeanLuc thought he'd seen something similar years ago in an art book. It was very strange and hauntingly familiar. He stared up at it in wonder.

A cultured English voice said from behind him: "It was done for my father by Jean Cocteau! Pretty spectacular, isn't it? It is one of my favourite things about this place.

JeanLuc started with surprise and turned.

"Welcome to my home, Your Highness. I am John Redcliff. Shall I show you to the dining hall where breakfast is waiting? Then we have much to discuss."

"Sure glad to meet you after all this time, Sir John. You have a fine place here," said JeanLuc to the bulky red-faced Englishman beside him. " But what is this 'Your Highness' stuff? Call me JeanLuc; everyone else does."

"All right. But you'll have to get used to it in the future. You are right; this place is beautiful, and steeped in blood and history. But that is a long story for which I'm afraid we don't have time right now. It is the future we must be thinking of. Follow me, I'll show you the way and then I'll meet up with you later in the library."

Halfway through a heaped plateful of kedgeree, a spicy rice dish with smoked haddock, chopped hard boiled eggs and a lot of parsley, JeanLuc looked over at Igor who was minutely examining the solid silver cutlery with the critical eye of a Krakow ghetto pawnbroker. He had just munched his way through a huge quantity of sausages, bacon and eggs—a feat that attracted furtively admiring glances from the buxom cook who was serving them.

"You okay, tovarich?" JeanLuc asked.

"Never better, JeanLuc. Are we staying long? This seems a nice place." He stared with frank lust at the cook who blushed crimson and ran out giggling.

"I agree with that," said the Professor, who was struggling through a bowl of porridge oats. "What is this revolting grey stuff?" he asked in puzzlement.

"It's porridge," said Igor. "Put some sugar and milk on it. Here." He passed over the jug and continued: "I would very much like to drive those cars that are outside. I miss my beloved Eldorado already. I hope she will be all right!"

"I don't know how long we'll be here. A few hours, I imagine. The plane needs re-fuelling and we have to fix it with the UK Customs and Excise and Air Traffic Control before we can fly again."

"Where are we going, JeanLuc?" This was the first time Professor

Spikel had shown any real curiosity about their destination. He'd been content to go where JeanLuc directed.

"We have to meet up with the Cardinal again." "Yes, I realise that but where?"

"To be honest, I don't really know, except it is somewhere in France."

"Oh, right. Thanks. Maybe I should check on the load?" He glanced around suspiciously. "Is this place secure, JeanLuc?"

JeanLuc laughed. "You can't get much more secure than this, Professor. This is the English headquarters of the Priory Arcadia—the people who are my patrons and who are backing the Cardinal."

"The Priory ... what?" asked the Professor curiously.

"Arcadia," said Sir John who had come back into the room. "If you are ready, follow me to the library where we can talk further. I believe also you have a presentation prepared, Professor Spikel?"

"Well, yes I do. But it was for Cardinal Mirphy, who commissioned my work. I'm not sure whether I should ..." he looked over at JeanLuc.

"If Sir John wants to see it, he should, Prof. I wouldn't mind hearing it myself, for that matter."

"All right. Do you have a television set, VCR or a PC available, Sir John?" "Hampton will set one up for us in the library."

"Fine. In that case, let's go. I have my video cassettes, CDs and discs right here." He lifted up a small aluminium briefcase.

JeanLuc interjected: "My friend Igor here will go and check on the progress with re-fuelling. Can he be permitted to have a look at your cars, Sir John? Igor is a car fanatic and connoisseur."

Sir John smiled. "Yes, of course; help yourself, Mr.Golemov. Drive them as much as you like. Hampton will give you the keys." Igor grinned and clapped his hands with delight.

The three men sat in front of a large screen Sony. Professor Spikel plugged his portable CD -player unit into the USB port of his notebook PC and a lead into the SCART socket in the back of the TV. He took out a couple of CDs and slid one into place in the player. He handed the other to Sir John. "I have made four copies of this. They are the only copies in existence. The master is in my safe in Duke University along with the videotape taken at the time of opening of the original storage tubes. You should keep this CD somewhere absolutely secure. I should also say that any unauthorised attempt to access the data will cause a subroutine to wipe the data—so be careful to enter your password correctly. I'll give you those afterwards.

"The information on that CD is collated from all the data we have amassed on the Jesus Icons over the last two months since the Carpocratian Legacy arrived in my lab. In my opinion, which is not humble, this could document the most important archaeological find of the century, possibly of all time. We are handling the religious equivalent of dynamite. To avoid any question of doubt I have subjected the Icons to every non-destructive scientific test possible in the time. The results of these tests are recorded on this CD."

A note of emotion entered the Professor's normally dry academic tone of voice. "I consider myself blessed and deeply honoured to have worked on this Project. I cannot begin to describe how this has affected me personally. I am expert in antiquities such as this but never have I felt the way I do about these particular treasures—and treasures they are indeed.

"Sir John, all the tests appear to prove without the slightest shadow of doubt that the paintings are absolutely authentic and genuinely date to the time of Jesus. However, as I shall show you, we do have some serious problems to address. Also, we do not know the reasons why they were painted and how they managed to survive so well all this time. These are still matters of speculation unanswerable by science. Maybe you will be able to contribute answers from other sources."

He turned to his PC and entered a password to access the presentation programme. A full- colour picture flashed onto the large screen. "This first picture is of the oldest of the paintings. We have managed to translate the Aramaic text written around the edge, thanks to my colleague at Duke, Professor Ephraim Bonar." He pressed a key and a close-up of the frayed border with the ancient script in faded grey black letters appeared on the screen. Moving the mouseball with his thumb, Professor Spikel moved the view to show the letters. "Regretfully, and here is the worst of our problems, although we can recognise these letters as Aramaic, the text makes no sense. It appears that they have been codified. This code I have been unable, as yet, to decipher. I will leave you with a printout of the symbols—maybe you have computers that could sort it out, Sir John?"

"I'm sure that could be arranged," said Sir John, his eyes riveted to the screen.

"As to the paintings themselves, I will go briefly through the main points that apply to them. Firstly and most importantly, until we decipher the Aramaic text we do not know for sure that these are portraits of Jesus and his immediate family. Although I have no doubt myself that they are meant to be, from the context, correct age and other circumstantial evidence but ..." he paused.. " It could be argued that they portray some other wealthy Jewish family of the time."

"My God, you mean there is some doubt?" yelled JeanLuc. "After all we've been through! I can't believe it!" He stared at the Professor in shock.

"I'm afraid so. You have been looking at them from your viewpoint and imposing your own perceptions—a form of wish fulfilment," he said harshly. "On the other hand, the weight of objective scientific evidence favours that hypothesis. But science can only go so far, the real clincher would be for the text to be deciphered and tell us the answer. Therein lies the final key to this considerable mystery."

The other two men looked at Spikel. They could not speak. Sir John waved a hand indicating for him to go on.

"Physics, chemistry and forensic tests give us the answers that the cloth, which is genuine silk, is carbon-dated at BC 50 plus or minus one hundred and fifty years. This makes the cloth fifty years or so older than Jesus' time. " The Professor tapped a key and a technical graph showed up on the screen. "This would be consistent with the cloth being manufactured well before its use for the picture-making. If it had been dated younger then they could not have been of Jesus. To illustrate my point, the Turin Shroud carbon dated to around 13-1400 AD. This, other evidence to do with pollen, the religio-political situation at the time and other things makes the Turin Shroud a clever fake constructed a thousand years after the supposed event.

"I can rule out the possibility that these are similar fakes to the Turin Shroud because the age of the cloth is consistent with the time-frame we are interested in. There is, however, the question of the age of the paint itself that we are unable to test for the obvious reason that it would destroy part of the picture. You could, for example, argue that someone had acquired old silk of the correct period and then used modern pigments for the painting itself." JeanLuc groaned and put his head in his hands. "However, fortunately, the various forensic style tests I applied, which, although not conclusive, support the view that most of the pigments and dyes are very similar to those used in the Middle East by the Phoenicians in particular. The extent of fading is consistent with great age but it would also be dependent on exposure to sunlight, air and other factors that cannot be guessed at. In fact, as you can see, the colour retention and preservation state of the cloth is miraculously good, considering its age. I put this down to the fact that they must have been in those storage tubes in dry dark conditions, untouched for hundreds of years at a time.

"Particularly interesting is the spectrophotometric analyses of the purple and blue pigments used. See here." He tapped a few more keys and the screen showed another graphical image but this time with numerous spikes in a mountain-range type of pattern. "This is the characteristic mass spectrometry analytical pattern from the Icons and ..." he hit some more keys "and this is the pattern from purple pigment extracted from a rare mollusc found on sea cliffs on the East Mediterranean coast near Tyre. As you can see the two patterns match exactly. However, this same pigment was also used by the Egyptians, Phoenicians and exclusively by the Roman Emperors for the Royal Purple on their togas. " He tapped another key. "As you can see, this pattern also matches the analysis of purple in a toga found preserved in the ash at Pompeii. Purple inks and pigments after about 200AD could be manufactured from other sources and they have spectral patterns totally different, see like this ..." The dissimilar non-matching pattern appeared on the screen "... or this, which is ink extracted from squids.

"If all this is taken together with evidence from the blue pigment analyses, then it appears to accurately locate the painting within the Holy Land."

"Why the blue? Surely these colours are all blends of various things and have little significance?" asked JeanLuc.

"Not so. In ancient times, even until quite recently, paints were made from blending chalks or vegetable dyes into an egg tempera or tree gums. There were relatively few sources of pure colours and these were often treasured and used for specifically religious reasons as here. Look at this pattern of the blue part of the robes worn by the figures." The Professor focused on the sleeves of the robe that Jesus was wearing in the painting. "It is very faded and now looks grey but the spectrophotometric pattern is identical to this ..." The screen showed a blue-coloured square with its spectral lines next to it.

"What is that?" asked Sir John with interest.

"This is the blue colour extracted from a species of snail only found at the site of the Temple of Jerusalem specifically in the Wailing Wall. It was only used in a strictly religious context, to stain the garments of the High Priests of the Temple. Its use was forbidden in any other application."

"So!" said Sir John excitedly. "Are you saying that the icons are painted with a blue dye only allowed to be used by High Priests of Judaism and purple that was precious even to royalty in the time of Jesus?"

"That's a good summary. Yes. And to me that is pretty convincing, but not conclusive, scientific evidence locating the time and place of the painting. It also means that the subjects painted must be of the highest rank in the Jewish Priesthood or Royal Family—not just anybody or else it would have been sacrilegious to use the blue dye. Moreover, the snails that made this particular pigment became extinct shortly after the Sack of Jerusalem in AD70 by Titus and the Tenth Legion. Whoever painted the pictures probably had to have painted them before AD70. However, it has to be said that is also still possible, though unlikely, for the paintings to have been done later, if someone, after that time, had access to a supply of the precious dye."

"A sort of holy paint pot, you mean?" asked JeanLuc." How did you get the test sample that you showed us?"

"There is still one minuscule source of the extract remaining and that is where I got the sample and then only a scraping. From Mecca."

"So it is still conceivable that a medieval or even modern faker could have got cloth of the right age and even pigments of extreme rarity and painted these pictures?" despaired JeanLuc.

"That is so. But don't be too downhearted, JeanLuc. I haven't finished yet. Also you have to consider the odds against such a clever fake, requiring almost superhuman cunning and resources. If they are fake, it could only have been perpetrated in the last decade or so, certainly not before. The only person I can think of who could have done this is Dmitri Yemeljan, and he would have needed considerable help from the Russian authorities. Why do it at all?"

"To discredit Christianity?"

"Possibly, but it seems an overly complicated way of doing so. Some Catholic priests themselves are already doing a pretty good job at that, even without outside help," he added sarcastically.

"You said you hadn't finished, Professor. Please continue." said Sir John.

"Of course. The other pigments in the painting are complex blends of vegetable extracts such as beetroot and of course squid or octopus blacks and browns. These all have their characteristic spectra as well, but since they have been used from antiquity to almost the present day they do not support our arguments as well as the blue or the purple."

"What about the silk material itself?" asked Sir John.

"Well, as I said, we have accurately carbon-dated it but since these are the only samples I have ever seen preserved for this length of time, there is nothing to compare them with apart from relatively recent materials found in late Byzantine sites and of course in China itself. I haven't been able to contact the Chinese to get an authoritative view as yet. This is something we may need to consider."

"Was painting on silk unusual in those days?"

"Very unusual. In fact, unheard of in that region of the world. Silk was an extremely rare and precious commodity, regarded as treasure by ancient kings and emperors. The length of silk in these paintings would amount to a king's ransom in those days. It wasn't used for women's knickers, that's for sure, unless you were Cleopatra!"

"So, whoever had the paintings done had to be very rich?" asked Sir John. "Either that or been given the materials for a sacred purpose as a gift."

"But convention has it that Jesus was dirt poor and the Essenes also called themselves 'the Poor' giving away all their worldly possessions."

"Yes, but convention also has it that Kings from the East, the three wise men, brought precious gifts to the infant Jesus, so a bolt of silk might have been part of this. The Bible also says that Jesus had many rich and powerful supporters such as Joseph of Arimathea. I don't want to go into the complex arguments about Jesus' real status and rank amongst the Jews but it is most likely that he had ready access to the materials necessary to paint these portraits."

"But we always come back to the central objection. Is this really Jesus and his Family or someone else in a similar time-frame—a rich merchant perhaps or a member of Herod Agrippa's family such as Antipas? God alone knows Herod tried everything to legitimise his position as King of the Jews," said Sir John mournfully.

"I'm afraid so," said the Professor blandly. "It becomes a subjective thing. Until we decode the accompanying text we are still vulnerable to scepticism from non-believers. They may come to accept the artefacts as genuine and scientifically proven, but contest the meaning of the images themselves. Circumstantial evidence all points to the truth that these are images of Jesus, King of the Jews. You and I may believe it, but that is not enough. As soon as you have to explain things in historical or even scientific terms and contexts, then you've lost your audience and your believers."

"What about the sacrilegious aspect? The forbidding of graven images? asked JeanLuc.

"That's not necessarily a problem. Modern interpretations of the Bible and archaeological findings in Jerusalem and at a place called Dura on the River Euphrates reveal that the making of statues and pictures was not banned by Mosaic Law. In fact, they did alot of decorating of the Temple and the Old Testament even tells them specifically how to do it. The Jewish Synagogue at Dura proves conclusively that Jews could have elaborate painted decoration of their synagogues, if they so wished. What I'm trying to say is that, at the time of Jesus, banning of practices such as portrait painting were not necessarily codified into Law amongst all the different religious groupings. Jesus is thought to have belonged to the Essenes who had very different practices and interpretations of Mosaic Law compared to say a Pharisee, like St.Paul, or the Sadducees. Early Christians Jews were dead against image-making as being idolatrous, and also by that time Jesus was starting to be regarded as a part of God."

"Dmitri Yemeljan in Russia told me a little about that," said JeanLuc.

"Ah, yes! Yemeljan. I would very much like to meet him. This is all his doing. He could be very helpful. He is very knowledgeable."

"Then we'll have to see about getting him over," said Sir John. "Do you think he may know something about the Aramaic code?"

"Who knows—it is possible."

"Please continue, Josef," said JeanLuc. "Is there more you can tell us?"

"Yes, indeed. These are fascinating artefacts that will occupy research teams for years. I have only begun to penetrate their mysteries ..."

"Yes, yes. I know. But I don't want to hear of academic dreams—what of the images themselves?" interrupted JeanLuc impatiently. "Do you have any comments on style or technique?"

"They are very skilfully painted with the sure detailed brush-work of a master artist. Unfortunately, it is very difficult to attribute them to a particular school or artist because we know so little about the art of that period. There are many influences there—Greco-Roman, Phoenician, a strong Egyptian style— the facial detail is reminiscent of Egyptian Mummy paintings. The faces are carefully painted and surprisingly realistic for the time. Normally, you'd expect a very stylised bland representation and yet here ..." he tapped some keys bringing up a close-up shot "if we look at this man's face which is probably Joseph, Jesus' father, you can see the artist has shown him as quite an old man with white beard and hair and wrinkled features— a real old patriarch. Such realism is quite unexpected and possibly has religious significance. If we use the microscope.." the image magnification increased to reveal a criss-cross pattern of brush strokes, "... we see that the artists, and I think there were two, used fine hair brushes probably soft camel hair, just like today!

"The paintings are relatively straightforward representations of people although done with great realism and by a skilled artist on an unusual and rare canvas. You get the distinct impression, however, that there is a purpose behind them beyond that of a rich family heirloom. And, indeed there is more ..." Professor Spikel paused here and looked at the others with a mischievous grin. "To quote a phrase, 'there is more than meets the eye' in these pictures and I have left the best 'til last. Let me show you and prepare to be astounded!"

The Professor tapped some more commands and the light on the CD player came on as the PC searched for the relevant information. "Can you pull the curtains and lower the lights please, JeanLuc." As JeanLuc got up to comply with this request, the Professor continued."The images I shall show you are very faint indeed. I had to use image intensification and computer tomography software to bring them up but there is definitely something there and I have confirmed it by micro- NMR!"

That icon of modern technology, the TV set, glowed brightly in front of them in the now darkened library that smelled of ancient musty texts containing hidden secrets, long-forgotten history and diabolical imaginings wrapped in parchment and yellowed paper bound with leather.

"First of all, I'll quickly go through some of the standard image analyses I did. I'll use the main portrait of Jesus himself as the example although I have scanned every millimetre of the others as well. This is the infrared scan. As you can see there is nothing showing, there are no differentiated heat areas at all ,which is to be expected. I also took low intensity x-ray pictures that revealed nothing unusual. I have placed pre-flashed sensitised x-ray film in direct contact with the silk for a month but there are no dark spots due to radioactivity. I have used nuclear magnetic resonance imaging techniques that they use for brain scanning. I have looked at them in reverse video and every colour enhancement mode or visible light frequency. I have scanned them through complex pattern recognition software, and even through the FBI faces database—the only interesting result I got was a thirty percent parameter match of Jesus' face to Elvis Presley! There's food for thought!" The others laughed uncertainly.

"I have used every image-manipulation trick in the book. If you recall, the Turin Shroud became famous for its 'negative image' and some people have conjured a 'face' out of faint Rorschach blotches on the Veronica cloth. I did all these things and got zilch ..." He stopped and keyed in a command causing the screen to go almost completely dark—they could just make out the features of the face of Jesus. The Professor moved the bright arrow pointer around the screen with the mouseball and settled it at the far right of the screen.

"That is, until I tried this ...!" and he hit a key. A brief flash of intense blue light flooded the screen and then faded abruptly. Magically, to the right of the screen under the arrow, they could now see a very faint yellow green after-image in the shape of a letter or some other symbol but which faded almost immediately.

"Well, what the hell is it?" asked Sir John, a note of petulance entering his voice suggesting he was getting fed-up with this lecture.

"To me, as a scientist, this could be the equivalent of a miracle," said the Professor in a portentous tone. "In areas of these paintings, there are symbols and letters that show up briefly only under short flashes of ultra violet light. Continuous UV exposure is no good—It bleaches the images. There is absolutely no doubt about this and I have collected image-enhanced versions of them here. " A collection of fuzzy edged symbols and letters in a green colour appeared on the screen.

"It is a virtual impossibility for anyone in ancient days to have known how to do this. These symbols were painted in ink that is only revealed by fluorescence under UV light. It is not even the same as the normal fluorescent paint that you find on watches or clock faces. The whole thing pre-supposes the ability to generate high intensity ultraviolet light and also the chemistry to put together an appropriate fluor. To me this is amazing—a miraculous accomplishment."

"Or else a completely modern fake," said JeanLuc tonelessly." Surely this puts the nail in the coffin? That son of bitch Yemeljan has put one over us! I'll kill the bastard!"

"Much as I hate to say it, I think you may well be right, JeanLuc. But I know in my heart that you are wrong. This is not a fake. I cannot put my finger on it, I cannot prove it with science but these are not fakes. You know Yemeljan. You went to Russia, to Siberia. You were there!"

"But you've just scientifically proved that they are fakes! " exclaimed JeanLuc "There is fucking fluorescent dye or something all over them! Just as if they were stolen marked banknotes! And Dmitri is a fucking artist, for Christ's sake he paints and sells icons for a living! And the Gallery sent him all over Russia. And his son works for the fucking FSB! My God I feel a complete idiot." He put his head in his hands and groaned. "I can just imagine how it will be. We make a big big story about the Icons ... then Dmitri comes along saying he faked them and can prove it by shining UV light on them, and this shows how gullible people are and that religious belief is just opium of the masses and we become the laughing stock of the world!"

"But if he was that clever then he must have realised and anticipated that we would put the Icons through every conceivable test before announcing their existence to the world; including the UV-exposure test which is a fairly standard thing. Also the Aramaic text is codified. Are you suggesting that he knows the key to the cipher and it will translate into something like yah-boo, sucks-to-you?"

"Too right I am! Maybe the whole thing is just a game to him—a complicated hobby! Maybe he is gambling we would not be thorough enough in our testing so that he can come and blackmail us after we go public. Pay or I tell the punters. My God, has he any conception about how dangerous this game is, what he is dealing with, how many deaths there have been, including that of his own daughter?"

"But we don't know this for sure, do we, JeanLuc?" argued Sir John suddenly. "I think before we finally make our decision whether to put the Icons in the bin along with Yemeljan, we should talk with him. I'll book him on the next flight out of Moscow into London. If he refuses to come, then it will because he thinks we've rumbled him and we dump the whole deal. If he agrees to come then we defer a decision until later. What do you think, Professor?"

"That sounds like a good idea to me, Sir John. Do you know his number?" "I'm sure we have it somewhere. What time is it in Moscow now, JeanLuc?"

"They're four hours ahead of us, so it'll be about three in the afternoon. You speak to him. I don't think I can trust myself not to scream." JeanLuc stood up and marched furiously from the room.

"He's coming, JeanLuc!" "What! I don't believe it!"

"He'll be here this evening. He is booked onto the Virgin Airlines three o'clock our time flight out of Moscow and I have already sent my chopper off down to Heathrow to pick him up and bring him here."

"What did he say?"

"He seemed genuinely glad to hear from us and anxious to know what the Legacy consisted of."

"What did you tell him?"

"I told him that we wanted his expert advice before going public with our findings. I told him we were very impressed?"

"Just that? Very impressed? Did he ask after me?"

"Yes, he did. I told him that you were well and would be here to meet with him. He says he will be bringing his wife Saskia with him, and that there was nothing in Russia left for them."

"Well, we shall see."

CHAPTER 34

JeanLuc watched with churning emotions, as the helicopter bringing Dmitri and Saskia Yemeljan dropped out of the black sky, following the path of its searchlight landing beams. Its green and red running lights reflected eerily against the grey castle walls. Sir John stood beside him. They were both smoking cigarettes—cheap and nasty English cigarettes cadged off Hampton the butler. Between them they'd finished the Glen Morangie and were well into a bottle of Black Label.

Sir John slurred, "My great-great-grandfather fought with Bonnie Prince Charlie, y'know!"

"Is that so, Sir John? I don't know who my parents are, let alone my ancestors."

"Y'mean no-one has ever told you?" Sir John looked at him in amazement. "You've been a ward of Joseph Mirphy's for nigh on twenty years and he's not told you?"

Outside the chopper had landed and two figures, bundled up in greatcoats, walked slowly away from it towards the waiting heraldic figure of Hampton. They were here.

JeanLuc turned away from the window and regarded Sir John out of narrowed eyes. He took a swig of whiskey. "No, should he have?"

Sir John gulped his drink and raised his eyes to heaven. "Haven't you ever wondered?"

"Sometimes, but not that much. They didn't encourage that sort of thing in the orphanage or the Military. We learned to make our own history day-to-day. Why do you ask? and why, earlier in the Chapel, did you call me by that ridiculous title?"

"We need to talk, my lad. We need to talk." Sir John laughed, an overtone of hysteria creeping into his voice.

There was a knock on the door.

"Come in!" shouted Sir John and he moved towards it. "Welcome, welcome!" he effused. "Mrs Yemeljan and you, too, Mr Yemeljan. I hope you had a reasonable trip. I won't say 'pleasant' because that chopper can be a bit bumpy at times, I know. You must be exhausted, so we have already prepared your rooms. I hope you find them comfortable."

"On behalf of my wife and myself, I thank you, Sir John," said Dmitri. "Hello, JeanLuc, it's good to see you again, tovarich!" He held out his arms.

JeanLuc felt tears of emotion flood unbidden into his eyes and he rushed forward to embrace the Russian pair.

"Oh, JeanLuc. Oh, JeanLuc!" wept Saskia and JeanLuc felt carried away in an emotional outpouring that he could hardly control—as if he'd been re-united with long -lost parents. Sir John wept too, in sympathetic alcoholic catharsis. Hampton regarded the chaotic dance of clumsy embraces with cold British aloofness and waited for it to subside. It would probably result in everyone pinching more of his cheap cigs. The Guv'nor would have to pay for it out of his supply of cellar-stored Chateau bottled wine. Hampton was quite partial to a drop or two of French vintage when everyone was in bed. He considered it a fair exchange.

Early next morning, five men met in the Library. Sir John Redcliff, Dmitri Yemeljan, Professor Spikel, JeanLuc and Igor, who stood by the door. The Professor went through his presentation once again. Outside, it had stopped raining. After his final sentence, all eyes turned to Dmitri.

"You could have faked this, Yemeljan," said Sir John bluntly. "That is why I brought you here. That is why we want an explanation."

Dmitri stroked his long white beard with nicotine stained fingers. "You are right," he began. JeanLuc closed his eyes in despair. "I could have forged these paintings, admittedly with greatest of difficulty. But I did not do so!"

The others regarded him in disbelieving silence. "Firstly, if I had actually done such a monstrous thing, I wouldn't be sitting here, my life and reputation entirely at your mercy. I swear to God and all that I hold sacred that this is not my work. This is the very first time I have seen what you call the Jesus Icons. All I ever saw was the copper storage tubes that we found in Rasputin's chapel. I am as surprised and staggered as you are at what we found."

"But I'm sure you understand our concerns, Dmitri," said JeanLuc. "You have the technical know-how, the resources, the contacts, the

Esoteric knowledge, even possibly the motive."

"That is true. But the fact remains. I didn't do it. If you like I will submit to a lie-detector test, truth drugs, whatever. I have nothing to hide."

"I'm afraid we will have to ask you to sit a polygraph test," said Sir John seriously and he pushed a call button on the wall. A few seconds later, Hampton came in, carrying a box from which he took the lie-detecting apparatus. Dmitri rolled up the sleeves of his shirt and allowed Hampton to connect the various sensors to the palms of his hands and forehead. Hampton switched on the instrument and studied the small VDU across the middle of which a wavering green line was pulsing.

"Now, sir" said Hampton politely. "I shall ask you a few questions which I'd like you to answer with a straightforward yes or no. This instrument is designed to detect if you are telling the truth." He looked down at the list of questions given to him earlier by Sir John. "Is your name Dmitri Yemeljan?"

"Yes!" The green line stayed steady. After a series of questions designed to check the operation of the machine, including asking Dmitri to tell some deliberate lies, Hampton came to the final set of questions. They all listened tensely.

"Did you paint the pictures seen here presented to you by Professor Spikel?" "No!"

"Did you forge or fake any of the pictures shown to you in this room by Professor Spikel?"

"No!"

"Have you ever faked a religious Icon before?" "No!"

"Did you know what the Carpocratian Legacy consisted of before today?" "No!"

"Thank you, sir. That is all I need. If you will kindly wait outside I will make my report to Sir John." Tiredly, Dmitri took off the sensors and walked to the door. Halfway, he stopped and half turned as if to speak but he continued, closing the library door behind him. Igor went out with him.

"He lied twice, sir!" Hampton said immediately. "To which questions?" asked Sir John dolefully.

"To 'is Sophia Yemeljan your daughter' and 'have you ever faked a religious Icon before'."

"Is that all?" asked Sir John, a note of hope in his voice.

"Yes sir. There is no doubt that the lie-detector is working perfectly. Most of the questions he answered truthfully, just those two."

"Thank you Hampton. On your way out, please ask Mr Yemeljan to step back in."

"Yes sir. I'll clear this up when you've finished in here, sir." "Right."

Dmitri sat down again in the chair facing his inquisitors. At once, he held up his hand to stop them. "Yes, I know, I know! I lied. Sophia was not my true daughter. I cannot have children. Both Sergei and Sophia are Saskia's by a previous marriage. Saskia and I married when the children were both babies and I still love and regard them as my own children. I did not know their father, who was killed by mercenaries in Africa whilst acting as a military advisor for the Soviets. You'll have to ask Saskia about all that.

"And yes I have conspired in the faking of an icon. To my shame, during the early sixties, when Podgorny was Secretary General, the Communists insisted that we at the Tretyakov sell off some of our treasures in return for bullion. In order to keep one of our most precious Icons in the country, we made a forgery and sold it amongst other less -valuable pieces to the Vatican Collection. It was a successful deception, because they still believe they have an Icon painted by the master André Rubelov! It was on that selling trip that I met Father Joseph Mirphy, as he was then. To think that now he is a Cardinal!"

"Sir John exchanged a glance with JeanLuc, who looked back at Dmitri with a mixture of puzzlement and relief at what Dmitri was saying.

"So, where does this lead us?" asked Sir John.

"Either the Jesus Icons are not a fake, or else they are and have been perpetrated by someone completely unknown to us," said Professor Spikel.

"They must be genuine. It is impossible for anyone else to have planted them and led us to their discovery," cried JeanLuc with a happy expression.

"Of course they are genuine! I've staked my life on it!" shouted

Dmitri.

"But what about the fluorescent symbols?" persisted the Professor. "Are you saying that these were painted in at the time of Christ—it seems incredible to me. I mean what is the purpose? There could have been no-one able to visualise them at any time in history up to the present day!"

"Maybe you're being too narrow-minded, Professor. There are many unexplained mysteries in this world, some of which I have witnessed first hand. Also, we should not underestimate the knowledge of the ancients," said Sir John. "Anyway, I for one am truly glad Dmitri is now here to help us solve some of these mysteries. Dmitri, on behalf of us all I would like to welcome you among us and I shall be the first to apologise for doubting you and for putting you through this ill-mannered treatment."

"I understand, Sir John, and I thank you. I bear you no ill will. I'm just glad to be here and will do everything in my power to help you."

"Yes I'm sorry too, Dmitri. I must admit to feelings of anger and rage at you, but that is all past," said JeanLuc quietly, the memory of Sophia still in his mind. "So let us put our minds back to the task of the Jesus Icons and their interpretation. As I see it, we have two remaining problems, if we make the assumption that they are genuine. First is the decoding of the Aramaic text around the borders, and second to try to find the meaning of the fluorescent symbols—am I right Professor?"

"That's about it, JeanLuc. The two may be linked. If we figure out one then the other may become clear. Also, don't forget the question mark of whether this really is the Jesus family or somebody else!"

"Switch on the TV again and let's have a closer look, now that Dmitri is with us. I'll draw the curtains." The Professor complied and again the symbols came onto the screen.

JeanLuc stared at the symbols. There were several Greek letter Tau's, a fish symbol, a kind of mandala, an eye in a pyramid and several Arabic numerals, a hive with dot-like bees around it and what could be described as a primitive star map. It was fascinating, and in this context of the Icons truly amazing. They all looked vaguely familiar, as if he had seen them before in books or in his dreams.

"As to their meaning, I can only make educated guesses," began Dmitri. "The Tau is a recognition symbol used extensively by the Zealots around the time of the Maccabees, many were tattooed with it; the fish symbol also. As most people know, the fish symbol was used by the early Christians in Rome, the Greek word for which formed an acrostic 'Jesus Christ Son of God Saviour'. The peacock is an ancient symbol of immortality. The pyramid eye might be something to do with Egyptian beliefs in Horus, Isis and Osiris—these Gods form a model for many eastern religions. The hive is a symbol of the ancient Sumerians who were forefathers of the Israelites. There are dots around the hive that might represent the Twelve Tribes or Zodiacal Houses. Bees were also a symbol of the Cathars who were a heretical sect wiped out by the Albigensian Crusade. As to the numbers and other patterns, I haven't a clue. They are obviously carefully positioned in the paintings as clues or keys to something else. I suspect we will now need to consult somebody versed in the Occult or Hermetic mysteries. I am at the limit of my knowledge I'm afraid," concluded Dmitri. He switched off the TV and sat down regarding the others with a sober expression.

"You have done brilliantly, my dear fellow. More than anyone could have hoped," said Sir John.

Dmitri looked at the others and then asked JeanLuc in Russian, almost tentatively: "Excuse me for asking, but don't you think the Jesus figure looks a bit like the Man in the Shroud? Has this been considered?"

"The Shroud of Turin?" replied JeanLuc. "I don't know." He turned to the Professor. "Josef, did you compare the features of Jesus here in our portrait with those of the Holy Face in the Shroud of Turin? " he asked. " You did say you'd done some computerised face-mapping."

Josef Spikel looked somewhat taken aback. "Well, yes I have, but only of faces I already had in image databases from TV news archives and the FBI. It wasn't an exhaustive search—I've not had the time. My brief was to restore the Icons not to interpret them. However, you are right, Dmitri. We should analyse the features against the Man of the Shroud and also various other Icons of Jesus"

"Like the mosaics of Hagia Sophia and Cefalu," said Sir John. "And the Genovese Mandylion," continued Spikel.

"And I should have some photographs here of the Mandylions in Gradac, Spas Neriditsa and the Studenica monastery," cried Sir John excitedly.

"And don't forget that beautiful picture in St.Catherine's monastery in Sinai!" exclaimed Spikel.

"What's the Mandylion?" asked JeanLuc impatiently. "I thought it was the Shroud of Turin we wanted to compare with. Although I can't see why. I thought you told me that it was a fake, and anyway, if I remember correctly, the features are very difficult to make out."

"I'm sorry," apologised Dmitri. "Let me explain more fully. It is sometimes difficult to remember that not everyone is a fanatical Sindonologist—that is somebody who studies the Shroud," said Dmitri.

"Yes, I did say the Shroud was a fourteenth century fake based on the scientific carbon-dating done in 1988. But if you ignore this finding, and there are some good reasons for doing so, then most of the other evidence and its history point towards it being genuine. Just to summarise for you: The Shroud image is now thought to be a vapourgraphic image of Jesus formed on the cloth by body odours and secretions mixing with a healing balm of aloes and myrrh. You can duplicate the effect, more or less, by smearing someone with the balm and draping them with a linen cloth. This cloth that is alleged to have covered Jesus or someone who'd been crucified, was kept as a relic and supposedly presented to King Abgar V of Edessa as a gift from the early Christians. For most of its history, it was kept folded with only the face portion showing through a decorated circular frame. It was known as the Mandylion of Edessa and was valued both as a relic of Jesus and as an apparent protection against armed overthrow and invasion. It remained hidden for many centuries in the gateway structure at Edessa. After its re-discovery, some think it was acquired by the Knights Templars who kept it hidden until the fourteenth century when it was displayed to the public to raise revenue for the widow of the family that had possession of it. Thereafter, its history has been fairly well documented. It was bequeathed to Pope John Paul II by the Spanish King Umberto II and is now in Turin Cathedral behind the altar of the Royal Chapel.

"Copies of this are thought to have provided the pattern for the earliest Christian Iconography. That is why the features of the Shroud face match up with some of these early Icons."

"But all that pre-supposes that the Shroud is genuine and also that it is of Jesus himself," interposed JeanLuc. "Even if the Shroud is genuine and the carbon-dating some kind of error or fiddle, there is no proof that it is Jesus - it could have been any crucified person. There must have been thousands of crucifixions going on around at that time. We have the same problem here. Until we decode the script, there can still be doubt about our own Jesus pictures even though they date correctly."

"Yes, you're quite correct, JeanLuc," interjected the Professor. "Although I might add that the linen of the Shroud is a very costly Syrian-made fabric not affordable by the ordinary run-of-the-mill crucifixion victim. Nor would this cloth have been used as burial wrappings—a quite different method was used, say, for the burial of Lazarus and most other Jews—it is all very confusing and mysterious. Nevertheless, to get back to the main point, the Jesus in our pictures looks like most other Jews: long Semitic nose, bearded, dark complexion and so on. What we will have to do is look carefully at all the twenty or so specific features listed by Sindonologists and see if they match up at all with our portrait. To be honest, I am not that hopeful, which is why I didn't pursue it in the first place—but we can but try."

"Dmitri, can you recall the main features of the Man of the Shroud?" asked JeanLuc.

"We can do better than that," said Sir John. "I have several illustrated books here on the Shroud. We should be able to find something." Sir John went over to the bookcases, opened the glass-fronted doors and ran his finger over some titles. He pulled out a book. " There should be something in here, in Ian Wilson's book." He flicked through the pages. In the meantime, Professor Spikel had put the magnified image of Jesus' face back onto the TV screen. It gazed out at them, flickering slightly.

"Ah, here we are. Fifteen special features of the Face of the Shroud that have also been found on Byzantine Icons. Here, I'll write down the list." Sir John took a pen and quickly copied some words from the book and then handed the paper to JeanLuc.

JeanLuc looked at these notes and then at the screen. "The first feature is a horizontal stripe on the forehead—can we see that?" They all peered closely at the screen.

"Well, the artist has painted an almost smooth brow. I cannot see anything that would constitute a stripe or a wrinkle," said Josef. "Let me look at that picture of the Shroud Face again, Sir John." He took the book and laid it open in front of the TV.

They spent an hour or so comparing the features of the Man of the Shroud and their picture on the screen. Finally, JeanLuc pushed his chair away from the table and stood up. "This is hopeless," he cried in disappointment. "The only feature that is similar is the long nose and maybe a slightly raised eyebrow but it is hardly convincing. We don't even have a forked beard in ours."

"We can't expect too much, JeanLuc." said Dmitri. "Remember, the vapourgraphic image must have introduced distortions from different concentrations of the aloe-myrrh balm smeared on the body. Feature I and 13 could just be from ripples of the mixture on an otherwise smooth surface. The fork in the beard may also be artificial, some long beards tend to split in two when damp or wetted. We don't know what cosmetic attentions were given to Jesus before he was laid in the Shroud."

The Professor thoughtfully stroked his cheeks. "If the Shroud image is vapourgraphic, then it must have been from someone still alive when the cloth was laid on him. I can't recall all the details but didn't Sindonologists try all sorts of ways of generating the image from corpses and even heated dummies?"

"Yes, and the only clear result came from a live person. Also the bleeding wounds that mark the cloth cannot have come from a corpse because corpses don't bleed. Apparently, Jesus was blood Group A— as determined by immunohistochemistry of the blood stains."

"So the Shroud Figure can't have been of Jesus, because He died on the Cross as dogma has it."

"Correct. Unless of course, Jesus was removed from the Cross alive!

This is the basis of the Conspiracy theory propounded by the Germans, Kersten and Gruber and earlier authors. However, the pesher of the New Testament also reveals this quite clearly. Even a straightforward literal reading of John's Gospel intimates that Jesus survived the Cross."

Dmitri took a deep drag on his cigarette and continued. "Crucifixions are survivable especially if you are anaesthetised by opium dissolved in vinegar, and the Essenes of whom Jesus was a senior member were well known as doctors, well-versed in the healing skills. Aloes and myrrh were used extensively as curative antibiotics in ancient times. However, it seems excessive to have loaded the poor fellow with what the Bible says was about thirty kilos of this stuff—he must have been swimming in it! God alone knows it must have cost a fortune— myrrh cannot have been cheap! Anyway, the Shroud became known as the Healing Cloth, which is correct but it came to be understood in the wrong context. People thought of it not as the cloth that was used to help heal Jesus after removal from the Cross but as a cloth which would heal others by sympathetic magic because it had been in contact with Jesus' holy body which had died and been resurrected by God. Although this is a pagan concept, it had to be thus otherwise the Resurrection Doctrine central to Christian faith would go out the window. You can begin now to understand the reservations that St.Paul and the early Church Fathers had about the use of Icons and why the Iconoclasts were so virulent in their suppression of Christian art and relics. They knew that a relic like the Shroud of Turin is a double-edged sword. It can either consolidate faith in the Church, as it has in the past, or destroy it by revealing the fundamental flaws at the core of Christian doctrine, to undermine belief in the Resurrection, the conquering of death and the God-like Nature of the Christ. That is why the Carpocratian Legacy, our Jesus Icons, have such potential power, such potential impact on Christianity. We must use them for the good of the world, for the re-birth of Gnosis—as Jesus must have intended. I believe with my whole heart and soul that we are doing God's Work!"

After this long speech, Dmitri fell silent. The others stared at him for a long moment and then Sir John broke the spell by saying: "You have been most illuminating, Dmitri. I thank you. For my part I can say that the Priory Arcadia has always believed that Jesus survived the Cross and more than that, he sired children with Mary Magdalene. The Carpocratian Legacy confirms this and illustrates it in the most dramatic fashion. As to the Shroud of Turin, who can say what it is, nevertheless it is true that our Brothers in the Templars did have the Shroud for many centuries—it is one of the relics that were divided between us when the two Orders split up in 1188. They took the Shroud and the fragment of the Cross given to St.Guilhem by Emperor Charlemagne and we took other items. It now seems that both sets of relics substantiate the idea that Jesus was mortal and survived the Cross. Nevertheless, this doesn't mean we have lost our belief in God or the Extraordinary Nature of Jesus or Christianity for that matter. It is just that the world, God and the Universe is more complex and stranger than anything we have so far conceived of and mankind is ill-served by being straight-jacketed by Catholic or any other doctrine. However, religion is the fundamental evolutionary tool for our species. It is the way we existentialise our reality, and it is the Holy Task for the Priory Arcadia to guide us through the stormy psychic seas that face us in the Age of Terror.

I don't know about you, but I could use a drink after all that pompous guff! I'll call Hampton and ask him to bring in some champagne."

*

A short time later, as Sir John sipped at his drink, his mind was already working, chewing over all this meant to the Plans of the Priory. Did they really need the Icons for the Fulfilment? They were an entirely new factor in the equation and it was difficult to predict what might happen. All their planning over the centuries had centred on a Fulfilment without the Jesus Icons. They had sufficient other relics and records, such as the Dynastic Scroll, to do without them; and yet they could make a truly sensational impact, generate intense public awareness like nothing else could—and as Mirphy had put it ' Fulfil the Fulfilment'. The Priory had been secret so long for so many centuries that maybe it couldn't cope with a high-impact, high-profile disclosure such as this. Maybe they had lost the skill for public relations. Even the

Fulfilment itself was a 'behind-the-scenes', affair involving only the persons of world leaders and other shadowy power-brokers.

However, the Rose Council knew of the Icons from Joseph Mirphy's sensational video in Paris, and it would be difficult now to suppress them or prevent their use in supporting the Fulfilment. And how would JeanLuc react or Jean for that matter? It was getting very complicated. The main concern was, did it make them more or less vulnerable to attack by the likes of Father Moloc and the Pope, or even raise the ante sufficiently so that other powerful forces came into play? And had the mysterious Icons already changed his own perceptions of the Fulfilment and of what the destiny of the Priory might be?

The Prince could give them access to the NeuroCray in Highgate House to model it all out for him, but he knew full well that they were all now on a roller coaster ride leading to the End of Time. The track lines had crystallised, and they were well strapped inside their little cart of fate hurtling with eyeball-squeezing, gut- wrenching speed towards their destiny and probably the Destiny of Mankind as well. No fancy computer could help them now, or anyone else for that matter. This was seat- of-the- pants stuff, genetic instinct and reliance on the habits of organisation and decision ingrained into the Priory over centuries.

And what of Jean de Sigor? This was why they called the Grand Master the 'Navigator'. They were truly at sea now. Divine Guidance would have to become consciously expressed through Jean's person. Sir John hoped he was up to it—he himself certainly wasn't. He'd be dead in a few weeks, possibly days given the shocks he'd had these last few hours. He knew that for sure, and was secretly relieved. He'd added his bits to the collective jigsaw and now it was his turn to reach for the light ...

The others were staring at him with concern.

"Are you all right, Sir John?" JeanLuc asked, reaching his hand out towards him.

"Oh, wha-what? Yes, of course. I was just thinking. You've given me a lot to think about, all of you. If you'll excuse me now, I have to make a few phone calls and get things ready," he said vaguely, and heaved himself up from his chair, walking unsteadily towards the door. He turned, "Professor, Dmitri. Please use my library as if it were yours.

As antiquarians, I think you'll find many interesting things here. We also have some rare and unusual manuscripts and books." He went out.

*

The Professor went to the windows and pressed the button that drew the curtains back. A weak, watery sunlight entered the room. It was cloudy outside and looked like more rain. The castle flags hung damply limp from their poles. He turned back to the room and started to look around the library stacks that reached from floor to ceiling, with a walkway halfway up the wall extending all around the room. There were several manuscript glass display cases set on wooden trestles and wired to alarms. He went to the first of these and looked at the brass plaque describing its contents. He gave an exclamation of astonishment. "My God! This is Priscillian's copy of the Kabbala! It says: 'to Charles, a gift from the Gentlemen's Club of Spalding'. Your friend sure ain't kidding is he? Jesus, what else is there here?"

He looked around in wonder. He rushed to another display case and peered in. He nearly choked as he read the dedication within:" 'To John from Fred and the International League of Antiquarian Booksellers (Ha, Ha!). Sauniere's parchments and genealogies of Hautpoul and Blanche de Castille'." He went to the glassed-in book cabinets where a printed label said 'Modern First Editions 1980-'. He turned the little brass key and opened the heavy glass-panelled door. Scanning along at random, he picked out the hardback of Foucault's Pendulum and opened it at the flyleaf. He read the handwritten dedication: 'To John— May God hear your Trumpet Call! Umberto.' And then there was the Messianic Legacy: 'To John with grateful thanks. Henry'. And Jesus the Man: 'For J.R. I don't believe you but thanks anyway! Barbara'. And many many others. Other cabinets held rolled-up parchments or papyruses of obviously great antiquity.

Suddenly, the Professor broke away from the stacks of books and turned towards JeanLuc who had been scrolling through the images stored on the CD while smoking a Benson and Hedges. Dmitri had gone to his room to find Saskia.

"JeanLuc," he said. "You don't need me any more. I've done everything in my power. You have the data and the test results to which I'll put my name and stake my reputation, even my life. In return, I don't want payment, it is I who should repay you. But please let me stay here in this Library. There is treasure enough here to last me the rest of my life. Please, intercede for me with Sir John. Let me stay here!" he pleaded.

"JeanLuc looked at him with astonishment and then laughed: "Sure, if that's what you want, Josef. You don't have to come with me to France if you don't want to!"

"Oh, thank you. Thank you and bless you!" cried the Professor, close to tears with gratitude.

"Maybe Dmitri could come?" he mused, "if he can ever forgive me for Sophia and for today."

"Yes, take Dmitri! I can talk to him over the phone; answer his technical questions. I can also continue work on the Icons right here."

Later, after listening politely to JeanLuc's request, Sir John shrugged his shoulders. He cared little for ancient history any more; it had become irrelevant, compared to the pressing concerns of the moment. "Yes, of course he can stay. As long as he likes, the rest of his life if he wants. Hampton will find him rooms in the Castle and see to his needs."

"Thank you, Sir John. And now where do we go? I understand you are coming with us?"

"Avignon, JeanLuc. I won't be coming with you today, but I shall follow you after tomorrow's International Rugby match, which I don't want to miss. Are you ready for lunch? I have chosen something rather special to celebrate our good news. Venison from my estate cooked in champagne and cream with grapes and noodles. One of my favourites—not good for the old cholesterol of course but my heart is practically all plastic now already. Come let us go in. Saskia and Dmitri are waiting."

CHAPTER 35

Joseph Mirphy, Cardinal Legate of New York, met up with Cardinal Von Helsinger of the Congregation for the Doctrine of Faith, at Fabrizzio's Restaurant in the Via Ottoviano a short walk from the Vatican City.

They were ushered with fawning solicitude to a discreet alcove in the dining room, which was cool dark and candlelit against the heat of the noonday sunlight outside—rather like a church. Dispensing with menus, Von Helsinger ordered for them both. He was obviously a regular customer.

"I'm not unhappy with the way things are going for our Church. Italia Forza is bringing us many blessings—not least is relief from all that nonsense about the Holy City having to pay taxes. Politics by media seems to suit the Italians quite well. Our old friends are suffering though but, to be candid, they've had their day and we must adjust to the new times and new men." He methodically chewed on a piece of crostini alla Napoletana and stared with hard unflinching black eyes across the table at Mirphy.

"Talking of the times, is His Holiness going to attend in January? Everyone else has accepted, even President Dillon."

"Why should he?" asked Von Helsinger bluntly. He held his glass up to the light and sniffed delicately at the deep red wine within. "Try some of this, Joseph—it's good."

"No, thanks. I'll stick to the mineral water." "You're so Anglo-Saxon! So intense!"

"Celtic Irish, if you please, Otto. And what about my question?"

"I have no control over what His Holiness does. He goes His own way; always has done."

"That's bullshit, Otto. He listens to you!"

The Swiss Cardinal gazed back at him blandly. "What makes you think that, Joseph my friend?"

"Well, he must! All Pontiffs have been guided by and listened to the Inquisition. The Vatican cannot function properly without your department, without your agreement," he said pointedly.

"Who says the Holy City is functioning properly?" "What do you mean?"

"If what you say about my Department is true, and I'm not agreeing one way or the other, then the Church would be functioning properly. But it self-evidently isn't."

The two Cardinals stared at each other across the table. A waiter brought a dish of Maionese di Pesce alla Genovese and placed it in front of Von Helsinger who tucked his napkin into his priest's collar and spread it wide across his paunch to protect the crimson surplice from any stray drops of food. He nibbled at a jumbo shrimp. Joseph Mirphy watched him and toyed with a fork at his plate of Palma ham proscuitio. Was this some kind of a hint? he considered. Was there a rift between Von Helsinger and Pope John XXIV?

"How is His Holiness' health these days?" he asked—trying another tack.

"He is well—a little withdrawn perhaps. The cares of office, you know. It is a difficult time for our Catholic Church."

"Tremendous workload, of course." "Of course."

"Is everything going as you would wish, Otto?"

"Well, like you, we win some and lose some." Von Helsinger mopped at the sauce on his plate with a bread roll.

"Would you personally advise the Holy Father to attend the Conference?" "It depends ..."

"On what?" Mirphy was getting tired of all this fencing, he wanted to talk turkey. The time for action was upon them. But he knew how the Vatican bureaucrats operated—prevarication had been raised to a supreme art-form within the Curia, and any pushing only resulted in more obstruction and a slough of vagueness.

"I would need to pray for Our Lord's guidance."

"Of course," smiled Mirphy carefully. "God's Will must be made known."

"Also, I would have to know what the Conference is all about, its objectives and so forth."

"It's a peace conference. A summit of world leaders to try and broker some peace initiatives."

"Yes, I know that, but what is it all about?" probed Von Helsinger.

291

"Are you suggesting there is a hidden agenda?" parried Mirphy. "Naturally, my friend. Naturally!"

"There is no hidden agenda. The Conference is exactly what it says it is—a summit for peace."

"Of course!" laughed Von Helsinger, showing small white even teeth. "I am getting to quite like you, Joseph," he said. "You amuse me and you are a worthy opponent!"

"I am not your enemy, Otto. We are both trying to do the Lord's work as best we can."

"Of course!" laughed Von Helsinger merrily. The waiter came by, refilled his glass and took away his empty plate. "Because you are an American, we are having the banana ice-cream sundae with nuts and chocolate sauce. I know you will like it!"

Mirphy regarded the fat man in front of him, disguising his distaste with difficulty.

"I hope you won't insult me by not partaking of this delicious Yankee dessert. I ordered it specially for us when I knew you were coming."

"No, I do like it, Otto. It is a hot day—just the thing." Mirphy hated American junk food. Von Helsinger had done this as a deliberate ploy.

The ice-cream came and both men started to eat the sweet sickly concoction. Then Von Helsinger, after looking furtively around the room, said: "I will advise the Pope to attend your stupid Conference, but I want some things in return."

"And what are they?"

"I must remain part of the set-up in the unlikely event you succeed to the Papacy. Also, I must know, in advance, what is really going to happen at this so-called Conference. What devil's business are you up to?"

" We will think about your terms. I cannot guarantee anything—it's not entirely up to me; we have a committee."

"A committee? The Priory Arcadia run by a committee? You've got to be joking! I know it is not so," scowled Von Helsinger.

"Shush, Otto; walls have ears!"

"It is all right, I do all my real work here."

"Well, you're right. I will talk it over with the Grand Master and let you know. But you must call off Father Moloc. We know all about the Atbash Plan."

"I know nothing about that," said Von Helsinger slowly.

"Moloc's mole, Duvain, was killed before he had time to switch off his personal computer. We accessed all his encoded files. Just as a minor matter of personal curiosity, why Atbash? That is a somewhat unusual name," said Mirphy carefully.

A glint of amusement showed in Von Helsinger's shark-like eyes. "You people are so much into Knights Templars, Hospitallers and so on—you should know. Atbash is an old cipher used for messages during the Crusades. I've no idea what it means or how the code is constructed—it just seemed an appropriate name, that's all. Why do you ask?"

"And Moloc?" pressed Mirphy, changing the subject.

"I can't do anything about Father Moloc—he is a fanatic. To him you are agents of the devil and I'm not sure he isn't right!"

"But he must be stopped!" said Mirphy with quiet vehemence.

"So! He's causing you a bit of bother, is he? I'm glad to hear it," smiled Von Helsinger. He beckoned to the waiter, who emerged from the shadows to take away his empty bowl. "Coffee, Joseph?"

"Well?"

"Don't worry, he is completely deaf—that's why I come here. Oh, and the food is excellent too, don't you think?"

"Well?" repeated Mirphy, pointedly waiting until the waiter had retreated out of earshot.

"As I said, Moloc is a free agent. But I will consider withdrawing further active support from him. That is all I can do."

"We'll meet again, Otto. The banana split was delicious. Thank you." Abruptly, Mirphy rose and walked quickly out of the restaurant. He blinked owlishly in the bright Roman sunlight and walked hastily to where his taxi, an Alfa Romeo twin spark, was waiting as instructed. The pavement was crowded with people but he wouldn't put it past Von Helsinger to have him assassinated right here on the streets of Rome.

"OK, move it! Rapido! Hit the gas!" he yelled as he flung open the rear door and jumped in. The Italian driver had seen enough

Hollywood movies to understand the words and the tone. He and the sporty Alfa complied with enthusiasm.

CHAPTER 36

Joel Maniato sold his Bang and Olufsen, his Sony and his Rolex through eBay. His Mercedes had been a company vehicle that had been driven away weeks ago by a Biophar Drugs employee. At least he no longer had to fork out the $100-a-week-plus-tips parking fee.

He took a cab to La Guardia and caught a flight to RDU on a stand-by. On arrival in Raleigh, he hired a car and drove straight to Duke University. After some debate with the authorities, they eventually agreed to let him into the Professor's laboratory. They recognised him from the Biophar Drugs days, but he wasn't going to tell them the new situation.

"The Professor wanted me to have a check around to see if everything was okay, in case he'd forgotten anything. Apparently, Mr Kuovic, his new assistant, may have inadvertently left some research videotapes behind which the professor needs," he'd said.

"Do you know when the Professor will return, Mr.Maniato? He has classes and responsibilities here that he has badly neglected. When you see him, could you tell him to get in touch as soon as possible? The Dean would like to see him. We had some dreadful trouble just before he left. Do you know where he is? We've had the builders around to repair the windows, so he can move back in whenever he wishes. It is still a bit of a mess in there though. No, we don't have the key to his safe—that would be most improper!"

He thanked the Miss Severity PrimKnickers profusely and jingling the keys headed towards the Department building and upstairs to the Professor's Laboratory of Classical Antiquities. He let himself in and started looking around for the safe, which he found set into the wall in the Prof's journal-cluttered office. It was a simple job for his electronic tumbler detector/decoder to hear the correct clicks and the safe was soon opened up. Bingo! There they were. He could hardly believe his luck. Boy, oh boy! Some people had no idea, no conception of security! Maniato reached in and took out the videotape cassette and some CDs, putting them in his briefcase. He shut the safe door and twirled the dial.

"Everything is fine! I'll tell the Professor." He dropped the keys on the counter, waved jauntily to the woman and breezed out with: "Yo'all have a nice day now!"

He was back at RDU airport within two hours of arriving. He handed back the car keys to the surprised bimbo desk clerk, and caught the Piedmont Airways afternoon flight back to New York. As he was taking his first drink from the airhostess, she said to him: "Let me get you a bandage for your hand, sir. Won't be a second." Joel looked at his hand in surprise and then with alarm. There was rich red blood seeping from a circular wound in the palm of his hand, both palms!

*

"So, what's he been doin'?"

"He's been selling off his personal possessions. I bought this rather nice Rolex off him, dirt cheap at $150. Must be worth at least a grand. Don't worry, he didn't suspect a thing. I was just some mug who bid for it on the internet.

"Then he took a day out to fly to North Carolina. We didn't follow him 'cos I wasn't sure of what budget level you were putting this surveillance on. Anyway, he returned that same evening. He hasn't moved from there since, except to buy liquid and white-powder groceries. Oh yes, and the drug store where he bought bandages. I slipped the doorman a fifty and he told me that this Maniato fellow recently lost his job and has been down on his luck. They're gonna foreclose on him within days, apparently. The doorman was moaning that he hadn't been tipped for months and how was he expected to make a decent living and do drugs without that? Jesus, this city! It gets worse all the time." Phillip sniffed with high toned disgust.

"Fine. Thanks, Phillip. Here's your money. I think we'll go pay him a visit right now. Are you tooled up?" The other man nodded his blond wig and slipped the proffered envelope into his sequinned handbag. "Okay, let's go, lover boy!"

Josiah Smith was tingling with excitement. It had been years since he'd done any 'missionary' work. The thought of the coming 'interview' with Maniato gave him a rock-like hard-on and he walked with difficulty after Philip, the drag artist who flaunted his extravagantly protuberant false tits into the grey harassed faces of the airport crowd. Smith loved his little Killer Queen who helped to tidy up after him and

296

do the little jobs that smoothed the path for his evangelical business. As a precautionary measure, they took the airport Greyhound into town and then the Subway.

They found Maniato dressed only in soiled skivvies and in a raving drunk. The apartment stank of stale liquor and rotted take-aways. In one corner, a cheap black-and- white portable TV/VCR combo showed a screenfull of flecked electronic snow. Maniato was a physical wreck. His staring eyes looked as though they'd been weeping blood, looked like something out of a Clive Barker movie. His hair was matted with clotted blood and his body looked half-starved. A half-empty bottle of Ernest and Julio's cheapest red dangled from a heavily bandaged hand as he opened the door to let them in. He looked at them with a dull incurious expression that hardly changed when Philip pushed him by the chest back into the room and closed the door behind them.

"So. What's the big deal, Joel? What's this information you have?"

"Who are you? Whadda you want?" asked Joel, a flicker of fear beginning to re-animate his features.

"Don't you remember me, Joel? I'm your friendly neighbourhood Mormon. You remember? I thought I'd drop by. On the off-chance, you know."

"Oh, yeah. Smith. Whaddya want, Smith? Can't you see I'm busy? I got my consultancy to run. Busy, Busy! That's me."

"Yeah, I can see that," grinned Josiah looking around with distaste. "We don't want to take up much of your precious time, do we, Philip?"

"No, sir. Certainly not. The time of such a busy person as you, sir, must be very valuable!"

"Yeah, very valuable" hiccupped Maniato.

"So, what have you got to show me, eh? I'm sure we can do a deal. Right, Philip?"

"Right!" said the drag assassin who'd drawn a Magnum from his handbag and was methodically screwing on a silencer.

"Ooh! What a big gun, Philip! You are a naughty boy!"

"Thanks, sweetie! " smiled Philip. "I do love a big tool for doing assholes!" He walked forward and kicked Joel in the stomach with his pointy woman's shoe. Joel fell to the floor groaning and squirming in pain. Blood seeped from an open wound in his side.

"So where is it, asshole?!" Smith shouted in his dried blood-encrusted ear. "Where the fuck is it?" He wasn't enjoying this as much as he'd hoped to. Where the hell was all the blood coming from? They'd hardly touched the guy. Had someone got to Maniato before them? Jesus, the guy was bandaged all over on his hands, bare feet, everywhere! The bed looked like the horse's head scene from the Godfather movie. What was he? Some kind of S and M freak? He turned to Philip. "Do him and let's get outa here. This is no fun—this guy's truly weird!"

"Okay, Boss." Philip lifted the Magnum, aimed at Joel's forehead and pulled the trigger. There was a pop like a champagne cork and Maniato's brains fizzed bloodily out onto the deep-pile carpet. He twitched once and then lay still. Philip prettily pursed his lipsticked lips blowing the wisp of smoke from the barrel before unscrewing the silencer and putting Magnum 'poppet' back in his lair.

Smith scanned around the apartment in boredom. Since they were here, he might as well see if there was anything worth taking with them. Maniato had talked a lot about a videotape, so Smith went to the VCR and pushed the eject button. A cassette slid smoothly out. He picked it up and looked at the label. He frowned. What was this? 'Property of Duke University -Professor J Spikel. Carpocratian Legacy Tape 1'. It obviously wasn't a rental. He put it in his coat pocket and looked around. There was a clutter of CDs lying on the bedside table with a similar label. He picked these up as well. There seemed to be nothing else of interest, so the one man and his drag went back out to the elevators and down to the lobby. "Paid up, did he?" the doorman called.

"You could say that," said Smith with a wink and a grin. He handed the man a twenty.

"Thank you, sir and have a nice evening!" "You too buddy, you too."

They went around the corner to a deserted unlit alleyway strewn with garbage cans. Watched by the cynical lemony eyes of a dozen scrawny cats, Philip gave Josiah Smith the blowjob he'd been needing. They split up after; Philip the Drag Queen a thousand dollars richer,

298

and Smith the Society Pillar feeling empty and strangely unsatisfied.

*

Smith took the red-eye shuttle to Washington—he had to be ready for his morning appointment with the First Lady in the White House. There was a mass of faxes and email messages waiting for him in the Physico Corporation Executive apartment in Georgetown. Smith stuffed them all into the shredder before going to have a shower and get changed for his meeting with the President's wife. He was not looking forward to it. She was a cold bitch, a religious Fundamentalist of unremitting fanaticism. She very rarely came to Washington, and only when she thought the President was not getting the support he needed in the Senate or when the Liberty Federation was hot on the heels of some dumb-cracker Congressman who'd got his dick caught in an Autovac or more importantly, whose religious platitude count and Nielsen ratings were unacceptably low.

"My idiot husband wants to go to France in January to a World Leaders Summit or some such nonsense. I know he is only trying to wriggle out of spending our annual holiday together but my spies tell me that this particular Conference may be something more than the usual jamboree of fat old farts" she began in typical Thatcher-like fashion. "God wants me to know what is going on, Josiah. You know how much I rely on you and the Mormons to see that God's Will is made manifest in this world. God has warned me that Satan is at the bottom of this Summit—the whole thing is a manifestation of the Anti-Christ. We are seeing a gathering of the Riders of the Apocalypse—a spawning of Devil worshippers! " With a linen handkerchief, the First Lady delicately wiped away the thin foam of spittle that had formed on her pale lips.

Josiah shivered. She always got so worked up, scaring everyone half to death. No wonder her children were psychiatric basket cases. No wonder President 'Popeye' was a workaholic!

"Yes, Ma'am!" He forced himself to look into her hyperthyroid glare. "What does the Good Lord want us to do?"

Later that evening, he rested after an exhausting schedule for Physico that had begun with his audience with the First Lady. He flicked through the channels to Vision News Network and listened. He sipped at a dry vodka Martini.

"... and just in from New York, we have the exclusive story of the gruesome ritual murder of a Catholic man marked with the stigmata of Christ's crucifixion

... after this commercial break ... And now from the Capital of Sin, here is Barbara Teery live from New York on the latest Revelations in the Stigmata Murder case ..." Josiah sat up abruptly and stared at the screen. Shit! That was Maniato's apartment building! ..."I am talking here with the Right Reverend Canon Stentorian. Father, what are stigmata?"

"Stigmata are the bleeding wounds that appear in the same place as those on Jesus' crucified body."

"Who gets them?"

"Well, there have been about three hundred confirmed cases in the past two thousand years. Some of our holiest saints have had the stigmata—like St.Francis of Asisi, and more recently, Father Pio of Italy and even right here in New York, we ...."

"I understand Father, that you have met the murdered man, who has just been named as Joel Maniato. Can you tell us about that?"

"Yes, I can. Maniato used to be a member of our flock and I spoke with him only a couple of days ago!"

"What was that about? Can you tell us?"

"I'm afraid not, Barbara. The secrecy of the confessional is absolute." "Have you any idea why he was murdered so brutally, Father?"

"I have some ideas which I am sharing with the police."

"Can you tell us? Millions of our viewers are very concerned about this." "I'm afraid I am not at liberty to say at this moment in time."

"Thank you, Father. This is Barbara Teery, VNN, New York. Back to you, Clive."

"Thank you, Barbara. Now we have here in the studio some representatives not only of the Catholic Church but of other denominations as well, and we shall be discussing this bizarre case with them. Right after these messages from your local stations. Please stay with us ..."

Smith stared in horror at the newscast and the subsequent panel discussion and then switched off the TV. The fucking media always blew everything out of proportion, sensationalised everything. My God, he was there, he didn't remember anything remotely like what these people were talking about. So there had been some blood, sure, but it wasn't anything particularly bad. Hundreds of people every day were blown away in New York, what made this one so special? He wished to Moroni he hadn't talked to that greedy bastard of a doorman. Jesus, it was possible he could be fingered by that sucker! No. No way. People like that kept their mouths shut if they knew what was good for them. Anyway, they were bound to think his long Mormon-style beard was a disguise, like Phil's drag outfit. Thank the Lord he had put on those false plain-glass spectacles. No. The chances of them connecting him with the murder were minuscule, non-existent. Not a VP of Physico Corporation, a confidante of the First Lady of the Land—no way José! Philip and he had done this before, admittedly not for some years but he wouldn't be found. Philip was a pro. It would all blow over pretty quickly. Josiah relaxed somewhat when he'd been through this chain of reasoning but he was still as taut as a guitar wire on Jimi Hendrix's Fender, when the phone rang.

Who the fuck!? He'd given strict instructions not to be disturbed!

"Sorry to disturb you, sir. I know you asked not to be, but I have someone from the police here and he is insisting on seeing you right away ... sir? ... Are you there, sir? ..."

Josiah Smith dropped the phone. Like a stunned Zombie, he walked over to the desk and opened the side drawer. He took out the little chromed .38mm pistol he kept there, placed the barrel of the gun in his mouth, pointing upwards. Closing his eyes, he pulled the trigger.

"Why did he do it? I can't understand why he did it. He had everything to live for. All I needed to see him about were some extra personal security arrangements, because he'd just been appointed to a Special Presidential Commission on Mafia Crime. It's a crying shame. What a waste, a good American like that! A man our country can be proud of! An example to us all."

"Thank you, Officer. That will be all. If we need you, we'll be in touch." The dumb cop went out closing the door respectfully behind him. Mike Folditch sighed and stared out of the window of the

301

interview room, lost in thought. Was this something he should communicate to 'Cornelius'?

Maybe, first, he would have a look at that video they'd found in Smith's coat pocket.

PART III

CHAPTER 37

It was a year of Omens and Portents. It rained on St.Swithin's Day. The rooks built their nests in the lowest branches.

The ravens of the Tower of London were sling-shot, made into shish-kebab with tasty slabs of salted rat and Alsatian guard dog, and eaten by cider-crazed winos from the Cardboard City underneath Waterloo train station.

The CBS TV network chosen groundhog emerged blinking on the fourteenth of February, turned around twice, observed his own Zen shadow, squatted to take an enormous crap on nation-wide Satellite Live TV and went back down his burrow hole, never to emerge again.

The Holy Goat of Mabinogion refused to perform his annual mounting of the milky buttocks of the Chief Druid of Carreg Cennen.

The Nile flood exposed a silt layer of bauxite which turned the river blood red, initiated a mass migration of frogs accompanied by bombing wave after bombing wave of locusts, and resulting in mass hysteria amongst Egyptians.

Sunspot activity was 'unusually intense' in the words of the harassed bespectacled NASA spokesperson, causing panic amongst Australian surfers who proceeded to paint even their genitalia with white zinc cream.

The hole in the ozone layer got larger. El Nino came early.

At least twenty endangered species finally became extinct and got dried and ground-up for sexual-potency powders for sprinkling on the withered dicks of Most Honourable Senior Japanese Executives. But happily and most mysteriously, the extremely rare golden tree frog of Papua New Guinea made a sudden re-appearance, coming back in languidly hopping millions.

The Amazon rainforest continued to disappear into pads of yellow Notette stick-ups and packaging for Hostess Twinkies.

The sophisticated pigeons of San Marco were decimated by poisoned popcorn, distributed by a vicious old lady from Minnesota on a 'See Venice before it Sinks!' tour.

The Nobel Prize for Peace went to Yasser Arafat and the Prize for

Medicine went to UK Professor Chris Evans for buckminster fullerene-coated pills containing attack chirals that could cure ageing liver spots. The Nobel for Physics went to MIT Professor 'Duck' Ozakawinowa a Japanese/Aussie/Aborigine for fundamental discoveries in 'cold fusion', 'high temperature superconductivity' and inventor of 'fart in a bucket' technology. Thalidomide was re-licensed for sale in the US.

And it came to pass that all the Crazies in the City streets went forth and multiplied as the Good Lord sayeth that they shouldethed.

And the streets of New York, London. Paris, Rio and yea even unto Moscow, did fill with End-of-the-World-Doom-is-Nighsters.

And everywhere it was endless 'Repent Ye for the End is Nigh', confronting the movie- going, basketball-going, football-going, baseball-going, tenpin-bowling-going, drive-in-bank- going, massed-S-and-M-orgy-going, drug-crazed-leather-shopping-going, creative-writer's-circle-going public.

And the Dalai Lama did miracle menstruate until he was exposed as a Preparation H junkie.

And all the crewcut high school jocks exhorted the cheerleading bimboknickers to fuck with them right now 'cos the End is Nigh and 'cos they didn't want to prematurely rapture all over the back seat of their Commancheros..

Attention ! 38... 39...40—deux fois!

*

"Nimes Tower, this is K209'er signing off. Over."

"Roger K209. Over and out. Welcome to France and have a pleasant stay."

JeanLuc taxied the Lear Jet over to the small plane's park at Nimes Airport. He cut the engine and the fanjet's moaning whine wound down. He stretched in his seat and yawned. It had been a long eventful week and he needed a break. Boy, did he need a break!

A dark blue Citroen van with Douane painted on its side pulled alongside the aircraft and two customs officers got out. They stood waiting patiently for the hatch to be opened. One of the men was armed with an Uzi. Spotting them from the cockpit side window, JeanLuc sighed and started to rummage around in his flight case for the necessary Bills of Lading, forms and letters given him earlier by Sir John Redcliff. He hoped things would go smoothly; he wasn't in the mood for a shoot-out followed by a car chase and that sort of shenanigans. He'd had a bellyfull of that recently; his life had been too much like an episode of an Indiana Jones movie. He was looking forward to catching a few rays of Mediterranean sun; ogling some girls. It seemed that he'd not had any dealings with women for months, not since ... He closed his eyes to blot out the memory.

After an hour of wrangling with the Nîmes Customs and Excise, they finally got the requisite stamp on their documentation and were free to unload the crate from the rear of the plane. By then, Sergeant Nollet had arrived in a black Mercedes 600 Pullman stretch limo with fluttering miniature French flags on the bonnet and a CD plate on the rear.

Sergeant Nollet had the slab-like build of a boxer, next to no neck and small-pox and knife- slash-scarred features. His CV read like something that should be in a red file at Interpol. He had been an Algerian soldier and street detective in the Marseilles Gendarmes—one tough looking cookie. Next to him, normal people looked like china dolls Igor excepted. The limo was accompanied by an anonymous-looking Renault Traffic van.

While the business of passports, entry visas, the unloading of the crate and other such matters were being dealt with by Jean De Sigor's capable Security Chief, JeanLuc, Igor and Dmitri relaxed in the cool dark air-conditioned interior of the limo, sipping Moét from the icebox and smoking harsh flaky Disque Bleu cadged from the uniformed chauffeur.

"I think I should ride with the crate in the van, JeanLuc," said Igor.

"That's a good idea, Igor. Go ahead. Not that we are expecting a hijack but it's best to be careful."

"Do we have far to go?"

"Not too far. Avignon is about thirty kilometres from here, I reckon."

Outside it was hot, the bright sunlight throwing sharp shadows on the concrete; the air smelled of high-octane jet-fuel exhaust. Every ten minutes or so came the thunder of Airbuses loaded with packaged tourists, lumbering into or dropping out of the late afternoon sky . At length, Sergeant Nollet joined them, and Igor got out to go to the van and then the small convoy set off, paying the toll and heading northeast towards Avignon on the Languedocienne Autoroute.

They drove slowly through the crowded narrow streets of Avignon, climbing steeply until they arrived at a private cul-de- sac bounded by ancient high stone walls festooned with ivy and other creepers and shaded by huge centuries -old plane trees. They drove up to an arched gargoyle-decorated coach entrance and the huge oak iron-barred doors swung smoothly open in response to the coded infrared signal from the chauffeur. The long limousine glided to a halt in a cobbled courtyard beside the immaculate white Rolls Royce Corniche with its Vatican City plates, the two inevitable black Volvo Estates and a dust-covered lipstick-red 1963 Mercedes 300SL.

"Welcome to France, my friends!" exclaimed Cardinal Mirphy. The tall elegant figure of the Irish- American Cardinal was waiting for them in the cool hallway of the villa. Beside him stood the young slim corn-blonde-haired figure of the Comptesse of Sigor. "Giselle, this is JeanLuc Kuovic," he introduced them simply.

"Hello again, Your Eminence. This is unexpected!" said JeanLuc.

JeanLuc smiled and put out his hand. "I am delighted to meet you, Comptesse—after all this time!" Giselle de Sigor blushed furiously and raised flashingly defiant dark blue eyes up to his. There was a moment of electric contact; an instant of shocking familiarity before Giselle cut it off sharply, to put on the closed face of the charmingly efficient hostess as she went about greeting the others and welcoming them as guests into the house and showing them to their separate rooms.

"We shall leave you to rest and get changed. I'll meet up with you again at dinner, which is at eight. My servants will bring champagne and cigarettes," she had said cryptically.

JeanLuc dropped his flight bags down onto an antique chaise longue and walked to the window. The view from his bedroom was stunning. Directly in front were the medieval towers, turrets, spires, crenulations, courts and gardens of the old Palace of the Popes and then in the distance the flashing silver, barge-dotted, ribbon of the mighty Rhone river as it wound its way through the patchwork of Provencal

308

countryside into the hazy distance. Beyond this were the dusty alluvial plains of the Camargue where the Rhone bled its open vein into the Med, fifty kilometres due South.

But his mind was not on the beauty of the view, but on the woman he'd now met for the first time and who was to be his bride. He thought she was very beautiful with wilful Bardot-lookalike features and hair cut and shaped like that of the painted women in an Egyptian hieroglyph. She wore a simple loose white cotton summer dress showing off deeply tanned bare legs and shoulders. For the first time in months, JeanLuc felt the stirrings of his libido. He desired this woman—he wanted to possess her, to crush her against his limbs, feel with his lips the softness at the nape of her neck, taste her, smell her ...

Groaning at the unexpected intensity of these feelings, he flung himself on the bed and buried his face in the cool scented pillows.

*

"He who drinks well will see God. He who quaffs at a single draught will see God and the Magdalene! A votre santé!" The Cardinal lowered his glass and studied his guests in silence as they began their dinner. He felt a glow of triumph. They were nearly all here! The Compte would fly down tomorrow and Sir John too. Over the next few months, all the senior members of the Prieuré hierarchy, the Rose Croix, would assemble here in the South of France using whatever excuses they could—the Cannes festival, doctor's orders, vacation, whatever.

Already, he could see Giselle and the Chosen One eyeing each other surreptitiously. It was going to work better than he could have dared to hope. All that was needed in this arranged marriage was for them to make and produce an offspring; but for them to fall in love—that was too much to hope for! It was not required that they live together; their past lives and upbringing were so different that they could hardly be compatible. However, she must be attracted, he could see that immediately; otherwise she would not be listening so attentively. He knew Giselle well; if she weren't interested, she would be away in seconds in that flash red sports Merc of hers.

"How did you get that black eye, JeanLuc?" asked Giselle. "It looks painful."

"I was beaten up by the Klu Klux Klan in America a few days ago;

just before they tried to burn me to death!"

"How dramatic! How horrible!"

JeanLuc shrugged and speared an oyster with a small silver fork. "It would have been if Igor here hadn't rescued me." He raised his glass to Igor, who winked back at him.

She looked incredibly desirable, in a low-cut, shoulderless black silk dress and she had painted her mouth a vampiric dark red which made her lips look black in the candlelight flickers, reflecting like fireflies trapped in the ebony darkness of the polished dining table and the fathomless pupils of her wide, clear eyes. With an effort, JeanLuc turned away to talk to the Cardinal.

"The Jesus Icons, Your Eminence? What will you do with them?"

"All in good time. All in good time, my boy." said the Cardinal. "Presently, we have taken them to be unpacked and stored in the small underground chapel here in the villa." He continued. "This house used to belong to the Catholic Church, you know. Cardinal Richelieu used to stay here when in Avignon and he prayed right here in the chapel. The Compte de Sigor, Giselle's grandfather, bought it just before the Great War as a base for the Southern France Operations of the Priory Arcadia—it seemed ideal."

"This Priory Arcadia.." asked Dmitri, his mouth full of la volaille demi-deuil. "What is it? What do they do? How are they involved? I hear nothing but this name ever since I came to Europe. My God! This dish I am eating is superb, what is it?"

"Boiled chicken stuffed with truffles, monsieur. A local speciality," said the butler standing behind him. "It is the chef's favourite—he gets his chickens direct from the Louhans district of Lyon. I'm glad Monsieur likes it—I will tell the Chef."

"It is wonderful. In Russia we have chicken so rarely, maybe once every six months. On the black market they are so expensive. Only the gangsters eat well in Moscow these days—and the tourists."

"Yes, so I've heard," said Mirphy dryly. "I'm so glad you decided to come out to us, Dmitri. And of course, without you, the Carpocratian Legacy would never have been found. I toast your incredible achievement!" They lifted their glasses and drank.

"But what a terrible price had to be paid," said JeanLuc sadly. "We

310

shall never forget and always honour your daughter, Dmitri. The Carpocratian

Legacy, the proof that Jesus lived, will be dedicated to Sophia's memory, I swear it," he vowed emotionally.

"Amen to that," concurred the Cardinal. "And she will not have died in vain. The Legacy will now form an integral part of the Fulfilment plans for the Priory Arcadia—plans that will have an explosively decisive effect on the Destiny of Europe and the Christian world. These are adjectives that I do not use lightly."

"Thank you for your sentiments. I have realised that life must go on and I must reconcile myself to our deep loss—in Russia we are used to the violent death of our loved ones. It is tragic but one must accept God's Will. But tell me about this Priory Arcadia" persisted Dmitri. "Is it some kind of organisation that you all belong to—a Secret Society, a Masonic Order perhaps?" Yemeljan stared questioningly at the Cardinal, eyes bird-bright with intelligent curiosity, within his patriarchal white bearded visage. Taken out of the cheap grey Russian ill-fitting suit, he could fill the role of a Druid or a Russian Orthodox priest or the popular image of Merlin the Magician.

"Yes, well. It is not a matter that I am fully authorised to discuss," evaded the Cardinal smoothly. "I am sure that the Compte will enlighten you further after he arrives tomorrow."

"Will the Compte be staying here with us?" asked JeanLuc.

"I am not sure of his plans. I myself drove up to meet you but I have to be back in Rome tomorrow." He paused. "But I shall return in less than a month to perform the Marriage Ceremony."

JeanLuc and Giselle glanced down at their plates and studiously resumed eating their dish of homard a la charentaise.

"What marriage is that?" asked Igor who liked a good party, especially a wedding party where he could sing maudlin Polish songs, get drunk and grope the larger sturdier bridesmaids.

"Between JeanLuc here and the Countess," said the Cardinal, picking carefully at a plateful of caraguolo la cacalaousada de Montpellier.

"So how come JeanLuc gets to marry the Princess? They've only just met!" laughed Igor in disbelief.

311

"This marriage has been planned for many years, Igor. At this level of European politics, royal marriages are only made to perpetuate the bloodlines of important royal families."

"But JeanLuc here is American—he sure ain't European or Royal, is he?" gaped Igor, a forkful of grenouille a la bressane halfway to the cream-stained hole in his black beard that was his mouth.

Even JeanLuc looked up at this, staring at Joseph Mirphy. What was that Sir John had called him in the Cocteau chapel in Redcliff Castle? They'd not had time to have that 'talk' which Sir John had promised before they left. He'd known the Cardinal for nearly twenty years; since leaving the US Airforce, but it was always as an employee or possibly as a protégé. They'd never discussed why the Cardinal had adopted him in the first place, had chosen him out of all the freaked-out Vietnam Vets that had de-mobbed into the streets of New York after 1965. He'd always considered himself as one of the Cardinal's 'good deeds'—an adoption based on Christian charity. Mind you, he'd done some strange things for this so-called high holy cleric. Some crazy antics, like that time ...

"Yes, he is. There has not yet been an opportune moment to tell him. But JeanLuc is of Royal Blood; a direct descendent in the ancient lineage of the Merovingian Royal Family who ruled France more than a thousand years ago. He is marked with the Sign!"

"Sign? What sign?" asked JeanLuc in disbelief.

"The birthmark between your shoulder blades. You have it, don't you?" "Yeah, sure. But birthmarks are pretty common—even where I have it." "Possibly, but the shape is distinctive, you've got to admit, JeanLuc."

"Are you trying to make out I'm some kind of Damian character, an Anti-Christ—you know, from the movie 'The Omen'. Or 'Rosemary's Baby'. It sure isn't a six-six-six!" he laughed wildly.

"No," began the Cardinal quietly, "but it is shaped like a rose. We have traced your parents and have much more corroborative evidence to substantiate your ancestry, which I won't bore you all with now. But most of all, don't you feel something, JeanLuc? What about your dreams? Rosa Roncalli, who was one of us, and who traced you through her psychic talents, told us that you would soon begin to change; that the weight of Fate would burst through you like water through a cracked dam; that you are part of us; an enormously important part of us—the final Key to unlock the Meaning of our Existence! To fulfil the Fulfilment!"

JeanLuc glared at the Cardinal angrily. "That's one ludicrous heap of holy bullshit, Mirphy!" he shouted. "I don't have to listen to this crap. You may like to believe you're some fucking Godfather to some Prince of Fairyland, but I don't have to participate. Find some other bloody idiot to play your fancy games!" He pushed himself away from the table and walked out, furiously shoving aside the butler and maids who barred his way to the door and the night outside.

The others watched him in stunned silence at the sudden outburst. Igor half rose out of his chair to follow but was stopped by a harsh command from the Cardinal. "No, Igor! Let him go. There was never going to be a good time to tell him, but better now when I'm sure he can feel the currents of Destiny controlling his actions and his dreams. We are all of us mere mortals and what is happening will soon be largely beyond our control. May God give us the strength to survive it. May God be with HIM. May God be with the Chosen One. Let the Divine Will be made manifest!" he intoned.

The others at the dinner table stared at the Cardinal with a mixture of worry and astonishment. He looked suddenly old and worn, and the dim candlelight only served to highlight the deep lines and creases in his face. He no longer looked the robust confident jovial American; more a reflection of the sad European sense of gloom that emanates from ancient portraits of Richelieu, that Machiavellian Cardinal who would stay in the villa when taking a break from dodging Parisian assassins and the irritations of Orthos, Porthos and D'Artagnan.

"We must now wait, my friends. We have mortal enemies in France and Italy who will stop at nothing to deflect our plans, even to kill us, so my presence here must not be prolonged or made known. To avoid this, I will return to Rome immediately tonight. JeanLuc won't want to talk to me after this—at least not for a while. The Compte will arrive tomorrow and will take command of the final preparations. Don't worry, the Legacy will be safe here." The Cardinal smiled wryly "I will be back, as Arnie would say!" Wearily, Joseph Mirphy rose from his

313

seat. The others followed suit. He kissed Giselle on the cheeks, shook hands with Dmitri and Igor and headed slowly for the door; to the white Rolls Royce, and into the dark sweet-smelling bougainvillaea-scented night.

The bird sings with its fingers—une fois.

CHAPTER 38

JeanLuc walked the streets and alleyways of Avignon. He ended up at a cafe-bar overlooking the old bridge over the Rhone river. The sun was setting, leaving vivid bands of colour crudely painted across the backdrop of the western sky. The ancient buildings of the city were infused with a soft magical pink glow. The cooling evening breeze caused a wraithlike mist to rise from the turbid river, enveloping the bridge.

To JeanLuc's daydreaming vision, the yellow headlights of the slow-moving traffic were the torches of the triumphant Albigensian Crusaders, waving their red-crossed banners and bearing their grisly trophies of Cathar heads on the tips of their spears.

He was shaken from this reverie by the sight of a classic Mercedes Sports going over the bridge, heading west towards the Auto route. He felt a bitter pang of disappointment. An abandonment, a betrayal ...

An impatient wave of his hand brought the black bow- tied waiter to refill his glass—with pastis, a disgusting canine-attractant aniseed liquor that suited his black mood. Each sip made his eyes bulge and lips pout like a true Frenchman. The street outside was noisy with leather and denim, youth coming and going on scooters and motorbikes. It seemed a friendly enough place. It got dark. After a while he switched to wine, a viciously coarse Cotes du Rhones house red that tasted silky smooth after the anise drain-cleaner. The barman didn't mind being paid in dollars. JeanLuc still had a couple of thousand bills rolled up in a wad in his pocket. That should see him through for a while at least—maybe a month.

Soon, he was buying drinks for everyone in the room and all French people were his brothers, his long lost brothers. Soon, his table was crowded with conviviality; with people young and old, and he had become a major distributor for Gaulloise and a consumer that had resulted in a forest of green bottles and why did the French all look like fish? Especially when they grow old; when they look like sturgeon or maybe snapper or maybe mullet. Even their cars had fish-shaped designs. Look at the old DS19—now that was a piscatorial design if ever there was one.

And didn't they know that he was King of the World and he was going to put everything right?

And didn't they know that he was going to French a beautiful French Princess? ....

*

So they took his wallet and dumped him in a foul-smelling back alley and drove off laughing; the long-legged girls riding pillion; their short tight dresses riding up their long French thighs; laughing gaily and laughing and the engines revving, those rackety engines and squealing wheelies. The world was spinning, spinning, spinning. JeanLuc blacked out, his chest covered in vomit.

*

And he rested, beside a sparkling stream that emerged from an underground source from under an overhanging copper beech tree. His horse slurped great gulps of water and wandered off a few feet to tear at a patch of lush green grass. He lay back on his back and stared up through the intricate pattern of leaves and branches into the bright sky above. He felt drowsy and his eyes closed. Too late, he heard the hoarse, laboured breathing; too late he smelled the foul breath. His eyes flew open in alarm and startlement, but only in time for one of them to receive the razor point of a short-handled boar-hunting spear which pounded into his right eye, bursting through his brain, cracked open the back of his skull and drove into the soft yielding earth of the grassy gnoll in the Forest of Woevres near Stenay, on which he lay... and died. The last fading vision of his other eye was imprinted with the leering features of that cunning fat bastard Pepin. Then, all was blackness. Whispering echoes in his ears ... "Die, Dagobert, Die!"

*

He was awakened by a kick in the side from the bar proprietor in the early hours of the morning. He suffered a torrent of incomprehensible French abuse of which the only words he knew were 'Merde', 'Americain' and 'Allez'! He felt as if a knife had been hammered into his brain through his right eyeball. He staggered into the dawn lit streets.

A black Volvo Estate drew up beside him. The electric window slid down and he was looking in at the bear- like features of Igor. "Do you need a ride, Princess?" he growled. "How much do you charge for a blow-job?"

JeanLuc laughed despite the throbbing pain in his temples. "Fuck you!" he said and opened the door to get in. "I can see that your English tutors taught you all the correct usages, Igor!" They drove.

"She left you a note."

"Who did?" asked JeanLuc muzzily.

"The blond bombshell of course, stupid. Who else? You lucky dog!" Igor grinned at him and threaded the big Volvo swiftly through the empty streets back towards the Villa.

"Where is it?"

"Here." Igor reached in his jacket pocket and handed over the envelope. JeanLuc took out a hand-written slip of paper with an address and instruction on where to leave the car. He held it up to his nose—it smelled faintly of perfume—her perfume! It was signed with a 'G'. Hell, he would go. He had nothing else to do. But he'd better recover from this hangover first.

"Is the Cardinal still here, Igor?"

"Niet. He left last night for Rome—soon after you went walk about."

"Good. I don't think I can face that son of a bitch just yet. What about Dmitri?"

He is in the villa—still asleep in bed. I came out alone to look for you."

"Thanks, Igor. I need some time to think and get cleaned up," he waved the note,"then we'll go see the Princess. Okay?"

"Okay, Boss!" smiled Igor. "Whatever you say."

*

'Swing low, sweet chariot. Comin' for to carry me home'. Sir John Redcliff OBE died just as a drop-goal put England three points ahead in a gruelling game that resulted in a famous victory against France in the Six-Nations Championship at Twickenham. As all around in the crowded private box were on their feet cheering, Sir John sank slowly back into his debentured seat and remained there, slumped. Thin dribbles of blood came from his mouth, ears and the tear- ducts of his

317

eyes. It was only when the crowd went quiet, as the ball was set up for the restart by France, that Damian Gerald Trotter, the Conservative MP for Eastleigh, suddenly realised, with horror, that his long-time friend had run in his last try, played his last stroke.

Although anticipated, this was still bad news for Jean de Sigor. He had lost his oldest and most trusted friend, who'd fought with him during the War, the senior Croisé, of the Priory Arcadia, only months before the most cataclysmic event in the Priory's history. Things were unravelling badly. Father Moloc's counter-attacks had got him virtually holed up in Sigor; it wasn't safe for him to travel abroad even to Paris, although he had to go to Avignon later today to meet up with JeanLuc. Pierre was embroiled in bitter and complicated trade talks between the EEC and the USA and couldn't move from Brussels, while Joseph was stuck in Rome for the time being, consolidating his position within the Catholic Curia.

He stared moodily at the crystal ball on its pedestal—it was now crazy paved with hairline cracks like an old billiard ball. He couldn't make up his mind if this was an evil omen or a portent of a new beginning, a hatching of the Phoenix. Today, it seemed darkly ominous, and he grieved for his old friend. It would be no fun any more to go to the Parc des Princes for the Rugby Internationals— the friendly rivalry had died with Sir John.

*

Giselle de Sigor sat at the dressing-table in her bedroom. It was very late. There was no sound in the vast empty house around her. The French windows of the bedroom opened onto a terrace but there was no sound of birds nor the rustle of windblown leaves in the dark garden beyond. The silk sheets on her bed were turned down, waiting for her, the pillows a white snowdrift heaped against the carved mahogany headboard. She ran her hands over her head, the curves of her palms smoothing down her blonde hair. She pressed her fingertips, wet with perfume, to the hollows of her temples and held them there for a moment, feeling relief in the cold, contracting bite of the liquid on her skin. She thought she would try to sleep. She had given up waiting for him to come.

Outside, the sound of fast -approaching hard-riding hoof beats caused batwing flutters of fear to rise in her throat. She heard his booted footsteps, the jingle of spurs, as they rose up the stone steps and onto the terrace. Frowning, she sat up looking towards the French windows.

JeanLuc stood there looking at her. There was no laughing understanding, no loving diffidence in his face. His features were drawn, cruelly austere, ascetic, cheeks sunken, the lips set tight. She jumped to her feet, hands pressed to her stomach, her fingers spread-eagled. He did not move, but a vein began to pulse in his neck. The smell of him penetrated the room—the smell of the horse and the sweat of his hot ride from the village.

Then, he walked over to her. He held her tight in a bruising grip, her thighs jerked tight against his, his mouth on hers. The shock of feeling his skin against hers, made her twist her body to escape. She tried to tear herself away from him—an effort that broke against his unfeeling arms. Her fists beat against his chest, against his face with its bruises still livid. He moved one hand, took her wrists and pinned them behind her, wrenching her shoulders back. She twisted her face away. She felt his lips on the upper curves of her heaving breasts . With all her effort, she jerked herself free and fell back against the dressing room table. Giselle stood crouching and panting breathlessly, hands clasping the edge of the table behind her, eyes wide in furious fearful denial.

Then JeanLuc laughed. He stood with his legs apart, his arms hanging down by his sides. She looked at the door behind him. However, at the first hint of movement from her, he put out his arm, not touching her, and she fell back, her shoulders moving faintly as she breathed. She glared at him, wanting to hiss and screech like a wildcat, but somehow not able to.

Then, with a swift sure movement, he approached, lifting her without effort and falling with her onto the bed. She sank her teeth into his hand and felt warm blood gush onto the tip of her tongue. He pulled her head back and forced her bruised lips open against his. Fighting without sound she did not call out for help—there was no help, she'd sent them all away. She was at his mercy.

She felt the blood beating in her throat, in her eyes; the hatred, the helpless terror. She felt hatred and his hands; hands which moved over her body. She felt hatred and his lips; hard lips which rolled and chewed her taut nipples. She fought in diminishing convulsions.

Then, in a thrusting lunge, he penetrated her; the sudden pain shot up through her body, to her throat and she screamed in a rage of fury at the tremors of unstoppable orgasm that flooded her body.

Then, she lay still. This was the thing she had thought about, had expected, had never known to be like this, could not have known because this was not a part of loving but a thing one could hardly bear for longer than a second. It was an act that could have been performed in tenderness as a seal of love, or in contempt, as a symbol of humiliation and conquest. It could be the act of a lover or the act of a soldier violating an enemy woman. He did it as an act of lust. Not of love, but as a master taking his due. And this had made her lie still and submit. A gesture of human tenderness from him and she would have remained cold, impersonal, untouched by the thing done to her body. But the act of a master, taking contemptuous possession of her, was the kind of rapture she wanted.

Then, she felt him shaking, with the agony of a pleasure unbearable even to him and she knew then that he desired her and that she had given him the solace he was seeking too, and she bit his lips and she knew what he had wanted her to know.

Then, he lay still across the bed, away from her, his head hanging over the edge. She heard the slowing gasps of his breath. She lay on her back, as he had left her, not moving, her mouth open. She felt empty, her body without sensation. She saw him get up and stand momentarily silhouetted against the window in the half-light.

Then, he went out, without a word or a glance at her. She listened blankly to the sound of his steps moving away in the garden and finally, the sound of hooves fading away down the driveway. She lay still for a long time.

Then, she moved her tongue over her dry lips. As if from a great distance, she heard herself groan. She began to shake as sobs racked her body in soundless hiccups. Dragging herself to the bathroom, she turned on the light to look at herself. Her father was right; 'Mirrors are the doors by which Death comes'. She saw the already bruising marks

320

left on her by his mouth and hands. She moaned; not at the sight of her reflection, but at the flash of knowing that she would not now take a shower. She realised that she wanted to keep the feeling of his body, his odour on her; and knew what such a desire implied. She could accept, thought Giselle, and maybe come to forget, in time, everything that had happened to her, save one memory; that she had found pleasure and release in their coupling; that he had known it and furthermore, that he had known it before he came to her. She had found joy in her revulsion, in her terror and in his strength. That was the degradation she wanted.

At last, she could no longer find it within her to hate him.

CHAPTER 39

A month or so after Sir John Redcliff's funeral, Jean de Sigor and Dmitri Yemeljan were in the small chapel in the Villa Portovecchio in Avignon. It was cool and quiet as a tomb, the silence disturbed only by their breathing and the occasional hiss of dripping wax from the mass of candles that provided the only lighting. The triptych of Jesus Icons was mounted on the wall behind the simple cloth covered altar before which they knelt. They had been there in silence for nearly an hour; each thinking their own thoughts and gazing meditatively at the pictures in front of them.

On the altar was a crudely worked silver chalice perched on top of which was a human skull, brown and cracked with age. In the top of the skull there were holes—ritual trepanned holes through which the soul had passed out of the body and made its ascent to Heaven. Beside the skull, there was an ornately carved acacia- wood box and a rolled-up scroll of obvious antiquity in a capped Perspex tube. There were many vases filled with red roses.

White cassocks of extreme simplicity covered both men's nakedness. They felt at blissful peace. It was with a supreme effort that eventually Jean de Sigor raised himself to his feet. He felt quite giddy. The candle smoke and the rose perfume were intoxicating. But his mind was calm and serene; he was a wax-paper boat, a perfect origami floating jauntily on a smooth underground stream irresistibly rushing towards the future. Jesus in the painting had been talking to him. It seemed so simple, so clear to him now, as if he'd taken cocaine. But this was no drug- induced high that would fade all too soon to jittery paranoia. No, this was the ultimate high, the high of clear purpose, the high of idealism, the high of religious enlightenment, a high that gives the world and nature that special optimistic glitter that is seen only through the dewy eyes of young lovers or children on the first morning of the school summer holidays.

In his mind, he'd been telling Jesus about his problems, about the setbacks they'd had, about what the Priory had been doing—there was so much to tell! As if two thousand years of human history had to be caught up on. He'd told Jesus how he'd felt lost and sad about the death of his friend Sir John, his anxiety about Giselle and about JeanLuc. He'd confessed to Jesus about the dreadful sins he'd committed in the name of the Priory and in the arrogance of his power and his wealth; the murders he'd ordered, the wrecking of lives and businesses, the political chicanery, the collaborations with agents of the Devil. It was a heavy catalogue of sins encompassing a lifetime of deceit, power broking and self-indulgence.

And Jesus had listened, had shared the burden. Jesus had listened with compassion and solicitude and understanding. His Holy Face had expressed love and forgiveness. Jean de Sigor began to feel like a new man, a man re-possessed, re-born with the Spirit of the Crusaders that had infused his youth, that had taken him through the War years in the Resistance and through the many years of his Grand Mastership.

He could see now why the Jesus Icons were an essential Key to the Fulfilment. He knew now they could never succeed without them. The Priory had possessed many of the symbols and the evidence, the proof positive of the Sang Graal ever since the First Crusades when Godfroi De Bouillon came back from Jerusalem after succeeding in his secret mission; even before the splitting of the elm. But these proofs were convincing only to initiates, to those with arcane hermetic knowledge; to Gnostics, Alchemists, Rosicrucians, the Templars, Hospitallers, the Jesuits, the Cistercians the Swiss Lodge Alpina and the Catholic Curia. But to the general mass of humanity, to the billions of mankind, esoteric knowledge and the arcana of Christendom was meaningless and totally lacking in rock'n'roll. This had been the fatal flaw in the Priory strategy, the hidden weakness that was addressed by the potential for mass appeal that the Jesus Icons represented. It was as if Jesus had known this all along; had planned for this two thousand years ago in the past. Now they had no choice but to go ahead. The timetable for the Fulfilment had been set as far back as Nostradamus; the Millennium had come and gone with the swiftness of a tsunami, the bedrock of social order had already become fluid, begun to disintegrate—the triumphant grins of the Lord of Chaos, Ishtar, Kali and Satan could already be seen through the thinning unglued curtain of reality.

323

As the two men left the chapel, Dmitri turned towards the Compte. "Jean, I have a question."

"Yes, mon cher ami?"

"Did Sir John have a cat?" "I don't know. Why?"

"JeanLuc told me he had had a dream. He dreamed that Sir John's cat is being neglected. He feels it is most important that we have this animal with us. JeanLuc said he has seen this cat before in a vision."

"I will do what I can, Dmitri. But you must be more specific. Where is this cat?"

"Hampton may know. I will ring him. Maybe Saskia could bring the cat with her when she comes."

Later that same day, after dinner, Dmitri and Jean de Sigor met in the book-lined study for a planning meeting. They smoked Disque Bleu and sipped Napoleonic brandy.

"So, is this cat thing sorted, Dmitri?" asked the Compte.

"Yes, I think so. Sir John Redcliff has a cat called Alexey who is at his manor house in Hampshire at the moment. Saskia will pick him up and fly over tonight with him in time for the wedding. She says that there is some cock-and-bull story about Alexey being over a hundred years old! Hampton the butler claims that Sir John acquired him from someone called Peter Damien Ouspensky just after World War Two and that Ouspensky claimed then that he'd been given the animal by Rasputin's mother when she was dying. Whatever the truth of the story, it must be a strange cat. It must have power to be able to get into JeanLuc's dream mind like that."

"Ouspensky," mused the Compte. " That name rings a bell. Let me look it up." Jean de Sigor searched around his library for a while and he leafed through several titles before finding the one he wanted. "Ah, yes! Here we are. He was a Russian theosophist—there is a picture of him here in Peter Washington's book, 'Madame Blavatsky's Baboon'. I thought his name was familiar. They're a strange bunch, the theosophists. The mystic pederasts we used to call them. Some of them came quite close to us just before the war but they became quite bizarre and un-Christian with their Hidden Secret Masters bullshit and blending of Eastern mysticism with Victorian spiritualism."

"But would not the Priory Arcadia qualify as their Hidden Secret

Masters?"

"Possibly, but we're all too fallible and human and always have been, all the way back to Our Lord Himself. We've never made any claims to being supernatural beings. OK, so we might adopt semi-divine titles for positions within our organisation—Elohim for example. But these are just names. The theosophists claim all sorts of things that it would be boring to go into. At least they are more sympatique than the American Fundamentalists."

"How so?"

"I suppose you in Russia have not been exposed to it as we have here in the West, so you won't know. The Christian Fundamentalism in America is a very dangerous Bible-literal religious movement comprised of several sects. They are apocalyptic and evangelical. Very dangerous and very effective in the mass media. We should learn a lot from them. They are also far right in political stance, which is why we have President Dillon whom they support. It is hard for me to talk about them without losing my temper. You've seen JeanLuc's bruises. He got those by tangling with them. Ask Joseph about them; he has to deal with them all the time. In business terms they're his main competitors in the market for men's souls."

"In Russia, there is the Orthodox Church and there are the sects, but the sects are not new. I belong to the Khlysty to which my father and grandfather also belonged. It is a sect founded by Daniel Philipov whom we believe to have been an avatar of Jesus Christ, just as you seem to believe might be JeanLuc's fate," said Dmitri.

"Although Philipov was not of the Bloodline of Jesus, as JeanLuc and Giselle and I myself are, we still believe that the Spirit of Jesus can enter any man and sanctify and transform them. It is when the Spirit of Jesus enters a man of His Own Bloodline that we believe that something extraordinary can be created," responded Jean de Sigor.

"I understand. So the purpose of the Priory Arcadia is to perpetuate and foster the Bloodline, which you call the Sang Graal, in the hope that someday the Spirit of Jesus will manifest itself in some person of that Bloodline—like JeanLuc for instance. And you are hoping that all the foretelling is true that it will be in this Millennial generation. A Second Coming that will redeem the world. A rebirth of faith, of gnosis as the Nestorians would say."

"I couldn't have put it better myself, Dmitri," smiled the Compte in admiration. "However, we do have mundane political aims as well. We believe that spiritual aims must be underpinned by real temporal power; guns and roses in effect."

"It is not for me to say, but you are paddling in dangerous waters, my friend."

"Yes, we know. But the Priory has been doing this for a thousand years so we have a little experience," said Jean De Sigor wryly. " We have planned for these final moments for many centuries. The psychic climate has been prepared. What has been foretold will happen—we will make it so. The exact details we cannot, as ordinary mortals, know but I have an unshakeable belief that the Fulfilment will go ahead." He leaned forward in his chair and waved his arms with passion. "I now believe the Jesus Icons were painted and preserved for this very purpose! Jesus himself knew what would be needed in this electronic age. We need Holy Images. Even fakes can generate fantastic belief; look at the Turin Shroud or the Veronica, even your fake Andrei Rubelov Icon in the Vatican Gallery inspires faith in the uncritical eyes of the masses."

"Am I invited to the Fulfilment?"

"Yes, of course. How could you have to ask! You are part of us now. What you and your family have contributed is beyond calculation. The martyrdom of Sophia. We could never repay you. You are a part of future history!"

"Thank you, Compte. That is all I need to know." Dmitri said gratefully. "In relation to the problems we have with the Icons, we have not ceased to work or reflect upon them. Professor Spikel in Northumbria and myself are in daily contact trying to decode the cipher and interpret the hidden symbols."

"Any progress?"

"Yes and no. Sir John's unfortunate death caused a delay, as you know; but we finally managed to put the coded lettering into a powerful computer again. But so far, the letters have not resolved themselves into any meaningful words within Aramaic, Arabic, Greek, Roman or any Judaic language like Hebrew. It is clearly encrypted in a simple but most effective way, each letter meaning another letter or group of letters maybe in another language. It is not a mathematical type or re-arrangement encryption."

"I know this may seem a foolish suggestion but have you tried the Atbash cipher?"

Dmitri stared uncomprehendingly at the Compte. "What is this cipher you speak of?"

Jean de Sigor leaned forward excitedly: "You mean you've not tried it? That's incredible. I thought that would have been the first one to try!"

"No. Maybe Professor Spikel has, back in the US, but remember neither he nor I are expert in Biblical research or spy codes for that matter. What is this cipher you speak of?"

"It was devised by the Jews even before the time of Jesus as a way of concealing secret names and information in scrolls and documents, and like pesher is a technique and a system for overlaying allegory onto history. The Priory used to use it centuries ago but it was discarded in favour of more modern cryptographic methods. The Templars used it even up to the fourteenth century. Dr.Hugh Schonfield has published the cipher principles in his book the 'Essene Odyssey'. I have it here somewhere." He got up to look again through the titles in his bookshelves. "Ah, yes! Here we are. I remember now. He correctly decoded an old Templar word Baphomet into Sophia, which is, as you know, Greek for wisdom. Even today, we include a Baphomet Ceremony for our own initiations. It is exactly what it says: a 'gaining of wisdom' ceremony where the novices are taught the basics of our history and the rules of our Order. I myself had to go through it many years ago," he said. "Of course, our Catholic enemies made out that this ceremony meant kissing the Devil's buttocks," he chuckled, "but I can assure you that these days ' Kiss my ass' is just an expression of language; in the Priory at any rate. I can't speak for some of the more bizarre Masonic brotherhoods however, where this practice may very well go on!" he laughed.

Dmitri wasn't listening, but flicking rapidly through the book. "I must phone Josef immediately. We should try this cipher. Shall I email these pages through to the Castle?"

"Yes, of course. Help yourself."

As he dialled 1044 and the number, Dmitri had a tingling certainty that this would do the trick. What might be obvious to the Compte, steeped in esoteric knowledge all his life, certainly wasn't to the rest of the world. The number of people who knew of the existence, significance and construction of the Atbash Code could probably be counted on the fingers of one hand. In Russia, he would never have had access to a book like the Essene Odyssey; just as he never knew about the Carpocratians until Cardinal Mirphy had sent him Morton Smith's 'Secret Gospel'. It seemed everyone had been there before him, he thought resentfully. But what would it decode as? What would it say? Dmitri suddenly felt a stab of panic. What if the text translated into:'Here is Sheik Abdul Rakir and his devoted family. Camel Dealers by Imperial Appointment. Get your pre-owned camel at Abdul's!' It would be a disaster. Did they really want to know? But they had to know because as soon as the pictures were published some bright bloody spark was bound to stick his hand up and say, what about the Atbash Code? And if they were right and it did translate as someone other than Jesus, then they would be down the tube and no mistake. "Hampton? This is Dmitri Yemeljan. Put me through to the Professor will you? Oh and an email will be coming through immediately after this call. Thanks."

Jean watched Dmitri from the depths of the ancient armchair whose leather had been worn smooth and softened by generations of priestly buttockfarts.

"Josef? This is Dmitri. Have you heard of the Atbash Code? No? Well, use it on the Icon lettering. I will fax you the details of the cipher construction in a minute." Dmitri listened for several minutes and his face lit up. "That's wonderful! That's incredible! I'll tell Jean at once. We won't be in touch for a week or so because we're due to be in Rennes le Chateau for JeanLuc and Giselle's wedding tomorrow. What's that you say? No, no. Apparently it's only a small private affair, about twenty people in all. I don't know any more than that. So you'll get on with the Atbash Code? Good. Good. Jean is here and I will tell him the good news!" Dmitri replaced the receiver and turned to the Compte.

"The professor thinks he has a possible explanation for the symbol fluorescence. He has been back in touch with the chemists in Duke University who did something called NMR analysis on that region of the cloth where the symbols are located. The chemical used appears to be a complex organic mixture similar to that found in extracts of deep-sea bottom dwelling fish that are occasionally netted by trawlers in the Red Sea. But the point is, the chemists say that the chemicals extracted have another property as well as fluorescence and that is they change colour with heat. The Professor reckons that if we heat the Icon silk, the symbols should show up and if we allow it to cool they will disappear again! He never thought of doing it himself because by then the cloth was sandwiched between glass plates and inaccessible."

Jean de Sigor got up out of his chair excitedly "So the fluorescence is just incidental and the symbols could easily have been illumined by anyone in the know, in ancient times!"

"It must be so. I think we ought to try it now. We could place a hot flat iron or something in the area of the symbols. I'll just send these cipher details to Josef and I'll meet you in the chapel."

In the chapel, they laid the heavy glass plates of one of the Jesus Icons face down onto the altar table. Jean plugged a domestic iron into a long extension lead and it began to heat up.

"Will it crack the glass, Dmitri?"

"I hope not. It shouldn't think so; this is reinforced plate-glass like they use for car windshields. It may take a while for the heat to penetrate." Dmitri looked through his notes and sketches. "Put it here, Jean. The Sumerian beehive symbol should be here on Jesus' robe." The Compte complied.

They stared down at the iron and waited. After a few minutes, Jean removed the iron and the two men leaned over to examine the heated area through Dmitri's magnifying glass. Sure enough, very faint dark outlines of a beehive with its surrounding circle of bees could be seen. It rapidly faded away as the glass cooled. Dmitri let out a whoop of triumph and danced around the table to grab the Compte's hand and embrace him.

"It seems the ancients knew a thing or two—things that we have forgotten in this modern age. This is indeed something to celebrate!"

cried Jean de Sigor joyfully.

*

Rennes le Chateau is an ancient village of mystery.

In the beautiful French Haut Languedoc region in the foothills of the Pyrenees between Perpignon and Carcassonne, it has become an irresistible magnet for fruitcakes and seriously mad, little old English ladies in hiking boots and Ron Ranson watercolour-painting kits. Like dogshit swarming with bluebottles, the area is plagued by coachloads of treasure hunters, ley- line sniffers, devil worshippers, Templar fanatics, Gabriel Knight heads, Atlantis freaks, Jesus freaks, UFO spotters, New Age Hippies, drug-crazed advertising executives, TV docu-historians, French Royalists, Elvis impersonators, neo-Albigensians, neo-Cathars, neo-Rosicrucians, astrologers, necromancers, alchemists, Holy Grail Seekers and day trippers from the coastal resorts. It has brought great prosperity to the tourist traders, the restaurateurs and bar keepers, the T-shirt makers, the knick-knack peddlers and the inventive pamphlet writers. No one will tell them that the dog that did the squat has long since gone.

JeanLuc and Giselle sat in the shade of an umbrella in the crowded Café Crusader watching the tourists go by and sipping at doll's-house-sized cups of strong black coffee. JeanLuc wore a multi-coloured T-shirt that depicted, on the front, a panoramic view of Rennes le Chateau with a UFO hovering over it in a blaze of orange light. Emblazoned across the back were the words 'Clapton is God! ' within a yellow pentangle. Giselle wore her simple white cotton dress and sunglasses. She had her hair in a knot on top of her head tied with a white ribbon. From time to time she stretched out her hand to touch his, to caress his fingers.

It would soon be time. Igor had gone to fetch the horses for the long ride into the hills. Giselle smiled to herself at the thought of her father's guests; those creaky and ancient men of the Priory Arcadia accustomed to smooth jet planes and limousines, who were now having to walk or horseback-ride their way from their choppers to the Meeting Place hidden high in the hills beyond Rennes le Chateau—to the Place of Marriage. From behind her dark glasses her gaze settled on JeanLuc with fierce possessive love. She was hooked on him. If he left her side

330

for more than an hour she felt withdrawal symptoms, a childish lost feeling, a hunger for his presence. Fleetingly, she wondered why the clinic in Perpignon was taking so long in sending back the results of her tests and why had they asked her last week for another blood sample? Surely these things were routine? But most of the time she felt wonderful, aglow with life and energy. In her secret heart, she knew she was pregnant. She was familiar enough with the rhythms and moods of her body to know that something, somehow had changed. Surely that meant that JeanLuc's child was growing within her already. Those tests could only confirm what she was already certain of—the consummation of JeanLuc's frequent visits to her bed, the consummation of their fierce couplings, their insatiable need for each other's bodies. Even now, she wanted him, only hours before their wedding, as he sat sideways to her, relaxed long legs stretched out, smoking a thin cigar, waiting for Igor, watching the colourful parade of people going by. In the hot sunlight.

The burly forms of Igor and Sergeant Nollet appeared. Pulling up two more chairs, they sat. Nollet's mobile phone buzzed and he unfolded, it listening without expression.

"We can set off when you are ready, sir" he said to JeanLuc who yawned and stubbed out his cigar.

"Let's go, then. This will be a laugh, Giselle. Can you imagine His Reverence Cardinal Mirphy Papal Legate to New York on horseback! I can't wait to see this!" he laughed. "Hey, Igor! You got the supplies? Plenty of vino and food for our guests? Come on, we're going to have a good time. Giselle, you lead the way."

Their route took them back towards Rennes les Bains, along the old Roman road following the River Sals, past the ruins of Blanchefort on their right, which was on land owned by the Priory, up the steep valley sides at the place found earlier by Giselle, past the ruined Sepulchre in the cathedral copse of beeches and back along the ridge on a deserted overgrown path. It could be seen that horses had travelled the way just before them and trampled a clear way through. After an hour's ride, they emerged out of the woods onto a narrow rock promontory that looked back towards Rennes le Chateau and commanded a magnificent clear view of the surrounding countryside of the Haut Languedoc.

Awaiting them, was the Wedding Party. Awaiting them, were the Commandeurs and Seneschals of the Rose Croix of the Priory Arcadia who had come from all corners of the globe. All were in full regalia, white-robed and hooded figures headed by the aged but still-commanding figure of the Compte de Sigor, the Nautonnier, distinguished by the blue trim on his robe, unhooded head and the gold-braided rope around his waist.

"Welcome Brothers and Sisters. Welcome to this happy and historic occasion. The Marriage Ceremony can now begin." He produced a folded white robe for JeanLuc who promptly put it over his head. The Grand Master handed his daughter a bouquet of red roses and another robe. JeanLuc and Giselle were immediately led forward to the main group assembled at the edge of the promontory. Igor, and Nollet went to join the civilian figures of Saskia and Dmitri Yemeljan who stood apart near the tethered horses. Following an impulse, Saskia reached up to the basket strung onto her horse, lifted it down and let the cat out onto the grass. Alexey looked around and then shot off into the bushes from whose cover he surveyed the strange scene before him.

The Marriage Ceremony, conducted by Joseph Mirphy, now the senior Croisé, was simple with few words. It was over quickly. The sun shone from out of a cloudless Mediterranean blue sky.

All embraced the bride and bridegroom, now husband and wife in the Faith of the Catholic Church and the Doctrines of the Priory Arcadia. All contributed their own hot fresh blood to the chalice of Clovis I and in it swore eternal fealty to the new King and Queen of Heaven.

Within thirty minutes, they had gone, leaving the newly-weds alone to consummate their Marriage in the most natural way on the warm, soft grass, in a chorus of birdsong and chirruping crickets, under the watchful mismatched gaze of Alexey the cat.

CHAPTER 40

"How is the Holy Father, Doctor? Is he well enough to travel? Can he function?" asked Cardinal Von Helsinger.

"It is difficult to say, Your Eminence," hedged the eminent white-haired psychiatrist with the face and mobile lips of a wise chimpanzee. "It will depend on the day. He has good days and bad days."

"Don't give me a long Latin name, but what do you think is wrong with him—in layman's terms please."

"Well, it's a rare form of catatonia of course—not quite a coma. It's as if his brain had seized up, to use mechanical terminology. The clinical symptoms of shell shock is the nearest equivalent I can think of. Apart from slight infirmity from old age, there seems to be nothing intrinsically wrong with him physically. The alpha brain waves are rather suppressed, I suppose."

"Is he a zombie? "A what?"

"A zombie. You know, like in American Video Nasties. Night of the Living Dead—that sort of thing!"

"I'm afraid I wouldn't know, Your Eminence," said the Professor stuffily. "I'm too busy with my patients to indulge myself in film fantasy."

"Yes, well. Can you wake him up? Maybe electric shock? Deprive him of his Sega games console?"

"Well, technically, he is awake most of the time. It seems that he hardly ever sleeps—maybe an hour a night."

"That's not what I meant. It is imperative that you snap him out of whatever evil spell or dream-zone he's living in. There is vital Church business to attend to. A Pope that cannot make decisions is a disaster for the Catholic Faith— Popes don't retire you know, they only die!"

"Well, there is no reason why the Holy Father cannot live like this for another twenty, thirty years. I have patients in the clinic who ..."

"Listen to me, Professor and listen good. You have got to do something. Either make him well or kill him—do you get my drift? Have I made myself clear enough?"

"I am outraged that you could say such a thing Cardinal Von

Helsinger! My professional reputation ... I couldn't possibly—" spluttered the Professor in shock and anger.

Von Helsinger looked at him balefully from behind his desk. He had bad indigestion, things were not going well, and now his patron D'Ascriba had begun to go cuckoo. This pale excuse for a man, this scientist, needed to be shown the true power of the Church. "I have here a file on you and your Institute, Doctor. As you know we of the Inquisition like to keep an eye on things."

"What do you mean?" cried the Professor angrily. "Have you been spying on me? This is an outrage!"

"Now, now Professor. It is just that we know about the secret work that you have been doing with some of your wealthier Alzheimer's and senile dementia patients and ..." The Cardinal flicked through the bulky file in front of him on the desk. "...we know about this link, this little arrangement that you have with that abortion clinic in the Via Tupino," he added grimfaced.

The Professor of Psychiatry went as pale as Death and sank back limply into his chair.

"You mean ...?"

"Yes. We know all about the foetal brain-tissue implants you've been doing. This is an abomination in the eyes of the Church. You have much to answer to God for, my son. A few Hail Marys is hardly sufficient for the sins that you and your colleagues have been committing in that Satanic Institute of yours. Let me see ..." Von Helsinger steepled his fingers and raised his eyes to Heaven, "... to start with, that will be pre-meditated murder of unborn babies. That would make a good headline in La Tampa, don't you think? And then there are the crimes against God and the Law of ..."

Dr.Emo Vittorio said dully: "All right, you bastard. What do you want me to do?"

"At the very least, you should call me Your Eminence, you devil-worshipping, baby-killing vampire!" shrieked Von Helsinger suddenly. Erupting from his chair like a black avenging angel of Death, the Grand Inquisitor thrust a large ornate wooden crucifix at the Doctor's terrified face. The professor cowered in his chair. The world of the Institute and of clinical Psychiatric Science was always quiet and orderly, in this day and age. The screams and ravings of the lunatics are attenuated by discrete truckloads of sedatives and drugs. The valium bill alone came to thousands of euros. The corridors and wards of his Institute were now mostly quiet with only the sounds of weeping and drug-sodden snores to disturb the peace. He rarely needed the protection of the two sumo dyke- matrons that accompanied him on his daily rounds. And now this monstrous black cleric was screaming at him and threatening to do physical violence with a holy crucifix, and worst of all threatening to expose him to the Press! He fainted.

"Sister Emmanuel!" shouted the Cardinal. "Get in here at once. Bring some water." The nun hurried in with the jug of water. Von Helsinger took it and threw the contents onto the Professor's face. he stirred in his seat, blinking his way back to awareness and the awful reality of Cardinal Von Helsinger's huge moon face millimetres from his nose, showing no compassion, no concern, no twinkly Christian kindness, no friendly interest; only a hard malevolent glare from eyes of Neanderthal flint and a soft breath of peppermint.

Diplomatically, Sister Emmanuel left the room, closing the heavy door softly behind her. His Eminence was obviously engaged in exorcising a devil—she must make sure he wasn't disturbed. She sat at her desk and prayed to Jesus, ignoring the sounds of bumps, thuds, pig squeals of agony and groans of pain that now issued from the inner sanctum. The devil came in many forms and they must be ever-vigilant, even here in the heart of God's kingdom on Earth. But God was with her beloved Cardinal and as God's High Priest he would win in the end against whatever manifestation of Beelzebub had possessed the poor doctor. The Professor was a lucky and privileged man; few were blessed with the brand of personal salvation dished out by the Cardinal himself.

A few minutes later, the Cardinal called her in. "Call the Professor's institute, Sister, and ask them to send an ambulance for him. Tell them he's had a collapse."

"Are you all right, Your Holiness? Can I get you some refreshment? Wrestling with demons must be hard work."

"I feel fine, Sister. Just a little out of breath. But you're right, it is thirsty work. Maybe you could serve tea when the Professor has been taken away."

335

"Yes, Your Eminence. I'll see to everything right away."

"God bless you, Sister; and now please leave us while I have a few more words with this unfortunate sinner so that he can be set on the path of righteousness once more."

The nun went out.

"Now listen, you miserable worm. This is what I want you to do."

The Professor couldn't answer; he could barely breathe. In the last few minutes, his own worst nightmare had coalesced into physical reality. The cup of his mind teetered on the very lip of the saucer of insanity; it would be relief to tip over completely so that he would never ever remember that he had just been sexually violated in the most brutal fashion; that he, an elderly eminent, world famous professor of psychiatry, had just been buggered by a high priest of the Catholic Faith; just as he had been as a cherubic boy of twelve, half a century ago. He whimpered now, just as he had done then. When he heard what the Cardinal wanted of him, he closed his eyes and prayed for death. When he heard that the Cardinal wanted him to immediately start implanting the foetal tissue of aborted babies from the disease-racked bodies of gypsy whores into the most holy brain of the reigning occupier of the Throne of St.Peter, he closed his eyes and prayed for merciful release. And then the men in white coats from his Institute came and took him away.

The whooping crane is a very rare bird. In fact it may well be extinct.

*

Von Helsinger was beginning to worry. The Pontiff appeared to have defaulted into a Sega world of virtual unreality and the Curia was now a hotbed of speculation about the consequences, and how long the Pope could last without being replaced. And, of course, Mirphy was milking the situation for all its worth, by constantly delaying his return to New York and by building on his power-base within the Vatican. Despite an apparent truce, Von Helsinger knew that Mirphy had been busy. This bloody Conference of his was being talked about by all the power brokers who mattered, as if it would really have an impact. And D'Ascriba seemed to be conspiring with his own fate by withdrawing into his idiotic computer sub-reality. He had turned into a zombie— Von Helsinger could think of no better description. It had all started innocently enough with the computerisation and electronic VCL archiving of Vatican records, but now even the lowliest baggarozzi were using email and carrying notebook PCs to Mass as if they were bloody life-insurance salesmen.

The Cardinal snorted with disgust. That idiot Duvain had been caught with his files undone, which had done some damage but at least not before the Atbash Plan had succeeded in its main aim. The Cardinal smirked. They won't know what's hit them—at least maybe not yet—and no computer had ever seen that part of the Plan. It had all been plotted in the good old-fashioned way; by a secret discussion with Father Moloc in the cloisters of the Parisian monastery where he still remained hidden; where he still deployed his sub-human troops of minor politicians, drug addicts, and sexual deviants in the service of Our Lord against the heretics. Von Helsinger might have lost the odd battle but he would win the war; he was sure of it.

"Where is my tea, Sister!" he called impatiently. "And get me Cardinal Paliato. He should be back from Bolivia by now." He sat thinking. Maybe now was the time to stage that stunt that they'd been planning and which had been instigated by the Pope about a year ago in one of his more lucid moments. Perhaps, he could upstage the Priory's Conference, maybe wreck it or at least discredit it. To do this, he would have to don his alter ego; he would become Cornelius again. He enjoyed writing vituperative slander about the enemy and planting subtle dis-information as his CIA chums called it. Stirring the muddy waters. He had considered being a journalist in the gutter Press before he was called to his true vocation as a priest and administrator within the Curia of the Holy Catholic Church. The duties were not entirely dissimilar at times, he thought wryly. On the other hand, should he jump ship? Jump onto Mirphy's bandwagon, do a deal? D'Ascriba was not much use to anyone at the moment but if he ever recovered, God help his enemies! D'Ascriba had been tough, merciless and ruthlessly single-minded on his way to achieving TopDogship. He would be a very, very bad man to cross—if he ever recovered. If he ever recovered—now that was a thought to ponder.

Sister Emmanuel arrived with the tea; lapsang souchon and a mountain of toasted and buttered crumpets. The crumpets were

337

especially sent to him in the diplomatic bag by Father Angus Neckbolt in London. And with the tea, there also came a Swiss Roll, sent to him from the town of Bolingen in his homeland. The Sister opened the window to let in some fresh air to blow away the stench of the devil that lingered in the office.

Guido Paliato, Von Helsinger's henchpriest, appeared in the doorway. His dachshund- like features were grey with jetlag, over-work and the stress engendered by working with the Grand Inquisitor.

"Ah, Guido. How was Bolivia. I hope our investments are flourishing? And our mutual friends—what of them?"

Cardinal Paliato settled himself in the chair recently vacated by Professor Vittorio, opened his Vatican briefcase and got out a sheaf of share certificates, treasury bonds and notes. "All is under control at the moment, Your Eminence, " he began. "But the situation is extremely volatile. I was lucky to get out of there in one piece. By the way, Il Presidente sends his warmest regards and loyalty to you. Please can you arrange for his account in the Banco Ambrosiano to be made well again."

"Same as usual, then!"

"Regretfully, I suppose so, yes. I brought back about two hundred million dollars that need washing, so I have arranged the purchase from the liquidators of two bankrupt companies in England. One is what they call an Estate Agency and the other a company that manufactures playground equipment. "

"That seems suitable. Would you care for a crumpet, Guido? Or some tea?"

"No, thank you. I seem to have lost my appetite recently. Maybe I should see a doctor."

"Perhaps I could ask the Holy Father's personal physician to take a look at you—you are right, you do look a bit peaky."

Guido Paliato flinched at this remark and he glanced warily at Von Helsinger. "Thank you, but no, Otto. I'm sure it will pass."

"As you wish. And the Church's business? Our Lord's work?"

Guido Paliato pursed his lips. "Things are very bad in Bogotá, Your Reverence. The priesthood is very fragmented, many have gone political and joined the peasants' underground rebellion, some are acting as spies for the CIA, some have even formed heretical cults of their own—it's a mess, and difficult to know what to do to change it. We need stronger leadership in South America as a whole, and maybe clearer direction from here," he said cautiously. To criticise the Pope was to criticise Von Helsinger and that would not be wise—he didn't want to be the one to have the death-warrant assignment to Bogotá!

"Well, let's forget about them for a while. We're unlikely to gain any more conclave votes from that quarter, and our investments seem reasonably productive considering the area," concluded Von Helsinger. "But to move on. We need to concentrate on preparing the Holy Father for this Summit in January. There is a new kind of treatment he will start soon. It is still experimental and highly controversial, but I'm told that there have been astounding successes. In the meantime, we must continue to programme him as best we can through that ridiculous computer of his. It seems to be the only channel we have into his mind at the moment. We'll need to have that young programmer back up here for his instructions."

"I'll start work on it today," said Paliato tiredly. "What has been happening on the Priory Arcadia front, while I've been away?"

"Not much visible apart from the build-up to this cursed Conference. Mirphy has been working from here in Rome but has also been travelling about a lot—we haven't been very successful at finding out where he is or what he's been up to. We know he has been soliciting votes for his pitch for the Papacy but he's been doing that for years. I suspect this bloody Conference is taking up most of his time."

"Are we going, then?"

"Yes Guido, we are. I figure it is best for us to know what is going on. Something is definitely happening and I must know what it is. They are all coming out of the woodwork, all dropping off their fences."

"What about Father Moloc? Can't he come up with something?"

"Well yes, he has already; but I've had to back-pedal on Moloc recently—he is very extreme and difficult to control. His deployment can be counter-productive at times."

The twenty-five crumpets awash in butter had disappeared so Von Helsinger cut off half the Swiss Roll. "Anyway, Plan Atbash has succeeded and we don't need him anymore."

"How do you know that the Plan succeeded? I thought Duvain the mole was exposed and killed by the Priory."

"Yes, but his secret mission about which I have not told you, did succeed," gloated Von Helsinger. "Giselle de Sigor went into hospital for a routine examination and blood tests in May. She is pregnant!"

"So? I thought she'd married some nonentity or other fairly recently. Why would this indicate that Atbash had succeeded?" Suddenly, Paliato blanched with horror at the thought that had just struck him. "You don't mean ..!"

"Yes, I do!" chuckled Von Helsinger. "I do indeedy." He picked up from his desk an emailed message. "This lab report obtained by Moloc concerning Giselle, Countess de Sigor, alleged heir to the heretical Carolingian Royal bloodline, not only states that she is pregnant but also that she has tested HIV positive!"

"May God forgive us!" muttered Paliato under his breath. "May God help us!" he said aloud "... when they find out. It will surely mean all-out war against us; you know that, don't you? Not the uneasy antagonism we've had so far. The Sang Graal is everything to them, I suspect."

"How can they ever find out? They cannot suspect that Philippe Dupont was one of Moloc's creatures; that his mission was to infect the Countess and ruin the Family's future genealogy. Dupont is dead, Duvain is dead. You, Moloc and I are the only ones who know."

"But they will know she has AIDS."

"Yes, by now, they probably will, but not by whom. According to Moloc, Giselle had many lovers before Philippe Dupont, and probably after as well, although Moloc says she dropped out of sight after his accident."

"That was a horrible course of action you took, Otto. Murder would be cleaner."

"But they are dangerous heretics, Guido. I took the only action that might stop them in their tracks. This will do what centuries of overt persecution have failed to do—and that is to write the final chapter of the Albigensian Crusade. Kill off the Cathars once and for all time!"

"Guido, there is one more thing we must do just to make sure— the final nail in the cross so to speak." continued Von Helsinger. "And

340

to send a message to any of the clergy who might be thinking of stepping out of line in the future."

"And what is that, Otto? You seriously begin to worry me, you know that, don't you?" sighed Paliato. "If we fail in some way, we will be out on the streets or worse."

"There is never any going back. You should know that, Guido. Now for God's sake, stiffen your resolve. We are playing for ultimate stakes here, and I don't intend to be a loser."

"I know that, Otto," said Paliato. "All right, so what is it that you have in mind?"

"We must begin formal excommunication proceedings at once against Joseph Mirphy!"

Paliato flinched: "But on what grounds? It will take years."

"I don't care how long it takes, just as long as it becomes known that he is in the process of excommunication. As for the grounds, well, that's pretty obvious—undeclared membership of a secret society with aims inimical to Catholic Doctrine."

"You and I know that; but I imagine he's been careful to have only a declared association with the Priory through this Conference; he will admit to that, but not to membership. It will be next to impossible to get hard legal evidence."

"I don't care. We can certainly stir things up against him and make his life hell by starting a formal investigation and proceedings. None of the die-hard Curia conservatives will touch him with a barge-pole if there is any sniff of doubt or taint of heresy."

"I guess you're right. In fact that's quite a good idea—it will be very damaging to his chances of the Papacy. Opus Dei will go berserk," said Paliato with false cheer.

"So, Guido! You have faith in me after all," smiled Von Helsinger cynically. "Listen, the way we should do it is immediately to issue a small notice to the Vatican Press Office. This will merely say that Mirphy is being investigated to clear him of certain unfounded allegations of being a member of a secret society. We will make all the usual vehement protestations that we believe he is completely innocent, etc, etc, but that the regulations insist that all such accusations, however insubstantial, must be disproved. I'll get Moloc to submit the formal accusation."

"As the English say, that will put a cat amongst the daptions!"

"Precisely... What the hell is a daption?"

"Latin for pigeon."

"Oh. To get back to my plan. You and I will start leaking to Brown, Baigent, Wilson, Salisbury and all those others I have in my cockroach file."

"Let them do all the exposing for us?"

"You've hit the nail on the head, Guido. Let them pester the life out of the Priory. We will do nothing but deny rumours. Something is bound to give way and if it doesn't they'll invent something, I'm sure. Those guys can dream up a conspiracy out of scotch mist and read meaning into the Pontiff's farts!"

"You are right as always, Otto. They have in the past and could do so again. You're a genius—I've always thought so. An evil genius, but genius no less," said Paliato, despair and hopelessness gnawing at his vitals. He noted the growing cheerful bounciness of the Grand Inquisitor who seemed, in Guido's mind, to be metamorphosing by the minute into an enormous African clawed toad—one of those awful warted amphibians that can gulp whole live chickens or baby piglets down into gullets the size of Dr.Who's Tardis.

Pausing in his discourse, Von Helsinger lit an Havana Gold and puffed at it like a steam locomotive going up a mountain, filling the room with perfumed smoke. Paliato began to feel nauseous. His bowels felt constricted and he had sharp pains in his lower spine. He thought maybe he would go to a doctor after all. He had been losing weight at an alarming rate recently and his shit was black and smelled disgusting. He'd read somewhere that this meant he had some bleeding in the gut somewhere. Perhaps he was dying. He felt like weeping with tiredness and anxiety. At night, his fitful sleep had been disturbed by dreams of bone-chilling vistas of frozen ice fields stretching to infinity, visions of the dark side of the moon and dark mazes of corridors from around whose corners came sudden cackles of fiendish laughter, like startled bats flying at him from out of a cave ...

"Guido ... Guido! Wake up! Are you all right? Come on, get a grip on yourself, man."

"Sorry, Otto. It's the jetlag. It was a difficult trip for me and I'm not getting any younger."

"Very well. A few hours rest and then we must get cracking. This is God's work we're engaged in and I want our reward to be on this plane of existence as well as in Heaven. And for God's sake see a doctor if you think you're unwell." Cardinal Von Helsinger glared at him with unpitying gaze. "I've no time for malingering!"

CHAPTER 41

The phone rang on Barbara Teery's bedside table. It went on ringing until, eventually, Vision News Network's ace reporter emerged from under her bedclothes where she'd been blowing mouth-organ solos composed by Frenchy Fellatio on her stallion-sized cameraman, Franco Heurtebise. As she turned away, she felt Franco's still-hard pecker teasing at her buttocks, rubbing up and down the slippery crack until with a sudden thrusting jab he was up the creek, brutishly tearing through what remained of her newly shop-lifted silken underthong.

Involuntarily, she moaned loudly into the receiver and then began to shudder with orgasm; as Franco's stiff plectrum fingers reached down to twang her perky trigger; as his own hot enema erupted into her.

At the other end of the phone line, a VNN News Editor replaced the phone in puzzlement and then, after looking through his list of numbers, he re-dialled. Teery answered breathlessly. "Teery here."

"Hi, this is the VNN News Desk, Jules Mitchelob here. Are you all right Barbara? You sound odd. Are you sick?"

Barbara suppressed a giggle: "Ah, no, Boss. I'm all right. I just got off ... outta the shower. Ah, what can I not do for you, Jules—I'm on vacation, remember?"

"Something big has come up." "Yeah, I know!"

"What? How do you know? I've only just been told myself!"

"Never mind."

"Anyway, can you come by the studios? The Big Chief is having a conference in about an hour and he insists that you be here. Oh, and do you know where Heurtebise is? We'll need him too. Give him a call, ring his bell or something. Sorry to disturb you but there is something big brewing and we want in; so get your sweet ass over here, pronto!"

"They want my sweet ass and for me to ring your bell, Franco!" Teery collapsed with laughter back onto the bed, her tits bouncing. The tall lanky form of the cameraman swung his three legs out of the bed and stood up shakily. He headed for the bathroom. "We'll take a cab," he shouted from the shower cubicle. "It'll be quicker. I wonder what's up?"

344

"Well, it isn't you any more, honey," said Teery looking disappointedly at his limpid form. "Hurry up. I gotta a lot of repair work to do. I feel like road kill on the Santa Monica Freeway."

"You look great, sweetlips. You were terrific!"

"Sure, sure, now get outta here! Fix yourself a beer and get me something sweet and alcoholic from the refrigerator." She paused. " Oh, and next time you go up the creek," she whispered huskily, "it would be nice to do it with a paddle!"

"Sure, baby. Whatever turns you on. I'll pack the Kriegs and rubber gloves as well!" The one-eyed snake on his thigh started to twitch interestedly.

"Down boy, down! We've got work to do. Our Audience Rating awaits," said Barbara with mock severity.

The conference was about to begin when Teery and Heurtebise arrived. They grabbed chairs and sat down.

Ed Piriana, the Executive Editor in Chief sat at the head of the long table and sucked moodily on a strictly forbidden Marlboro. 'Cornelius' was always right, he thought. He'd never been wrong before. This was going to be a BIG One but it was going to play merry hell with his quarterly resource budget—all that foreign travel and satellite time. Jesus, the stick he'd had from the fucking accountants across town in Finance, after the Baltic and Iraq and now this. He would have to put his top people in and they only went first fucking class. And it wasn't somewhere cheap, like Russia, that they were going to. He stared gloomily at the famous faces around the table. Unleashed, these motherfuckers could drain the budget in a day. All that polished punditry and pedantry produced an unquenchable thirst for the finest wines and most matured of liquors, and a ravenous hunger for picky gourmet eating; plus a deep yearning for the softest Hilton featherbeds nearest the war -zone. But they were not going to any war zone, so they wouldn't be able to skip blithely out without paying, as they usually did. More's the pity.

If Cornelius were wrong about this, the Network would axe him for sure and then put the organisation back onto fire-chasing and serial-killer profiling. Piriana popped a couple of Zantacs and washed them down with Perrier water. He preferred Perrier when it had the benzene in it. He preferred Coke when it had coke in it. Ah, but those were the good old days when a medical tonic was firewater and laudanum; hamburgers were made from bovine beef, apple pies had apple in them, and Twinkies had whatever it was in them.

He put on his Walter Mathau face, lit another Marlboro and started the meeting. "Okay, guys and gals—listen up!" he shouted. The room quietened down. "I've had word from my very own 'Deep Throat' ..." Franco winked at Barbara who brushed dark auburn hair from her face and frowned back at him ..." that a Big Event is to happen in Europe soon. I have code-named our operation Project Vision, and I want this given top priority, especially during January."

"So what is this Big Event, Ed?" interrupted Hiram Plonkerpuller the token-black news presenter originally chosen because of his resemblance to King Cronkite. "Third World War? Neo-Nazis being funded by the CIA? Popeye lost his spinach?" A few people laughed.

"I'll get to that in a second. This is no joking matter. On the strength of my unimpeachable source, I will be committing major and I mean major VNN resources to this new story and that includes my ass." He looked meaningfully around the table. "And that means your collective asses too. You all know me. If I go down, I don't go alone," he said with quiet menace. He stared at Plonkerpuller until his eyes lowered and he started to fiddle with a gold pencil. "Okay. So now we know what the score is. I'll give you your assignments and you can sort out your own arrangements as usual. I suspect that other Networks will be in on this pretty damn quick but I want those exclusives for VNN. I want us in there, right at the heart of events. Now most of you will be relieved to know that this is not a war. I'm told it's more of a political thing. Sorry about that Butch. I know you like dodging bullets."

Butch Billiard, a VNN war correspondent and a walking commercial for plastic surgery, grinned back wolfishly. "That's okay, Boss. If there's no war, I'll pay someone to start one!"

"That's ma boy! " smiled the Chief Editor without humour. "There is also a strong religious aspect." He raised his hand to forestall the inevitable. "Yes, yes, I know! Nobody is interested in religion anymore. TV, Virtual reality and drugs are quite sufficient opiates for the people. But my source says, and I have to go along with him, that fundamental things are happening in Europe now, and like an underground stream it has to come to the surface, and it will be soon."

"Yeah, like the Anti -Christ has pitched his tent at Megiddo! Come on Boss, give us a break. All that stuff is old hat."

"I don't agree, Carel," interjected Teery. "You remember that story I covered some months ago—the Stigmata Murder Case. That got huge ratings and aroused genuine feeling in our audience. The Mormons had a real bad set-back from that one and the Mormon Fundamentalists are very powerful in Washington these days."

"Thank you, Barbara, you make my point. People are still psychologically in the Middle Ages in spite of TV, and all the techno-crap we put out. Therefore, this is going to be an important human story for us. An evolutionary thing for the Network. It has everything: power politics, corruption, high finance, you name it. Also, you guys will actually have the opportunity to research and write proper material—you know, Pulitzer-Prize stuff," he smiled sarcastically. "That is, if any of you are still up to it."

"Christ! This sort of stuff belongs to those assholes in the BBC. What sort of real action footage can we expect?" Carel Studheimer leaned back in his chair, thumbs pulling at the red braces he wore to hold up his Armani slacks. His speciality was going in with the choppers and shoving microphone into the faces of mortally wounded combat-troops. Anything to say to the folks back home, trooper? How does it feel to die agonisingly on a foreign sand dune far from home in a pointless undeclared war of political ambivalence?

"To be honest, I don't know, Carel. And normally, I would agree wholeheartedly with you. But go along with me on this one, and I think you'll find we'll get good footage—sensational footage, I hope. That's all I can say. "

He put on his glasses and peered down at his notes. "I'm assigning Lois Lane and Clark Kent here ..." there was a titter around the table "... to Rome for the time being. Is that okay Barbara?" he asked. "I want the woman's view of Catholicism—you know the usual thing; the Pope; contraception; male chauvinism; monks' sex lives. A miracle on camera would be good. An update on the status of the Turin Shroud would be useful, too. I have contacts for you and a couple of good researchers already there who'll write your material and set things up for you."

"Sure, Chief. That sounds great to me. When do we go? I love opera!" She started to hum the theme from the latest Lloyd Webber hit musical currently on Broadway.

"You're already booked on an Alitalia flight out from La Guardia tomorrow morning. And don't make trouble—those Eyetalians can get real dangerous, if rubbed up the wrong way. The Mafia may be yesterday's news here but not there. Capiche?"

"Yeah, yeah. Don't worry. The Pope is as good as in the can!"

"Remember, CNN, ABC, BBC, CBC, NBC and every other BC in the world will be there. But we will be what ...?"

"Be there ... be first!" they had chorused in unison after he'd given them their assignments. Then they'd picked up their things and filed out.

This was it. His ass was now firmly on the line. It was his Project, his Story. Once they'd all left the building, the budget would start to drain, the countdown on his career would begin. He'd gotten $5 million for this one. He'd be Executive Producer and Director. Every bit of expenditure from condoms to the 'dead- bunny' microphone covers would be down to him. Ah, what the hell, he'd been doing it for five years now and was close to burn-out anyway. Let the fucking accountants worry. He was going to take the ageing corporate Lear to cover Paris and anything that happened there. He could orchestrate the whole of VNN operations from there as easily as here in New York. And 'Cornelius' had said that it would be Paris or near Paris that the whole thing would go down in January. On the seventeenth. He had a date. They had one week to get organised. It would be tight, but not impossible. They'd worked to tighter schedules than this before—they were media pros after all. Get it as it happens.

He looked at his Rolex. It was a nice one—a good buy, he thought. From that woman who worked in Editing. Muscular ugly-looking bitch, but connected. And two hundred dollars cash was a bargain; must be worth at least a grand. Maybe she had some other stuff. Probably all nicked, of course. He liked to buy stolen goods; it gave him a vicarious thrill, as well as saving himself money. Ed Piriana

348

wondered where the watch had come from, who'd had it before him? In the old days, when he was a newsman on the Post, following little leads like this had gotten him some of his best stories. It was such an inconsequential thing that had led him to his Pulitzer and also his first meeting with Cornelius—his Deep Throat in the black heart of world politics. But it sure was a tough life. He'd divorced two wives, his four kids disowned him, he had an ulcer, haemorrhoids, dizzy spells, angina; he could hardly focus on a VDU anymore and his lungs felt like sacks of moist shit.

He lit another Marlboro' and looked down the assignment lists and air-time schedules. Yeah, he would do his first piece on the fifteenth and then Barbara Teery could do a fifteen-minute in-depth from Rome on the sixteenth. He liked Teery, his chirpy little Lois Lane. He wished he were younger so he could take her into his bed. He could still do it, of course, by sheer power-play but sex no longer interested him that much, and it would make him ashamed. That Franco stud is probably fucking her, the lucky dog. Yeah, she was nice-looking on camera too—stylish. The smooth dark-auburn hair, wide-set hazel brown eyes, creamy complexion, and full pouty painted lips—a dark Madonna! Ah well, Monsieur Perrier, down the hatch!

His secretary came in with his tickets, and authorisations for him to sign. He put his spectacles back on and ran a sharp proof-reader's eye over them. Shit! That son of a bitch Studheimer had already put in a fucking two hundred dollar expense claim for a dinner at Sardi's he'd not even eaten yet and he'd hardly left the goddamned building. Well, he'd give the clever little bastard something to claim for—fucking hospital insurance. He would re-assign him to East Africa. Yeah, Somalia. He'll be HIV-positive before you could say 'Mama'. Serve him right, the lying cheapskate!

*

Outside the Studios, it was snowing. It had been snowing for weeks. This was the worst post- Christmas blizzard in living memory. There was no charity or hot soup left for the meek and the miserable. That night the homeless froze to death on the City streets in their thousands beneath the white drifts and the bitter Polar wind.

Send $10 and we'll say a little prayer for you. Forever, and ever and

349

ever ... again.

Buy Heaven. The soap the Angels use!
Repent Ye. For the END is NIGH!
Repent Ye. For the WICKED shall BURN!
Repent Ye. For JEEEEEZUS is a'comin' Bro!
Get your HOTDOGS at JOE'S place!
HONK if you love JESUS!
My other car is an Edsel!

*

"Okay, Folditch. So brief me. What's the latest situation? This better be good—my wife is giving me unbelievable stick for agreeing to attend this Summit. A 'Spawning of Satan' were the exact words she used. She had to be sedated before I left."

AirForce One, in which the US President and his CIA chief were travelling , was now a converted stealth bomber that could travel at over Mach 1. The old 747 aircraft had been 'retired' and sold to Madonna who used it for touring. She liked to hold parties in it. There was no Rolling-Stone staffer worth his salt who had not moved heaven and earth to join this particular Mile-High club. The famous bullet hole in the toilet door was now neatly framed and personally autographed by His Reverence HST himself. Although extremely painful, many of the world's leading rock'n'rollers had submitted in-flight to being sizzle-branded on the buttock with the big 'M' logo.

"Okay, Mr.President. I have here the latest list of attendees."

President Dillon put on his spectacles, and scanned the page placed in front of him by the CIA Chief. He whistled. "Jesus. How in hell did they get all these guys here at once? We couldn't do that. It'll be a security nightmare! Some of them will be cutting each other's throats in the goddamned aisles!"

"It won't be too bad, sir. No worse than a meeting of the UN Security Council. There are only forty VIPs in all."

"Yeah, but pretty VVIP. Who are all these guys from South America?"

"They are heads of powerful families with real old money and huge estates. Fabulously rich. This guy here ..." Folditch pointed with his pencil "... is believed to be worth more than Texas! Part of the Austrian Royal Family, now lives in Argentina, probably owns half of it as well, or those bits the Germans don't."

"And the Priory Arcadia? Do we have more information on them?"

"No sir. No more than was in that Briefing File I gave you last year. They're a cagey lot." concluded Folditch, watching the President from under hooded eyes.

"Strange story. Is there anything of substance to it?"

"To what, Mr.President?"

"All that bullshit about Jesus, Royal blood lines, Crusaders and French politics. Maybe my wife is right. Maybe we're entering the lion's den here. It all seems kinda Un-American don't you think?"

"Unfortunately sir, we need closer European ties. The Deficit Dictates, as they say. Your predecessor concentrated, quite rightly, on the Pacific Basin but now we must repair our Atlantic alliances if they are to act as a bulwark against the Russian Nationalists. Anyway they are beginning to outstrip us economically."

"I see the Ruskies are listed here in strength. Do I have to drink their goddamned vodka, Folditch? The stuff plays havoc with my guts these days."

"I don't know sir. Maybe Secretary Bollinger can advise you on matters of protocol. Anyway your hosts are French ..."

"I hate goddamned garlic! All their food tastes of slime and shit!" whined the President petulantly. Mike Folditch shifted uncomfortably in his seat. He sighed inwardly. This President was capricious. The NFL semi-finals were coming up and he might just turn the jet around to go press the flesh at a popular ball game. 'Popeye' knew he needed a boost in the popular polls. The winter snows were hard this year and there had been many deaths in Chicago and the North Eastern Cities. The remnants of the US Social Welfare programme had been allowed to collapse so that the insurance companies could introduce their new lottery ticket schemes. So the underclass of the permanently poor who no longer registered on the computer databases as existing in terms of credit rating or property ownership, were beginning to cause trouble.

351

Nothing that couldn't be handled but nonetheless the Police and FBI budgets were being stretched and paranoia was rampant. He was beginning to lose votes.

"Oh well, we'll be landing in Paris soon. May as well get on with it. I don't want to go home and face my wife just yet, or those buffoons in the Senate for that matter. Maybe a Foreign Policy success will boost my ratings. There will be plenty of media there, won't there?"

"Yes, Mr.President."

CHAPTER 42

"This is Barbara Teery coming to you live by satellite from Northern France at the World Leader Summit devoted to Peace for the New Millennium. In an unprecedented move, the organisers of this event have imposed a total news blackout from this Summit. This unwarranted censorship has infuriated the media here and also many of the delegates. I talked with US President Bob Dillon, who arrived just a short while ago. Talking exclusively to VNN, the President told me that he knew little of what was on the agenda for the meeting. He was surprised and incensed at the media restrictions that have been imposed. However, I can now tell you that, thanks to the resourcefulness of one of our team who has smuggled in a hidden camera, we will be able to give you exclusive inside pictures of what's going on."

But first a word from our sponsors ...

"This is Barbara Teery, VNN News in Northern France. We are about forty miles north west of Paris at a place called Sigor. Here in the old Norman Castle once occupied by Crusaders, world leaders from every corner of the globe are arriving for the self-styled Millennial Peace Summit. We have in our Paris Studio a full panel of experts and correspondents to keep you informed on what is happening. Over to you, Hiram."

"Thank you, Barbara. Now as Barbara said, we will shortly be getting exclusive pictures from inside the Castle and inside the Summit Meeting itself. I cannot emphasise more strongly the importance that this Summit will have on world opinion. Never before have so many top leaders and influential men and women assembled in one place. Carel, Have you spotted any of the leaders or spoken to any of them?"

"Yes, indeed, Hiram. I have seen the arrivals of European Commissioner Pierre Lorraine, the Presidents of the France and Germany, and I am told that all the European Heads of Government are due to arrive in the next hour or so. I spoke a few minutes ago with Cardinal Otto Von Helsinger, spokesperson for the Vatican Delegation and he told me that His Holiness the Pope has already arrived and is inside the Grand Hall of the Castle."

"There have been rumours about the Pope's health, Carel. Did Cardinal Von Helsinger comment on this?"

"Yes, Hiram. When I asked about the Pope's condition, His Reverence assured me that His Holiness is fit for the trip and his health has responded very well to some recent treatment that he has been receiving in Rome."

"Thank you, Carel. Barbara, do you have any developments yet from inside the Castle?"

"Not yet, Hiram. But I would like to tell our viewers about the incredible security that surrounds this place. I have seen the French Military here in huge numbers. There are tanks blocking all roads into and out of Sigor. I have been told that there are at least two battalions of crack infantry soldiers guarding the Castle and grounds. There is a complete ban on air traffic within a fifty-mile radius, which has caused tremendous problems and disruptions at Orly Airport, the main air corridor into Paris. We have seen anti-aircraft and anti-missile rocket-launchers sited on the battlements of this ancient fortress."

"Have you managed to interview any of the organisers, Barbara?"

"I'm afraid not, Hiram. Neither we nor the other networks have been able to talk with the organisers, who are known simply as the Priory Arcadia."

"Thank you, Barbara. Let us know when we can expect pictures from inside the Castle. Now we can go over to Ed Piriana who is in our Paris Studio. Ed?"

"Thanks, Hiram. Here in Paris VNN has gathered some informed commentators on the world scene. Let me ask you first, Henry. Who are the Priory Arcadia people and what do they represent?"

"That's a good question, Ed; and I'm not really sure I can answer it. My information is that they are a real old long standing and influential secret society or Masonic Lodge whose avowed and stated aim is to establish France as a Monarchy as it was in olden times."

"David, anything you'd like to add to that?"

"I'm sure Henry is right, but there must be some other purpose to this Summit beyond just the restoration of the French Monarchy, an undertaking which hardly merits an International Summit on this scale."

"Then is this some kind of peace-brokering to solve some of the issues of the Middle East and International Terrorism? After all, there are many of us who either doubt the ability of mankind to survive without nuclear annihilation, or else expect an apocalyptic encounter with the Forces of Darkness. This is surely a worthy attempt to bring sanity into a world of political and economic chaos. I, for one, welcome any attempt to bring peace to the world whoever they are."

"Bill, have you been surprised that so many influential people have turned up? I mean it must be a fair indicator of the clout of the organisers."

"Yes, Ed, you're right. I am totally amazed that His Holiness the Pope is here today. Also the Russian and US Presidents together. We don't yet have a full list of delegates but those who have been seen arriving are among the richest most and powerful men on the planet. From South America, Saudi Arabia, the Middle East—it is incredible! Whatever goes on inside that Castle today will resound forever in history—I am certain of that!"

"I understand from this message on the monitor in front of me that we can now go live to Sigor Castle and Barbara Teery where something is beginning to happen. Barbara?"

"Yes, thank you, Ed. You are now seeing the first pictures from our secret camera smuggled into the Grand Hall. You can see that it is a cathedral-sized room and the delegates are milling around this huge circular conference table. In the centre there is a dais on which there appears to be a number of objects and a wooden box. The upper spaces of the room are filled with the flags printed with heraldic devices and other patterns. They do not seem to be recognisable as belonging to particular countries; although I have recognised the EEC flag and the Fleur de Lys of France. Ed? Maybe our panel could come in with some comments at this point."

"Okay, Barbara. Henry, anything there you recognise?"

"Well, not really Ed. Some of them look familiar but they seem to be family crests, mainly."

"I notice that there is a big cinema screen on one wall and a speaker's podium beside it."

"Carel, do you have any observations to make? What is happening outside?"

"I make it about forty delegates who have arrived so far, Barbara. There do not seem to be any more choppers arriving or limos coming through the police roadblocks. In fact they seem to be closing the gates of the Castle. Yes, the gates are closing and a tank is moving to block the access road. I think maybe the Summit is about to begin. Over to you, Hiram."

"Thank you, Carel, and now some messages from our sponsors. Stay tuned to VNN for exclusive live coverage of the Peace Summit here in France ..."

"Everything working all right, Franco?" asked Jean de Sigor. He was wound-up clock- spring tight, every movement, every gesture jerky with the tension of the hour.

"Yes sir. The camera is perfectly positioned to capture everything that goes on. I can control it remotely, from our hidden position up here."

"Remember, no sound until I come on after Mirphy. Just pictures."

"Yes, I have told them outside that there is a minor fault I'm working to fix."

"Good. Merde, I wish I wasn't so nervous. You're sure you'll be the only camera in the place? We want just the one outside link here, we want to make it look as if it was smuggled in—it adds drama."

"Yes, I'm switching channels on this monitor here. VNN is the only one that will be able to broadcast live pictures from inside. Everyone else has views of their studios or of the outside; the Castle, the tanks, the missile launchers, and the helicopters—we are the only camera inside. Nollet has told me that his sensors and metal detectors would have picked up anything being carried in by the delegates. He relieved them of mobile phones, PDAs, dictation and translation machines. All delegates have been totally cut off from the outside world for more than an hour."

"Right, let it begin. I'll go now to get changed and prepare myself and the others."

Franco Heurtebise looked with pity at the old man. The Compte had wasted away since they'd last met when, as a Chevalier in the Priory

Arcadia, he'd been given the assignment to penetrate the VNN organisation. Just the shell of the man remained, kept alive by the flame of zealotry that burned within him, driving him onward towards this final achievement of a long life. The Compte ducked out of the small dark room which overlooked the Grand Hall and made his way down the narrow winding stone stairway. He knocked softly on the door of one of the service rooms behind the Grand Hall, and walked straight in without waiting for a reply.

"It is time," he said.

Giselle lay on her back on a steel-framed hospital trolley. She was unconscious, her breathing soft and shallow. Her form was draped in white linen. Her face was pale and ravaged, with hollowed cheeks, grey lips and sweat-slicked brow. Twin spots of unhealthy colour glowed in her cheeks from a tracery of broken veins. Her long golden hair had been shorn to prison length but was still lifeless, and streaked with white. The Compte fought to control the grief and rage that threatened to overwhelm him at the sight of his beloved daughter reduced to this state.

JeanLuc knelt beside her, holding one of her hands against his lips. His eyes were closed in a posture of prayer or trance. He was already robed. He looked up as Jean came in. The two men embraced. Then the Compte kissed the pale cheek of his daughter, stroking the lank hair out of her eyes. "Adieu, my darling. Adieu Giselle. Soon you will be at peace. Soon you will be in the arms of God and with your Mother. I promise," he whispered.

"Courage, Nautonnier. You must have courage. We must go on!" JeanLuc cried. "Remember what the specialist said ... the child will survive."

The Compte nodded mutely, tears pouring down his cheeks. "I know, I know. But such a sacrifice! Such cost! I cannot bear it!" he wept. "I know the agony of Abraham!"

"Welcome back. This is Barbara Teery VNN live from Castle Sigor. We understand that the Conference is about to begin. Our secret camera from within the Grand Hall will bring you exclusive pictures as it happens. The leaders have all taken their seats around the table and their personal assistants are being ushered out. This is unprecedented.

357

The World Leaders are to be in there on their own. I can see that there is much heated discussion and shouting going on in there already! Yes! This is astonishing! A fist fight has broken out between a Russian delegate and one from the Baltic States; others are trying to separate them. Over to you, Hiram."

"Thank you, Barbara. Ed? We are already witnessing an unseemly fracas between the delegates at this so- called Peace Conference. Does your panel think there is any chance of a positive outcome from all this?"

"You have a point, Hiram. Let me ask you first, Henry. What do you think would be a good result from this?"

"Well, Ed. It is obviously a disappointing start but from my long experience, emotions often do run very high at these Summits. There is a huge amount at stake and unpalatable compromises and accommodations often have to be made between sworn enemies. As for your question, I think some kind of Joint Declaration to work towards peace is about all we can really hope for at this time. However, getting such disparate leaders here in the first place must surely rank as an achievement of historical dimension—whatever the outcome."

"David, any comments?"

"I still cannot understand why the Summit is being held at all. I still think there must be some other motive. Also, why this particular day in midwinter? It's damned cold out there!"

"Yes, I see. Henry, is there any significance to the timing of this, do you think?"

"I cannot think of any. I have looked through my diary and the only entry for the seventeenth of January is that it is the Feast Day of an obscure Catholic Saint called St.Sulpice."

"St.Sulpice?"

"Yes. Otherwise I cannot see anything particularly special about today. It doesn't seem to be the anniversary of anything."

"Thank you, Henry. And now we go back to Barbara Teery at Sigor Castle after these messages from our sponsors. Stay with us for exclusive coverage ..."

Sweating with fear and from the exertions of prising apart fighting delegates, Cardinal Joseph Mirphy walked over to the Speaker's podium. It was his job to start the Proceedings. He felt the baleful murderous gaze of Cardinal Von Helsinger and the hooded amused stare of Pope John XXIV on his back, as well as the collective curiosity of the assembly. His legs were wobbly as he mounted the steps. He gripped the sturdy podium with both hands to steady himself. He waited. He waited for an angel of calm to alight on his shoulders, for a bird of inspiration, for the Holy Spirit to descend with a gift of tongues. As the Gathering grew quieter, Mirphy reviewed swiftly in his mind the order of events. But this was no familiar Mass with its comforting ritual, habits of speech and centuries-old rhythms of motion. Here, he couldn't lose his Self in the anonymity of the vestments, behind a choral wall of sound within the vastness of a dim incense-filled Cathedral. This was an intimate gathering, a smoke-filled room of supremely powerful, calculating political egos; many of whom were his sworn enemies. He was in Satan's Boardroom and he had no real idea of what was going to happen. This was uncharted territory, a nexus in history. Anything could happen and there was no going back; he was about to launch his personal horseshoe at the far distant peg of Destiny.

Gradually, the assembly settled down and all eyes focused on the tall figure of the Cardinal. He raised his hand. "Your Royal Highnesses, Lords, Ladies and Gentlemen! This is an historic occasion! You are participating at the first Summit for Peace in the Age of Terror. This is ..."

"Cut the crap, Mirphy!" shouted a loud arrogant voice from the far end of the Hall. "What have you got? What the hell are we all here for? There's nobody here but us chickens. You can tell us." There was laughter from around the tables.

Mirphy felt a slow burning fuse of fury suddenly flare alight within him. Anger cleared his mind in an instant. You bastard, he thought. Just you wait and see, you son of a bitch!

"Hey, Mirphy! You fitted yourself out with that Papal Cassock yet?" heckled another. At this the figure of Pope John raised itself from his seat and shook his fist at the perpetrator. He yelled abuse in Spanish.

Everyone was as jittery as hell.

Mirphy turned a small silvery key set into the podium. A small red light blinked slowly on the key console. The lights dimmed in the

Grand Hall. Hell, they may as well go for it right now. He hoped Jean was ready because … THIS WAS IT!

"You are watching a VNN live broadcast from Northern France. This is Barbara Teery. Cardinal Joseph Mirphy, Vatican Legate of New York, has just opened the Summit of Leaders. The disruptions seemed to have ceased. The Pope seems to be angry about something. We apologise for the lack of sound but I am told we are working on it and it should soon be operational. In the meantime, we shall continue to give you a blow-by-blow account together with live pictures exclusive to VNN. Over to you Ed, in Paris."

"Thank you, Barbara. Henry, any comments?"

"Well, I must say it is the most animated that we have seen the Pope for a long time."

"It looks as though Cardinal Mirphy is being heckled in there."

"Yeah, it sure does, but remember these are powerful opinionated World Leaders and they certainly aren't shy! Plus they also don't realise they're on camera!"

"I see the Hall has gotten dark now, and a picture has appeared on the cinema screen. Back to you, Barbara for more exclusive coverage by VNN."

"Thank you, Ed. Yes, it has gotten dark in there and projected onto the screen we can now see a heraldic device which I am not familiar with. And here comes a new figure approaching the podium. Hiram, do you have any idea who it may be?"

"It looks like the Compte de Sigor, who is the main organiser of this Summit. Cardinal Mirphy is giving the podium to the new man who is dressed in a white robe ... Ha! It sounds like we now have sound for you. We'll be back right after this ..."

Jean de Sigor, Croix du Guerre, Legion D'Honneur, KG, OBE, Nautonnier of the Priory Arcadia, surveyed the assembly in the darkened Grand Hall of Castle Sigor. Not since the Splitting of the Elm in 1188 had so many Kings and Princes of Temporal Power been gathered together in this Castle, Home of the Prieuré since the Beginning. As it was then, so it was again, with a Grand Master addressing Princes of Men who watched like a pack of starving Siberian wolves around a dying campfire. He gripped a wooden rod, cut and carved from the remains of that same Elm.

Suddenly, with infinite relief, he could feel the OLD POWER begin to enter him. The base of his spine tingled with sensation, sending sparks of nervous fire into his brain. His eyeballs rolled upwards into their sockets and he stretched out his arms, holding the rod aloft. He stood silently for several minutes against the backdrop of the heraldic device of the Priory Arcadia. The assembled delegates fidgeted nervously in their seats. Few knew Jean de Sigor personally, only what he represented—the secret power that had shaped Modern Europe and made this Gathering. And now he stood there like Charlton Heston parting the Red Sea for Paramount Pictures.

The perfume of roses pervaded the Grand Hall. Then he began:

"We, the Priory Arcadia, MAKE OUR CLAIM!" he shouted. The Assembly flinched at the loudness of his amplified voice.

"We take our RIGHTFUL HERITAGE! "We INVOKE THE ANCIENT RIGHTS!

"NOW IS THE TIME for all to be REVEALED in the SIGHT OF ALMIGHTY GOD!

"STAND UP, SONS OF LIGHT! "STAND UP, BROTHERS OF JESUS!

"STAND UP, PRIESTS OF THE ONE TRUE GOD!

"STAND UP, KEEPERS OF THE SANG GRAAL! "STAND UP, TRUE KNIGHTS OF CHRIST!

"APPROACH THE DESTINY PROPHESEYED BY MALACHI!"

The thirteen Croisé, and Commandeurs, men and women of the Rose Croix, including Joseph Mirphy, rose from their seats and walked in solemn procession to pick up a white robe from the pile stacked beside the podium. They lined up in front of the Compte, their arms held out, showing the golden bee in one hand and the flat white stone from the Jordan River in the other. Faces and identities were now revealed to each other and to the world.

"We make our Claim. We PROVE our Claim in the eyes of the Lord and in the eyes of Man!" cried out the Nautonnier.

"BEHOLD!" he bellowed.

361

"BEHOLD, THE TREASURES OF THE TEMPLE OF JERUSALEM1 "BEHOLD, THE GENEALOGY SCROLL!

"BEHOLD, THE HAIR OF JESUS, OUR LORD!

"BEHOLD, THE TREASURES OF THE DESCENDANTS OF MEROVEE AND CLOVIS!

The Nautonnier took a deep shuddering breath and then screamed at the top of his voice:

"BEHOLD, JESUS HIMSELF!

"BEHOLD OUR LORD AND HIS FAMILY!"

The images of the Jesus Icons were suddenly projected in full-colour vividness onto the huge screen behind Jean de Sigor. He now looked like a stick insect silhouetted against the magnified features of Jesus in the central panel. The ring of onlookers stared with mouths agape at the strange but attention-riveting performance. Peculiar information was being thrust upon them with the dizzying intensity of a revivalist meeting. But was this some kind of cabaret act or what? When were they going to get down to some serious negotiating and talking? But it didn't look as though there was going to be any negotiations. They were being told—this was it, buddy, take it or leave it. Who were these guys!? At the mention of the prophecy of Malachi, Pope XXIV's heart had turned to jagged ice. He stared at the dais with growing dread.

The images of the Jesus Icons were flashed across the world, across every network, every syndicate, onto every TV, into every living room, bar or bedroom—imprinting themselves into the minds of millions, awakening a genetic memory, striking a subliminal chord that would reverberate through the Christian World—forever.

"Uh-um. This is Barbara Teery, VNN. We are witnessing a remarkable performance here from the Compte de Sigor. Also, a number of famous politicians and celebrities have formed a group by the Compte and are dressing themselves in white robes. I don't know what to make of it. Ed, can you help?"

"Henry?"

"This is astonishing stuff, Ed. This Priory Arcadia organisation appears to making some kind of Claim for Legitimacy and backing this with a show of ancient relics. These relics appear to be connected with Jesus. Those haunting images you see on your screens right now are claimed to be the faces of Jesus and his Family! If I understand the situation correctly."

"David?"

"Well, like you, I am a bit confused. If these relics are real then obviously their authenticity will have to be scrupulously verified by top international scientists under the most rigorous of conditions. At the very least, we would have to have an international commission oversee the whole thing and verify their claims. Myself, I think it is preposterous! They are hijacking this Summit for personal aggrandisement! We are missing a genuine opportunity to move towards world peace."

"I think you're wrong, David. I mean look at those men and women who have lined up alongside the Compte. I would hardly think they would condone some grand confidence trick. They have declared themselves publicly as members of the Priory Arcadia. You don't think people like Cardinal Mirphy of New York would be party to anything that didn't have the highest aspirations of humanity at heart? I mean they are talking about him as a candidate for the next Pope! I find this tremendously exciting!"

"I think you're being a bit naïve, Henry, if I may say so. There has been a lot of talk about Cardinal Mirphy recently—some of it not good."

"Hold on fellas! Something else is happening. The dais in the middle is now spot-lighted and there's someone wheeling a trolley towards it! We'll take a break now for some important words from our sponsors; but stay with us, astonishing things are happening here right here on VNN, your twenty-four-hour all-action news channel ..."

*

On cue, JeanLuc wheeled the hospital bed with the unconscious form of Giselle into the Grand Hall. All eyes in the room swivelled towards him. He could physically feel the pressure of the millions of eyes, the eyes and psychic attention of the world upon him, curious, wondering what was going to happen, willing him on.

Over his head boomed out once more the voice of his Father in

363

Law.

"The God of Abraham is a JEALOUS GOD!

"The Lord Our God Demands a REVELATION! "The Lord our God demands an ACCOUNTING! "The Lord our God CRIES OUT for RELEASE!

"LO! You see before you THE LIVING INCARNATION OF JESUS!

"...KING OF THE JEWS!...KING OF THE FRANKS...KING OF FRANCE

"...KING OF THE WORLD!"

*

JeanLuc stood tall on the dais in the full glare of the spotlight. White robed, his long hair flowing over his shoulders, his strongly featured face raised towards the images of his ancestors. He was the image of a King.

At that moment, he became a KING—a King as the High Priests of the Priory understood it, a symbol of all that is brave and hopeful about humanity, all that mankind might aspire to, emulate and carry in their minds. A KING who was there to act as psychic focus for the Collective Unconscious. A KING who was ready to be an intermediary between man and Almighty God. A KING who would do what normal men could not. A KING who would SACRIFICE ...

The troglodyte faces of the World Leaders stared up at him in cold calculation and hostile cynicism that quickly turned to fear and horror, when from under his robe, JeanLuc produced the Dagger of Godfroi de Bouillon. A jewel-handled dagger that glittered laser flashes of light. He began to spin, whirling on one foot, holding the dagger out in front of him. The Dervish spin became faster and FASTER. The members of the Rose Croix began to chant and cry out urging, urging him on. His long hair whirled outward in a carousel around his head ...

And as his earthly body rotated, his mind spun free and expanded onto an astral plane; his mind filled with blinding light and shooting colours ... and still it expanded, as if caught in the wizard Whirlwind of Oz ... and then he was free of the world ... rushing outwards into the blackness of interstellar VOID ... and he saw the EARTH as a blue green tektite emerald EYE set against the diamond-flecked black velvet of space ... and the atomic heat of the sun lashed out at him

And virtual-video visions of past lives fast forwarded through his mind at supra light speed ... and he was being born again and he died ... and he was born again and he died ... and he was BORN.

And his own laboured breathing was the soundtrack of the universe ... and then the blackness of the Void began to dissolve pinpricks of comet-light lasering through and he could hear the threads of MUSIC that stitched the fabric of TIME ...

And he KNEW. The KEY turned and the river of GNOSIS flooded through him.. He knew that HIS spinning was winding up the Clock of Time once more. HIS actions would propitiate the Lord of the Universe and it was enough ...The Bloodline would go on.

JeanLuc stopped.

He raised the Dagger high and then plunged it down, down through Giselle's soft white breast, piercing her heart asunder. A plume of arterial blood fountained from her pierced breast. JeanLuc pulled the Dagger free and with a swift motion lowered his head and mouth onto the narrow wound. Giselle's life ebbed swiftly and his mouth overflowed with virus-virulent crimson. The people moaned in shock. Giselle's body trembled briefly and then lay still.

Jean de Sigor cried out in anguish and a deathly silence descended upon the Grand Hall.

JeanLuc lifted the Dagger and held it aloft once more towards the Jesus Icons. He screamed aloud; blood-smeared features contorted into a grimace of agonised grief shown across the entire TV world.

Within the cracked crystal heart of the ball of Childeric I, which lay on the dais alongside the other Relics, a blue-white atomic glow could be seen to grow with ever increasing intensity ...

With a voice like thunder, Jean de Sigor cried out his final words: "BEHOLD! The FULFILMENT!"

With a now steady hand, firm with purpose, he turned the other small, silver key. The matching key to the one turned on in the console. The light now stopped blinking and stayed, demonically, steadily alight, Maraschino-cherry red.

*

The worldwide TV audience stared at their suddenly blank screens.

365

Ed Piriani, stomach tightening with fear and wonder, feeling his heart jackhammer painfully in his chest, looked out of the window of VNN's rooftop TV studios in Paris, towards a foaming mushrooming pillar of fire-veined cloud which now formed a terrifying looming backdrop to a diminutive Eiffel Tower.

*

Malachi's hot nuclear whirlwind reaped Castle Sigor with its contents of world leaders, laid waste Paris and consumed a large area of Normandy.

*

At the same time, far away from the predicted effects of the Fulfilment, in a small specialist HIV treatment-clinic and hospice of the St.Guilhem le Desert monastery, a recently born baby opened his eyes for the first time. He smiled as a sudden gust of wind blew into the nursery from an open window causing a wind chime, constructed from tiny golden bees, to tinkle prettily.

EPILOGUE

Even as Father Moloc lay dying, he could not regret what was done, his involvement—even the killings. Choice had not been an option. Programmed from birth, he was the Instrument that had to precipitate global events that had been more than a thousand years in the planning.

Since the Splitting of the Elm.

He did not feel guilty: The Fulfilment was nothing to do with morality; it was a necessary evolutionary step, a Birth Pang for the New Consciousness. In the impassioned coded words of the Nautonnier, who was now a radioactive residue along with the Pope, the Presidents, the Prime Ministers and the rest of the world leaders at the crater that had been Castle Sigor, 'Blood must not be denied. The fruit of the vine is ripe. It is the Time of the Harvest!'

From the bed, propped up by coarse bolster pillows, he could see out of the narrow glassless windows of St.Guilhem le Desert, an ancient monastery that housed a fragment of the True Cross. The Holy Relic was given to St.Guilhem by Emperor Charlemagne and was entombed with him, making the town a lucrative pilgrimage destination. The Monastery itself was given to the Knights Templars and the Cathars as part of the 'splitting of the Elm' arrangements in 1188 at a formal ceremony on the Pont du Diable, which spans the river Hérault.

The view overlooked Van-Gogh-coloured vineyards, in steep ordered rows, covering the Pyrenean foothills glowing hot and hazy in the afternoon summer sunlight. Heat was what he needed. Marrow-warming heat was what he craved; to burn away the ice that wrapped his frozen heart.

The small narrow room, in one of the oldest buildings of this ancient monastery, was stripped of ornament; no books, no papers, no PC, no telephone, no internet. The walls were of rough-hewn blocks of grey granite, floors of ancient timbers worn smooth by generations of dutiful monastic feet.

Looking across, he could see the faint outline where a holy picture or crucifix must have hung for centuries on the cool stone walls. A monastic cell; a suitable anteroom to Eternity.

He was safe. He had no pain. The drugs were keeping him dozy, but his mind was clear. Escape to Oblivion was near. Task completed.

Where had he read that, at the end, when the smooth hull of Life's surface has become completely barnacled with experience, you know everything, the Secret, the Power, why you were born, why you are dying and how it could all have been different. You have become wise. But the greatest wisdom, at that moment, is knowing that your achievement is too late and that life's greatest tragedy is that wisdom is incommunicable.

He knew now ... that there is a mystical moment of pure Being, a moment that justifies the pain of sentience, that is only experienced by a few men or women and which is the subconscious Grail of existence. This is a Revelation of Truth, seldom granted, so seldom understood. A glimpse of the underlying Meaning of Life in the formless Chaos of Being; a mystical straw given to those who nudge mankind along its unknowable path of destiny. He'd had his Revelation and was content.

An hour passed. Somewhere in the tower of the Abbey, a heavy brass bell tolled for Mass.

He wouldn't be attending.

Dust motes drifted gently in the hot golden shaft of sunlight that pierced the throat of the room like the Sword of Mithras. A cockroach skittered an uneven path across the floor. His eyes closed. Yes! There it was! Faintly at first, but growing stronger, he could hear the pipes of the Shepherdesses as they gathered near the Tomb.

Calling him.

A heady perfumed fragrance—jasmine, orange blossom and beetroot pollen—of intoxicating intensity pervaded the room.

It was so simple really, not a puzzle at all. But try telling THEM! They would still search for hidden meaning, the truth behind the

Cosmos; spin another clever theory for Existence, weave another excuse for a Crusade, uncoil another Red Serpent—to give Certainty, to give Meaning, to ward off the Terrors that come with Power.

But for him?

It would be another Beginning.

'Et in Arcadia ego…'

THE END